One Boy's Quest to Change History

REVERSING
TIME

MIROLAND IMPRINT 30

**Canada Council   Conseil des Arts
for the Arts   du Canada**

ONTARIO ARTS COUNCIL
CONSEIL DES ARTS DE L'ONTARIO
an Ontario government agency
un organisme du gouvernement de l'Ontario

Canadä

Guernica Editions Inc. acknowledges the support of the Canada Council
for the Arts and the Ontario Arts Council. The Ontario Arts Council
is an agency of the Government of Ontario.
We acknowledge the financial support of the Government of Canada.

One Boy's Quest to Change History

REVERSING TIME

Charlotte R. Mendel

MiroLand
publishers

MIROLAND (GUERNICA)
TORONTO • CHICAGO • BUFFALO • LANCASTER (U.K.)
2021

Connie McParland, series editor
Michael Mirolla, editor
David Moratto, Cover and interior design
Guernica Editions Inc.
287 Templemead Drive, Hamilton, ON L8W 2W4
2250 Military Road, Tonawanda, N.Y. 14150-6000 U.S.A.
www.guernicaeditions.com

Distributors:
Independent Publishers Group (IPG)
600 North Pulaski Road, Chicago IL 60624
University of Toronto Press Distribution (UTP)
5201 Dufferin Street, Toronto (ON), Canada M3H 5T8
Gazelle Book Services, White Cross Mills
High Town, Lancaster LA1 4XS U.K.

First edition.
Printed in Canada.

Legal Deposit—Third Quarter
Library of Congress Catalog Card Number: 2021939094
Library and Archives Canada Cataloguing in Publication
Title: Reversing time : one boy's quest to change history / Charlotte Mendel.
Names: Mendel, Charlotte R., 1967- author.
Description: First edition.
Identifiers: Canadiana (print) 20210140674 | Canadiana (ebook) 20210140690
| ISBN 9781771836050 (softcover) | ISBN 9781771836067 (EPUB)
| ISBN 9781771836074 (Kindle)
Classification: LCC PS8626.E537 R48 2021 | DDC jC813/.6—dc23

*To my dearest family, my husband Eli
and my children Eytan and Abigail,
for the love and support that enables me to write.
To our shared history
and whatever the future might hold—I love you.*

CHAPTER ONE

SIMON LEAPT UP from his seat so quickly he smashed his knee on the desk. He rushed out the door, expertly flicking his coat off the hook without slowing his pace, and was pelting past the rows of cars in the parking lot before the end-of-school bell had finished chiming.

Despite the quick get-away, he could hear the bullies behind him; they had also catapulted out the door as soon as the bell had rung.

"Slow down rat-face!"

"We're gonna get you, shit-brains."

Simon smirked; they'd never got him yet. They always did stupid things like yell as they ran, wasting much-needed breath. Day after day the same thing happened. They'd fix their beady little eyes on him as the end of school drew near, hitching their backpacks over their shoulders and leaning forward in their seats. But Simon had chosen a desk near the door on the first day of school. And he was fast. Luckily, they weren't smart enough to develop a better strategy.

Just before the corner that led to his driveway, he risked a glance over his shoulder—they were far enough away for him to turn briefly and give them the finger. He continued more leisurely down the long driveway, but he didn't stop focusing on the sounds behind him for a minute. If they thought they had a chance of catching him, they wouldn't hesitate to follow him right to his doorstep, and nobody would hear his yells if they caught him. The privacy of the house was both a curse and a blessing; theirs was the only house in the subdivision with a long driveway and a wooded backyard. His mother had insisted on it.

Of course his mother might hear him yelling if the bullies caught him on the doorstep, but what could she do? Even if she wanted to do something.

That's not fair, Simon chided himself. *Sure she'd help. If she happened to be awake and dressed.*

Not many days like that.

He passed his father's workshop, where they had spent many happy hours tinkering, and approached the house. As soon as he opened the door, his dog Toby bounded up, his whole body shaking with joy. Simon's face broke into a smile as he reached down to scratch vigorously behind the dog's ears.

"Hey Mutt-face. Hey Fleabag."

With his long body, fat little legs, and pointy ears, Toby looked like a quarrel between a fox and a basset hound. Simon glanced once more over his shoulder before entering the house, but the driveway was empty. He walked into the kitchen, Toby still doing his happy dance.

"Hey, Mum."

"Hello, Simon. Did you have a good day?"

His mother sat at the kitchen table, a mug of coffee clenched between her hands. Her open journal lay beside the mug, a pen reposing on the writing. She'd jot things down throughout the day. Simon wondered what she wrote about; she never did anything.

"Yup."

Simon rummaged around in the fridge for a snack and grabbed a yogurt, a cookie, and an apple to take to his room. As he exited the kitchen, he glanced at his mother again. She sat in the same position, staring at her mug. He didn't know why she even bothered to ask about his day. It's not like she cared.

That's not fair, he told himself again. But it felt like the older he got, the worse she got. He could remember when he was younger; his mother used to get up in the mornings to make everyone breakfast. Brushed her hair. She had loved to dance, grabbing him by the arms and whirling him around the kitchen. He remembered she'd drive him and Toby out to the country and they'd go on these long walks, where she'd point out amazing things in nature. If there was a hawk suspended in flight above their heads, she'd see it. If there was a tree frog, small as a fingernail, camouflaged against the forest floor, she'd see it.

But as Simon hit his teens, they had stopped going out. She'd pretty much stopped doing anything.

"How come we don't go walking in nature anymore?" he once asked her.

"Now when I look at nature, I see the destruction of humankind. The impact of our greedy nature. Our stupidity."

"Well, you're not helping much to make things right, sitting there staring at your mug."

And for some inexplicable reason, she'd burst into tears and had run out of the room.

It felt like she'd given up on him, as well as nature. Thank God for his Dad.

The best Dad in the world.

∞ Simon did his homework and played a few video games, before succumbing to Toby's hopeful expression and going out to throw the ball for him. Thank God for Toby too, especially since Simon didn't like bringing kids home, in case they thought his mother was weird. Even Sandra, his only friend, wasn't encouraged to visit. But playing ball with Toby compensated for a lot. Simon held the ball up and Toby whirled in a frenzied circle, chasing his own tail.

"Lucky for you that you never get dizzy," Simon said, laughing, and made as if to throw the ball. The dog rushed down the yard in anticipation and Simon tossed the ball after him. Toby's fat little legs flew over the earth until he was under the ball, then he launched himself vertically into the air, whizzing past the ball on his way up, snapping his jaws fruitlessly as it sailed by a metre below him. His plump legs pummelled in space and his long body twisted itself into spirals as he attempted to chase the ball mid-air.

Simon doubled over in hysterics. It didn't matter whether he threw high or low, the exact same thing happened every time.

The game only came to an end when they heard the familiar beep beep of a car.

Boy and dog turned in unison and started racing towards the driveway.

"Hey Dad," Simon called out happily as his father parked in front of the garage.

His father uncoiled his long body from the front seat.

"How's it going? Good day?"

"Yup."

"Bullies chased you again?"

"Yup."

"Good thing you're so fast."

But Simon saw his father's jaw clench. His father had done everything he could to stop the bullying. His persistent calls to the school had produced some concrete results. During recess and lunch, Simon was allowed to hang out in the library. But the school couldn't control what happened outside its boundaries. Getting home in one piece was the challenge.

"Yeah, no worries there. I can outrun those idiots."

Simon always tried to minimize the fear in front of his father. He appreciated everything his Dad did for him: the fact that he cared so much, the fact that he came home promptly at 6, even though he worked at a stressful job. His Dad knew that he was the main caregiver, and that their evenings were important to Simon. Sometimes it seemed like his father did everything, and his mother was just a useless burden, whose presence prevented him having a normal life and inviting friends over. She was probably the reason he was bullied, too.

Yeah, yeah, not fair, he muttered automatically to himself. It was becoming a mantra.

Simon began to lay the table while his father nuked the stew for the third night in a row. Simon knew better than to complain. It was the same every week. His father would make a huge pot of something on Sundays—usually soup or stew—and they'd eat the same thing for several nights in a row. Simon made dinner on Thursdays—pasta or omelette—and Friday was take-out night. Week in, week out, the same routine, while his mother sat like a lump of …

"How is my darling Alley doing today?"

His mother raised her tired eyes from their intense contemplation of the coffee cup.

"I'm fine."

As Simon watched his father bend to kiss his mother's head tenderly, he wondered if he'd ever love like that. A love so strong that, no matter what happened, it never stopped.

Like he loves me, Simon thought. *Like I love him too.*

His father maintained a running commentary on his day during dinner, even though Alley barely lifted her head. Then he peppered Simon with questions about his day, naturally focusing on the issue that bothered him the most.

"How many were after you today?"

"It's always the same three, Dad," Simon answered, glancing down between his legs where Toby's hopeful face peered up at him.

"Why do they do it?"

Always the same question, night after night. Simon didn't know. Does anyone ever really understand why they're picked on?

"I mean, what if you trip or something? While you're running? What would happen then?"

Simon shrugged. "They'd beat me up, I guess."

He didn't remember when it had started. The first day of primary, perhaps? He had clutched his mother's skirt, horrified that she was abandoning him in this prison-like building. The teacher had wrested him away by force, holding his hands and telling his mother to go, go, quickly now, it was better that way, the child would stop crying if she'd just leave. Her face was horrified; she was almost crying herself, backing out the door with her eyes fixed on him.

The school can tell my mother what to do, he remembered thinking, shocked that she wasn't the all-powerful being he'd thought. Perhaps that was the beginning. Perhaps his mother's power had begun to seep away from that moment. Perhaps the other children, sitting demurely in their desks, had already earmarked him as "different."

"It's ridiculous that we can't think of a solution! Can't you wait in the classroom until they're gone?"

Simon scooped a piece of meat, potato and carrot onto his spoon, Toby scrutinizing every movement in an agony of desire. Surely they'd had this conversation ten times already?

"We should demand that the teachers escort you home. The small-mindedness that dictates boundaries in a situation like this—we can protect the kids until this point, and no more."

Simon lifted the bowl to his lips to drink the broth. Why should the school look after him outside of school? That's what parents were for. His mother should escort him home.

"I'm sorry, darling, this conversation is bothering you." His father pressed his hand gently over his wife's. "There's absolutely nothing to worry about. Our son is so fast, he'll never be caught."

She didn't respond. Sometimes Simon felt like smashing a plate over her head, just to see if she'd react. He hooted in derision. "I'd be caught quick enough if they had an ounce of brains. It'd be so easy to develop a strategy ..."

Fantasies of consorting with the enemy against some other kid filled his head for a moment.

"If they ever get close and you're still on the road, just run up to someone's house and bang on the door," his father said. "Yell blue murder and someone will hear you. If they start closing in when you're near our driveway, keep running past it and bang on the next door. And if you've already turned into the driveway ..."

"Yeah, yeah, run into the workshop," Simon said, completing the sentence. It wasn't like he hadn't used the workshop already, pounding mere metres ahead of his enemies, slipping the lock into place just as they threw themselves against the door on the other side.

"Do you feel like going out there tonight and finishing that surprise for Mummy that we're working on?"

"Sure," Simon said, wishing his father wouldn't call her Mummy.

"Is there anything we can get you before we go, Alley?" His father bent over his wife solicitously, stroking her hair away from her eyes.

"No thank you. I think I'll write in my journal for a bit and go to bed." *That's all she did. Stare and write, all day long.*

∞ They were making her another bird feeder. His father hung the feeders in strategic positions outside the windows; if she happened to be looking out the window when a bird was feeding, a smile would play about her lips and she'd watch until it flew away. Sometimes she'd get cross, banging on the windows and yelling at the blue jays, who were hogging the food from the chickadees. Sometimes she even laughed, as battles raged between the mourning doves, the crows, and the squirrels, quarrelling on the ground over spilt feed.

This feeder was to go directly outside the kitchen window, placed high in the tree so she only had to raise her eyes from her coffee cup to see it.

It was an intricate, beautiful feeder, with lots of perches for different-sized birds. Simon was working on one half of it, and they would glue the halves together when they'd finished. He loved the workshop; the lower floor was well-lit and tidy, the upper floor was used mostly for storage, because his mother hated to throw anything away in case it might be useful later. "Everything we throw away adds to humankind's endless landfill," she'd say, back when she cared about things.

The two floors were joined by surprisingly beautiful oak stairs, and, bizarrely, a dumbwaiter.

"This was probably a fancy house once," his father had said.

"It's not very big," Simon had replied doubtfully.

"Maybe it was bigger once. Maybe part of it burned down or something. There's a mystery about this place. Can't you feel it?"

Simon had always been a little frightened of the dumbwaiter. When he was little, his father had warned him never to climb in.

"It'd be great for hide-and-seek."

"But look how small and claustrophobic. And it's so old. Who knows if the door would get stuck, or if the pulleys are safe? There's a funny smell, too ..."

There was. An old, musty smell. The idea of being locked in that space was horrible, even though it hadn't seemed so small to a seven-year-old Simon. So many things were frightening, back then. Cramped spaces, spiders, nasty movies. *Still are*, he thought.

Father and son worked companionably together for an hour, and had warm milk and honey before bed.

CHAPTER TWO

SIMON DIDN'T LIKE the glances the other boys were giving him. All day, as he ploughed through his math sums, or wilted with boredom in geography, he could feel them eyeballing him. Snickering.

That can't be good, he thought, finishing his sandwich in the library at lunch time with his only friend, Sandra. He had been telling her about his worries regarding the bullies, and she had reassured him that it was probably only his imagination. He was so glad that Sandra didn't seem to mind hanging out with him. Perhaps it was because she was a bit weird too, with her cropped orange hair and various piercings and tattoos.

The librarian stopped by, plucking Simon's empty sandwich bag off the table. "I'll put that in the garbage for you."

"No, thanks," Simon replied, reaching out his hand for the bag.

The librarian handed it back reluctantly, watching as Simon carefully folded the bag and replaced it in his lunch box. "What are you going to do with it?"

"I'll clean it if it's dirty, and use it again tomorrow."

She looked at him oddly. "It's a plastic bag."

Sandra stuffed the last bite of her peanut butter and jam sandwich into her mouth, and held out its crumpled wrapping to the librarian. "You can throw mine away, if you like."

The librarian ignored her, waiting for Simon's answer. "In my family we never throw anything away."

"They don't buy anything either," Sandra said with a snort, sending a spray of crumbs across the table.

The librarian sat down by Simon. "That can't be true. Didn't you buy those clothes you're wearing?"

Simon could hear his mother's voice in his head. *Everything you buy—EVERYTHING—ends up in a landfill.*

"My clothes are all second hand. Already recycled. We wear our clothes until they start falling apart, and then we tear them up for dish cloths, or whatever."

"But you're not ..." The librarian flushed slightly. "Your father has a good job."

Simon frowned. "It's not because we're poor. It's to reduce our footprint."

"Isn't that a little extreme?"

Geez, she didn't know the half of it. He could still remember the horrific fights his parents used to have.

★ ★ ★

"I can't be married to a man who works for an oil company!"

"My dear Alley, please be reasonable. You know my influence there has resulted in environmental regulations ..."

"And you're also making such a lot of money," Alley said with utter contempt. "Mr. Fortune 500."

"We donate 30% of my salary to environmental organizations. That's a lot of money going towards causes that are important to you. That amount of money wouldn't be possible at any other job."

Or:

"You bought a lawn mower? We have a lawn mower."

"It's broken, Alley. It's very old."

"Then fix it. Or find someone to fix it."

"Its parts will be recycled ..."

Colour would bombard her cheeks and he'd start to back paddle. "OK. I'll fix it."

Alley hadn't managed to persuade her husband to leave his job, but he had stopped buying things. Drove around in an ancient car, switched to electric as soon as they became widely available. Wore old clothes in the house and preserved his suits for as long as possible. Occasionally, Simon would accompany his father to work, and even his young eyes could tell that everyone else was better dressed and better shod than his father. No doubt they had better cars and massively bigger houses as well.

"Idiots," his mother called them.

★ ★ ★

Simon looked across at the librarian and shrugged. "It's not extreme if our only chance of survival is to lessen our impact on the earth."

The librarian laughed uncomfortably, and got up. "Our survival? That still sounds a little extreme, dear."

"Yeah well, listen to the scientists," Simon muttered under his breath.

"What did you say, dear?"

"I said, if a scientist had told you three years ago, in 2019, that the whole world would shut down the following year because of a pandemic, you would have thought that was extreme too."

"Yes, that's true, dear. After COVID, anything seems possible. What a terrible year 2020 was! Thank goodness they developed vaccines so quickly."

"And what a shame we returned to the same globe-trotting, meat-inhaling habits after COVID."

The librarian looked at him with a vague smile and moved away.

Sandra was rummaging around in his lunchbox in case there were hidden treats at the bottom.

"What you do makes no difference," she said, without looking up. "There are seven billion other people polluting away."

"So I should only do the right thing if everyone else is doing it too? Besides, every day more people realise that what we do as individuals matters."

"One person don't matter enough to warrant suffering."

"I'm not suffering; it's just a way of life. You get used to it."

"Yeah, whatever. You know the bullies hate you 'cause you're different." Sandra had found a mangled toffee in the depths of his lunch box and happily popped it into her mouth. "I can skip my bus and walk home with you today, if it'd make you feel safer."

Simon shook his head. He'd have to invite her into the house if she walked home with him, because Sandra lived outside the subdivision and bussed back and forth to school. He didn't know what state his mother might be in today and, if she was slumped in her chair in the kitchen, he didn't want Sandra to see her.

There was a time when he'd blamed his mother for everything, even the fact that he was bullied. But that wasn't fair. His clothes were just as good as everyone else's. They just skipped the brand-new first day stage.

There was also a time that Simon had wished his parents would stop fighting.

Now, he just wished his mother could still be passionate about something.

∞ The afternoon was the same. The bullies watched and snickered. They nudged and winked. Simon didn't look at them, but he felt anxious. What were they up to? Whatever it was, it wouldn't be good for him. He began to fidget as the end of the day drew near. Instead of putting his heavy binder in his school bag, he took only the sheets he needed to do his homework, to make his bag lighter. He checked his shoelaces. Five minutes before the bell, he glanced surreptitiously in the direction of the bullies. Shawn, Tyler ... with a jolt of fear he realised that Jake was missing. He looked all around the classroom, then back at Shawn and Tyler. They were looking at him, grinning. Tyler rubbed his hands together. Shawn mouthed: "We're going to get you today, shithead."

Simon's stomach clenched. He made a quick decision to leave before the bell had even rung, and was up and out the door before the teacher could call him back. He heard the surprised yelps of his enemies, then heard them pounding down the hallway after him, the voice of the kind (but ineffectual) teacher demanding that they return this instant.

Simon grinned to himself as he pelted past the cars. He'd made it again. Suddenly he felt his leg catch on something and his grin collapsed as he fell violently, smacking his knees painfully on the cement ground. Raucous laughter pummelled his ears as he instinctively leapt to his feet, punching wildly behind him to shake off the hands that clutched him.

"Got you!" Jake's voice sniggered in his ear.

Simon knew he had mere seconds before the others caught up. He turned and kneed Jake as hard as he could in the groin. Then he was running again, too fast to even register the look of agony on Jake's face as he crumpled to the ground. But the others were there, right behind him. Another hand reached out and grabbed his backpack, but Simon slipped it off his shoulders and kept running.

They'd never been this close before. Simon could almost feel their hot breath on his back as he ran. They weren't yelling now, they were focusing on running. A surge of fear gushed through his stomach. What to do? Should he try to run up to one of the houses that lined the streets, like his father had suggested? But what if there wasn't anyone home? He'd be caught for sure, then. His best hope was to keep running. His breath rushed in and out of his lungs; he tried to control his mind: *I can do this*, he thought, *I can outrun them*.

But he couldn't outrun them. Although he didn't dare turn around, to risk the infinitesimal second that turning around would take from his speed, he could hear them. They were right behind him, and they weren't falling back. His driveway loomed ahead. What to do, what to do? Simon felt the need to pray, even though he wasn't religious. *Please God, help me. What should I do?*

He'd already rejected the idea of knocking on doors, so really there was no choice. He could go to the house, or the workshop. They were so close, he wasn't sure he'd make it to the house. *Please God, give me enough time to get inside the workshop and lock the door.* Simon knew then he'd be safe; the boys wanted to beat him up, but they wouldn't vandalise the workshop. Breaking windows wouldn't be satisfying enough to risk the punishment ... whereas beating him up ...

Simon pounded down the driveway towards the workshop. He could hear them panting. They were so close. How could he open the door, shut it behind him, and lock it before they got there? It was impossible.

Come on, just a few more metres. One last little sprint. Please God, give me speed. And Simon launched himself forward, calling on every reserve of energy he had.

There was the door, and Simon was grasping the handle and hurtling through and slamming it behind him but they were there, right there, and Simon knew that they'd be throwing themselves against the door while he fumbled with the lock and he made his third split-second decision that day: without hesitation he flung himself across the room and into the dumbwaiter. He was sliding the two half-doors of the dumbwaiter together as the boys crashed into the room; they would have seen him if they'd glanced in that direction. But they hesitated, looking around the room; then they dashed up the stairs.

Simon knew he had a minute or two, enough to start running towards the house, perhaps. Would they follow him in there, too? Possibly. He'd have to risk it, and the effect on his mother. Simon jiggled at the crack between the two half-doors, hoping they would glide open as silently as they had shut, even though there wasn't a handle on this side. The doors didn't move. Simon jiggled again, more strongly now. It was stuck. Just like his dad had warned, the damn thing had stuck.

He felt the urge to pound against the unyielding wood, but then he heard the boys descending.

"Where the hell did he go?"

"Hey, look at that little house. It's part of a bird feeder. Neat."

"Let's smash it."

"Duh—they'd kinda know who did it, wouldn't they, dick?"

Should he call for help? Wouldn't it be worse to be stuck in this horrible, cramped space for hours than beat up?

"Help," he yelled. "Help."

"What the ...?"

Simon heard footsteps approaching. A jolt as some moron punched the dumbwaiter. The sound of hands scrabbling on the other side. He tried to pry the door open from his side, they were pounding and yanking on the outside, and all of a sudden the dumbwaiter gave a lurch and began to move.

Down. It was moving down. The house only had two floors. *There was no down.*

Simon began to pound on the door madly. "Help!" he screamed. "HELP!"

He heard laughter from above. This was like a nightmare. *Where the hell was he going?*

The dumbwaiter juddered and whined. Simon sweated in fear as thoughts whirled through his head. He was going down into the bowels of the earth, and unless those idiots told somebody, he'd never be found. Pretty ironic, really; he was dependent on the bullies for his survival. Except they wouldn't tell anybody, in case they were blamed. Of course his father would search for him, everywhere. But how could he find him, if even Simon didn't know where he was?

The dumbwaiter thumped to the end of its journey so abruptly Simon banged his head on its ceiling. He held his head, blindly feeling for a lump in the pitch darkness. Panic and fear welled up and he had to quell the desire to scream. He couldn't see anything. He couldn't hear anything. He closed his eyes and took a couple of deep breaths.

"Calm yourself," he said.

It wouldn't do any good at all to succumb to hysteria. After a few breaths, he did feel calmer. It was a technique his mother had taught him long ago.

Slowly, Simon began to feel along the walls of his prison. His fingers inched down the length of the door, and discovered a small crack. He closed his eyes and took another deep breath, this one tinged with relief. When the dumbwaiter had crashed to the ground, the impact must have jolted the door open slightly. Simon inserted the tip of his index finger and began to pry the two half-doors apart. He tried to focus on how great it would be to get out of this cramped space.

"Don't think about what's on the other side," he told himself, as the doors creaked open.

The air outside was as musty as the air inside. Light filtered in from a tiny, cobwebbed window near the ceiling of what looked like some type of basement. Simon poked his head out of the dumbwaiter, taking deep breaths to calm his fear. In the dim light, he could see the huge stones that made up the basement's walls, slimy with moisture. There wasn't much else to see.

"Nothing to fear," Simon said, trying to encourage himself as he uncoiled his body from its cramped position and tentatively extended one leg to the dirt floor. The dumbwaiter appeared to have landed in the middle of a large, empty space about the same size as the workshop above. There was a chest in one corner, and what looked like a water pump, though Simon wasn't sure. He turned slowly in a circle, his heart tightening as he noticed something weird on the floor in the other corner.

"It's not going to eat you, wuss." Simon forced himself to approach, step by step. He remembered his mother telling him about a prayer that an African boy had once uttered in the middle of a race, hoping to make a deal for his tired feet: "You pick 'em up, Lord, and I'll put 'em down."

Something sticky covered his face and he jerked backwards, wiping cobwebs from his eyes. He looked around more carefully, noting the webs draping the walls and the supporting posts, linking the stones with intricate patterns. Simon saw a spider swinging on the edge of a strand, lowering itself determinedly towards his face. Simon stepped back abruptly, but still the spider approached. It was huge; its body two centimetres across, its legs spanning a man's hand. Very carefully, Simon stepped around it, giving it a wide berth. He approached the thing in the corner more slowly, looking about at every step for more curious spiders. "You pick 'em up, Lord, and I'll put 'em down."

His trepidation continued to mount as he drew closer; it was a well, the water lapping at the very edges of the topmost ring of stones, threatening to spill over onto the dirt floor. What the hell was a well doing in a basement? Maybe it was bottomless … Simon leapt backwards and sprinted to the other side of the basement, almost banging his shin against an old chest lying on the floor.

"Geez, it's just a well."

He wiped the cobwebs off his face, irritated at his own foolish fear. Spiders marching towards your face were one thing, but a well couldn't do anything, unless you were stupid enough to fall inside. Simon shuddered at the thought.

He stood staring down at the chest. It was one of those old chests people used to travel with before suitcases were invented. It seemed to be made of brown leather, with metal casings. There were handles on either end. Dare he open it? "Of course, I bloody dare," he said, angry at himself, and reached a tentative hand towards the chest's lid, half-hoping that it would be locked. But it creaked slowly open, and Simon took another deep breath and peeked inside. It appeared to be filled with old newspapers.

"Oh well, that's it then, nothing interesting," he said out loud.

The sound of his own voice made everything seem more normal. He eyed the window. It was tiny, a typical basement window of about two by one feet, smack against the ceiling, but he was pretty sure that he could fit through it. The chest was just the thing to help him reach the window easily. Simon took hold of one of the handles and hoisted one end, dragging the other end over the uneven floor as he eyeballed the air in front of his face for unwanted companions. The chest was heavier than it looked, and Simon wondered how people used to shift it when it had been full of stuff. He dropped it to the ground for a rest, and heard something clink inside.

Simon dragged it the last few feet and jostled it into place, directly under the window. The chest clinked again. *There must be something else in there, besides newspapers*, Simon thought. He wasn't sure he wanted to know what it was, but then he recalled his irritation over his cowardice about the well, and reached down to jerk the lid open again. Gingerly, he began to pull out the paper, handful by handful, nervous about what the next handful might reveal. How he wished he could be brave, not frightened of stupid things all the time! He glanced at one of the newspapers, and was surprised to see that they all seemed to be dated from 2006—he'd assumed the papers would be a lot older than that. That was just one year before he'd been born! He scooped the papers out faster, strewing them over the floor.

Finally, the bottom of the chest came into view; nestled in one corner was some sort of pendant, its chain twisted around itself. Simon picked it up carefully and examined it. The pendant was round and heavy, about the size of a large sand dollar. Smooth on one side, with some type of intricate pattern on the other, it looked like it was made of silver. It was beautiful. Simon held it up towards the meagre light coming through the window. The pattern appeared to be an apple tree in full blossom, its branches twisting in every direction.

Simon peered at it, marvelling at the detail. Whatever light was coming through the window seemed to shine directly on the face of the pendant; it almost seemed to glow. Simon could see the veins on each leaf. There was a bird's nest snuggling on one branch and ... was that a beak wide open, striving upwards in expectation of food? Simon searched for the parents, surely on their way to satisfy this mute appeal. There the mother was! Gliding through the apple blossoms with a worm dangling from her beak. Simon became so engrossed with the pendant that he forgot his desperation to get out of the basement. Such a wonderful tree, what artistry to create such perfect, tiny detail!

It was only when the face of the pendant dimmed that Simon looked up at the window. It was getting late. He slipped the pendant's chain around his neck. He liked the feel of it against his chest; its heavy solidity was reassuring. He looked up at the tight squeeze of the window that he'd have to crawl through to get out, and dropped the pendant underneath his shirt to protect it.

Then, taking a deep breath, he closed the lid of the chest and stood on it, examining the window at close range. There was a plastic fastener that you could press, which allowed you to slide the window half-open.

"Sorry," Simon said to the spiders as the opening window ripped apart their brand of artistry. His mother had taught him at a very young age not to hurt any living thing, not even insects or arachnids.

"But what if a mosquito bites me?" he'd asked indignantly.

"Well," she'd said after thinking about it, "I guess if the insect initiates hostilities, then you can murder it." And they'd giggled together.

There was no way he could get out the half-window. Simon rattled the frame, but he wasn't strong enough to push it out of place. He got down from the chest and started to search for a stone. The floor was cast in shadow, but it was still easy to find a hefty rock. Simon lugged it back to the window and hopped back on the chest. He bashed at the window again and again, narrowing his eyes to slits in case pieces of glass flew back at him. Most of it burst outwards, shattering onto the ground outside.

There seemed to be a large bush directly outside the window, obstructing his view; maybe that was why he'd never noticed this window before. Peering out, he could tell that the window faced away from the house and the driveway. Simon chipped away at the last few shards, running his fingers gingerly around the frame of the window to make sure there weren't any glass splinters to stab him as he crawled out. Then, touching the pendant for courage and smiling at his own foolishness at the same time, he hoisted himself through the tiny window, wriggling, kicking his legs to give himself momentum, grabbing the bush outside to pull himself through, the frame scraping against his stomach and back. *If I'd been one inch wider,* he thought, hoping he wouldn't cut himself as his bottom broke free and he slid onto the glass-covered ground like a newborn baby.

CHAPTER THREE

SIMON ARRIVED HOME two hours later than usual, bursting through the front door, full of his unexpected adventure. But although Toby catapulted out the door even more desperately than usual, his mother was sleeping. She hadn't even noticed his late arrival.

"I could frigging die," Simon told Toby, savagely throwing the ball and refusing to laugh as Toby launched himself like a cannon, shooting well past his target and pedalling madly mid-air to get back down again. "It'd take her days before she realised." Still, his father was coming home soon. His father would lap up every detail of his story.

But Simon didn't tell him right away, although he rushed over as usual to greet him as he drove up.

"Good day?"

"Yup."

"Bullies chased you again?"

"Yup."

"Lucky you're so fast."

Simon hugged himself with delight, anticipating his father's surprise when he told him what had happened. Not now. At dinner. So that his mother could hear as well.

Simon ladled out the stew, grinning to himself, as his father stroked Alley's hair and remarked that she looked rested and well.

He sat down, repressing the urge to cackle with glee, enjoying the suspense while his father delivered his usual commentary on his day at work. Eventually, he turned to his son.

"How many were after you today?"

"Always three, Dad."

"What if you trip or something? While you're running? What would happen then?"

Simon's delighted grin belied the shock of his words. "I did trip, Dad! Those morons managed to put together a strategy. Jake slipped out before the end of school and rigged some type of string or something between the cars where I always run. I didn't really see what it was, but I went down like a sack of potatoes." Simon glanced at both his parents. His father was leaning forward, concern etched on his face. Even his mother was giving him her full attention, her eyes travelling across his face and body to see if there was any hurt.

Simon rarely had both parents focussing on him entirely, and he enjoyed telling the story very much. There was utter silence in the room as he spoke; his father's face went pale with anxiety as he described his frightening descent in the dumbwaiter, his mother leaning forward with more interest than she'd shown in months.

"Luckily, there was a window. Imagine if they'd built the basement without a window! I'd never have escaped."

"But we've lived here for years," Alley said. "How come we've never noticed any window?"

"There's a big bush just in front of it, and it was right at the back of the workshop. I guess there's never been a reason to go back there. Anyway, there was a well in one corner, full of water. What type of people build a well in the basement?"

"Were you scared?" Alley asked, her eyes wide with empathy.

"I was," Simon admitted sheepishly. "I was petrified."

"A lot of old houses have wells in their basements," his father said. "Probably so the inhabitants of the house wouldn't have to go outside for water in the winter."

"But how'd they get down there? They wouldn't travel up and down in the dumbwaiter, obviously?"

"No. Looks like we'll have to explore the workshop a little more. Maybe we'll discover a hidden staircase!"

Alley's eyes had drifted back to her plate; she stirred the stew around with her fork. Simon wanted her attention back on him.

"That's not all. There was an old chest in the basement."

His mother glanced at him listlessly, but anxious fear was still etched across his father's face.

"I found something in that chest." Simon hooked his index finger around the chain encircling his neck, pulling the pendant up slowly from underneath his shirt, enjoying the attention trained upon him. Even before he had pulled the pendant completely free, his mother was on her feet, swaying slightly, her eyes fixed with unnatural intensity on the object emerging from his shirt.

"It's OK Mum; it's just a pendant," Simon said, reassuring her, as he pulled it out with a flourish.

There was utter silence in the room. Simon couldn't decipher the expressions flitting across his mother's face, they changed so fast. Joy. Fury. Implacable hatred? She looked kind of insane. He glanced uncertainly at his father. He had risen to his feet as well, but he wasn't looking at the pendant. He was looking at Alley.

Slowly, Alley held out her hand towards the pendant. "Let me look," was all she said.

His father walked around the table to Simon's chair. "Yes, let us look," he said.

Simon began to draw the chain over his head.

"Don't you touch it," Alley said, practically hissing. Simon looked at her in surprise. Her chest was heaving, her eyes glittering at her husband.

"What do you mean?"

"As if you don't know. You've lied enough. Just shut up."

"I have no idea what you're talking about, Alley. This emotion can't be good for you. Please calm down."

"Give. It. To. Me."

Both his parents hovered over him; Simon wasn't sure what to do. Suddenly his mother reached out to snatch the pendant, but his father was faster, closing his hand over it and almost wrenching it out of Simon's hands.

"Give it to me!" Alley screamed, and launched herself at her husband. She scratched at his face. She bit his hands, trying to pry them open. A desperate, keening sound rose from her throat. Simon was horrified. He'd never seen anything like this. His father was stronger; he slipped the pendant into his pocket and held his wife with firm, gentle hands.

"Calm down, Alley. You are not yourself. Calm down."

"Don't touch me," she said in a venomous tone, wrenching her hands from his grasp. The keening had turned to sobbing now. She rushed over to a kitchen drawer, yanking it open and plunging her hand inside. When it reappeared, it was holding the carving knife.

"Give it to me, or I will kill you."

His father laughed incredulously. "You can't even hurt a fly."

Alley clenched the handle of the knife and raised it above her head. She began to walk deliberately towards her husband. "I will kill you without compunction."

His father hurled the pendant at Simon, shouting, "Your mother has gone mad. Go to your room and lock yourself in. Keep this safe and don't open the door for any reason!"

Simon snatched the pendant to his chest and pounded up the stairs, Toby hot on his heels. He poked his head into his parents' room, eyeing the large wooden wardrobe that dominated the wall opposite their bed. It would make a good hiding place. On Saturday mornings, Simon would often take his book and snuggle in between his parents to read. He liked the huge, king-sized bed, and he liked the ancient wardrobe his mother had fallen in love with at a yard sale.

"Let me build you a lighted, walk-in closet," his father had said.

"What for? I love my wardrobe; all my clothes fit in there beautifully," Alley had replied. And indeed, she didn't have many clothes. Simon's mother didn't see the point of having more than three of anything—three skirts, three dresses, three pants, three sweaters—it all fit perfectly in the wardrobe, and there was still room for Simon. He used to pretend he was Peter in *The Lion, the Witch and the Wardrobe* when he was younger. The dark closeness made him feel safe, and now he edged towards it, wondering if that would be the best place to hide. But then another piercing shriek from downstairs had Toby dashing into Simon's room and diving under his bed. Simon wanted to be with Toby so he followed him, locking his door with trembling fingers. He sat on his bed, clapping his hands over his ears to dim the horrible sounds coming from downstairs. His mother was cursing his father in a high-pitched, continuous scream; his father's low reasonable voice punctured her hysteria, trying to calm her.

It was as though she hated him—her husband, who had always been so good to her. She must have lost her reason. Her illness had made her crazy.

Toby put his head on Simon's knee, whimpering. Simon stroked him, trying to comfort him, or himself. "It's OK, Toby. It's OK." He felt like he was in a nightmare for the second time that day, except this time he had no idea what was happening. Anxiety pricked his chest as a flood of obscenities poured like a poisonous river from his mother's mouth. He grabbed his iPod and plugged his ears with loud music.

Time ticked by unbearably slowly. Every few minutes Simon would turn down the volume and listen. His mother was still shouting like a mad woman; his father still placated.

Simon lay down, staring at the rows of books that covered the wall opposite his bed. He preferred physical books to his eReader, despite his mother's gentle hints about trees and paper. A window on the wall to the right of his bed framed the darkness outside. His room was neat, his possessions shelved and his clothes folded in the chest of drawers.

Simon covered his head with the pillow, the buds still blaring music. Toby got up on the bed and lay down next to him, pressing his warm, comforting back against his.

He wasn't sure how long they lay like that, but he was jerked from his reverie by a knock on the door.

Rat-a-tat-tat. Cautiously, he slid the pillow from his face and pulled the buds from his ears.

Rat-a-tat-tat. "Are you there, Simon?"

His mother's voice. Sounding like … his mother again.

"Yes?" he called out.

"Open the door, Simon. I need to talk to you."

Simon remembered the knife in her hands and the wild look in her eyes. He didn't move.

Rat-a-tat-tat. "Can you hear me, Simon?"

Simon stood up and cleared his throat. "I hear you."

"I want you to open the door, Simon."

She sounded normal. He took one step, then two.

"Simon, come closer." A muted whisper, as though his mother's lips were pressed against the crack of his door. He shuffled forward, staring at the door.

"Your father wants you to think I'm crazy, Simon, but I'm not. Think hard. Do you really think I'm capable of hurting you?"

She must have been right up against the door; it was hard to hear her. Tentatively, Simon advanced his ear to the crack.

"Your father did something evil. That … pendant you found is mine, and he stole it from me. If you open the door, I can prove this to you."

"Don't you touch me, you bastard!" The sudden yell hurled Simon back to his bed. Sounds of struggle; a shrill wail from his mother. A hand scrabbling against the door.

Simon could hardly breathe.

"Why are you doing this?" Alley cried. "Whatever happens, our sham marriage is over."

"Don't talk like that! Nobody loves you like I do."

"Do. Not. Touch. Me."

Simon wondered how his father could still love her, even as she spewed hatred at him.

"Why does this pendant make you hate me?"

"Stop lying. Don't you understand? We are finished."

"Don't say that. I love you more than life itself. I would never do anything to hurt you. What am I accused of? What do you imagine I've done?" Simon heard the tears in his father's voice.

His mother's voice dripped with venom. "You have stolen my life. I shall never speak a single word to you again."

"You think I stole that pendant from you? You're talking like a crazy woman."

Alley rattled the handle desperately. "Simon, let me in! You know perfectly well I'd never hurt you. Please, Simon. If you open the door, I will explain everything. I will prove to you who speaks the truth."

"Don't open the door, Simon!" his father called urgently from further away.

Simon was fighting tears, Toby looked at him with compassion, licked his hand. "Stop it, Mum," he said, pleading, his voice breaking. "Please stop it."

"Oh, my darling boy." And now it was her voice, laced with tears.

There was silence. After a few moments, Simon got to his feet and crept noiselessly to the door, thankful for the coloured shag rug muffling his footsteps. Holding his hand up to Toby so the dog would stay put, he cautiously pressed his ear against the door. Almost at once, his mother's voice whispered through the crack, as though she had placed her lips as close as she could to the very place where his ear was pressed.

"My darling boy. You must be so confused and upset. I'm so very sorry. I am going away for the night, but I will talk to you soon. Remember that I love you with all my heart. You do not understand what is going on tonight. I can't explain it to you in the presence of your father, but one thing I ask. Do not give him the … the pendant. If you do, it will disappear and neither of us will ever see it again. Please. You didn't give it to me, and I understand. But do not give it to him, either. If he tries to convince you, remember, there are things you don't know. Things your father doesn't want you to know. Things that I can prove are true—that he can't prove are not true. I will contact you very soon. Until then, keep our pendant safe!"

He heard her steps receding from the door and descending the stairs, his father's supplications flowing in their wake. Simon had never heard his father beg like that.

"Stay, Alley. Don't leave me. I can't live without you."

He felt utterly confused. He examined the pendant again, before slipping it over his head, hiding it under his shirt. Ironically, the small round weight against his chest comforted him, despite the fact that it had caused such uproar in his family.

Toby whined a little, and Simon scratched his head, exchanging 'what next?' looks as footsteps approached the door again.

"Are you all right, Simon?" His father's voice.

"Yes."

"Good night, son."

"Good night." Simon smiled with relief. His father was going to leave him alone.

Thank God.

CHAPTER FOUR

SIMON WOKE UP the next morning from a pleasant dream and stretched, wondering why there was a constricted feeling around his heart. For a moment, he couldn't remember why. He felt Toby's warm tongue lapping his ear, and laughingly pushed him away, puzzling over that unpleasant pressure on his heart. He shifted to his side, and felt the chain of the pendant slither across his chest, and remembered.

His parents had had a violent fight over this pendant. His mother had left.

Simon got dressed slowly, wondering what new craziness this day would bring.

The smell of bacon and eggs wafted up the stairwell; his father hadn't gone to work yet. For the first time ever, Simon wasn't sure whether he wanted to see his father.

He dragged his feet into the kitchen and sat at the table, Toby commanding his usual vantage point between his knees, from where he could scrutinize every movement of food from plate to mouth. A glass of orange juice and a plate brimming with toast appeared before him.

"Good morning," his father said in a cheery tone. Simon squinted up at him. Did he think he was four years old, pretending that everything was hunky dory? Did he think he was an idiot, and had already forgotten last night?

"Why aren't you at work?"

"I wanted to eat breakfast with you," his father answered, scraping a mish-mash of eggs and bacon over Simon's toast. Simon lifted a loaded forkful to his mouth. "Mmmmm."

A morsel of egg fell to his knees; Toby's tongue shot out and it disappeared.

His father sat down opposite him, with his own over-flowing plate, neatly stacking morsels of bread, slivers of bacon, and smears of egg on his fork, while Simon grasped his toast with both hands, shovelling it in willy-nilly. They ate in silence for a few minutes; Toby gazing upward from between Simon's legs, eyes swivelling back and forth like windshield wipers, following every tidbit's journey from plate to mouth.

"Everything is going to be OK, son. She'll come back. I don't know what the hell's going on, but we are her family. She'll come back."

Simon nodded.

"Seems like that pendant drove her over the edge, for some reason."

Simon could feel the light, round weight against his chest, soothing him.

"Do you have any idea what's going on?"

Simon looked up, surprised. "No."

"I'm a bit worried about you, with your mother in such a state. I want you to phone me if she tries to contact you. Can you do that?"

"Sure."

"I don't know whether to go to work today or not. What if she shows up and tries to take the pendant from you by force?"

Simon wiped up the yolk on his plate with the crust of his toast. Toby emitted a gentle burp between his legs, and Simon giggled.

"This is serious, Simon. Something weird is going on in your mother's head and I'm worried."

Simon watched him fastidiously prepare another forkful of perfect proportions. He felt sorry for him. "I won't give it to her, Dad. Actually, I'm already stronger than her."

"Mad people can't be trusted, Simon."

Your father wants you to think I'm crazy, Simon, but I'm not.

"I don't believe she'll hurt me, even to get it."

"You have no idea what she'll do, in her condition. I think you should give the pendant to me, for safe-keeping."

If you give the pendant to your father, it will disappear and neither of us will ever see it again.

"Don't worry, Dad. I'll take care of it."

His father stood up and held out his hand. "I want you to give me the pendant, Simon. I don't know what the hell is going on with your mother, but I definitely don't want her to see that thing again. It seems like whoever holds the pendant becomes the target of her madness."

Simon felt his over-full stomach clench with tension. "Please Dad, I don't want to fight with you. I don't know what's going on either, but I just feel … I just want the pendant to stay with me."

His father came around the table and towered over his son. "I'm not asking you, Simon. I'm telling you. Your mother tried to kill me last night because of that pendant. God forbid that you should be the next target."

If you give the pendant to your father, it will disappear and neither of us will ever see it again.

Simon got to his feet and began to edge away. His father grabbed him by the arm. "I don't want to do this by force, Simon."

A sudden growl erupted from Toby's throat. Simon was shocked by the hard grasp pinching his arm. "I'm not going to give it to her. I'm not going to give it to either of you—you're both mad," he shouted, throwing himself backward. The sudden movement caught his father by surprise, and Simon managed to wrench his arm free.

"Simon! Don't you trust me? Why wouldn't you trust me? I'm not the one who tried to plunge a knife into your mother."

Simon backed towards the door, slowly.

"Please Dad, I do trust you. I know you'd never hurt me. I just need some time to think, that's all. Please let me go. We can talk more tonight."

His father leaned over the table, his face twisted with emotion. "Simon, your mother told you that, if you give the pendant to me, you'll never see it again, right?"

Simon was silent, standing with his back to the door, ready to run.

"Right?" his father insisted.

Simon nodded. Toby pressed against his legs, asking to go outside to pee.

His father spoke slowly, enunciating every word. "If you give it to your mother, Simon, neither of us will ever see *her* again."

Simon opened the door and slipped out, following Toby's mad rush to his favourite peeing place.

"Do you understand, Simon?" his father shouted after him. "Even if your mother's telling the truth, which is worse? Never seeing that cursed pendant again? Or losing your mother forever?"

Simon turned around to look at his father. "I won't give it to her, Dad. Don't worry. I promise."

He smiled at his father's worried face, and turned with relief in the direction of school.

∞ Simon was so preoccupied with all the stuff happening at home, he almost didn't notice the snickering of the bullies. Almost.

At lunchtime he dragged Sandra to the library.

"Whassup?"

"I have something to tell you."

He began, from the very beginning.

"They rigged a tripwire to nab you?" Sandra said.

"Yeah. So anyway ..."

"They're giggling together like cretins today, too. Didja see 'em?"

"Just wait, that's not the point of ..."

"I'm walking home with you today." Sandra took a huge bite of her peanut butter and jam sandwich, regarding him defiantly.

"Are you going to let me get to the main part of this story or what?"

And as he continued, Sandra stopped eating and stared at him, mouth hanging open. Simon could see the glint of her tongue stud.

"I'm totally walking you home today. You don't need to worry about your Mum no more, because she's not there, right?" Sandra finished off her sandwich triumphantly. Then her smile faded. "What're you gonna do?"

"Maybe I should just throw the damn thing away. Maybe it's a bad luck thing."

"Yeah, it's totally crazy. What's your instinct telling you?"

"What do you mean?'

"One of your parents is lying, man. Hate to break it to you."

Simon tried to think. He couldn't remember a single instance where either parent had lied in the past.

"It's gotta be your Mum. She's always been nuts, and that necklace pushed her over the edge. Hey, can I look at it again?"

Simon leaned forward and held the pendant out on its chain. For some reason, he felt reluctant to take it off.

Sandra held it up to her eyes and examined it closely. "It's really beautiful."

"I don't think it's evil. It feels … comforting."

"That don't mean nothing. Evil things don't advertise." Sandra linked her arm through his as they exited the library. "I'm coming home with you today, remember."

Her arm felt comforting too.

∞ Misery had replaced comfort by the end of the day. None of the bullies were in the classroom, so for once Simon could saunter out like a normal student, except his heart was heavy with dread.

Sandra linked arms with him again, but he shook her off. "This isn't a stroll along the promenade. You've got to be ready to run."

Sandra giggled. "Promenade? Where do you come up with them words?"

Simon didn't answer; he walked slowly, swivelling his head in all directions as he checked the ground, the sky, behind and to the sides. Sandra sensed his nervousness, and punched him playfully. "Hey, loosen up. I'm with you, remember? I can beat those wusses with one hand."

"Don't be ridiculous. There's three of them, and they're all Neanderthals." But Sandra's compact, muscly body gave him courage; she probably was a much better fighter than him. In any case, two against three was a lot better than one.

They walked slowly, Simon shushing Sandra every time she talked. His 360-degree scrutiny paid off; they had a second's warning when Shawn and Tyler erupted from behind parked cars on either side of the road. Simon and Sandra spun in unison and started running back towards the school.

Then the bullies' plan became clear, as Jake leapt from behind a bush, directly in their path. They must have passed Jake's hiding place, but Simon hadn't noticed, despite his care.

Two chasing them from behind, one in front: Simon pivoted sideways and began to run up someone's driveway.

"Let's fight," Sandra screamed, grabbing a rock and hurling it at Jake, smacking him right on the chest.

He howled in pain and doubled over.

"Run," Simon yelled over his shoulder, half-ashamed that he'd already taken to his heels, leaving Sandra to attack alone. From his periphery vision, he saw her pelt past the crumpled Jake, back towards the school. A rock came sailing past his shoulder.

Shit, she's given the morons a new idea, Simon thought. He could see that both Shawn and Tyler were chasing after him, leaving Sandra to her own devices. He was alone again. A constricted, miserable feeling stained his heart like mould.

He vaulted over the fence separating the yards and raced over someone else's property. He would probably get lost. He was sick of this. Running, frightened, bullied every day. A sick mother, who was now crazy. She'd probably do something terrible and get locked away. He hated his life.

Simon stumbled over the unfamiliar terrain. There was some type of backyard waterfall coming up. Simon veered around it and headed for the road beyond. He didn't have to turn around to know the bullies were closing in; he could hear their rasping breath. Two, three? He was sick to death of running. He was sick of his miserable life.

A rock sailed through the air and cracked against the asphalt. Then one thudded against his shoulder, sending a jolt of pain shooting up his neck and jerking him forward. He stumbled, and almost fell; tears rose unbidden to his eyes. How could those morons throw rocks and run so fast at the same time?

I hate my life. I hate my life.

Simon knew the tears would blind him, slowing him down. He wasn't sure he cared. Let them catch him. Let them beat him up. Maybe the physical pain would alleviate the heaviness weighing on his heart.

The pendant thumped unpleasantly against his chest in time to his strides. He pressed it still with one hand.

I hate my life. I hate my life.

Another rock whooshed over his head.

I wish I was dead.

The ragged breaths of his pursuers seemed to be getting closer, but he didn't dare look over his shoulder to check. Looking back slowed you down.

I wish I was done with school. Done with that miserable house and my crap parents. I wish I was 18.

A strange whistling invaded his ears. His vision went dark, as though someone had slipped a blindfold over his eyes. The strangest sensation enveloped his body; it felt like a strong wind was spinning him around, lifting his feet off the ground. He opened his mouth to cry out, but before the sound materialized he felt cold tile under his knees, and the darkness fell away from his eyes.

He lifted his head. He was crouching on the floor outside a half-open door. A long corridor stretched in either direction, with similar doors lining it on both sides.

∞ He was alone in the corridor, although many of the doors were half-open, and he could hear a jumble of voices. Music was blaring from a door down the hall. Rigid with surprise and wondering what the hell was going on, Simon watched a girl and a boy, just a few years older than him, emerge from one of the doors in deep conversation and stride up the hallway. He jumped to his feet as they passed him, embarrassed to be crouching on the floor, but they didn't pay him any attention.

"Excuse me," he whispered. "What is this place?"

The couple ignored him.

He cleared his throat. "Excuse me!"

They glanced back at him, without breaking stride.

"Where am I?"

"You're in Clancy Hall," one replied unhelpfully.

Simon watched the couple disappear around the end of the corridor, and turned back to the half-open door nearest him. He poked his head inside. The first thing he saw was the coloured shag rug that was usually slung across his bedroom floor, except this wasn't his bedroom. He didn't recognize the room. It was much smaller than his room at home; there was a single bed in the corner, and the sun blazing through the window on the opposite wall illuminated the piles of books and papers strewn over the floor. A young man sat at a desk in the corner of the room with his back to Simon, peering at a laptop.

Simon felt embarrassed and confused. He was about to clear his throat to announce his uninvited presence, when someone shoved by him, propelling him into the room. Another young man entered, and flung himself across the bed. "Jesus Simon, haven't you finished studying yet? I told Owen we'd meet him for lunch."

Simon jumped when he heard his name, smiling uncertainly at the man on the bed. The man looked at him in surprise. "You didn't tell me you had a little brother, Simon."

The man sitting at the desk turned around. "Do you mind waiting outside, Chad? I just need another five minutes, and I'll finish faster if you're not breathing down my neck."

"All right, but get a move on. We were supposed to meet Owen ten minutes ago."

The man strolled out, winking at Simon on his way. As soon as he was gone, the man at the desk jumped to his feet and locked the door. As he did so, Simon looked directly in his face. The cry that had lodged in his throat burst forth.

The man … had his face.

And he was looking right at him.

"This is your first time, isn't it?" he asked.

"The first time for what?"

The young man laughed delightedly. "I remember it! I remember every detail—those bastards chasing me and throwing rocks …"

Simon felt faint. "Chasing you? Please, what's going on?"

The young man jerked slightly, almost as though he'd forgotten Simon's presence. "Damn, I'm breaking the rules. Communication is strictly forbidden."

"What? You have to tell me …"

"No! There are rules. Ask Mum."

"My Mum?" Simon asked uncertainly.

Older-Simon laughed uproariously, as though he'd made a joke. "Go on now, scoot. Go back to your own time," and he snatched his wallet from the table and zipped out the door, apparently forgetting the five minutes of studying he'd intended to do, in his haste to preserve the rule of no communication.

Simon looked after him in consternation. His own time? How was he supposed to know how to get back? He closed his eyes. What had he been thinking when this had happened? He'd been wishing he was older. *I wish I was fifteen.*

Nope, still in Older-Simon's room.

He tried to recall his exact actions as he ran away from the bullies. He remembered the pendant thumping against his chest. He had grasped it in his hand, to stop the thumping. Of course, how stupid of him. He plucked the pendant from under his shirt and held it firmly in his hand. *I wish I was fifteen.*

The same sensation of spinning around, the blindfold, the wind, the whistling in his ears. He had time to briefly wonder if he'd land on his feet, running away from rocks down a suburban street, before he felt solid ground beneath his soles and opened his eyes to his own, familiar room. He felt exhausted, he wanted to lie on his bed and close his eyes, but somebody was pounding on the door downstairs. Toby was barking frantically. Simon closed his eyes and contemplated ignoring whoever it was; he needed to think. What the hell had just happened?

But the pounding wouldn't let him think, and then he heard Sandra's voice, filled with irritation. "Open the friggin' door or I'm smashing it open!"

"Coming," he shouted, and raced downstairs.

"What took you so long?" Sandra said angrily, stalking inside and blowing a cloud of smoke in his face as she pocketed her vape. Simon looked down at Toby, who was gazing at him with a bewildered expression.

"Hey Toby," Simon reached a hand towards the dog. "Why are you looking at me like that?"

"Why'd you leave him outside?" Sandra answered on Toby's behalf. "He's been alone all day and he wants to be with you. I'd be mad too."

But Toby didn't look mad. He looked puzzled, as though he didn't understand what Simon was doing in the house.

Because he hadn't seen him come in.

"Sandra, did you see what happened?" Simon asked, following her into the kitchen.

"You ditched them, big-time. Hey, is it OK if I make us a snack?"

Simon knew she was dying to poke around. "Sure."

Cookies, apples, cheese strings and juice appeared on the table as Sandra whipped open drawers and fridges, investigating every nook and cranny with frank curiosity.

"So, you saw them again after I'd … disappeared?"

"Yeah. I came back when I saw nobody was coming after me." Sandra crammed an entire cookie into her mouth, sending a spray of crumbs fanning outwards as she laughed. "They were circling like dogs that'd lost the scent."

"Did they see you?"

"Yup. They asked how you'd disappeared like that. You must be one fast runner."

Simon tossed a piece of cookie into Toby's waiting mouth, as recompense for tricking him.

Then he began, from the very beginning.

∞ By the time he had finished, Sandra's mouth was literally hanging open. "Oh my god, are you kidding me??"

"I know it's hard to believe."

"There's one way to convince me." Sandra stood up and linked arms with him. "Let's go visit Older-Simon."

The idea was appealing; the girl somehow dispelled the anxiety and nervousness that always preyed on Simon. With a brief prayer that the magic would work again, Simon clenched the pendant in his hand. *I wish I was eighteen.*

Nothing happened.

"Maybe I have to hold the pendant, too," Sandra said. She put her hand over his. The warmth of her hand made Simon blush.

I wish I was eighteen.

"Maybe I have to actually touch it."

Simon shifted his hand so it covered only half the pendant, while Sandra placed her hand on the other half.

Still nothing.

"Maybe I have to, kinda like, be closer to you or something."

Sandra put her arms around him. Simon froze. "Here," Sandra said, and looped the chain of the pendant over her own head.

Her face was inches away from his. Simon could feel the warmth of her body pressed against him. He felt stiff with self-consciousness. He wanted to swallow, but he was afraid the sound would ricochet down her ear drums. Even breathing normally seemed to be an insurmountable obstacle. But he managed to focus enough to whisper, "I wish I was eighteen," before Toby barked suddenly and took off towards the door, breaking the agonizing paralysis which had taken over his body. He pulled back from the discomfort of Sandra's proximity.

"It's not working."

Sandra frowned in disappointment, fingering the chain that still linked them.

"Do you believe me, what I told you happened before?"

"Yeah, I do, but it is kinda hard to take in."

Simon gazed into her dark eyes, willing her to believe him.

"What are you two doing?"

The two kids whirled around at the sound of Alley's voice. She was standing in the doorway, a bemused expression on her face. Among the multitude of feelings that rose in Simon's breast, embarrassment fought its way to the top. He saw how it must look through his mother's eyes, the two of them standing so close, linked together by a chain thrown over both their necks. His whole body blushed.

But nothing fazed Sandra. She flipped the chain off her neck in one, fluid motion, and walked towards Alley with her hand stretched out. "Hello. My name is Sandra. I'm your son's friend at school."

"Only friend," Simon whispered.

Alley tried to smile as she took Sandra's hand, shaking it heartily to hide her displeased surprise.

"It's great to meet you, Sandra. I need to have a chat with Simon in private. Do you need a drive home?"

Sandra peered at her watch. "I didn't realise it was so late. My mother will be expecting me."

Simon looked at Toby, who was casting supplicating glances towards his ball. He grabbed Sandra's arm after his mother had exited the room and whispered: "Do you mind if I don't come with you?"

Sandra shrugged. "Don't matter to me. Your mother seems cool."

Simon smiled. He remembered waking up that morning anticipating the next meeting with his mother with dread; now, he was waiting for her to return with bated breath. Whatever was going on—and he was very confused about what, exactly, was going on—Older-Simon had advised him to talk to his mother. Maybe she would have the answers. Maybe she could explain.

Alley even looked different. Gone was the debilitating exhaustion imprinted on her face from the moment she woke up. She looked energized, excited. Hopeful.

Simon went outside with Toby, who shuddered and trembled in anticipation, eyes fixed on the ball in Simon's hand. *If humans showed their feelings like dogs, I'd be trembling like that too*, Simon thought.

He held the ball up in the air, triggering an orgy of anticipatory wriggles in the mutt. He pretended to throw it, moving his arm in a great arc as Toby flew down the yard, ready to leap towards the sky at first sighting. After a minute he came to a stop in diminishing bounds, and rushed back to Simon, wriggling anew as he caught sight of the ball. He was delighted with the trick Simon had played on him and again raced off, just as trustfully, in the direction that Simon's raised hand indicated.

This time, Simon threw hard and straight down the yard, in the direction of the fleeing dog. He smiled as Toby's head swished back and forth like a metronome, as he scanned the skies for the first sign of the ball. As soon as it landed in his periphery vision he eyeballed his target with single-minded intensity until he gauged that he was directly underneath, whereupon all four fat little legs vaulted simultaneously and he soared up, up, snapping uselessly as he flew past the ball, twisting and turning as he struggled to reverse his trajectory mid-air.

Simon convulsed in hysterics.

He threw the ball for Toby until his mother returned; he could watch the dog's ball-catching failures forever without getting bored. Once, his stupendous leap in the air ended when he smacked his head against a tree branch. Once, Simon threw the ball high enough that Toby's surge into space didn't overtake the ball, though he still failed to catch it. "You know the definition of crazy is doing the same thing over and over and expecting different results," he informed Toby, who grinned up at him, tongue lolling. He didn't mind being crazy, if crazy meant his family laughed, instead of shouting like they had last night.

When his mother returned from taking Sandra home, Simon followed her into the kitchen, where she began to make a cup of tea. He had absolute faith that his mother was about to transform the craziness of the past few days into something sensible. Answers, finally! Simon perched on the edge of his chair and bit his lip with impatience.

"We don't have to wait until it's boiled, do we? We can talk now?"

Alley smiled, and came over to his chair to hug him. "First of all, I want to apologize for last night. That must have been really upsetting for you."

Simon glanced at his mother's new face. He didn't feel upset right now. He felt that they'd returned together to an earlier time, when she used to do things with him, when she had looked at him with interest and love. "Do you know what I did today?" he told her in a rush. "I just disappeared from this place and reappeared somewhere else, like a university dorm or something, with ... wait for it ... an older me!"

His mother laughed, hugging him tightly.

"So Mum, can you explain?"

"Yes, I can explain everything. But I should start at the beginning."

"No Mum, please. Can't you just tell me what the hell is going on with this pendant?"

"Would you like some tea?"

Simon tried to curb his impatience, and nodded. Alley put a plate of chocolate chip cookies on the table, and handed him a mug with just the right amount of sugar and milk. He sipped appreciatively, waiting.

Alley perched on her usual chair and took a sip of her own black tea. "I want to start at the beginning so you understand everything, especially why I'm so angry with your father. It is important to me, that you understand that.

"So, the beginning. I come from a special island. We are identical to all the other humans in the world, except that we have a special skill. With the aid of our talismans—what you call a pendant—which we receive in a special ceremony at the age of thirteen, we can time travel."

Simon almost choked on his tea. This was so incredible. *If she'd told you last night, you wouldn't have believed her. You'd have thought she was insane.*

"Water under the bridge," Simon murmured.

"What?" Alley asked. "That wasn't quite the reaction I expected."

"Sorry Mum, just ... a little overwhelmed. So, I'm fifteen! Can we go right now? Can I visit the dinosaur era? Oh man, I'd love to see a dinosaur. I can't believe this. This is so ... I feel like my whole world is changing. It's fantastic. Can I visit 2050? See what's going on then?"

Alley laughed. She looked so different, when she was laughing. Younger. Lighter. "Slow down, Simon. We can't visit the Mesozoic Era, because we weren't alive then. We can only travel along our own time-lines, within our own lives. We can only go where we ourselves have been, or will be. So, for example, if you travel to India when you are 35 years old, you can visit your future self in India today, when you are fifteen. You can go back to when you were a baby, and visit yourself there. But you can't go beyond your own birth at one end, or your death at the other. That is the timeline of your own life."

His mother stopped to sip her tea and Simon leapt into the silence; he was bursting with questions.

"So can we visit the island? Do I have relatives there? Why have we never been? Do you have a mother and a father there? Let's go there now! Let's check it out!"

"Slow down, Simon. I haven't used my talisman in fifteen years. Don't you think I'm dying to go home? But I'm not entirely sure what I'm going to find when I get there. It's complicated. I need to talk to you a bit more about that."

Simon didn't care where they went, he wanted to time travel! He jumped up from his seat and threw the pendant's chain over his mother's head, so that it encircled them both. "I wish I was eighteen!" he yelled.

Nothing happened.

"That's how you do it, isn't it Mum? You say the age you want to visit?"

"Yes, or the year. But slow down, Simon," Alley said more urgently. She ducked out of the chain that linked them and took the pendant in her hands, reverently, stroking its surface. Simon saw a tear splash on the trunk of the tree. She regarded it intently, and raised it gently to her lips.

"Mum?" Simon asked uncertainly.

She lifted her face to his; her lips were trembling, and her eyes filled with tears. She let the pendant fall back against his chest.

"What is it, Mum? Aren't you happy?"

She stroked his face with gentle fingers. "I'm very happy, Simon. But I'm a bit overcome. Remember, I haven't seen my home in fifteen years."

"So you can only travel to the island with the pendant? Is it in a different world?" At that moment, Simon could have believed anything.

"Not exactly." An image of a rift in the horizon filled Alley's head. But it was complicated to explain and she didn't want to overload Simon with too much information. "It's in this world, you can travel there by air and bus and sea. I did go there once, after I'd lost the talisman." Alley's face grew pensive. "There are a lot of things I have to explain to you, Simon. Bit by bit, so it's not too much all at once."

Simon jiggled from foot to foot, elation charging his whole body with the enormity of all the new information.

"I have *grandparents* I've never met? What else? Do you have siblings?"

"No, there's just me and my parents. There are strict rules on the island, Simon. For example, two people can't travel with one talisman."

If you give the pendant to your mother, Simon, neither of us will ever see her again.

"Can I get a pendant too?"

"I don't know, Simon." She began to draw the chain over his head. "The story you told me about travelling to your future self made me very happy, because I wasn't sure you'd have that ability. You see, Simon, the island where I was born and grew up is the most wonderful place. Since people can visit themselves at different points of their own lives, they become much wiser than most of the people here. You know how there is less corruption and wrong-doing in countries where the governments are transparent? It's a bit like that. If those stupid oafs bullying you at school knew the eventual result of their actions, they wouldn't do it."

Simon interrupted excitedly. "So there are no bullies there, because they know they'll get caught? They can jump ahead a few years and see what'll happen to them if they don't stop?"

His mother sat down in her chair and nibbled on a cookie. The pendant dangled from her hand. "Something like that. How can you bully someone, if you have the perspective of your entire life in front of you? How can you do wrong, if the people surrounding you could easily find out, including your own family?"

Simon remembered Older-Simon's refusal to talk to him. "Why is it forbidden to communicate with the ... inhabitant ... of the time you are visiting?"

"We are not allowed to change history, and to that end we can only observe. We must not be seen or heard."

Simon's mind raced. "Can I see my own death?" Did he want to?

"People usually know the approximate year of their deaths, due to their inability to visit the years beyond it. Sometimes, a talisman will

CHARLOTTE MENDEL

take a person to the very point of their death, and then they know. But if the talisman doesn't take you to the exact day, you might never know the manner of your death, until it happens."

Simon broke a cookie in half and surreptitiously slipped the second half to Toby's waiting mouth. Alley frowned. He was not supposed to feed the dog when they were eating. "That reminds me of another rule that prevents us from changing history: you cannot transfer information that you learn during your time travels to others, if that information pertains to their own lives. For example, if you time-travelled to the future and witnessed the death of a friend, you couldn't tell that friend what you had seen, because you might impact his choices or the direction of his life in an unforeseen way."

Where would his talisman take him? What would he experience? This was *incredible*. "Do you think the talisman shows you what you need to know? I know we choose the year, but the talisman chooses what to reveal to you in that year. Is it showing you what's important for your own personal growth?"

Alley smiled. "That's an interesting question, Simon. There are huge debates about that very issue on the island. Some people interpret the talismans' choices as purposeful, and some insist they're random. The faithful believe that if you are supposed to know about your own death, your talisman will take you to that point. If you aren't, it won't, and nobody else can enlighten you. They have lots of examples where their talismans revealed to them events which—as you said Simon—enabled them to grow. The scientists, on the other hand, insist the time you land is completely random, and document reams of evidence proving this."

"What do you believe?"

Alley extended her foot to stroke Toby's head. He had settled on the floor between their chairs. "I suppose I'm more inclined to the scientific side, but I think the faithful do experience life-changing time travel. Perhaps it's the placebo effect. And what does it matter, which is true? What matters is that we have tried to build a just, equal society;

away from the senseless greed and the misery dominating so much of the world right now. In order to protect our society, and—even more importantly—to ensure that our special ability doesn't impact history —we have very clear rules. You ... you are the first child born outside the island ... in living memory."

Simon was listening so intently he didn't notice that the pendant now encircled her neck. The island sounded like such a special place. "But if I can time-travel, does that mean I can be part of the island too?"

"I don't know. Now I have my talisman again, I'm not sure what they will decide: not about me, nor about you. I need to go back and explain that I have found it again, that I did not lose it—which would have been an unforgivable idiocy, in their eyes—but that it was stolen from me. I still broke the rules, but I want to beg for mercy. To beg for forgiveness, in the hopes that they will allow us to live there."

Simon nodded vigorously, building images in his head about this new world. Imagining walking back and forth to school in peace. Was there anything here he'd miss? "Mum, I can tell Sandra about this, can't I? I already told her about visiting Older-Simon."

"No. That's one of the rules I mentioned to you. It's vital that you keep everything about the island, the talismans, our special ability, to yourself."

"But I've already told ..."

"So explain to her why you can't discuss it anymore," his mother said sternly.

Simon thought of Sandra's strong will and determination. He wasn't sure how that conversation would go. His mother was still speaking.

"Before I go back to my island and talk to the Leaders, before I beg them to let us live there, you have to do some thinking. Are you sure you want to come with me? It means leaving your father."

A lump rose in Simon's throat. Leave his father? He hadn't thought about that. Everything was moving too fast for him. He felt confused. "Why can't Dad come?"

"First, because that is one of the rules of the island; you can't bring people there. Second …"

"But you said it's in this world, so people can travel there."

Again, Alley thought of a rift in the horizon that would be hard to explain. "The island is very isolated. It's … difficult to find."

"But people must get there sometimes. How have you kept your skill a secret?"

Alley sighed. It seemed like every time she tried to simplify it backfired. "If an intrepid traveller happened to arrive at our shores, they would see a quaker-like people living primitively on an isolated island. There is no hotel where they could sleep and nobody would be very welcoming, so they wouldn't stay long. I will explain why outsiders are not welcome at another time. Second, I believe your father stole this talisman from me to prevent me from leaving him. I truly cannot forgive him for that. Ever. I know this must be very painful for you, but I cannot be with someone I despise, even for you."

"You don't know Dad stole it!"

His mother looked at him compassionately, until Simon's jolt of anger subsided. He gulped at his tea, trying to sort out the bewildering onslaught of his thoughts.

Alley laid a soft hand on his shoulder. "You can't decide now. This is a huge decision. You need to take your time and think carefully about it. About everything. And I need to go back to my home and seek guidance as well."

If you give the pendant to your mother, Simon, neither of us will ever see her again.

Simon rushed over to his mother and clasped her in his arms. "Mum, don't go, Mum. Not without me."

She held him tightly, rubbing his back as though she could expel all his worry and tension. They stood there together, arms entwined.

"Do you know for a fact that he stole it?" Simon whispered.

Alley stood back a little to look into his face. "Oh, Simon. The actions of your father destroyed many lives, not just mine."

What did she mean? Simon sat at the table and picked up his half-full mug, sudden fear constricting his throat. "Is he a murderer? Is he a rapist?"

"No, no Simon. It's not like that. In his eyes, he loved me and did everything he could for me and you, our child. You know that. The man you know and love is your father, Simon. He's not *only* wicked. But he did something wicked."

"Just spit it out, Mum. What did he do?"

"He stole my life."

Simon thumped his mug on the table and a bit of tea sloshed over the rim. "Your life looks pretty good to me. It's still going, isn't it? You had me with Dad—doesn't that justify those years together? Making a family?"

"I had a family."

Simon's heart thumped. He thought of the Selkie story he had read in school. The one where the fisherman falls in love with a Selkie—half woman, half seal—and steals her skin so she cannot wrap it around herself to change back into a seal and return to the sea. The woman stays with him for years and they have children, but she pines constantly for the sea—her true home—and the family she had had there. One day she finds the sealskin and leaves her new family to go back to her first family, and her true love. A sudden terror gripped Simon's heart. "You have other children?"

"No, no! Only you, my dearest Simon. Oh, I'm doing this badly—this is hard!"

Anger supplanted terror. Simon leapt to his feet. "So you had me with Dad. We're your family. And now you can see your original family. Lots of people leave home and create new families in different places, and don't see their parents and siblings too much. What do you mean, Dad stole your life? What do you mean, he did something wicked? Creating a loving family for me—that was wicked?"

Alley got to her feet too. "This isn't going right. You're not listening. I am not always a good speaker. I want to tell it like a story, but spoken narrative no longer works that way in our culture. But I have written it down, Simon." Alley reached her hand up the front of her shirt and wriggled a thick notebook out of the band of her skirt. She held it out to Simon.

"I always write my journals like stories. Maybe I dreamed of getting published one day, even though I know it's impossible to publish this story, because it would betray the secrecy of the island. Because this story is true, Simon. This happened. This is your history, and your destiny. Read it calmly. I love you."

Simon reached out and took the journal.

Even if Toby hadn't barked, they would have heard the car in the sudden silence. Simon got to his feet and clutched his mother tightly, preventing her from reaching the pendant, crushed between their bodies.

"Simon," she said with infinite gentleness. "Every decision I have made since you were born, has revolved around you."

Simon looked into his mother's eyes. He sensed she was speaking the truth, but along with his excitement about this new world unfurling before his eyes, was fear. His current world was falling apart. There might be new worlds, as yet unimagined, waiting for him, but what was happening to the world that he had always taken for granted? His world was this house, these parents, this dog. His definition of family was the one factor you could rely on to love you, support you, and keep you safe. In a world full of hostility, ignorance, and cruelty, his family was his safety net. They loved him. They were supposed to love each other. Unto death. What was happening?

Suddenly, everything that he had assumed to be safe, wasn't. His life, as he had known it, was about to change.

His mind kept returning to the one sticking point that—unbelievably—was destroying his safety net. "You said you believed Dad stole the pendant from you, but you don't know for sure, do you Mum?"

"You will read the story, Simon. You will judge for yourself."

"Can I join the hug?" his father's deep voice spoke from the doorway. As Simon watched, his mother's face changed. Hatred and contempt filled it, and she began to detach herself from Simon's embrace, without once looking towards her husband.

In two strides John was by her side, his own face revealing love and sadness and fear. "Alley, you have to listen to me. You owe me that. Haven't the years of love I've given you earned me the right to be listened to, before you cast me off so heartlessly?"

She recoiled from him, as though he were a poisonous snake. She clutched the pendant in both hands. "If you try to take it by force, I'll just disappear. You know I can do that. You'll be holding empty air."

"Oh my God," John cried. "Do you think I'm a monster? Do you think I'd try and take it from you by force, if it's so precious to you?"

"Why not? You took it from me by stealth and deceit; why not by force?"

"I. Did. Not. Take. It. From. You."

Alley turned to Simon and smiled, but he noticed that her eyes still watched her husband's every move. "I'm going now, Simon. I have to see my family, discuss the new situation with the Leaders of the island, like we talked about."

Simon looked at his father's wretched face; he felt torn and unhappy. Suddenly, he wanted his mother to stay with them and forget this other world—what had that place to do with their family?

"Don't go Mum. Please."

"Simon. I know this is difficult for you. A lot of things are changing, very quickly. But you are the most important person in my life. Trust me."

"Trust you to do what? I trusted that you were my Mum and this was my Dad and we were a family. That trust was destroyed just like that ..." and Simon snapped his fingers in the air.

"Alley, for God's sake," John said. "Think of the boy. Think of our son. He is the only important thing in this mess you are creating. You've got it all wrong. I would never do anything to hurt you. Don't hurt him, out of spite for something you think I've done. Don't leave us!"

"Oh, I'm not leaving him, John."

If you give the pendant to your mother, Simon, neither of us will ever see her again.

At that moment, Simon didn't care about the magical new possibilities that the pendant had opened up for him. He cared that his father was in pain, that his family was breaking apart, that his mother's feelings for his father had transformed from affectionate indifference to hatred … and that her reasons were probably wrong. His father, a thief? The idea was preposterous! She kept telling him how important he was, but she wasn't doing what he wanted, or thinking about his needs. He'd make it clear, in case his mother hadn't understood. In case she was confused by his earlier enthusiasm. If he made it clear, and she still didn't listen, then maybe his father was right. Maybe she was planning to disappear forever. The thought made him want to weep and weep. "Mum, listen. I don't want you to go. I don't want to time travel. I want us to stay together as a family."

John stepped closer to Simon and hugged him to his side. Alley withdrew at the same time, although Simon tried to clutch her back to his chest. John's arm brushed against his wife in the process, and she grimaced as if he had burnt her.

Alley smiled at her son, but it didn't reach her eyes. "Your father's fear is infecting you, Simon. Before he came, you were talking quite differently. I will be waiting for you tomorrow when you get home from school."

"Don't go!"

Alley stepped away from them, holding the pendant in her hand. "What are you saying, Simon? That I shouldn't go and see my own parents, whom I haven't seen for sixteen years?"

Simon wasn't sure what he was saying. He only knew that fear and confusion were gaining the upper hand, and he could hardly remember what he'd been so excited about. "We can travel there together, without pendants. You said so."

Alley gave him an odd look. "That takes several days. I have some questions that I need answered immediately, without dragging you away from school for a couple of weeks. What is the matter, Simon? What are you frightened of?"

Simon glanced at his father's distraught face, trying to formulate an answer. Alley saw his look. "I'm afraid I can't alleviate your fear on that one, Simon. I know it's tough when parents get divorced. But this marriage is over ..."

A cry broke from John's lips, he moved towards Alley, his arms outstretched. She backed away, holding up the pendant between them like it was a shield. She never once looked at his face, but continued to speak to Simon.

"Nothing can change that. It'll take time for you to get used to this new reality. I understand. I'm sorry."

"What have I done? How is this happening to me?" John said, staggering, and grasped the back of a chair to steady himself. Simon's heart wrenched as he saw the tears in his father's eyes.

"Look at me, Simon!" Alley said. "You are my beloved son. I have no idea what the Leaders of the island are doing to decide, but I do know this: even if they give me permission to live there again, in that special, wonderful, safe, place, I won't if you can't live there with me. And you know what else? Even if they give you permission to live there, but you decide that you don't want to live so far away from your father, I will stay in this town for your sake, until you finish school. Do you hear me Simon? I want desperately to go back to my home, but if you choose to stay here, and want me by your side, then I will be here for you."

Simon looked at his parents in wonder. It was as if they had changed places. His strong father, who ran both home and job, looking after everything, was slumped over the chair like a rag doll. His mother, whose life force had drained away over the past few years until she was almost entirely reliant on her husband, was overflowing with energy and certainty. Her words calmed him. He believed her.

One of your parents is lying, man. Hate to break it to you.

That's what Sandra had said. But she had also told him to trust his own instincts. He felt in his heart that his mother spoke the truth. She wouldn't abandon him. "Will you come back tomorrow?"

"I said I would. But one more thing I have to say. I know it's painful, but your father and I will never live together again. It will take time for you to accept that, but I want to be completely honest with you, so you don't build impossible expectations."

A groan burst from his father's throat and he collapsed on the floor, still clinging to the back of the chair. "Why should he believe you, when you've lied to me? What about our marriage vows? How can you live with someone for years, then judge, condemn, and abandon them without a trial?"

"Can't you curb your feelings in front of your son? You're upsetting him."

John looked incredulous. "Sorry that I'm upset, Simon, but your mother is destroying my happiness and my life without reason."

Alley snickered grimly. "Because my talisman walked to this house which *you* bought, marched down to that mysterious basement underneath *your* workshop all by itself, and locked itself into a chest."

And she was gone, just like that.

CHAPTER FIVE

THERE WAS COMPLETE silence for a minute, as they both stared at the empty space where Alley had been a moment before. Then Toby uttered a short bark, and began sniffing the area where Alley had been standing. He kept glancing at his two humans, as though they were playing an elaborate trick on him, just like they often did with his ball. He made Simon smile, as usual. He held his hands up, palms towards the sky. "Where is she, Toby? Where'd she go?"

Instantly, he regretted the humour in his tone and glanced guiltily towards his father, who had folded himself into a small space on the floor, like a foetus.

"Can I get you a cup of tea, Dad?"

John lifted his head from the floor and tried to smile. "I think I just want to be alone for a while, son."

Simon was relieved. He felt sorry for his father, but he didn't know how he could help him. And there was a tad of discomfort too.

Because the talisman walked to this house all by itself, marched down to that mysterious basement underneath your workshop, and locked itself into a chest.

He laid his hand on his father's shoulder as he left the room.

Simon wanted to mull over what had happened. He wanted to think deeply about everything his mother had revealed to him. But as soon as he heard his father close the door to his own bedroom, Simon retrieved his mother's journal. He gazed down at the cardboard cover, empty except for his mother's name. Fascination and trepidation battled for precedence. Fascination won, and Simon turned to the first page.

* * *

Today was the day! Today was the day! I could barely contain my excitement as I pranced home from work, my last day teaching. I always enjoyed the walk home, past the little homesteads with their allotments overflowing with produce and clusters of animals. Most houses on the island boasted near self-sufficiency in terms of food. Many families had several acres; in addition to large gardens and orchards which provided fruit and vegetables, people kept chickens, pigs and goats for eggs, milk, cheese and meat. Often neighbours would grow different crops, swapping their watermelons for someone else's peaches when harvest time came. Very few items were imported to the island; if a fruit or vegetable wasn't in season, it wasn't available. That was fine by me—when every food item is available all the time, how can you appreciate the seasons?

I rounded the last corner and there was my own, dear little house. I was passionately fond of it, even though it was just a shack really, with one bedroom, a study, a diminutive kitchen and sitting room. All the houses on the island were small, but mine was especially tiny. I loved it. My vegetable garden and the orchard nestled behind my house, merging into a field that plunged into the forest. The goat enclosure straddled both field and forest.

My boyfriend François was standing in the kitchen, shovelling the last of the pasta into his mouth. "I'm off," he said.

"What? Do you know where you're going already?" Of course he was excited too, just like me, but would he have waited to say good-bye if I'd come home five minutes later? Sometimes it was hard to know how much François cared for me. Or how much I cared for him.

"The Leaders said that 2022 was a pivotal time in our history, so I

thought I'd fast-forward 36 years and check out where I'm going to be then. Perhaps I'll be in a place where I can do some good."

I felt a surge of excitement at his words. Last night the Leaders had held a special meeting and changed the rules. We'd never been allowed to communicate with our other selves when we time-travelled (we weren't even allowed to show ourselves) and we could only stay for four hours in any given place. Rules like these derived from the fear that our time travel would impact history in some way. But last night all those rules had changed. "Humanity is hurtling towards self-extinction," Jacob, one of the Leaders, had said. "Many of you standing here today are going to live to over 100 years old. In your time travels to the future you have seen wars over lack of water and food. Whole coastal towns swallowed up by rising water levels. Hundreds of thousands of species that we take for granted today, gone in the next 100 years. Increasingly terrible natural calamities. In light of this dire situation, we have decided to change our time travel policies." Jacob paused for effect, then pronounced solemnly: "We are going to try and change history."

It was terrible to hear that the future of the world was so bleak. I hadn't known. Although we had the ability to travel the length and breadth of our own life spans, I rarely visited the future. I wanted my life to be revealed to me like the surprises behind each door in an advent calendar. But many people on the island did travel to the future and some of the younger ones had come back with shocked faces. So now we were allowed to try and convince the world to change the future. The usual four-hour limit had been extended to four days at a time and, best of all, we could team up with our future selves!

"Maybe I'll go with you to 2022," I told François. "I can check out whether you'll still be handsome at 61."

Francois smiled and kissed the top of my head. "That's a great idea, Rakita, but we probably won't land in the same time or place. Let's go."

I fingered the chain that secured my precious talisman to my neck. It was true that we had no control over where our talismans took us. We requested the year, but who knew where we'd land during that year? Some island people thought the date we landed was completely random; others felt that the talismans had a Grand Plan of their own.

"Perhaps holding hands will impact where we end up. How about we travel to 2022, and see if we land together?" This seemed a sensible idea, until I stopped the rush of adrenalin coursing through my body and allowed my brain to think for a second. "We might not be together in 2022. We'll be wherever our future selves are."

François was practically dancing on the balls of his feet, he was so eager to go. "Maybe our future selves are together. If not, we'll both come back here in exactly four days. By that time, we'll both know where we are in 2022, so we can coordinate. But try coming with me anyway—just for fun!"

I was affected by his enthusiasm, so we clasped our left hands and held our talismans with our right. I closed my eyes. I wish I was 61. *I waited for the familiar whoosh of air to envelop me, but I didn't feel anything. After a moment I opened my eyes. François wasn't there; I was standing by myself.* Damn, *I thought.* I guess I'm not in Paris at 61. Or the US. *But then it struck me. I was standing in exactly the same spot as I'd been two minutes before, with François. Weird. I would be living in exactly the same shack in 36 years? Not that I minded, I loved my shack, but still. So where was my 61-year-old self? I looked around carefully. For the first time, a frisson of panic bubbled across my scalp. Where was I? Where was my 61-year-old self?*

"Calm down," I chided myself irritably. "You haven't even looked thoroughly through the house yet, let alone the gardens." But the panic continued to throb in my temples. It didn't work like this. You always arrived out of sight, but usually not out of earshot, and always, always in close proximity to your past or future self. I'd never had to search *for myself.*

In the hopes that it would calm that throb of panic, I began to methodically check every possible location in each room; then the impossible ones—behind the sofas and under the table in our snug sitting room. Then I went to the bedroom, opening closets, rifling through the clothes, checking under the bed. I stopped searching and listened intently; several species of birds were singing joyfully outside the window. I could hear the hum of the wind turbines on the little hill that signalled the beginning of my five acres. There was no other sound.

There were only two more rooms. There was nowhere to hide in the bathroom, but I flicked back the shower curtain in any case and, absurdly, opened the little cupboard underneath the sink, which wouldn't have contained my four-year-old self, let alone a grown woman.

I almost ran to the kitchen, rummaging through drawers now, pulling out the fridge to gawk behind it, as ancient dust bunnies rolled across the floor. I knew it was ridiculous, absurd; of course my futuristic self wasn't crammed into a drawer. But where the hell was she? What was going on? It was the first time in my time travels that I hadn't found myself easily, although I'd almost always travelled backwards in time. I was frightened. Maybe the time travelling hadn't worked, for some reason? I grasped the talisman again. I wish I was 61. *My eyes flew open and travelled around the room. Same place, same year. Same Rakita. Could my talisman be malfunctioning? Or perhaps there were so many island people transporting to different eras right now that the talismans were getting confused? I smiled, despite my worry. Confused talismans sounded implausible, even to me.*

Perhaps there was something wrong with the year 2022. I made a mental note to check it out with other people, trying to ignore the absence of François, which indicated that 2022 had worked just fine for him.

I wish I was 50.

No whoosh of air, lifting me off my feet. No rushing wind in my ears. I didn't even need to open my eyes to know I was still in exactly the same place.

I wish I was 46.

Nothing. The panic had moved from my temples to behind my eyes, which were wide with fear.

I wish I was 40.

I almost stumbled; the whoosh of wind was so sudden and unexpected.

Joy lambasted the panic as I opened my eyes and found myself in an unknown room. The unmistakeable sound of my own voice was snapping at someone on the phone in an adjoining room. I found myself in a good-sized area, doubling as a sitting room and a kitchen, with lots of windows. I sprang to a window and looked down at a familiar Central Park, though I'd never been in NY before. Apparently, I would be living in NY in the year 2001, right downtown. A tug of anxiety replaced the throb of fear that had lodged in my chest. Was I destined to die somewhere between the ages of 40 and 46? I glanced surreptitiously through the door at my enraged self, still bellowing down the phone. She was sitting in what appeared to be an office; a tiny room dominated by a huge desk.

"We'll drape our bodies across the bloody land if we have to! That area is home to millions of species ... no, I'm not exaggerating ... maybe I am including insects, everything is vital in the food chain, you idiot ... they'll build homes in that area over my dead body ..."

I smiled to myself. It made sense that I would become an environmental activist, given what I was doing in my twenties. I listened to my angry self for a few moments, hopeful of hearing a hint about the state of the world in the 21st century, but no luck.

Since my future-self was so absorbed in her phone call she probably wouldn't notice if I lurched across her line of vision, I decided to explore a little bit. I began to poke my head into the different rooms in the apartment. It wasn't large; either I would never lose my preference for small, cozy, and manageable, or downtown New York apartments were really expensive. There was a bedroom with a double bed, strewn with papers and books. The bathroom was small and Spartan; a peek in the mirror cupboard showed that I would still use the same face cream in 15 years. I opened the last door with a curious longing in my heart, which barely registered until the longing sharpened into disappointment as I discovered that the extra door led to a closet. Forty years old, and no kids? I had always loved kids—wasn't I going to have any? Forty years old, hmmm; leaving it a bit late. My career must be pretty amazing, if I'd waited so long or (please no) changed my mind.

Anyway, at least I was alive and kicking and still making a difference at age 40. There was nothing more to discover here. I put my hand over my talisman.

I wish I was 25.

Back in my dear little shack, I went outside and fed the animals before making myself a cup of tea and swallowing the pill that would enable me to travel without exhaustion all day. That was another change the Leaders had implemented last night. Time travel was so tiring that we could only do it once a day, but the Leaders had given us pills that would lend us the strength to time travel several times a day. Tea always helped me to think, and I wanted to work out a plan. I would be alive at 40. Should I try and visit 41, 42, and so on, until I couldn't find myself anymore? Did I really want to know, if I were destined to die so young? No, I didn't. I grasped my talisman quickly, before I drowned in my own thoughts.

I wish I was 80.

The whoosh of air. The sensation of spinning. Gratitude filled my heart. I opened my eyes and found myself squatting behind an overturned car, watching my older self crouching behind a similar vehicle just ahead of me. The air was filled with smoke and the sound of gunshots. It was dreadfully hot. I watched as Future-me pulled herself with difficulty to her feet, calling to a young man racing by. "What is happening?"

"It's another invasion. From the East this time." The man took the opportunity to catch his breath, leaning against the car and examining his gun.

I craned my neck to see better. Not a single blade of grass or sound of a bird call. Grey cement, grey humans, grey weapons.

"What are they invading for this time?" Future-me asked.

"Same thing as always. Their homes have been swallowed up by rising coastal waters. They don't have clean food or water. This is a war without an end. Too many people and not enough resources."

"God gave us such a magnificent world. How did we manage to destroy it all?"

I looked at Future-me in surprise. God? I'd never believed in God. A bullet whooshed by my ear and I grasped my talisman to go home. I'd seen enough. Now I understood why the Leaders had changed the rules.

I felt dispirited from the depressing scene I'd just witnessed, the avoidable devastation that humankind was visiting on itself. But I was alive at 80. How come I couldn't find myself between the ages of 44 and 61? How many more years would I be lost? On an impulse, I grasped my talisman.

I wish I was 62.

I only stayed long enough to note that I appeared to be striding across a large field full of cows ... and cow patties. My 62-year-old self was trudging through the patties without taking the slightest notice and talking energetically to a female companion of approximately the same age. My guess was that I was in England. My heart lightened, filled with gratitude at my obvious good health, but I didn't tarry. I had a mission, and getting too obsessed about my own future at this juncture wasn't helpful. I needed to visit my parents, pack, and focus on doing some good during whatever future years I could access.

I wish I was 25.

∞ *My parents were both delighted and saddened to see me, knowing I had come to bid them farewell. My mother made tea and we carried our mugs to the table under the oak tree in the back of their house, looking out at the rows of fruit trees and bee hives that comprised their orchard. Chickens scratched in the dirt around the trees.*

"Do you know where you're going to?" my mother asked.

"I had planned to aim for 2022, but something very weird happened, Mum. There was a gap of ... well, of years ... where I don't seem to be anywhere at all. But I don't die young, because I'm still alive at 80."

My mother looked fixedly into her steaming mug. I waited for a moment. "Mum?"

"I noticed that too," she said in a small voice.

"What?"

"There seems to be a period of, well, years, just like you say, where I can't *find you." My mother looked at me, and I saw that her eyes were filled with tears. I suddenly realised that she had known about this before me.*

"Why didn't you tell me?" Although I knew very well. Another rule. If you discovered something about someone else during your time travels, you couldn't tell them. If they were supposed to know whatever it was, their own talismans would reveal it to them.

"I went to the Leaders to discuss it and they seemed to think it could only mean something ... bad. I'm so sorry."

"Bad how?"

"They said that the only circumstances where a person has 'disappeared' like that, are limited to the few cases where people have been banished from the island."

I stared at the chickens, digesting this new thought. Repercussions to breaking one of the island's rules could be severe, and the Leader's words from last night rang in my head: "It is extremely important that you respect the new rules just like you've always respected the old. Never exceed your four-day limit! First, because we need frequent check-ins, and second, because it is essential to remember that we are only visiting our future selves, and we must remain attached to our real-time lives. We cannot live two lives simultaneously. Once you start living for four days at a time somewhere else, that will become your permanent abode, so you won't be able to control the exact date of your time travel back to the island. Even so, it is still vital that you come every four days, according to the time in your permanent abode. We don't know if this change will result in a dangerous mixing of our future and present lives, so the repercussions for break-ing the rules are severe. If you stay more than four days at a time in your future, you will be stripped of your ability to time travel and banished from the island."

I look up at my mother. "But I will never be late coming home. Never. That Instruction Book they gave us with the new rules ... I'll memorize every one. I'll stick to them like glue!"

My mother put her hand over mine. "Don't worry, my dear daughter.

What will be, will be. It can't be so very bad, because you don't disappear forever."

I shook my head, trying to clear the worries away. "It took me by surprise. I've never tried to figure out exactly what I do in my future life. I've just kind of bopped around a bit for fun, until now."

My mother laughed. "There seems to be two types of island people, those who want to know every detail about their entire lives, and those who prefer to find out the traditional way."

My father, Harry, brought a tray with three bowls of strawberries and cream. I took a bite appreciatively; there was nothing more delicious than freshly-picked strawberries, succulent with juice, with a dollop of my mother's thick cream.

My parents held their cups of tea in the air. "To a successful mission!" We all clinked cups.

Harry began to analyse the reasons for the Leaders' unprecedented, extraordinary decision to change the rules so dramatically. "For the first time in our island's history, we are going to double up with our future selves. They would never have done such a thing if the world wasn't truly under threat."

Underneath the excitement I felt a frisson of fear. Was humanity itself threatened? How could our intervention make any difference?

When my father had finished his soliloquy, I asked my parents if they would look after my animals while I was gone. My parents had never been big travellers, and would probably not find themselves in a different country in their futures, so they were expecting the question. The Leaders had covered everything last night, including what would happen to our present, deserted lives: "For those of you who cannot visit your future selves in a different country, because you spend your lives here on the island, you are just as vital to this endeavour! The essential jobs, like teachers and nurses, must continue to be filled. You will also have extra duties caring for the livestock of absent owners."

My parents glanced at each other. "Doesn't your nanny goat have a nasty habit of plunging her hoof into the milk?"

I thought of Nanny's leg-waving shenanigans. "Just with François, and that's only because he takes so long to milk she gets bored."

"Of course we'll look after your animals, darling," my mother said, standing up to hug me goodbye.

I felt strangely reluctant to go, even though that was absurd. No matter where I ended up, I could visit home every day if I wished.

I kissed my parents and trotted back to my own house. I pottered around for a while, packing a knapsack with a few clothes and books, my diary, washing stuff, and some sandals. I dressed warmly and donned boots, sweating in the warmth of the island's sun. Finally, I grasped my talisman, and in quick succession visited myself at 42 (still in the New York apartment); 43 (ditto); 44: ah-hah, a different apartment. My future-self was apparently sleeping on the couch. I tip-toed over to the window and peeked out. I was high up in a tall building and the view was amazing; beyond an expanse of buildings and parking lots, the distinctive pyramids of the Muttart Conservatory staked their impressive claim across the river. Apparently at 44 I will have moved from New York to Edmonton. I moved silently around the apartment, noting with satisfaction that I had remained true to my Spartan taste: this place was even smaller than my digs in New York. There were only 3 rooms—a sitting room (where I lay slumbering on the couch) with a kitchenette in one corner; a bedroom, and an office, which sported a huge tack board covering an entire wall. I moved closer to take a look. Bolded names of local oil corporations were followed by lists of facts. My future-self had done some serious homework. I air-kissed her goodbye as I departed.

I tried 45 next; I was still in Edmonton.

At 46, I didn't budge from the island. Ditto for 50, 55, 60. Whatever caused my disappearance, it seemed to have wiped me off the planet for around 16 years. I knew I was in England at 62, and in Edmonton at 44/45. Where should I travel, 2006 or 2023? 2023 was closer to the years I'd originally intended to travel, but I was in England, not the West. The cow-patty infested field in England didn't scream "Help" in the same way that the Edmonton apartment had, with its lists of local oil corporations tacked onto the wall. I grabbed my knapsack with one hand and my talisman with the other.

I wish I was 45.

∞ *The rules in the Instruction Book that the Leaders had given me stipulated what to say to our future selves. Determined to stick to every rule like glue, I placed my knapsack gently on the couch and went to look for myself. I was in the office, furiously typing on a laptop. As I drew closer to peer over her shoulder, I saw that she was toggling back and forth between different environmental sites, and pasting lines of information into what looked like a blank sheet of paper on the computer. My mouth gaped open at the speed of this modern machine. Suddenly, my future-self whipped around and saw me. To say she was surprised would be an understatement.*

"What the hell?"

"Hello Rakita, I'm Rakita," I couldn't help grinning.

"And you are talking to me because ...?"

"Well, that's a long story, so why don't we ..." and we both spoke at the same time, "... make a cup of tea."

Yup, I would have a lot in common with future-me. We perched on either end of her tiny couch as I jogged her memory about the events from 1986. "The Leaders told us to pick dates 20, 30, 40 years from our current time and—if we found ourselves in places where help was needed, we were to double up with our future selves as environmental activists and spread the word ..."

"I remember now," Future-me interrupted, blowing on her tea. "I've been doing that ever since, and I'm still doing it. People choose to make individual changes quick enough once they understand the impact on their children's lives if they don't."

It was so weird, seeing my face 20 years older, although I hadn't aged badly, if I did say so myself.

"Yeah I know, but now there's two of us."

She smiled. "The four-day limit was like a pilot test. They'll monitor you carefully to gauge the impact of the new rules. You're going to have to

fill out a ton of forms listing every action and conversation that you par-
ticipate in."

I whispered mischievously, "Does the pilot test go well?"

"You know I can't answer questions that reveal your future. But there
are reasons for those rules and I'm not sure they should have changed them,
even for such a vital cause. A person can't inhabit a time without impact,
and two timelines can't coexist simultaneously."

I searched her face for a clue to her meaning, because I knew she'd
clam up if I asked for clarification, just like I would if a younger version
of myself asked me. I had been worried for a minute that she had been
referring to our disappearance. I shook my head to clear it. I had to forget
about the bloody disappearance: I had an important mission to focus on.

"We're not really coexisting. We're just spending a little longer together
than usual."

"We're coexisting. Just don't forget what'll happen to me if you stay
longer than four days." She drew a hand across her throat. She meant she'd
disappear. That's why the rules were so strict—two timelines can't exist at
the same time.

There was a short silence. "Do you remember Rambo?" I said, to
lighten the mood.

She threw her head back and laughed, spilling her tea. "That bloody
buck! He spent his whole life aiming his horns at my legs. Every time he
butted me, I would grab him by those same horns and flip him over onto
his back, bellowing in his face, 'I'm the alpha here—got it?'"

I began to laugh too. "And he'd stare up at me sheepishly; he did look
extremely silly on his back like that, so I wasn't surprised at his embarrassment. Eventually I'd release him and continue with my chores. I could see
him struggling with himself as my enticing legs swished back and forth in
front of his vision. He knew he'd be flipped again, but he couldn't resist
the temptation."

"Yeah! I remember his head lowering incrementally every time a leg
crossed his vision, until he couldn't stand it anymore and he'd run full-tilt
at them."

"Damn him. My legs were always covered in bruises during Rambo's brief sojourn."

"But didn't he taste the best?"

"Revenge is sweet."

∞ *We spent the rest of the day hunched over the computer, talking and quaffing endless cups of tea. Future-me brought me up to speed on all the work she'd been doing. She was focusing on three major oil corporations: PetroWorldBase, ConocoJames, and BigOilGramby. She had created a website, and launched what she called a Facebook campaign. My mouth was hanging open at the incredible things future computers could do. Answers would miraculously appear to whatever question she typed on this page called Google. Facebook enabled you to reach tons of people with one click of the mouse. It was impressive. She had organized demonstrations, visited schools (which tallied with the Leaders' focus on education) and stood at street corners handing out pamphlets and belting out her message to anyone who would listen. She was way ahead of me, and I wasn't surprised when she began to dictate my duties for the next day.*

"You can take over one of the oil companies that I've been targeting. They're all fortune 500 oil corporations that are way more focused on making money than minimizing damage. No surprise there. Which fat dog would you like to go for?"

I looked at the three images on the screen—the fat dogs of PetroWorldBase, ConocoJames, and BigOilGramby. The Vice President of BigOilGramby was younger, and I liked his uni-brow.

"I have tried to set up meetings with some of their fattest dogs, but without success," Future-me continued.

I pointed to Uni-brow on the screen. She wrote down his name and the address of BigOilGramby on a slip of paper and handed it to me. "The fattest of the fat dogs. If you can get this idiot to listen to you, you'll be worth your keep. Now, how about some food?"

I stood to one side and watched as she zipped around her tiny kitchenette, whipping up sandwiches that had just the right amount of mayo, of course. It was strange, watching myself like that. Identical mannerisms, identical habits, identical person. Mind-boggling. I began to understand why the rules prohibited any contact or communication during our time travels. "So this Google entity, anything that I want to know, I just ask it? That's pretty cool; almost like magic."

"Yeah, except anyone can write anything there, so you have to know which sources to trust."

Future-me leapt right back into her instructions after we'd eaten, but whatever adrenalin had been coursing through my body had dried up. I was utterly exhausted. Time travel is tiring and I'd bopped around so much today that even the pills they'd given us seemed to have lost their power. Future-me didn't notice my eyes glazing over, but she certainly noticed when my head pitched forward, and then jerked upright. "Oh, for goodness sake," she said crossly. I wondered if 'changing the rules' could actually change my future character, because it was clear I needed a touch more sensitivity in my make-up. But her next words were: "Bed." She made a comfy nest on the sofa for me; I crawled under the covers and was dead to the world within minutes.

The next day when I woke up, I was alone in the apartment. A large note was propped against a book on the coffee table beside my sofa-bed, telling me to help myself to whatever I wanted, followed by a list of what I should try and accomplish that day. It seemed a very long list for my first day on the 'job', but I wasn't going to get all tense about it. (Was I going to end up a workaholic?) I'd start at the beginning and do what I could. The first job on the list was to waylay Mr. Fat Cat as he exited a meeting at BigOilGramby at precisely 10:30 a.m. Damn, it was already 9:30. Future-me had left instructions on how to use Google. I still couldn't get over how answers miraculously appeared to whatever question I typed. How could there still be dumb people in the 21st century, when they had all this knowledge at their fingertips? How come everyone wasn't reacting to the climate crisis as though it were the most important war they'd ever fought, if the proof was in front of their faces?

I 'googled' how to get from downtown Edmonton to BigOilGramby:

it would take approximately half an hour. I showered and ate in record time, and pulled a smart business suit from Future-me's closet. (Somehow I knew she wouldn't mind.) I put on some make up, pulling my hair into a bun, so I'd look professional. I was rather pleased with the results. Future-me had left what she called an iPhone, which I wasn't sure how to use, and some money, which might have been enough for lunch, or just enough for my bus fare; I hadn't a clue how much things cost. In any case, I didn't have time to make a sandwich, so I grabbed the money and a bag of pamphlets and was standing outside a multi-storied building some thirty-seven minutes later, having sprinted all the way from my final bus stop. Fortune was on my side. Fat Cat was just exiting the building as I raced up, so I braked madly in time to walk sedately over to him, rehearsing my practiced speech in my head.

"Hello Mr. Scendel," I said, smiling kindly in the hopes that it would mask the fact that I was breathing heavily from my sprint. "I was wondering if I could have a word with you about something very important?"

He looked down at me—he was much better looking than on the computer screen—and smiled. "My name is John. As it happens, I'm looking for some lunch. I hate eating alone; perhaps you'll join me?"

My heart soared. Future-me had said if I managed to talk to this guy I'd be worth my keep, and he'd immediately invited me for lunch! Then I felt suspicious; it was way too early for lunch. "You don't even know me."

He smiled at me. "First, you look very familiar, so perhaps I do know you. Second, the way you're wheezing and gasping is very endearing."

I giggled. I couldn't help it. He steered me into a nearby restaurant, explaining that he'd been working since 5 a.m., hence the early lunch. We sat by a huge aquarium filled with fascinating fish. I rarely went to restaurants, and between perusing the complex menu and returning the gawking of the fish, who seemed to be congregating next to our table, I forgot that one is supposed to small talk. I glanced at my companion guiltily; he was looking at me with an odd expression, but he lowered his gaze as soon as our eyes caught.

"Would you like me to order for you? I eat here a lot."

"Thank you, yes," I replied in relief, my gaze drawn irresistibly back to the fish, who blew bubbles at me gently. I remembered my mission. "So, I know you've probably heard a lot of criticism from other environmentalists, but ..."

"None as pretty as you," he said.

The fish and I looked at him frostily. "Would you consider yourself a reasonably intelligent person?" I asked, rolling my eyes at the sympathetic fish.

"I am the Executive Vice President at BigOilGramby. I handle millions of dollars every day. I make decisions that affect thousands of lives. Do you know how much I make?"

"I couldn't care less how much you make. You Westerners are so vulgar."

To my surprise, he burst out laughing. The fish and I were not amused. "Where are you from?" he asked.

"So every intelligent person has a way of making decisions in their lives," I said, ignoring his question. "Choosing between right and wrong. What is your way?"

"Well, right now I'm trying to decide how to get you to go out with me tonight."

"Be serious," I said angrily.

Immediately, he smartened up. "I suppose when I make a decision, I look at all the facts, weighing the pros and cons."

Yay, he'd played right into my hands. "So when you decide to forge ahead with digging for more oil, refining it, and selling it, how do you reconcile the pros of that process—financial gain, with the cons—the destruction of our planet?"

The waiter materialized to take our order. John ordered wine; I told him I didn't drink. He ordered beef Wellington; I told him I never ate beef, first because feeding massive numbers of cows gobbled up vast tracts of land, and second, because their methane-ridden flatulence was harming the environment. Didn't he know this? He said if I'd only agree to taste the wine, he'd never eat beef again. The waiter looked baffled, but the fish seemed to approve of this compromise.

Finally, he answered my question as we sipped on the wine, which was truly delicious. "There are scientists that say that human impact on the earth's climate is minimal, and that global warming would have happened anyway."

"The vast majority of scientists agree unequivocally that humans are the main cause, and that we must reduce our carbon emissions if we want to survive."

"That's an exaggeration."

I glanced at the fish for support, and they rolled their eyes at me. I wished I could tell him that I had seen what the world would look like in half a century. "We are already feeling the effects of global warming, in the form of catastrophes like fire, flood, and more extreme weather. How can you define yourself as intelligent if you ignore science when its truth doesn't suit you? Are you so desperate to make money now that you're willing to destroy the lives of your own children?" My voice was getting a little emotional, so I stopped abruptly.

"What can one man do?"

"As top dog in an oil giant, you could do so much! Start by convincing your company that the era of oil is coming to its end, and they should be investing in renewable sources of energy ..."

He snorted with laughter.

I plunged on. "It's not just change at the corporate level, though that obviously has the most impact. As individuals, we should all be thinking of how to tweak our lives: reducing our energy use ..."

"Why do we have to reduce our energy use? I thought you said we just had to switch our source of energy to renewables?"

The waiter set down a plate exuding smells to die for. Every shellfish in existence festooned my plate, each in its own little nest of exquisite sauce. I glanced at the fish with a touch of guilt, but they undulated their approval. "No, we have to reduce our energy use. We can't continue to binge on energy like we've been doing ever since we discovered fossil fuels."

"And that's supposed to persuade me?"

"No." I pointed my fork at him. "The fact that your children won't be

able to breathe clean air should persuade you. Can't you reduce your entitled consumerism so that your children live reasonable lives? Climate change isn't some future issue. It's already happening."

"Of course I believe in the science, I know this is happening. Now eat your dinner."

The first mouth-watering morsel of lobster in cognac-cream sauce, washed down by a wine that enriched its flavour, almost rendered me speechless. It was a struggle to remember my mission. "Answer my question."

"Of course I want my children to breathe fresh air. And I support the changes that are happening. I support the carbon tax, for example. But Rome wasn't built in a day and these things take time."

I frowned. "Change at the corporate level might take time, but change at the personal level must be immediate. Collectively, humans produce more emissions than corporations. What you do matters. So stop bloody buying crap all the time that you don't need. Stop eating beef. You said you were intelligent; it's all about thinking before you do anything. Do I really have to take this plane trip today? Do I really have to drive to the shop, or can I walk?"

Damn, the food was good. I could count on one hand the number of times I'd had food like this. But ... my mission. "Think about every decision. What charities do I donate to? Are they environmentally conscious? Is my bank? Since I'm so very, very rich, and so revoltingly privileged, how can I turn my privilege to good use? If I gave 50% of my salary away every year, would I even notice?"

He held up his hand. "OK, I get your point. You are very persuasive."

The fish swam closer to the glass as I leant forward in anticipation: had I changed his perspective?

"Are you always this preachy?"

"What?"

"I've never met anyone quite like you before, so don't be offended, but you're not saying anything interesting or original ... just a bunch of environmentalist jargon clichés ..."

Oh my god—had I screwed up? Was I just spouting old news?

"... anybody but me would find you insufferable, arrogant, self-righteous, and demanding."

I looked at him, really looked at him for the first time. I liked his piercing blue eyes mounted by thick black brows that met over his hooked nose. His words hadn't offended me, they'd made him seem more trustworthy. Obviously, I had to work at my job before I could get good at it.

Smiling, he reached over and speared one of the buttery scallops on my plate with his fork, then held it before my lips.

Surprised, my lips parted involuntarily to receive it. He was staring at my lips so hard I couldn't enjoy it, so I closed my eyes. The most tender, luscious tidbit.

"I'll tell you what," he said, leaning over the table confidentially. "From your very long list of things I could be doing, I will incorporate one life-long change in my current habits, every time you eat a meal with me."

The fish and I were astounded by his impudence. But then I thought, if there really was a chance of convincing him to make some changes, wouldn't it be worth a meal or two? I had a mission, after all: to change the earth-destroying habits of BigOilGramby. I glanced down at the assortment of flavours on my plate. And what a pleasure it would be, to fulfill it!

∞ *I spent a couple of hours handing out flyers, and then I took the bus to an elementary school where I was supposed to talk to the children about everything from recycling, to asking Mummy to shut off the engine instead of idling. School children and I understood each other just as well as the fish, and their response was enthusiastic. I was tired by the time we were finished, so I asked a teacher to help me phone Mr. Fat Cat's number, so I could cancel the evening meal I'd agreed to.*

"What about our deal?" he asked. "Tonight I was going to give up beef forever."

"You'd already promised that, when I had wine," I shouted towards

the phone. It was a flat rectangle without a mouthpiece, and I had no idea which end to speak into.

"True. Well, if you have dinner with me tonight, I'll buy an electric car, even though they're expensive and difficult to maintain."

I waved my hand, even though he couldn't see me. "They get cheaper and better soon."

"How do you know that?"

I had said something stupid. "Everything does with time," I said, laughing, hoping it sounded more genuine to him that it did to me. "Doesn't it?"

Then I felt a wave of irritation. I didn't want to be having this conversation. Everybody made mistakes when they were tired. "You should be doing this because it's the right thing, not just so I'll have dinner with you," I shouted at the rectangle.

I went to hang up, but the effect was somewhat dampened by the fact that I had to call the teacher over to locate the hang-up button, which wasn't even a button, just a round icon on the screen that apparently knew when I was touching it. I could hear his voice, backtracking and promising the earth if only I'd come to dinner (no pun intended) but eventually I managed to cut it off. He phoned back promptly, but the teacher told me how to silence the ring, and I travelled home in peace.

Future-me had macaroni and cheese with a salad on the side waiting for me, and demanded a blow-by-blow account of my day as we ate. I started with a comparison between my lunch and dinner fare, but she wasn't amused.

When I had finished, she looked at me for a moment. "Be careful."

I was a bit peeved, because I'd expected approbation. "How long have you been trying to get this guy to listen to you, huh? I come, I see, I conquer."

She continued to look sceptical.

"I know it's just because he likes me, but so what? Does it really matter why these people implement change, so long as they do?"

"I guess not. But be careful."

I fell into bed and slept like a stone.

∞ *The days fell into a routine, and then the weeks, also, settled into a pleasant pattern. Each day I would wake to a list of duties. Each day, I'd get through about half of them, but only if I rushed about like a lunatic.*

"You might get more done if you chucked the lengthy mid-day lunches with Mr. Oilman," Future-me said.

"Those lunches bring about more changes than all our other efforts put together," I snapped back, and there was no answer to that, because it was true. John had kept all his promises, both at a personal level and at a corporate one. He'd bought an electric car. He was looking for a smaller apartment. He gave a staggering (to me) amount of money to different environmental organizations. He had launched a series of meetings at BigOilGramby, inviting teams of environmental scientists to educate and inform.

"John truly understands the need to find ways to reconcile industry development with environmental protection," I told Future-me.

She fell back on the sofa, howling with laughter. "That's like saying that John truly understands the need to find ways to reconcile the slave trade with social justice."

When she'd finally finished her hysterics, I frowned at her. "He's not just doing these things for my sake, is all I'm saying."

Future-me wiped her streaming eyes. "I certainly hope not. This whole relationship feels dangerous to me."

She'd given me these warnings before and she'd give them again, but I felt good about my work and I was enjoying myself. It was obvious John loved me and, even though I knew this wasn't my real life or my real time, I couldn't help responding. He was so kind and attentive. I think he would have given up his job in a flash if I'd asked him, but we both realised he had more clout in the company than out of it. But I was also bothered by his increasing focus on me.

"Every four days you disappear," he said, reaching for my hand across the table in our favourite restaurant. The fish looked at me kindly. They

knew instinctively that I wasn't from this time, but they couldn't offer advice on what to tell John.

"I'm sorry. There are things I can't explain."

"Do you have another life, Alley?" Alice was the Canadian name I'd adopted for this life, since it was close to Alison, the name Future-me had chosen for herself. John liked to call me Alley.

I looked at him in shock. Had he guessed something? Thank goodness I kept my mouth shut, though, because he spoke again after a few seconds. "Do you have a husband, somewhere else?"

The fish rocked back and forth with laughter. "No! No, of course not!" John looked puzzled at the obvious relief on my face.

Then another time he asked: "Sometimes when you let me hug you goodbye, I have felt a hard disc under your shirt. You always have the same chain around your neck, too. Why do you always keep your necklace under your shirt?"

"It's very precious to me, and I don't want to lose it."

"Can I see it?"

Reluctantly, I pulled the talisman from under my shirt, but I didn't remove it from my neck, so he came very close to me to examine it. It was nice to look at his face, without him ogling me in return. I was becoming fond of his strong, dark features. "It's amazing," he said. "Such exquisite detail. Where did you get it from?"

"It's an heirloom," I replied, slipping it under my shirt again.

A couple of days later he gave me a beautiful gold necklace. I never bought anything myself that wasn't a necessity, so I certainly didn't want him to buy me things. I refused the gift adamantly, but he begged me to wear it for one evening only, before he returned it to the store. At first, I thought I'd keep my talisman in my pocket, but I was terrified it would fall out, and besides, it was a rule to wear it at all times. So I dropped it down the back of my dress and wore his necklace on the front. Of course, he saw the chain, which still encircled my throat. "Do you never take it off?" he asked.

"Never."

"Any special reason for that?"

"I can't explain."

"You can't explain." He looked into my eyes, as if they would supply the answers he so desperately wanted. "I'm thinking there is a connection between this necklace and your four-day disappearances."

"I'm thinking that if you want me to feel happy, you'll stop prying."

He didn't say another word, but I could feel his curiosity pulsing through him as I held his hand.

Sometimes he made dinner for me at his apartment, though of course I never invited him to mine. He continued to pry gently into my history with a hundred subtle questions, but he was as fine-tuned to my needs as a musician with a favourite guitar. As soon as I became irritable, he'd take my head between his hands and pull me towards him for a kiss. The first time he did it, I resisted, but when I felt his lips on mine, something warm exploded inside me and I wanted him to kiss me again. I had never felt such a detonation with François.

∞ *Every four days I went home like clockwork. First thing, I would phone the Community Hall and set up an appointment with one of the Leaders, as per the rules. Then I'd phone my parents to let them know I'd visit later, and that they were relieved from goat duties for that day.*

Finally, I'd rush outside to hug my animals; I really missed them and did every task with joy. Nanny always clambered onto the milking stand happily enough, but it was a race to finish milking before she finished eating, otherwise she'd casually lift her back hoof and wave it airily over the milk bucket. "NO!" I'd yell, to stop her dirty hoof from plunging into the milk. Nanny looked affronted as only goats and camels can. After all, she was just communicating her foodless state so we'd both be on the same page. Usually my bellow reminded her that waving hooves resulted in smacks and she'd desist. That's why I liked Nanny and hated Rambo; she had a brain.

After the animals I would prepare a meal to take to my parents, cutting up vegetables and herbs from the garden. Food tasted so much better when it was fresh; it was one of the things I craved in the city.

Finally, I would walk to my parents, bearing pans which radiated enticing aromas of simmering spices. We ate together and I told them about my work in Edmonton, while they updated me on everything that was happening on the island.

Occasionally my visits would overlap with a visit from François, who was advocating for a new, more binding Global Climate Agreement. It was exciting to hear that in 2022 the world was beginning to unite against this global threat, but it wasn't happening fast enough. We'd sit over dinner and words would pour out of him like an avalanche. I began to notice that he talked about himself all the time, and only asked briefly about my experiences. I also noticed that I always made the food, and that he always ate it too fast. I compared his apparent lack of interest in me, with John's unfailing admiration.

Every visit included a session with the Leaders; first completing endless forms, then undergoing a verbal interview, in which I was encouraged to confide things which the forms might not include. During my first trip back, they supplied me with an up-to-date Canadian passport with my new Canadian name, Alice. There was a lot of probing into my mental state, and my connection to this 'other' life. I tried to tell the absolute truth, but I didn't dwell on my growing feelings for John. Even to myself, I avoided defining them. Despite this omission, the Leaders still cautioned me about him, every time. It wasn't good that he had strong feelings for me, it was worrisome. "He would never hurt me," I said, trying to re-assure them. "And I'm totally focussed on my mission. Surely that's the whole point of this enterprise? I'm making a difference." And they conceded that I was, and didn't forbid me from returning to Edmonton, something I felt sure would happen eventually, and dreaded.

At first, I tried to brainstorm ways to coincide my visits with François, but coordinating time travel back to the island was impossible. The amount of time I was spending in Canada made that my permanent abode, which meant that every time I wanted to return to Edmonton, I arrived back after a few hours or a few days—however long I'd spent on the island. But the talisman considered my trips back to the island as time travel, so it landed me wherever it wanted, so long as it was during the year that I had requested. As often as not I'd find myself still in Canada, since such a large chunk of my 25th year was being spent there. Once I found myself weeping in a hospital, John grasping my hand. I got out of there pretty quickly; I had no interest in discovering events that were just around the corner. Why couldn't the talisman sense that I wanted to go home? Sometimes it was only thanks to the pills that I managed to get to the island at all, and several times I was reduced to choosing the previous year, or some other year in the past when I knew I was on the island, to ensure that I actually arrived in the right place. This was a drag, because I wanted to see my parents in the present.

Gradually, I stopped leaving little notes for François in an attempt to meet up. François pounced on the change immediately, and stayed on the island for several days in the hopes that I'd show up. "Why aren't you leaving messages? You know I have no way to contact you and find out what's going on."

"You want me to leave you messages, I'll leave you messages. This can't go on for much longer anyway, my parents are tired from all the extra work. You do stay for a bit when you come, don't you? Give them a break?"

François's mouth fell open. "You're not suggesting that I milk Nanny?"

"That's just one job, you can still water the crops and make life easier for them. Look, if you really can't milk Nanny then at least walk her over to my parents' place, save them the trip."

His mouth still gaped. I wished he'd close it, he looked stupid. "What, with her two kids traipsing along behind?"

"I don't care how you do it. Why don't you ask your parents to lend a hand, or your sister? Why should my parents shoulder the entire burden?"

"Because they're your animals. Besides, I don't want to spend much time here, in case my talisman thinks the island is my permanent abode. I must return to the exact day in 2022 when I left, minus the time spent here, obviously. My work is too important to risk missing any time."

I was speechless with anger, but it was true that François had identified a key problem. Many people opted to stay only four hours on the island, as that seemed to guarantee a return to the same day in our other lives. Since François refused to help, I began to visit the island more frequently—when I could, every day, but I only stayed for a few hours. It was enough time to tend to the animals and the crops, so regardless of the day in the year I landed, it saved my parents work. It also ensured that I arrived back on the same day I'd left. Future-me complained vigorously about the drop in the amount I was able to achieve in Edmonton. "What?" I said to her. "You don't care about your own parents?"

I tried to convince Future-me that my declining affections for François had nothing to do with John.

"I don't like it," she said. "The Instruction Book clearly states that you're not supposed to develop any deep relationships with people during your time travels. Don't you get it? This isn't your time; it's mine. You're not even supposed to be here."

"Well, I am here. It wasn't me who changed the rules. I'm sure many of our people are experiencing deeper relationships as a result of the longer stays—it's only natural, isn't it? We are human beings, after all." But I had to turn away to hide my flushing face. I felt like I was lying, and it didn't feel good. But how could I tell critical Future-me that one day, when I was aching with pleasure from John's kisses, he had led me towards the bedroom? I hadn't said no. I had wanted to keep kissing him all night long. I had wanted to explore his entire body with my lips. I'd never felt the intense physical joy that he gave me before.

She took a sip of her tea; of course tea accompanied all our discussions. "Maybe I should nip back to 1986 and tell the Leaders my perspective."

"Maybe you should," I replied rudely, and got up to shut myself in the bathroom. This was the only place I could be alone in that apartment.

But the very next day confirmed all her suspicions. At the end of our lunch at our favourite restaurant, where the fish had become so used to us that they'd rush over to undulate their hellos as soon as we sat down, John slipped off his seat and knelt on one knee. "Will you marry me, Alley?" he asked, holding an outrageous diamond ring in his outstretched hand.

"What did we say about buying?" I said.

"It's only a tiny ring that will never end up in a landfill because you'll be buried with it." The look on his face was so tender and loving, my heart ached. I wished I could tell him the truth about why I couldn't marry him. If this had been my actual life and time, I might not have refused. The longing in my heart told me that I, also, felt love.

"I can't, John," was all I could say. It felt unfair, terribly unfair, to hide the truth from him.

His face turned a dull, brick-red from mortification. He rose from his knees and sat back in his chair, glancing to his right and giving a slight shake of his head. The waiter standing there scuttled into the kitchen, but not before I'd glimpsed a bottle of champagne in his hands. I realised that John had been sure I'd accept him. This must have been so humiliating for him. I placed my hand over his. "I think that I do love you, John. There are reasons for my refusal that I can't explain."

"What? Are you already married? Are you a criminal? Is your entire family stark raving mad and you've recently discovered that you've inherited the insane gene? Or is it connected to that mysterious necklace that chains you by the neck to frequent absences? Don't you know that there's nothing … nothing … that you could tell me, which would stop me loving you?"

I squeezed his hand, not knowing what to say. The more he pushed to know, the more he pushed me away from him.

That night in the apartment, I had a long heart-to-heart talk with Future-me. She opened the Instruction Book, and read out the pages which described the dangers of establishing deep relationships with people from other times. Why it was forbidden. Why the punishment was so harsh. Banishment. Tears rose to my eyes as she read, because the words sealed the end of my time here. It was over. She looked up and saw the tears, and scooted over on the couch to hug me. "I know it's hard, but you'll find another place to do your work. Hey, you've done a great job here! I'm going to miss you, despite the joys of getting my living room back."

I tried to smile, to repress the lament that I might find another place to do good work, but it wouldn't contain John. "You're right. Tomorrow will be my last stint here."

"*Why tomorrow? The sooner the better.*"

"*He deserves some type of explanation, so we part in a good way. With as little pain as possible.*"

"*So write him a letter. I think you should leave tonight.*"

"*Slow down! Tonight? That's ridiculous; I have to see him one more time.*"

She put her arm around me again. "*He is a powerful man, used to getting his own way. By your own account, the 'mystery' surrounding you is driving him nuts. What if he hired a detective or something, to track your every move? How long do you think it would take him to realise you aren't travelling anywhere:* you simply disappear?"

As she spoke, there was a knock at the door. We both froze. "*Who could it be?*" *I asked, trying to remember whether Future-me had ever mentioned a friend. She grabbed my hand to quiet me, staring intently at the door. The handle was turning.*

"*Didn't you lock …?*"

"*I never lock …*" *It was one of the things I never remembered. On the island, nobody locked their doors.*

We sat as though transfixed as the door slowly swung wide on its hinges. John stood in the doorframe, looking at us uncertainly, as we sat side by side on the couch, two peas in a pod.

For a second nobody moved. Then Future-me jumped to her feet, her hand scrabbling inside her sweater as she yanked out her talisman and practically screamed, I wish I was 70!

John gawped at the empty space that had contained a human being two seconds before. I watched him warily, until his eyes slid over to mine. "*I'm guessing that vanishing act is one of those things you can't explain?*"

"*How do you know where I live?*" *My voice was icy with anger. He had hired a detective, just like Future-me had warned. The rules about keeping our special powers secret were blatantly clear. He was going to destroy me.*

He heard the ice and in two steps was kneeling in front of my knees. "*Alley, I love you. I want to marry you. But you were torturing me, keeping every detail about your life shrouded in secrecy. I didn't understand why. Here I was, inviting you to my house and showing you pictures of my family and recounting my entire history, like normal people do with their lovers, while you refused to divulge a single detail about any aspect of your life. I was burning with curiosity; it got so huge it became unbearable. So one day I followed you home. Forgive me."*

Panic billowed in my chest. "I think you should leave." I had to think. I had to do damage-control. I had to be alone.

He pressed his face into my lap. "Forgive me!"

"Get out!"

He leapt to his feet as though I had hit him, and backed towards the door. I couldn't look at his face, but I knew by his ragged breathing that he was crying. "Alley. Don't disappear on me. Please don't hurt me like that. I'll never tell anybody what I saw. I'll never ask you to explain. Promise that I'll see you again. I'll go if you just make that one promise."

I was desperate for him to be gone. He wasn't letting me think. I had just broken one of the most important rules, and the punishment would be severe. I had to think. "I promise," I said, without thinking.

"Thank you," he whispered. "I'm sorry." Then he was gone.

His departure cleared my head. I took a couple of deep breaths, and then realised that I'd promised to see him again. That couldn't happen. I had to leave right away—I'd already screwed things up badly. I could just leave, but that would mean that the last thing I had said to John would be a lie. On the island, few people lie. The truth always outs in the end, even with normal people, but that is doubly true when you have the ability to time travel. John loved me. I needed to tell him honestly that this was good-bye. If that would be painful for me, I deserved it. Selfish was what I'd been, basking in John's admiration and refusing to acknowledge the dangers. It would be hard for me to say goodbye, but it would cause great pain if I didn't, and to save myself pain by causing another worse pain was also selfish. I wanted to stop being selfish!

This entire thought process only took a minute, then I was on my feet and rushing out of the apartment after him. I saw him as soon as I'd exited the building; he was on the other side of the street, his head bowed in dejection, his hand shielding his face from view. My heart swelled with pity. "John!" I yelled, "John!" He turned as I careened across the street towards him, my eyes fixed on my unhappy lover. I saw his face morph into horror as his mouth opened in a scream.

There was a screech of metal, then everything went black.

★ ★ ★

Simon lifted his eyes from the page and realized with a jolt that it was past midnight. That meant he'd be tired at school the next day. But he couldn't stop reading! He couldn't leave his mother in a near-death situation! His eyes scanned the first paragraphs of the next segment.

★ ★ ★

Everything hurt. My head, my back, my legs. Even my toes. I tried to open my eyes, but bright whiteness assaulted the quiet darkness of my brain and I slammed them shut again. A warm hand enclosed mine as I drifted back to sleep.

The next time I woke I remembered the brightness, and cracked open one eye to the merest slit. I was in a white room, a hospital room. There was a black head lying on my legs, the face turned away from me. John. Memories started to filter through the fog: I was in a hospital room, because I had been hit by a car. Mentally, I took stock of my body. There were tubes coming out of my arms, probably to feed me. My arm was in a cast. My head still ached, but a cautiously-raised hand informed me there were no bandages. So, no head injury. All in all, it looked like I was still very much alive. My relieved smile was punctured by anxiety in less than a second. Had four days passed? Had I missed my deadline? I seemed to be making terrible mistakes every time I moved. Whatever punishment they gave me, I would deserve it. I had to get back right away. I patted my chest area, then felt around my neck for the chain. It wasn't there. Dread sprouted in my stomach and travelled quickly up to my throat. "John," I wheezed, feebly plucking at his hair. He was instantly awake, his haggard face dropping years as he grinned in relief.

"Alley! You're awake!"

I didn't return the smile. "Where's my talisman?"

* * *

Simon glanced at his phone again; it was almost 1am—the accident hadn't hurt his mother badly—he must go to sleep!

Reluctantly, he dogeared the journal and put it under his pillow. But he couldn't go to sleep. It was all so unbelievable. An entire new world; he felt like Harry Potter springing free from his cupboard-room beneath the stairs. An entire history—his history—opening before him. Was it during the accident that the talisman disappeared? He ached to open the journal and scan ahead, find out the great evil his father was supposed to have done, that justified destroying their family unit. But yeah, it must have sucked to lose the talisman. Simon couldn't imagine being cut off from one's family like that. But hadn't his mother said you could get to the island by land? Surely she would see her parents again? And now he, Simon, could maybe see them too. He tossed and turned, excited thoughts buzzing in his head. It must have been close to 3 a.m. by the time he dozed off.

CHAPTER SIX

IT WAS DURING lunch in the library the next day that Sandra finally realised that she couldn't convince Simon to spill the beans about his mother's revelations. She immediately flew into a fury, ripping off a piece of crust from her peanut butter and jam sandwich and throwing it at him. "What do you mean you can't tell me? Am I your best friend or what?"

"My only friend." Simon had felt tired all day, like he'd expected. He wished he could have steered Sandra towards a less exhausting subject, but there was no hope of that.

"So how do you think that makes me feel?"

Simon extracted a bag of cookies from his lunch box and handed them to her. "Here. As compensation."

Sandra knocked the cookies out of his hand and onto the floor.

"Hey, hey," the librarian said. "Any more of that and you'll be eating in the hallway."

Simon leaned towards Sandra, and took her hand in his. It was the first time he'd ever done anything like that, and Sandra froze in surprise. "You are my best friend. I would tell you everything, if I could. You know that. But my mother really stressed the rules."

"But I won't tell anyone else."

"I'll ask her again. And again and again, until I get permission to tell you. Promise." Simon picked the broken cookies off the floor and offered them to her again. Mollified, Sandra took them.

They both looked up in surprise as the door to the library opened and Rakita herself bounded in, past the school secretary, who had shown her the way.

"You can find your own way back again, Alice? Don't forget to sign out at the front desk as you leave."

Rakita nodded towards the secretary and turned to Simon. She was beaming.

"What are you doing here, Mum?" Simon wanted to act cool in front of Sandra, but he couldn't help himself. A huge grin spread across his face; he was so damn glad to see his mother. He didn't acknowledge the nagging fear that she wouldn't come back, which had pursued him all morning.

"Silly me, I thought you'd forgotten your lunch!" Rakita handed him a brown paper bag with a wink. She nodded towards Sandra and strode out of the library without waiting for Simon's response. He didn't even have time to call after her, though he was dying to ask about her visit to the island.

"Two lunches? You'll need help eating this one." Sandra leant towards the bag in anticipation of something nice; she always packed her own lunch and in her opinion mothers invariably packed better treats.

Simon opened the bag and peered inside, perplexity turning to amusement as he pulled out the pendant and a note, which he read and handed to Sandra.

Just in case you need to escape the bullies today. Remember, you must abide by the rules: stay hidden during your time travel and don't communicate with your Other Self. Have fun! I'll be waiting for you at home.

Sandra laughed. "Good thing you've got this to keep you safe, because I can't go home with you every day." She fingered the pendant wistfully. "I guess if it's so damn secret I'll never get to experience its magic myself."

"You never know," Simon replied, slipping the chain of the pendant carefully over his head. He could dream about bringing Sandra to the new world with him, even if his mother had said that the rules excluded outsiders. He hoped there were good reasons for all these rules; they seemed pretty strict to him.

Simon and Sandra walked together back to class.

∞ As the day drew near its close, Simon kept his eye on the bullies, trying to decipher what they were planning. They whispered and looked at him a lot, but when their eyes met by mistake they didn't snicker menacingly, as was their habit. Instead, their eyes slid away, and focussed elsewhere. Simon wasn't sure if this change was intriguing, or worrying. But with the light round weight of the pendant resting against his chest, sending out warm ripples of comfort and courage, he rather hoped they'd follow their usual routine and pursue him homewards with murderous intent. A plan began to form in his head. Perhaps this would be the day he'd be caught. His mother had said he couldn't tell anybody about the pendant, or the island and its inhabitants, but she hadn't said anything about using the pendant secretly. If the pendant catapulted you into different times and locations; if, with one whoosh, you disappeared from one place and popped up in another, how secret could it be? Simon remembered how he'd landed in an empty corridor of a dorm during his first trip. In general, that must have been a pretty busy corridor, with tens of students marching along its length. Perhaps the pendant had deliberately chosen a moment when nobody was around? Another question in a growing list to ask his mother.

The plan swirled pleasantly in his head; it depended on the reliability of the bullies. They had been hounding him on the way home from school every day like clockwork since the beginning of the year. Surely they'd stick to their routine today, too?

He waited impatiently for the end-of-day bell, fingering the pendant underneath his shirt. Incredulous about the fact that he was actually going time-travelling today. *What year shall I visit?* Simon thought to himself. He wanted to choose carefully, because he realised from what his mother had said that he might not be allowed to live on the island. He might never get his own pendant, never experience the whoosh of the wind in his ears as he teleported to another time, unless his mother occasionally lent him hers. Even if they did accept him on the island, would he leave his father? He wished that there wasn't a question mark hanging over the truth about the pendant. Had his father stolen it in order to force his mother to stay with him? Like in the Selkie story? If not, what other explanation made sense? And in the end, did it really matter? Whatever he'd done, Simon loved his dad. It seemed cruel to rip his entire family away in one fell sweep. He'd have to talk to both his parents before making any huge decisions like that.

Last night, his father had brought supper to his bedroom when he'd failed to come down to eat. Simon had shovelled food in groggily and fallen back asleep. By the time Simon descended in the morning, his father had already left for work. There hadn't been an opportunity to talk, and Simon still had no idea what he'd decide. However, he did hope that he'd actually have a choice. He hoped the Leaders of the island would accept him, and give him his own pendant. But if not ... it could mean that he wouldn't be able to travel very much. Simon felt the comforting disc against his chest. Should he visit himself at 35, see what he'd made of his life? Would he be married? Children? What about career? Should he visit himself at 60, see where his journey of life had taken him? Would he find himself on the island? Of course! He should visit himself in a couple of years, and then he'd know what the Leaders of the island had decided!

The bell rang.

Simon could feel the eyes of the bullies on his back as he sauntered out the door. Perhaps, if he wanted them to stick to their routine so badly, he should have kept to his. He should have pounded out the door like the devil himself was after him, as per usual.

They weren't following. Damn.

Simon walked along slowly, and more slowly, knowing they'd

either have to match his snail's pace or pass him, since they all walked home in the same direction. He whistled the national anthem, knowing that would annoy them. After he'd exited the school parking lot, he glanced backwards. There they were, three peas in a pod; large, hulking youth with identical greasy hairstyles. "Hey morons," Simon called back pleasantly.

"Hey, shit for brains," Jake said, and he gestured towards the other two, speeding up a little. But they still didn't catch up to him. So Simon changed tactics. He cast a fearful glance over his shoulder, pretended to startle at their proximity, and broke into a lope. It worked. As though he'd pressed a button, the bullies sped up too, and soon they were all racing down the road pell-mell, just like every other day. Except not like every other day, because this time, Simon wasn't gripped with fear and tension. This time, he was in control. He pretended to trip and fall to the ground. Before he could leap to his feet again, they had surrounded him.

"Well, well, what have we here?" Jake asked, using his foot to propel Simon to the ground again.

"We have a shit for brains," Shawn said, too stupid to think up insults on his own.

Simon glowered up at them, trying to mask his triumph.

"I'm going to enjoy this," Jake said with a sneer. And then, without warning, they were on top of him, punching, kicking, scratching. The onslaught was so sudden and unexpected that Simon panicked for a moment, warding off punches and protecting his head, unable to reach for the pendant. Pain shot up his arm as someone trampled on his fingers; lights ricocheted across his vision as a fist connected with his nose, knocking his head back and generating a spurt of blood. Simon scrabbled desperately underneath his shirt for the pendant, suddenly frightened that the beating would be over before he could use it. There it was, the round, soft metal. *I wish I was seventeen.*

As a blessed blackness enfolded his eyes, the world began spinning and the grunts and oafs of the bullies faded. Wind whistled in his ears and he landed with a thump on his bottom, on a wooden floor. His eyes sprang open eagerly, gobbling up his surroundings before a wave of disappointment engulfed him. He was in his own house, outside his own kitchen. So the Leaders of the island weren't going to accept him? Why? He hadn't done anything wrong. He could time-travel too; he was one of them! Simon felt like kicking something. He lurched to his feet with that intention, but his whole body clenched in pain. He'd forgotten about his beating. Lifting his hand gingerly to his face, he touched the blood still trickling from his nose. He could hear urgent voices coming from the kitchen, but he wanted to look at the damage first. Stumbling to the bathroom, Simon surveyed his battered face. His nose had bloomed like a clown's schnozzle, there was a cut over his eye and his whole body ached. He washed his face as best he could, and pressed the soft part of his nose for several minutes, until the bleeding slackened. As soon as he was more presentable, he tiptoed back to the kitchen and pressed his ear against the door.

"It's not that easy to change people's way of thinking, especially when it hurts their bottom line." His father's voice.

"Surely most people don't want to fly in the face of facts? So first, present the facts: this is what is going to happen if the temperature of the earth increases more than two degrees."

His own voice stopped speaking, and Simon heard the scratch of a pen, or marker. He pushed the kitchen door open a crack. The first thing he saw was a broader version of his own back; apparently he was writing on a flip board. His father sat at the kitchen table, facing the flip board. Simon peered to see what his older self was writing.

He was drawing. Two divided halves of a square, captioned <2 and >2.

Under <2, he was scratching sentences:

You have to check your phone before you open a window, to make sure the hot, congested air outside won't harm you.

"It's not very interesting watching you write," his father said. "Can't you just tell me?"

One quarter of earth's plants and animals will go extinct, wrote Future-Simon, **Hundreds of millions of people will lose their homes**.

Simon could see irritation radiating from his older-self's back. He frowned. Did this mean that he and his father would be having problems in two years?

"This type of information turns people off. It's too big."

Simon turned around and looked at his father. All trace of irritation was gone. His face was focused in thought. "Mum always said she could see peoples' eyes glazing over when she tried to tell them the truth."

John sat up straighter. "What? What did she say?"

Simon rapped the marker against his palm. He appeared not to have heard his father.

"You're right. We have to make it personal. How about this?"

Are you going to be alive in 2050? Are your children? You love your children, right? If there was something you could do to make your kids happy throughout their lives, of course you'd do it.

John was tapping his fingers on the kitchen table impatiently. Simon whirled around. "So fucking DO it. NOW."

"I won't tolerate that language in this house."

Simon looked at his father for a minute. "You need to leave your company, Dad. It's not enough, to claim to work there to mitigate the harm they do. Let's face it. Most of the time you perpetrate what they do."

Now it was John who appeared not to hear his son. "The climate deniers say all this isn't true. Huge tracts of the world are in denial. We can't succeed unless we get them on board."

Simon spread his hands. "I live here; I can only work in one place. But there are millions of people world-wide who are rising up and demanding change. We're not working in a vacuum—everything we do is part of a giant web of action. We can't change everyone, but we can choose whether we ourselves want to be part of the problem, or part of the solution, and spread the word to others that they face that same choice."

Simon could see anger flitting over Older-Simon's face again. "Those climate deniers must be either wicked or ignorant."

John hooted. "Don't you know that generalizations are always wrong?"

"Since when is a personal opinion as relevant as proven facts? The scientists have been predicting for ages what's happening now. It's already happening, Dad. There is irrefutable proof." Older-Simon smacked the flip board in frustration. "Why can't people change? If they knew that changing *one* thing would prevent the biggest tragedy of their lives ..."

"Simon, you've inherited your mother's flare for drama. You can't control what other people do—you'll go mad or sink into despair if you rage against what you cannot control."

Simon jiggled on the balls of his feet. "You told me that there's nothing worse than the suffering of your own child. If every human on earth changed one thing, that would totally reduce the suffering of their children. Because their children are going to live in an altered universe if we don't change *now*. Forget drastic changes—they can start with something small, that barely impacts them. Travel less. Eat a bit less meat. Buy a bit less crap. Why won't they *do* it?"

"Calm down, Simon."

"What type of world is this, where the people making decisions about whether the human race will survive or not can ignore scientific proof? Ooh, if I pump money into the fossil oil industry, it'll create jobs and make money now, and that means I'll be re-elected! Yay! Who cares that this decision puts the very survival of the planet at peril ..."

"People don't like change. And even if they did, isn't it too late? Isn't the permafrost melting and releasing methane? Isn't the carbon we've already released into the atmosphere ..."

"No!" Future-Simon yelled. "I hate it when people say it's too late—it's just an excuse for their selfish desire to do nothing. We can change fast enough if people realise this is a crisis. Look how the world came together to beat COVID!"

"I wish you'd calm down, Simon," John said, standing to place his hand on his agitated son's shoulder. "Your mother used to get really upset about these things; she'd make herself ill and depressed."

There was a short silence. Then John added in a constrained voice: "How is she?"

Simon pressed his ear closer to the crack in the door. His mother wasn't living with them, so she must be on the island. Perhaps the question meant that his older self visited the mother regularly? Even lived in both places?

Older-Simon hugged his father. "She's fine, Dad. She's grown the most amazing garden, just like she used to do ..."

"... here, before she got too depressed." John's voice dropped to a whisper. "Does she ever mention me?"

"All the time, Dad. All the time."

"She is helping you a lot in your work, isn't she?"

Older-Simon put his arm around his father. "You are invaluable, Dad. Don't forget, you have a friend whose friend has the ear of the Prime Minister. That's better than anything else."

Simon pressed even closer to the crack in the door, to catch the reply. The door swung open suddenly and he stumbled into the room. Older-Simon and John jumped apart and looked at him in astonishment. Then they both spoke at the same time.

"What happened to your face?" his father asked.

"For God's sake, you have to learn to hide yourself. It's the number one, most basic rule. If it's too bloody hard for you then maybe you shouldn't use the bloody talisman anymore."

"I'm sorry ..." Simon started to say, but Older-Simon interrupted.

"Don't stand around talking to us. Don't you know the rules? Just bugger off back to your own time, before you do or say something to change history. For God's sake!"

Simon smiled apologetically at his irritable older self and rubbed his pendant. *I wish I was fifteen.*

CHAPTER SEVEN

"**W**HAT HAPPENED TO your face?"

Simon opened his eyes in surprise; he was in the exact same kitchen, but instead of Older-Simon glowering at him in fury, his mother was staring at him in consternation.

He touched his swollen nose. "They got me, Mum."

"But didn't the talisman ..."

"I did it on purpose. I wanted them to see me disappear, because I thought that might make them back off in the future. I hope that's OK?"

Simon felt a nudge on his leg and looked down at Toby's puzzled face. He laughed and bent down to scratch the dog's ears. Toby would probably never get used to these sudden appearances.

"There are no specific rules around timing one's exits from this world, but secrecy is always stressed as important. Still, given these special circumstances, I suppose it's OK." His mother smiled at him, but he could see a crease of anxiety between her eyebrows. "This time, they've gone too far. We must go to the school and the police. The bullies must be punished."

Simon felt his heart constrict. One didn't snitch. Not at his age. He was handling it himself. That's why it had happened—he had let it happen. His parents couldn't wrench this out of his control and complain to the school or the police over a bloody nose! He'd be despised. The gang of bullies would increase, not disappear like his mother thought.

"I'm going to take some photos of your face," continued his mother. "What are their full names?"

Simon realised he still had some control. "I'm not telling you."

"Why not? This can't go unpunished."

"It's not going to happen again. I'm handling it."

His mother looked at him. The kettle began to whistle and she ignored it. Simon held her gaze until she turned to pour the tea into the waiting mugs.

Shall we go outside to drink our tea? It's a lovely day. Summer is coming."

Simon nodded and grasped the tray, which held a plate of cookies as well as two mugs of tea. A wave of exhaustion washed over him as he tottered toward the door. How strange that he should feel so tired and excited at the same time. He hoped his mother wouldn't notice the slight tremor of his hands, as he tamped down his impatience. Every day brought a ton of questions. What was the significance of that conversation he'd just witnessed? Was his destiny to become some sort of environmental activist? He'd always complied with his mother's long list of rules: he rarely bought things, he recycled, reused everything, walked everywhere, rarely ate meat and never beef. But he'd never been passionately interested in the subject, like Older-Simon had seemed to be. He'd certainly never considered taking it up as a career, or anything like that.

He was also desperate to know what they had said to his mother on the island. The glimpse of the future seemed to indicate that he was going to live with his father, but maybe he had just been visiting? Was there any rhyme or reason to where the pendant took them? And why did it matter so much if people saw him?

Oh, the questions he had! He could barely keep his tongue still as they pushed through the back door and took their seats at opposite sides of the round table.

The garden stretched out before them, meandering down both sides of the driveway to end at his father's workshop. On one side was the fenced-in vegetable garden. His mother used to plant herbs, all the ingredients for a salad, as well as potatoes and corn. Over the past few years, he and his father had taken over the job of planting the garden and watering it throughout the summer. Simon had resented his mother's abdication of yet another duty, one she'd even enjoyed.

He remembered her rhapsodies about the fresh taste of tomatoes and cukes during harvest time in the fall. How she bemoaned the fact that the vegetables only had this fresh taste for a couple of months. "Some places have fresh veggies for most of the year," she used to say, with a forlorn expression on her face. Simon had assumed that she was just feeling melancholy, as usual. Now, with his new knowledge, everything took on a different meaning. His mother had been homesick, all those years, ripped from her roots and family. Replanted in this hostile world, where some people still denied climate change, and there were only fresh vegetables for a few months a year.

On the other side of the driveway, flowers and bushes were sprinkled haphazardly over the stretch of land like raisins in a bowl of cereal. At this time of year, it just looked like a brown-green expanse, but Simon knew that if he bent down to examine the area, he would glimpse the tips of this year's flowers pushing through the soil towards the light.

They sat side by side in two lawn chairs, a low plastic table between them.

"Can I have it back?"

Simon knew she was referring to the talisman. He felt a curious reluctance, as he drew the pendant over his head and handed it to his mother. She grabbed it with barely-concealed eagerness and kissed it, before slipping it over her head and under her shirt.

"Separation anxiety," she said, joking.

"So, what happened?"

A sad smile played across his mother's face. "It was so lovely to see my Mum and Dad again. We all just clung together and wept. They are so old …" Her voice broke and she looked down into her mug of tea.

Toby had located his ball and dropped it expectantly at Simon's feet, gazing at it ferociously as if he had the Force and it would take off on its own accord. Simon bent over slowly, his ribs aching, and lobbed the ball down the driveway. Rakita burst into laughter as Toby executed his aerial antics. Laughter is infectious, but Simon's ribs wouldn't allow him to indulge.

Toby raced back, dropping the ball right on Simon's feet and ogling it fixedly. Simon ignored him; he was still waiting for his mother to continue. He wanted to know whether he would be allowed to live on the island or not, but he knew his mother would get to the nitty-gritty in her own time.

"Did you read any of my journal? I wanted you to know the whole story, so you'd understand my past. Why I feel so strongly about your father. If you understand more, you can reach your own conclusions."

"I got to the bit where you'd just been hit by a car."

Rakita put her mug of tea carefully on the table and leant back in her chair, closing her eyes. "So you've read about the day they called the Special Meeting and how I met your father," she said in a soft, nostalgic voice. "I was young, full of energy. I was teaching at the school … "

"I know, Mum. I've read this."

"Though I knew the environmental devastation that would start to happen in my lifetime, I wasn't down about it, because even before the meeting I felt that our special island was destined to change history."

"But I thought all the rules were to prevent you changing history?"

"You're right, Simon, but don't interrupt. So the day they changed the rules so we could time travel for four days was very exciting. Also, since time-travelling is so exhausting, we can't do it more than once a day, but they gave us a pill that enabled us to do it several times."

A lightbulb irradiated Simon's brain: "That's why I'm so tired all the time!"

Rakita smiled at him. "You're excited, aren't you? I don't want to repeat things you know already; perhaps the best thing would be for you to read the rest of my journal. Then you can ask me all your questions at the end. How does that sound?"

Simon liked reading quietly on his own, but Rakita persuaded him that it was the quickest way to get all his questions answered at the same time. He went to fetch the journal. Leaning over to scratch Toby on the head, as compensation for not throwing the ball, Simon settled comfortably in his own seat to read.

∞ *"Alley! You're awake!"*

I didn't return the smile. "Where's my talisman?"

"Your what?"

"The thing I always wear around my neck. Where is it? I must have it!"

John looked puzzled. "I don't know."

I tried to slow my breathing, to calm down. "When did this accident happen?"

"Yesterday." A sliver of relief pierced the fog of fear. Just yesterday. We still had two whole days to sort things out. The Leaders would never have to know.

"Tell me exactly what happened, from the beginning."

"You were running after me. I can't tell you how happy I was that you came after me ..." He tried to exchange a meaningful look, but by this time the panic was causing my breath to come in short, painful gasps. "Calm down," he said anxiously, kneading my hands.

I shook him off. "Tell me!"

"You didn't even look before you darted across the road. I thought you were dead. The driver had a blanket in his car and we covered you and phoned 911. When the ambulance came I pretended to be your husband so they'd let me stay with you. As soon as we got to the hospital they took you into emergency while I waited outside. They were worried about how long you'd remain unconscious, but now you've woken up, thank God. You have some bruises and a broken arm ..."

"Where are my things?"

"They put your things in this closet. Do you want me to look?"

I cast an anguished glance towards the closet in reply, and he brought all my things over to the bed; a little bundle of neatly-folded clothes. I shook every item out, checked and re-checked every pocket, my motions getting jerkier as it became obvious the talisman wasn't there.

"Call the nurses and the doctors. I need to talk to everyone who saw me after I entered the hospital. Were you with me for every minute up until that point?"

He nodded, his eyes searching mine anxiously. "What will happen if you can't find it?"

"My life will be over," I replied grimly.

It would be impossible to describe the growing horror of the next couple of days, as I questioned every human being, right down to those who had only glimpsed me from afar. I questioned John first, but he had no memory of seeing the talisman after the accident. "It's hard to remember the exact sequence of events. You'd just been hit by a car, and I was mad with worry, totally focussed on getting you to the hospital as quickly as possible. Then when we got here the hospital staff took over, and whisked you away."

It was pretty natural not to notice any talisman when I'd just been hit by a car. But as soon as he realised how vital it was that I find it, John looked after everything. It was thanks to his persuasive efforts that I was able to talk to every single person, from the intake people who had handled my paperwork, right down to the cleaning woman who had possibly glanced at me from across the hallway. At my request, he had returned to the scene of the accident and thoroughly searched the entire area, in the hopeless hope that it had fallen off my neck during the crash and would be lying there, alone, waiting for me. Without my even having to ask, he offered a million dollar reward—a million dollars!—to anyone who could supply information on the whereabouts of the talisman. I described it in minute detail, and he broadcast the description on the radio, the television, and social media. I felt very hopeful for a time, because if it had fallen off *my neck during the crash and someone had picked it up, they would soon find out it wasn't worth anything like a million dollars.*

"Thank you so much for everything you've done, John."

He took my hand. "I would do anything for you. I love you."

Hope swelled at the beginning of every new interview, then began to sink within the first few sentences, to shrivel and die by the end.

"Why would I know where your necklace is?" one of the cleaners asked defensively.

"You wouldn't," I answered with a sigh. "It's called scraping the bottom of the barrel, I'm that desperate."

John got the driver of the car on the speakerphone, so we could both hear him, although he seemed more intent on proving his innocence than answering my questions. "You just ran out of nowhere!"

"I know. You are completely guilt-free, it was my fault. Just forget all that, it doesn't matter. The point is, did you notice anything around my neck? A pendant of some sort?"

"She lost something very dear to her," John said, hoping to make things clearer. "She just wants you to try your best to recall if you noticed any jewellery. Anything at all."

"I wasn't looking at her jewellery. I was looking to see if she was dead!"

Calm, irritation, desperation; whatever emotion we displayed, it made no difference. The driver who hit me, the paramedics who drove me to the hospital, the ambulance driver, the anaesthesiologist, the doctors and nurses—nobody remembered any necklace.

But there was a necklace. So somebody must be lying.

I questioned them one after the other, my fear suppressing my exhaustion as I struggled to strip the interrogatory tone from my voice. "You were with me from the moment I entered the hospital, doctor?"

"Yes. They brought you in on a stretcher, and I walked alongside the stretcher as they wheeled you into emergency. I was there as they removed your clothes. There was nothing around your neck. You weren't wearing any jewellery at all. You didn't have anything on except the clothes you

were wearing. Speaking of which, there are a lot of forms waiting to be filled because we didn't have any information on you."

I tried to drag my mind back from the brink of the abyss to focus on the trivialities he was spouting. "I come from a different country. I have no information."

He laughed, as though I'd made a joke. "Not even a marriage certificate?" he said, glancing at John.

"We're not married."

"Just friends? I wish I had friends like that. In lieu of any insurance information, your friend agreed to pay all your medical expenses."

I tried to compress my fear enough to permit my gratitude to surface. "Thank you so much, John. I hadn't realized that people have to pay for hospital care here; it was free on the island."

John swept my hand to his lips and kissed it passionately. "It's free here too, but this is a private clinic. That's why the service was so good."

I hadn't noticed that it was any better than on the island, but I nodded.

The doctor beamed as though this was the happiest scene he'd ever seen, and practically tip-toed out.

Nobody had seen the talisman.

Somebody was lying.

Despair must be held at bay.

∞ *I slumped on the edge of my bed as they filled out more endless forms, this time so they could release me. John had bought me some new clothes, and he stood beside me, holding the little bundle of old clothes and answering their questions because I didn't care and if my mouth opened screams would spew out. I felt paralysed by terror. I had been in the hospital for four days. The deadline for returning to the island had passed. And I didn't have my talisman. Fear sapped my energy, so I felt exhausted all the time. It clogged my throat, so I could barely eat. The only way I kept the fear at bay enough to function was by repeating my next steps, like a mantra.*

First, go and see Future-me. Maybe she'd have an idea about what to do. Next, borrow money from John to fly/bus/ferry over to the island, which would take a few days. Then I would learn my fate.

To my knowledge, nobody in the history of the island had ever lost their talisman. It didn't seem real. I was in some nightmare.

"What will happen if you can't find it?" John asked me for the umpteenth time, standing by the door after the forms were finished, waiting patiently for me to join him so we could go.

"I don't know," I whimpered, still slumped on the bed. "Something very bad."

He was silent for a moment. "I will look after you, you know that."

I shrugged irritably. Sometimes, it was hard to make gratitude triumph over anger. If he hadn't come to the apartment that night, I wouldn't be in this nightmare.

The doctor, bustling down the hallway on his way to see another patient, saw John standing ready to go and poked his head in my door. "Are you off, then?"

When I didn't respond, he entered the room and stood beside me. "This depression is worrisome."

I didn't know if he was addressing me or John, and I didn't care.

"We can help you with the depression. I'm assuming you don't have a doctor, since you come from away, but I can give you the name of an excellent family doctor."

Tears started to drip down my nose. The last couple of days, my eyes had turned into leaky faucets.

"I'm sorry that you lost a necklace that was so important to you, but try to be thankful that your injuries were so minor. Just a broken arm and a few bruises." He smiled at me. "And you should be truly thankful that your baby is fine."

He wasn't expecting the face I turned towards him. His glance skated towards John before my eyes trapped it again. "You didn't … you surely didn't think your baby was dead, did you? I just assumed that that would be the first thing you asked your friend here. Or the first thing he'd tell you."

My eyes bored into the doctor's. "You should have told me."

"I thought you already knew—I'd told your friend and you didn't ask."

I didn't ask, dickhead, because I didn't know I was pregnant.

"It doesn't matter," John interjected smoothly. "We know now."

Oh God. This was worse and worse.

"Is that what's upsetting you?" the doctor asked. "You thought you'd lost the baby?"

Momentarily, irritation dispelled the pall of anxiety that constantly sapped my energy, and I lurched to my feet. "Let's go," I ordered John.

"If the depression lingers and you find that you can't shake it, we can help!" the doctor called after my retreating back.

I was quiet as we walked out of the hospital and into the parking lot. John opened the door of his electric car for me, and I dropped into the deep seat, comforted for a moment by the rare luxury of riding in a car.

"Take me to my apartment," I said.

"Are you sure? Wouldn't it be best if you came to my house for the first couple of days, so I can look after you? Or will your ... friend be able to do it? Because if she works or something, I could take the day off ..."

"Take me home."

He shot a glance in my direction. "Are you OK?"

"Why didn't you tell me?"

"About the baby? I was going to ask you the same thing. But then I realised ... you never said anything because the baby isn't mine, right?"

Screw the baby. That was just an unnecessary complication right now. On the island, people rarely became pregnant when they didn't want to. We learned about birth control at school and it was free, so once you were in a serious relationship, taking the best birth control for your needs was a no-brainer. But if a mistake happened despite your precautions, then safe, free abortions were available, to be booked at the earliest opportunity. I certainly wasn't ready to have children, but I hadn't realised that I wouldn't even know I was pregnant. "Did the doctor say how far along I was?"

Hope glimmered in John's eyes. "Are you saying that it might be mine, depending on the dates?"

"No, it's yours for sure. I'm just wondering how urgently I need to schedule an abortion."

The car swerved suddenly towards the shoulder. The right front wheel skidded stridently on the gravel before John straightened it with a jerk of his hand. My whole body winced with anxiety; really, these big metal monsters were death-traps. John noticed my pallor. "Sorry," he said. "You just took me by surprise. So, the baby is definitely *mine?"*

I nodded, recognizing the delight that surged across his face, but not sharing it. Because I had just realised that I was very far from home in a land that didn't necessarily allow women to make their own decisions about their bodies, despite over-population issues that were already affecting the world. Perhaps I couldn't just 'schedule an abortion'.

"How do you know?"

I gave him a scathing look. "Umm, the usual way? Only been you for the past few months."

John raised my hand to his mouth and kissed it. "So this baby is ours. Darling. I'm so very happy. Maybe now you will reconsider my offer of marriage. You are the only woman I have ever loved ..."

"Turn right here," I said, interrupting when I recognized the street that led to my apartment.

I tried to tug my hand from his as we pulled up. I could feel him raining butterfly kisses along my wrist. "Darling, please listen. You can't make decisions concerning our child without me, it's half mine. Perhaps I didn't hear you right when you talked about abortion."

But I was already out of the car and racing through the main door and up the stairs; turning the doorknob to our apartment to check if it was locked before banging on the door, imploring Future-me to open it. She should be here; it was Saturday.

John came up behind me as the door swung open slowly. A squat, balding man stood there, dark as mahogany. "Yes?" he asked.

For a second I just gawped at him, but when he began to close the door, my tongue loosened. "I was just living here last week and … I had a roommate and … where is she? Who are you?" Perhaps Future-me hadn't come back yet. Perhaps this squat man was a squatter.

The man peered at me for a minute, and then shifted his head slightly to size up John. "I dunno. I just moved in." He obviously felt that we didn't look like criminals, because he flicked the door wider open. "See? All my stuff's still in boxes. Saw the ad on Wednesday, moved in yesterday." The room was indeed littered with boxes, spewing their contents onto my old, familiar sofa-bed.

"Did the former occupant leave her furniture?"

"Yup. Landlord asked if I wanted it, I said sure. Most of it's junk though. You want to know about the last renter, ask the landlord. Got his number?"

"All your possessions are still in there," John whispered into my hair as I scribbled down the number.

I thanked the squat man for the number. "One last thing. Did the previous tenant leave a desk in the office? She did? At the back of the top drawer in that desk, there is an envelope. In that envelope there is my passport. Could you bring that to me, please?"

The squat man brought me the passport, carefully checking the mug shot with my own face to ensure it was mine, muttering about the weirdness of people leaving all their belongings and disappearing into thin air. I was charging down the stairs before he'd finished, holding out my hand towards John as we stood on the landing inside the front door of the apartment building. "Give me your phone." I willed my hands to stop shaking. But they wouldn't; they swerved back and forth like drunken ponies, refusing to be controlled by the reins of my brain. Or perhaps my brain also veered back and forth, shying away from frightful thoughts about why Future-me wasn't here, galloping down the road of #2 on my agenda: going home.

Going home. And what if that had disappeared as well?

"Hello, this is Alice … Alison from Apartment Number three."

"Alison? Didn't you just move out of Apartment Number three?"

"Yes, that's right. I was just wondering if I could ask you a really weird question. I have been suffering from inexplicable memory lapses lately. Can you tell me what day it was when I ... moved out?"

"If you want your stuff you can ask the new tenant. You said you didn't want nothing."

"No. I don't want anything. What day did I move out?"

"You never moved out; you just phoned and told me to rent out the apartment cause you wasn't returning. And you didn't want your stuff."

I took a deep breath, so that my impatience wouldn't shoot down the phone and impale his eardrum. "What day did I call?"

"Tuesday."

Tuesday. The day of the accident. Future-me had phoned the landlord in the evening and erased herself from this time. Why? The cell dropped from my nerveless hands and I would have fallen to the floor if John hadn't caught me. My brain tried to run from the Frightful Thought, but it ran faster, growing bigger as it advanced, like in some awful nightmare, where you can't get away from the pursuing enemy.

This is why you disappeared. This is why you couldn't visit yourself for years and years. You lost your talisman. You were stuck stuck stuck stuck stuck stuck stuck stuck stuck stuck stuck stuck stuck.

∞ *Everything hurt. But not like when I woke up in the hospital. A different hurt. An unbearable ache somewhere in my ribcage. When consciousness first beckoned, I didn't remember why this ache was pulsating through my body, creating this feeling of misery. Then it came crashing back: the awful reality of my current situation. Cut off from home, family. Cut off from my people. And it was all my fault. Future-me had warned me about the dangers of intimacy with people from different times. I had thought I could handle it. I'd thought I was cleverer than the rules that the first Leaders had established in their wise experience. I'd thought I was above the law. And now I would be punished. My eyes flew open, but no bright whiteness invaded the dark. I was in John's familiar king-sized bed.*

I sat on the edge of the bed, probing the corners of my body for pain. There was none; just the heaviness of the cast pulling at my arm. "John?" I called, but there was no answer. The bedside clock told me it was 7:30 a.m., which was early for him to go to work. I hobbled into the bathroom, where I washed my face in the sink, using a wet flannel to clean the rest of my body. The hot water cheered me up. It was silly to forecast banishment when I hadn't even talked to the Leaders yet. It wasn't like there were precedents to this situation; nobody had ever lost their talisman before, to my knowledge. I'd been in an accident. It wasn't my fault. Surely they would take that into account? In any case, it was useless to wallow in misery or speculate about something outside of my control. I had a long journey ahead of me and that was a good thing; planning and implementation would keep my spirits up.

With that in mind, I headed downstairs and prepared a really nice breakfast: John always had a delicious selection of fruit. I found some olives and fresh French bread, and washed it all down with some good, strong coffee. I was going to look around for a pen and paper so I could start a To-do list while I ate, but realised it wasn't necessary. John's home office had a computer; all I needed to do was look up routes to the island, book the tickets, gather together a change of clothes, and I'd be on my way. Just thinking about my plan made my elusive energy levels inch higher.

As I was finishing my breakfast, I heard the door opening and John entered the kitchen, a bag of fresh croissants in his hand. "I was going to make you breakfast, but you're already up. Even better."

I gestured towards the coffee pot. "There's some coffee left."

I watched as he dropped a dash of milk into the blackness of his coffee, creating a weak cloud which rippled to the sides of the cup. He offered me a croissant. I shook my head.

"Croissants have a lot of necessary vitamins and minerals, and they give you an energy boost. You need energy."

I turned my head away. I knew my head was filled with nasty, negative thoughts these days, but really! Western humans were so health-conscious, preserving their individual lives while they squandered the earth's resources, as though more vitamins in their diet would keep them alive after they'd poisoned the air they breathed.

John took a bite out of one of the croissants. "I wish you would tell me why you are so frightened. What are the repercussions to losing your necklace?"

"I don't know yet. I have to travel home to find out. It's a long trip and I need to borrow the money from you. Can you give me the password to the computer in your home office? I'll use Google to find the fastest and easiest way to get there."

"You shouldn't travel alone in your state. I'll go with you." John pulled his phone out of his pocket and started tapping. "Where do you live?"

I wiped a baguette crumb from my lips. "I have to do this alone, John."

"Why?"

"I come from a different place; somewhere you can't visit. It's very far away, and it will take me several days to get there. If you lend me the money, I promise I'll pay you back, even if it takes me a while." I wasn't sure exactly how I would do this, but even if I had to work at some crap job, I'd manage it eventually.

"Pay me back? Aren't we partners? Aren't we together? You are carrying my child."

That was something I'd think about later. I couldn't think about everything now! I just had to get home to my mother, not obsess over whether I could be a mother myself. I didn't understand how it could have happened. I had always been so careful with my birth control. Would the fact that I was pregnant make the Leaders think even worse of me? Or would they pity me?

"Alley? You keep going off in your own little world. I know that something terrible has happened to you, even though I don't know what, exactly. I want to help you in any way that I can, but please don't ask me to support your disappearance to some unknown place, while you're carrying my child. You're in such a weird state of mind; you even mentioned

abortion, although I'm sure you didn't mean it. You need me to be with you, look after you."

I smiled at him; this couldn't be easy for him, either. "You'll never know how much I appreciate the support and love you've given me, John. But this next step is something I have to do alone."

A look of anguish crept over his face. "Get rid of our child?"

I didn't know much about the time I was in, but obviously some people still equated abortion with murder (while locking their doors against refugees who were escaping from countries where actual murder happened daily). "No. My next step is to travel to my home alone, so I can find out what ... what my fate is going to be."

He jumped to his feet in agitation. "What does that mean? Could they kill you because you lost that stupid necklace?"

"They could banish me."

"In which case you'd come back to me?"

I shrugged. I didn't want to think about the possibility of banishment. It was too horrific.

John sat down again and placed his hand over mine. "You're pregnant and your arm is broken. You can't travel alone. I'll go with you."

I explained again. He protested. I tried a different approach; he demurred. We made a new pot of coffee, even though I really wanted tea. It took quite a while for my assumptions to crumble under the weight of the truth, because I'd thought I could convince John to do anything for me. But on this he was adamant: he wouldn't give me money and watch me stride away into the sunset, carrying his child in my womb. The fact that he couldn't accompany me, no matter how much we both might want it, didn't seem to sway him. If they were just going to punish me, why did I need to go back at all?

"It's my family! My parents, my friends, my people! What, are you saying that I should just disappear from their lives? Never see them again?"

"What type of family is it, that they'd punish you because you were in a horrible accident? I'm your new family."

All the energy that had crept tentatively back when I had decided to focus on my new plan began to dissipate. I could feel the precious stuff dribbling away like sand through an hourglass. Anyone who stole my energy wasn't an ally; I just wanted John to go. I yawned prodigiously, watching determination dissolve into concern on his face. "You're not strong enough for this yet. These things don't have to be decided in a second. Why don't you go back to bed and get some rest, and we'll discuss it again this evening?"

I nodded slowly, as though my head felt heavy. "Whether you come with me or not, I'll need to find a route. I've never travelled to my home in this way before."

John took my arm and helped me to my feet. "I'll tape the password onto the computer in my home office."

I leant against him as we manoeuvred the stairs, as though I was dropping from exhaustion. "What shall you do while I sleep?"

"If you're sure you're OK, I'll go into the office. I missed a lot of time last week, and a few of my projects are falling behind schedule."

My heart jumped with glee, even as I leant more heavily against his supporting arm. He was going out!

John laid me tenderly in the bed, as though I were a porcelain doll. I closed my eyes and focused on making my breathing even, so he'd think I was dropping off to sleep. All my senses concentrated on his movements: he went into the home office, hopefully in order to tape the password onto the computer. He went downstairs again. A few minutes passed, while I cursed the delay with every bad word I knew, wondering what the hell he was doing.

Finally, the front door clicked and his car purred to life in the driveway. Instantly, I was out of bed and running towards the office. John might only be gone for a couple of hours, so there wasn't a lot of time.

Less than two hours later, I was marching out the front door, closing it carefully behind me. A sturdy walking stick, borrowed from John, tapped rhythmically and comfortingly against the pavement. The knapsack on my back contained food and water, a change of clothes, a blanket, various pens and markers, and a map; my route was marked in red. I wasn't going to plant myself in the nearest airport, that would be the first place John would look. I would find my way to the international airport in Winnipeg. I wasn't sure how I'd board planes or ferries without any money, but I'd start with hitchhiking. Surely people would be more likely to pick up a person with a broken arm.

It was good to be out of the house, making my own way. The craziness of travelling tens of thousands of miles without any money, the possible dangers of hitchhiking—these thoughts were kept locked in a little box within my heart. With my talisman, nothing frightened me. I could vanish from every situation, evade any danger. Without it, I was absolutely vulnerable. But I was still a free human being, making my own choices. If John didn't want to help me, I'd do it by myself. There was no other option.

∞ A few hours later, my broken arm was throbbing and my feet were proclaiming an achy fatigue. I had reached a major road leading out of the city, according to my maps, but my outstretched thumb wasn't slowing down any of the metal monstrosities racing by me on the highway. I levered myself to the ground on the shoulder, and rummaged in my knapsack for a marker. In big, block letters, I wrote the name of the next city on the back of one of my maps, skewered it on the end of my walking stick, and held it as high in the air as I could.

Within minutes, a large truck roared to a stop beside me. I struggled to my feet and hobbled to the door, grinning widely. I was on my way.

∞ Days later, I was marching along the TransCanada highway near Fredericton in the province of New Brunswick. The truck driver, a taciturn, non-talkative man, thank goodness, had been going a lot further than the next city emblazoned on the back of my map. I had driven with him for several days, sleeping in the cab of his truck when he stopped at a motel for the night. He'd tried to convince me to let him rent me a room, but I already owed him so much. Besides, I didn't need a bed, when I could stretch across the double seat of the truck. I had felt optimistic and *happy, trusting that the kindness the truck driver had shown me would be replicated again and again, carrying me step by step towards my destination, which had changed to Halifax, NS once the truck driver had told me that he was heading East. Surely tickets to Europe, the next step in my long journey, would be cheaper from Halifax, since it was nearer? In any case, with every rotation of the wheels I felt like I was getting closer to my island.*

Somewhere in NB my truck driver and I parted ways, and I continued on foot. Nobody picked me up that day; when evening fell a steady rain fell with it. Feeling distinctly miserable, I veered off at the next exit; I could see the lights of a few dwellings from the highway, but it took me longer to get to them than I had thought it would. By the time I was knocking on a door and requesting permission to sleep in the shed, I was so exhausted I could hardly see straight. I was refused. The look of repugnance they tossed in my direction before closing the door firmly in my face made me stop by their car to peer at myself in the side mirror. Perhaps I looked like a tramp? "Get away or we'll call the police!" they bellowed out the window.

I looked the same as I always did. Maybe it was just weird to have someone knocking at your door like that, when you didn't expect it. Again, a sense of my own vulnerability engulfed me. I was in a time that wasn't mine. I didn't really understand what made these people tick. How many of them lived in a state of fear and suspicion, like the family I'd just encountered? How many would want to help me, like the truck driver? I didn't know, and the drip drip of the rain clouded my thinking. I didn't want to return to the never-ending concrete highway, so I walked in an easterly direction on smaller roads until the scattered houses changed to subdivisions, which in turn shifted to taller buildings as I entered the noise and light of a city. I walked until the city converted to subdivisions again. I continued to walk, until the subdivisions gave way to patchy trees, and then stretches of forest. I climbed down from the road and made myself a rough bed under a tree, hoping that its thick boughs would protect me from the rain. I covered myself with my blanket and, using my knapsack as a pillow, tried to fall asleep.

I woke up cold and miserable. My feet still ached from all the walking and my carefully rationed piece of bread and cheese didn't begin to fill the hole in my stomach. Still, I struggled to my feet and continued. I returned to the highway and walked and walked. Finally, someone picked me up and took me to Moncton. Then I walked until someone else picked me up, and took me all the way to the International airport in Halifax, NS. Buoyed with new elation, I entered the delicious warmth of the building to inquire about really cheap flights. It didn't really matter where they were going to, so long as it was in the right direction. Google had advertised some last-minute deals that were half the usual rate. I didn't have the money for even a last-minute deal, but if I found something for a couple of hundred dollars, why, I'd just pick up some odd jobs for a few days and make the money. Anything was possible. I had to keep saying that to myself. I could do anything.

Until I stood in front of the neat, spick and span ticket agent, who explained that if I wanted to book from the airport it would be full price, and most flights were overbooked anyway so it would be impossible to find seats, all the while looking askance at my dishevelled hair. I checked every flight going to Europe from the airport that day. I talked to other ticket agents; some were nicer than Ms. Spick and Span, but the essential message was the same: empty seats were few and cost a small fortune. Struggling to organize my thoughts, which were getting jumbled (probably due to the rotten night's sleep I'd had), I found my way to an uninhabited corner and sat staring at my hands. I trembled under my wet clothes; it felt like years since I'd last been warm. Go away misery, *I told myself. Focus on a To-do list. I would stay and check the flights every day. I'd talk to travel agencies. I'd find a job, to tide me over, to pay for that cheaper flight I had to trust I'd find.*

I was so engrossed in my own thoughts that I didn't hear the footsteps approaching from behind, until a heavy hand descended on my shoulder. I skittered sideways on my seat and twisted around. A short man in a trench coat stood there, pasty-white skin partially covered by an enormous moustache. "Alice?" *he asked.*

I gaped at him, and didn't answer.

"You look like you could do with a hot bath and a nice, warm meal."

So I'm not in trouble, then. *I shook my head, amused at my own idiocy.* And if I were, they'd know my name was Alice? *Who cared how they knew or what they knew, Mr. Mustachios had read my mind.* "Yes, please," I said. "A nice, hot bath, followed by a hot meal, followed by a hot bed. Everything as hot as possible, please."

He led the way, glancing behind every now and then to make sure I was following him. I stuck to him like a burr: I could practically feel the hot water against my skin already. The success of this whole trip depended on the good will of my fellow humans, and I would take any that came my way. I didn't feel bad vibes from this guy; it didn't occur to me to distrust him. Mr. Mustachios drove me to a hotel and arranged a room, then he left me alone. He didn't explain a thing and I didn't ask.

Nothing had ever felt quite as good as that bath. I luxuriated in the deepest, hottest water I could stand, and when it began to cool I let some out and filled the tub back up again. Eventually I must have dozed off, because I was definitely running through the field with Nanny and her kids when a knock at the door jerked me back to the present.

"Yes?" I called out, wondering if that kind Mr. Mustachios had ordered me room service.

"Alley? Can I come in?"

Of course. *John had come home to an empty house and hired a detective. Well, nothing had changed, except that I felt a lot better. One more reason to trust in destiny.* "Just wait," *I called, heaving myself reluctantly from the hot water and drying myself off with a towel. I surveyed my cold, wet clothing with distaste. I'd have to wash and dry my things before returning to my nomadic life. I draped the towel around me and opened the door. John was standing there with a large, fluffy housecoat open in his hands, which he'd obviously taken from the cupboard beside the bathroom. Behind him was a tray, piled high with different salads, breads and cheeses. Sometimes it seemed like John knew me almost as well as I knew myself. I bundled myself into the housecoat and, suddenly ravenous, started making little bread-based pyramids quivering with different flavours. John sat opposite me; I glanced up at some point, irritated by his silent scrutiny. "Want some?"*

"No, thank you."

"Well, it's rude to stare, and it's putting me off my food," I snapped.

John picked up the room service menu and studied it intently. "What were you thinking?" he asked softly, eyes still fixed to the menu.

"Did I make a secret about what I was thinking? I thought it was pretty clear: I'm going home. Do you think my decisions are dependent on your approval?" I began to laugh. "We've been brought up in different worlds, John. You think money decides everything, don't you? You thought if you told me that you wouldn't give me the money, I wouldn't get home. You thought your money controlled the outcome." I laughed again, but not unkindly. "You thought wrong."

"So how, exactly, were you going to take a plane?"

I popped another pyramid into my mouth. "It only costs a few hundred dollars. I was going to work for a few days."

"You were just going to pop into different establishments, with your dirty clothes and dripping hair, and ..."

"Why don't you leave, John? I refuse to explain how I'm going to get home. It's actually none of your business."

Red stained his cheeks and he leapt up. "You are endangering the life of my baby by this reckless behaviour. Of course it's my business!"

"What reckless behaviour?"

"Hitchhiking with strangers, sleeping outside, eating irregularly. It's not good for you!"

"Goodness, what a good job your detective has done. If you are so worried, give me the money so I can get home easily and safely. Otherwise, get the hell out of this room and out of my life." I wasn't sure why I was being so unpleasant. I was very fond of John; at times I even thought I loved him. But something truly terrible had happened to me and he didn't seem to get it. Besides, nobody controlled my decisions, and nobody ever would.

John placed his hands over his eyes and rubbed them vigorously. After

*a moment or two he murmured: "You're right. Of course I should have
agreed to pay your way, right from the beginning."*

Let this be a lesson to you, *I thought.* Don't try and control me.
And then I sat on his knee and fed him a pyramid as compensation.

∞ *It was very strange travelling home the traditional way. The never-
ending flights were exhausting; on one of them I sat near a baby who
screamed lustily for large chunks of the flight. I offered a silent prayer that
it wasn't too late to delay my own motherhood for a few more years. The
ferries were better, as I could walk around and stretch my legs. Then, finally, there were our private boats, moored to the next island over for the
specific use of our people. I found the key in its usual hiding place, and
started to chug towards the horizon. I was anxious. We had all learned the
emergency way to get to our island at school—the secret, physical way that
guaranteed we could return home under any circumstance, even the un-
imaginable. But nobody in living memory had ever had to use this secret
path. I was tense, training my eyes against the glare of the sun, scared I
would miss it. Eventually my aching eyes were rewarded by the sight of a
barren island—more a pile of rocks than an island. There was a rock on
the far-left corner that jutted up like a triangle. I drew closer and stood up,
reaching my hand towards the horizon just above the upper point of that
rock, praying that I would find the right place in that endless stretch of
horizon. My hand sailed through the air, closer to the triangle rock, my
shoulders rising in tension. Air, only air. Then I felt it; a soft fold in the
sky itself. My hand plunged into this seam and clutched the edge, peeling
it back to make a hole big enough for the boat to pass through. Beyond the
rift, the horizon looked exactly the same, rolling waves meeting blue sky,
except in the far distance I could just make out the contours of another
island. My island.*

*My boat nudged through the opening and I drew it shut behind me as
I passed, letting it fall against the stern when I couldn't reach back any
further. It looked like someone smoothing out a crumpled drawing over an*

identical original. When I looked back, the jutting triangle rock looked exactly as it had before I'd touched it.

But I was through the rift. My island was before me.

I can't describe how I felt as the boat nudged against my island's wharf. I tied it to a mooring and looked at the familiar shore, filled with love and a feeling of comfort so profound I laughed at myself. It was as if I'd been away for years, instead of mere weeks. It was as if some part of me had been worried that the island wouldn't be there, just like Future-me hadn't been there. But of course that was silly. Soon everything would become clear. What it all meant. Why I couldn't visit myself between May, 2006, and 2022.

I enjoyed the walk home, revelling in each familiar landmark.

"Nanny! Nanny!" I shouted as I approached my little house, waiting for the stubborn old beast to rush up from the field at the sound of my voice. This time, I didn't have a treat in my pocket, but she wouldn't know that. She was especially partial to banana peel. I drew close to the gate, and peered at the barn for a few moments in confusion. This wasn't my little shed. This was a two-storey barn. I felt anxious. I pushed open the door and stepped inside. Large pens lined each side of the barn, and each pen was filled with different animals: goats, chickens, geese, pigs. Above my head a loft stretched across the entire barn, bursting at the seams with hay.

I turned and ran out of the barn, and I didn't stop running until I reached my parents' house. At least this looked exactly the same, and I pushed open the door and hurtled inside, calling for my mother, trying to hold my panic at bay.

My mother appeared in the doorway of the kitchen. I rushed towards her, and then stopped in confusion. "Mother?" I asked, tentatively. She looked ... different. Her hair haloed around her face like white fluff. A couple of weeks ago it had been light brown, streaked with gray. Deep lines sprang from the corners of her eyes and mouth. She looked smaller. Her mouth was open and her eyes shone with tears.

"Rakita?"

I rushed over and our arms enveloped and clung to each other. Then my father was hugging me too and we were a hugging trio and I closed my eyes and immersed myself in the joy and comfort of my parents' love.

But when I opened my eyes, I saw that my father's face bore the same signs of ageing. "I was just here a few weeks ago," I said, drawing back slightly so I could look in both their faces. "You were in your fifties. What's going on?"

"My darling Rakita," my mother said, tears streaming down her face. "We haven't seen you in over twenty years."

My world reeled. I staggered back, suddenly understanding the full import of what it meant to be stuck, stuck, stuck. "Is this ... 2006?" I asked, fearing to hear the answer.

"This is 2006," my father said, "but you're still in your twenties, aren't you? For you, it's ... what?"

"1986," I whispered.

"Do you know what happened?" my mother asked.

"I lost my talisman."

We sat in the back garden, looking out at the rows of fruit trees and bee hives in their orchard, watching the chickens scratching in the dirt. I felt so grateful that this, at least, had not changed. I looked and looked, as I told them the whole story from the beginning. I didn't know when I would see it again.

My parents listened, and wept again, and hugged me. And when they knew every detail of the past few months of my life, and I knew the highlights of their past 20 years, my mother urged me to go and see the Leaders.

"What will they do to me?" I asked her, reverting to my childish self, hoping that my mother could protect me.

Tears sprang to her eyes.

"What, Mum? What do you think?"

"My darling girl, you are my child. When you have your own child, you will understand. I have visited every year of my life multiple times, but you know we cannot choose the exact point where our talismans take us. I never managed to visit this day, for example. I didn't know that this day

would happen ..." I watched in despair as my mother's face crumpled in pain. "I am very grateful that I ..." She burst into tears. My father moved over to her and hugged her. When she could, she spoke again. "It's not over," she whispered. "There are many more years ..."

My eyes were wide with fear. "Many more years when we don't see each other?" I whispered.

She nodded. I fell into their arms and we hugged and hugged, as though we'd never let each other go.

And then I walked slowly towards the Gathering Place where the Leaders awaited me.

I sat in front of a row of four; the questions came fast and furious, and I answered them as clearly as I could. It felt like an interrogation, but there was no resentment in my heart. I deserved this. The questions seemed to go on forever, but eventually there was silence. It stretched on, as they looked at me.

"This is an unprecedented situation," Jacob said quietly. His was the only face I recognized, despite his now great age.

"I already know that I am banished," I said quietly. "My parents said that I am absent from their lives in their visits to the future, and I was unable to visit myself for a period of approximately 15 years. However, I did manage to visit myself at 61, so I have hopes ..." My voice caught, and I had to stop for a moment to control my breathing. "I believe the situation will be resolved eventually."

Not for years. Not for years. Your parents will be approaching their 90s. You will have lost half your lifetime with them. Years. Years. Years. Stuck. Stuck. Stuck.

Tears rolled down my face, but I stared back at the Leaders calmly enough.

"More than any other aspect of what you have done, this child in your womb is the greatest deviation from what your life would otherwise have been. It is an aberration. It was not supposed to happen."

"I can have an abortion," I said.

Jacob looked at me carefully. "No, we do not advise that. Despite the

121

fact that it was never supposed to exist, we feel that this child might have a role to play."

I stared at him in astonishment. I knew that he had seen something, understood something about the future. I also knew that he could not tell me. It was a basic rule; you cannot reveal anything that you find out about another person's life.

But I burned to know more. He had said that this cluster of cells in my belly had a role to play. "Is there anything else you can tell me?"

"No. But if you love this man, John, then we advise you to stay with him. Have your baby. Live your life. There is no punishment. We feel you have been punished enough, by the fact that you are basically cut off from your family and from the enlightened society we have created here."

"I can't live here?" I whispered.

"No."

"If you forbid me to stay here, do not say there is no punishment! You are banishing me!" I cried in despair.

"Not at all, my dear," said the wise-looking old woman with the gentle face, sitting beside Jacob. "You have changed the future through your actions, although you can't know how, because you can no longer visit your future. But we know two things: you are not here for the foreseeable future, and you are pregnant."

"You have broken the rules. History has been changed," Jacob said. "We aren't sure what that might mean, but the present is quite simple. You are not here, therefore you must be somewhere else. I say again: if you love the father of your child, your natural place is with him."

I felt angry. There was no reason to banish me. I'd had an accident. It wasn't my fault. "Please let me stay! Maybe, if you permit me to stay, history will be changed again, and I will be here, on the island. We don't know what would happen, do we?"

A grimace of contempt swept over Jacob's face. "Don't minimize what you have done. You have taken over another time period, one that is not your own. We cannot yet comprehend the repercussions of that."

I held my eyes wide, to keep the tears from brimming over. "What do you mean?"

He leaned forward and held my gaze. "You exceeded your four-day limit. Why do we reserve the worst punishment for people who exceed the limit of their time travel?"

If you stay more than four days at a time in your future, you will be stripped of your ability to time travel and banished from the island.

Rakita felt trapped within his dark pupils, certain that something awful was going to come out of his mouth.

"What do you think has happened to the future version of yourself? You lived with her during her time, and now you have taken over her time. Everything you will experience in the next 20 years is different from her experiences. That's what I meant when I said that this child in your womb is the greatest deviation from what your life would otherwise have been. We know that two versions of the same life can not exist simultaneously. So this must mean that those years of hers don't exist."

Images passed through my mind: Future-me warning me about my deepening relationship with John. Flitting around the kitchen whipping up a snack and talking non-stop at the same time. Reeling off instructions with the focussed look of a woman who felt she was living a meaningful life. And I had taken that life away from her. She had been snuffed out, as though she had never been. Because I got trapped in her time, and supplanted her. I had as good as murdered *her.*

Jacob leant back in his seat. "I wouldn't feel too complacent, if I were you. If I didn't think your child might have a special role to play, I'd banish you without compunction. You lied to us, by omitting to report the true nature of your relations with this man. You broke the rules. You have irrevocably changed history, and annihilated a life. You deserve to be banished." Jacob closed his eyes, effectively dismissing me.

I staggered to my feet, wiping my tears as I took my leave. My mantra of, "I'd had an accident. It wasn't my fault" twisted and changed shape as the different faces of Future-me marched by my vision: her face dissolving into laughter as we reminisced about Rambo; her furrowed brow when she tried to explain some modern phenomenon. My anger at the leaders dissipated. They had been kinder than I deserved. I got involved with someone from another time. I broke the rules. The accident wouldn't have happened if I hadn't broken the rules. Future-me would still be alive. It's all my fault.

But why couldn't I stay? What negative impact did my presence have? The only difference it made to anybody, was to me and my parents. They would be devastated, losing their only child. The Leaders had made a snap decision, without thinking. The Leaders always think carefully and consider all available knowledge, every perspective.

I hated them. I hated myself. I felt so utterly vulnerable without my talisman. Its loss brought home the manifold advantages I had always taken for granted. My talisman had eliminated fear and uncertainty from my life. It had granted possibilities and perspectives that I'd relied on for every decision I had made. Now, the uncertain future was frightening. How awful it would be, stuck in a different world, in a different time. Cut off from everything I knew. Stuck stuck stuck.

Then, if I did marry John and we brought up the child together, and then somehow, some miracle occured and I could come back to the island, what would happen to John? He couldn't come with me. And what about the child?

Stuck stuck stuck.

I walked slowly along the road back to my parents' house, looking at everything with the greatest attention, knowing I might not see it again for years. It would be impossible to make the gruelling trip very often, especially with a child. Perhaps the child wouldn't be allowed to come, even. I wish I'd asked that question when I'd been with the Leaders. In any case, John wouldn't want to give me the money. Everything was going to be awful.

My parents knew, as soon as they saw my face. They hugged me tightly, for a long time, as though they never wanted to let me go. We wept together, entwined like three gnarled branches on a tree.

"You will visit us?" my mother asked. "We want to see our grandchild."

"I don't know. The Leaders kept saying that they weren't punishing me, so I'm not officially banished, but they kept repeating that I am not to be found here for a long, long time. What does that mean, Mum?"

Her old, moist eyes gazed at me with such sadness. "That is what I have seen too, Rakita. Perhaps you won't be able to come. Perhaps ... you will change in this new life. It might be hard for you. Maybe you will sink into one of your depressions, and I won't be there to help you." My mother's face creased in an anguish I wouldn't understand until I had my own child.

Stuck. Stuck. Stuck.

CHAPTER EIGHT

SIMON LIFTED HIS eyes from the last words on the page and stared straight ahead, watching the lengthening shadows cast patterns over the grass. His left hand rested on the teapot between them, filled and drunk several times that afternoon as each of his mother's words became paint strokes, slowly creating a picture in his mind. The feelings bubbling in his chest were too complex to decipher; he didn't know what he felt. Sadness? Pity? Amazement? Certainly anger, but against whom?

His mother was waiting for him to speak, staring straight ahead at the expanse of grass, as he was. Toby lay by their feet, exhausted from his futile efforts to entice them to play ball.

"Thank you for telling me, Mum."

"I wanted to, it's important for you to understand." Rakita didn't add that every word he'd read had chipped away at the burden of secrecy weighing on her heart. On the island, the value of truthful communication was held dear. She had grown up espousing truth, despising even white lies. She hadn't realised the burden her silence had been, until it was gone. "Is there anything you'd like to ask me? Your father will be coming home any minute, and I'll be gone before he gets out of his car."

Simon got to his feet and stretched, feeling his cramped muscles release. Toby was already on his feet, ball clamped in his everlastingly hopeful mouth. Simon retrieved the ball and threw it hard, the familiar smile spreading across his face as Toby performed his usual aerobics. His mind slowly turned from the past to the present. He had many questions, but there was one question that tapped insistently at the forefront of his mind.

"Did you really want to get rid of me?"

Rakita looked startled. "No, never. What do you mean?"

"You wanted to have an abortion."

"That wasn't you, sweetheart. That was a clump of cells."

Simon jutted out his jaw obstinately. "It became me. If you'd gotten rid of those cells, I wouldn't have existed."

"Every time I use contraception I'm preventing the existence of a potential human. You existed for me when I felt you move inside me for the first time. Then, I would have felt sadness at your loss. Once you'd entered our lives, I would have felt anguish at your loss. But during those first couple of months, you were an embryo. A seed."

"But ..."

"I have loved you for over 15 years. You want to quibble about your first weeks in my belly? Didn't love you. Sorry. Glad I had you, though. Next question?"

Simon bit his lip, unsure if he was really upset about this, or not.

Rakita began to drum her fingers on the arm of her chair. "Your father will be back soon. Is that really the only question you have?"

Simon realised he had lots of questions. Maybe he'd come back to the fact that his mother had wanted to terminate his existence later. "So you saw your parents today for the first time in 15 years?"

"It was so sad." Rakita's lips trembled.

"Why are you so sad now, Mum? Weren't you happy to see them again?"

"They are so old; they are both pushing 90. I lost 35 years that I should have had with my parents. I don't have much time left with them, yet I realize that I'm lucky they are both still alive."

Simon did a quick calculation in his head. His mother was only 40. He glanced over at her. She was fighting tears. "Perhaps that is the main reason why I'm so angry with your father. It wasn't just the talisman that he took from me."

"Actually, I still don't quite understand the time thing. Grandma obviously didn't have you when she was 50?"

"When I first visited this city 15—no, it was 16 years ago—the year for me was 1986, and I was 25 years old. But I had come forward 20 years in time, to 2006, and was visiting myself at 45. But because my talisman was stolen I was trapped in this time, so I stayed at 25 in the year 2006, while my parents were the age they would normally be in 2006—20 years older than when I had last seen them. When your father stole my talisman ..."

"After it disappeared."

"Really, Simon? You still think there's a question mark around that?"

Simon hung his head. How could his father do such a thing? He mustn't have known what he was doing. He hadn't known he was cutting her off from her family and home. Simon didn't want to think about it. It was too painful.

"I went back to the island and found my parents in their 70s instead of in their 50s like they were the last time I saw them," Rakita said. "Then I was so angry with the decision to banish me ... well. My parents wanted me to visit them the normal way, even without my talisman. They couldn't believe that they'd never met you. Sometimes the decisions we make in our lives come from anger and pain. They're not the right decisions."

"Do you mean the decision not to visit the island again after I was born?" If that was the decision she was talking about, he agreed with her. Definitely a stupid decision based on anger. He might have been introduced to the island and his family years ago!

Rakita nodded. "Don't forget, it's not that easy to visit the island without a talisman. It takes days. And I lost my energy, somehow."

Simon picked up a cookie too and changed the subject. "Did you see the Leaders today? What did they say?"

Rakita sighed, raking her hand through her hair. "They are as they have always been, saying the opposite of what you want them to say, with perfect logic and rationale. You don't have a talisman, Simon, so you can't go and live there."

"But why can't I get a talisman like any other 15-year-old island boy? I obviously have the right genes, or whatever one needs to belong to your tribe!"

"I'll stay here with you."

Simon looked at his mother, disappointment throbbing through his temples. Toby was looking fixedly at the ball he'd dropped at Simon's feet. He gave a little bark, just in case Simon hadn't understood his role in the game. "They're stupid. And cruel. To separate a mother and child, especially in your case where your parents have already been separated from you for decades; that's cruelty." And Simon picked up the ball and hurled it violently into the darkening sky.

"Simon, listen to me. The decisions of the Leaders are never driven by emotion. Nor cruelty. Ever. Whenever they have to make a decision, they weigh all available knowledge very carefully. They made this decision because they believe it is best for you to stay here for the next couple of years. Maybe not forever, but for now. Trust them."

Simon felt close to tears. "But you don't want to stay here."

"I will do what is best for you. Do you think it matters where I live, when I've been granted my freedom again? I can zip back and forth every day, visiting both families in both worlds."

Simon wanted to contradict everything she said. "It's ridiculous for you to stay here and rent another place, when it takes you two seconds to come back. You should live on the island, and come back every day to be with me after school."

His mother stood up and enveloped him in a bear hug. "That sounds like a perfect idea. There's only one small hitch. Once again, without wanting to, I seem to be changing the rules."

"What ... why?"

"People can't travel back and forth to the same, exact time. I'm not sure which world my talisman will consider to be my 'permanent' world. If I'm based on the island and that is my life, then I can visit this year every day, but that doesn't mean it will translate into consecutive days for you. Knowing this, that there might be days you don't see me, are you sure you want me to live on the island?"

For a minute it was hard to swallow; everything was changing too fast. He wanted his mother to be happy, but he desperately wanted her with him. Rakita sensed his hesitation, and hugged him harder. "I will be here every day, no matter what that might mean. We'll figure it out. My darling boy; it's going to be all right."

Toby heard the car first, wrenching his eyes from his beloved ball to turn towards the noise.

"I have to go," Rakita said. "I will be back tomorrow."

As they hugged goodbye, she whispered in his ear: "You can come and visit me in the summer."

The summer! That was only a couple of months away. Simon lifted his head and grinned happily at his mother before she disappeared.

∞ The next day Simon rushed home from school, making up a funny story about the bullies' transformation from tyrants to chickens as he ran. He wanted to make his mother laugh. It had been amusing to see how they'd avoided his eyes, when they had once sought them out, especially towards the end of the day. As soon as he got home he flung open the door and was almost bowled over by Toby, who had evidently not been let out. "Mum?" he called to the empty house. "Mum?"

But there was no answer.

"She just hasn't come yet," he explained to Toby as he played ball with him, executing ever more funky tosses into the sky, to see if the dog's antics would be even funnier in response. Still, he worried. What if time on the island was completely different to time here? How would his mother know when to come? What if the talisman refused to take her here? And tomorrow was the weekend. If she didn't come today … tears pricked Simon's eyes, but he took a deep breath and threw the ball again.

Eventually, prompted by hunger, Simon wandered back into the house and opened the fridge, which was usually full of snacks like fruit and cheese. It always boasted a large pot of something, made by his father over the weekend to tide them over the first few days of the week. But there was very little food in the fridge today, and no pot. Simon decided he'd better make the dinner himself; at least there were some eggs and bread. He couldn't find any salad things, other than a tomato and some onions, so he cut them up small and doused them in balsamic vinegar and olive oil. Toby barked and Simon's heart leapt, then dropped as he heard his father's tread in the hall. Now his mother wouldn't come for sure.

"How are you, Simon?" his father asked in a tired voice, slumping in a chair.

"I'm fine," Simon said. He divided the food between two plates and put one in front of his father. As they ate, he tried to tell his funny story about the bullies, but his father's dispirited pecking and his mother's absence defeated the humour. His voice petered out.

"That's great, Simon." His father's fork moved, but the food on his plate didn't decrease.

"Dad, are you going to make a pot of food tomorrow? It's the weekend. But we need to do a shop first."

"Sure."

But the weekend dribbled by and his father seemed to spend most of his time staring into space. It was almost like his parents had changed places: Rakita was now the one full of energy and life, while his father wilted in despair. Simon felt sorry for him, and would have liked to have heard his father's perspective on the story he had been told. But his father didn't speak, and Simon was frightened to probe. *Because the talisman didn't walk into the basement and lock itself into a chest by itself. And unless his father put it there, what other scenario made sense?*

"Dad," he ventured on Sunday afternoon, "are you going to cook?"

"I don't know, Simon. I don't really feel like cooking. Shall we get take-out?"

Simon didn't remind him that his mother had always restricted take-out meals, because of the plastic they used to wrap the food, and also because she liked to know the ingredients she was putting into her body. "Why don't I make you a list of stuff to buy, Dad? If you're really tired, you can drive me to the store and I'll get everything myself. Then you can just sit in your chair and instruct me how to make the stew." John grumbled that it would be easier to get take-out, but Simon insisted, and eventually he complied. The stew turned out pretty well, but Simon didn't enjoy it. He didn't want to do everything himself. He wanted parents who would look after him.

On Monday, he raced home after school, but his mother wasn't there.

Nor Tuesday.

Nor Wednesday.

If you give the pendant to your mother, Simon, neither of us will ever see her again.

Every day, he felt angrier and sadder. Where was she? Was she having so much fun on the island that she'd forgotten him? She pretended that she was from such a great place, so superior to Canada, and she could abandon her own child like this? On Thursday he wept so much that even John noticed his swollen eyes at the dinner table, steeped in his own depression though he was. "She has deserted us both, Simon."

"No, she hasn't!" Simon screamed, and smashed his plate on the floor. His father didn't move as he rushed up to his room, an anxious Toby at his heels. He flung himself on his bed and buried his face in his pillow, ignoring his beeping phone. But it kept beeping insistently, so eventually he grabbed it in frustration.

Yr Mum? Sandra had written. Then: *Talk to me*, sent regularly every few minutes for the past half hour. Didn't she have a life?

Not here, he texted back. Contrary to his mother's advice, he had told Sandra the gist of his mother's story, and he didn't regret it either, although he could see she was struggling to make sense of what he had said. On the one hand the whole story was ludicrous and obviously a complete fabrication; on the other hand, Sandra had never known Simon to lie. On the third hand, she had hinted during one of their lunch breaks, it was totally normal to make up stories when something really hurt … like if his mother had abandoned him …"

"She hasn't!" Simon had screamed.

If you give the pendant to your mother, Simon, neither of us will ever see her again.

But he was sure his mother loved him. So where was she?

Sorry, Sandra texted back with a sad face. *I help w. dinner 2moro?*

Not 2moro. TTYL, Simon texted back, and prayed she'd leave him in peace, which she did.

On Friday, he didn't bother to run. He sauntered home, scuffing his shoes by scraping them along the curbs. He was so full of rage and misery that he didn't even notice Toby rushing along the driveway to greet him, although he certainly noticed when his mother crashed into him and strangled him with her hug. It felt like someone had injected a shot of joy right into his heart. When they finally pulled apart, Simon's anger evaporated in a flash at the sight of his mother's ravaged face. They both started talking at the same time: "It's been a week since you were here, Mum!"

"I couldn't get back to the right day—I was desperate!"

"I waited for you …"

"That stupid talisman. We're told to trust it but it's obviously totally random and just sticks you wherever it bloody likes …"

When they had calmed down a little, and were ensconced in their favourite chairs overlooking the garden and drinking tea, his mother described her rising panic as the week had worn on. "The first day, I found myself outside the office, and you were on the computer. Then another me brushed by and went in, and you said to this other me,

'Over a million people have signed our petition, Mum,' and of course I knew right away that it wasn't the right day."

Simon had pulled his chair around so he was facing his mother (simultaneously avoiding Toby's plaintive gaze as it ping ponged between him and the ball). He wanted to hear the whole story, but he couldn't help interrupting: "A petition about what?"

"From what I could see, you had several on the go: prevent drilling in the arctic, stop deforestation in the Amazon ..."

"This year? I start being an environmental activist this year?"

Rakita realised she'd unwittingly broken a rule; she shouldn't have revealed anything about Simon's future. "Even though I was exhausted from that one time-travel, I kept imagining you waiting here for me, so I tried again, but I couldn't manage more than once or twice a day. I couldn't stop crying, thinking of you waiting."

Simon flushed as he took a bite of his cookie, slipping a piece to Toby at the same time. He felt such relief, but also shame that he'd doubted his mother. "So a day on the island is the same as a day here?"

"Oh yes, I knew exactly how much time was going by, without being able to get to you. Twice the bloody talisman took me to this summer, when we're together on the island. Once to next Christmas. It was torture, I can tell you. I even considered giving up on the talisman and taking a plane. But finally, yesterday, I found myself outside, watching you run down the driveway towards me. I was sure the talisman had finally taken me to the right date. As soon as you reached me, I grabbed you in a hug like I did today, but you kind of shrugged me off with an embarrassed, 'Mu-um ...'. So then I knew I'd still got it wrong. I asked you the date—it was next September. And then I felt someone breathing down my neck, and I was behind myself."

Simon was sitting on the edge of his chair, his forgotten cookie dangling from his fingers.

"This other me said, 'You aren't supposed to be talking to anyone.'

"And I wailed, 'I'm sorry! But I can't get to the right time ... Simon is waiting for me ... I have to be here every day when he gets home from school ...' I was blubbering by this time, desperate because I couldn't get to my son who needed me, terrified that I'd broken the rules yet again. What was wrong with me, constantly screwing up all the time? Would some terrible consequence result from my mistakes, like it had before? So I grabbed my talisman to leave, but I heard your voice yell after me, clear as a bell: 'You have to sleep here, Mum!'"

Rakita leaned back in her chair and nodded significantly at Simon.

He still looked bewildered. "What?"

"I have to sleep here, if I want this to be my permanent place. If I want to be here every afternoon like clockwork for you, I have to sleep here."

Simon remembered how much he had missed his mother, and how long she had been away from her own mother. "But you want to be on the island."

Rakita leaned forward and punched him lightly on the arm, as if to knock the seriousness out of his face.

"If I time-travel back every day, I'll be popping up so often in their lives they'll be sick to death of me."

Simon grinned, and then grew serious again. "But then you'll have to rent a place here, or something. Do you have the money for that?"

"I can get money if I need it, but I've thought of a better solution. I'll come here in the morning when your father leaves for work, and sleep all day while you're at school. That'll be my main 7 hours of sleep, and the talisman will recognize this as my 'permanent' place. So I'll be here every day when you get home!"

Relief flooded into Simon's heart, followed immediately by another worry. "Didn't you tell me that you can only time travel for a few hours at a time? So where will you stay all the rest of the time when you're here?"

His mother crowed with delight. "That's the best part! The Leaders have made a special exception in my case. I have received permission to time travel for 14 hours at a time. See? I told you they weren't cruel."

They grinned at each other. Then Simon felt a wetness on his fingers as Toby delicately extracted the dangling cookie from his hand.

He shouted with surprise. And they both laughed.

∞ The last couple of months at school passed slowly for Simon. He discovered that the only difference between being bullied and being feared was that the threat of violence disappeared, otherwise he was as alone as ever. Alone, but not lonely, thanks to Sandra. He continued to leave the classroom as soon as the bell rang, but even when Sandra accompanied him home and they loitered en route, he never saw hide nor hair of the bullies. They avoided him like the plague. Sandra began to come home with him after school on a regular basis, hanging out with Rakita until they grew more comfortable with each other. Rakita began to understand why Simon had had to tell Sandra about the island. She knew the burden of secret-keeping from loved ones too well to judge any decision to spill the beans, although she refrained from discussing the subject herself. The trio often made dinner together; as soon as Rakita realised John had stopped cooking she stepped smoothly into his shoes, creating delicious meals from ingredients she dictated to Simon to pass onto his father, so he could buy them.

Sometimes Simon's hand would brush against Sandra's as they cut up vegetables on both sides of the giant cutting board, and an electric jolt would shoot through his body at the contact. He was worried that Sandra would guess at these new feelings, and took care never to betray by a word or sound what he felt. Such a revelation would change their comfortable, friendly relationship and that would be a shame, because he felt it was perfect the way it was. Sometimes they made cookies, or went for walks together, or drank tea and talked in the garden, until Toby's pricked ears informed them of John's arrival. Rakita was determined never to break another island rule, so she would go into another room, or around the corner of the house, before disappearing. But she could not disguise the fact that she was there one moment, and nowhere to be found the next, and this, more than anything, convinced Sandra of the truth of this outlandish story of Simon's.

Occasionally, Sandra was able to stay for dinner, and she and Simon would hole up in his room until John could drive her home. They usually talked very easily about things, but sometimes, as Sandra sprawled on her stomach across his bed and scrolled through her phone, Simon would become intensely aware of her, lying there. He'd have to go and stand by the window for a few moments, doing math equations in his head, so she wouldn't know what he was thinking.

Usually, Sandra's mother wanted her home before supper, to do her chores. Sandra had never let Simon come to her house, and he thought it was probably because she lived in a poorer part of town, and was ashamed. This made him sad, because it meant she didn't understand him very well. As if he cared about stuff like that! He couldn't even get a clear picture of the types of chores she was talking about, but gathered that she had several younger siblings. As soon as John returned from taking her home, the long, dreary evenings began. Simon hated this part of the day more than any other.

"Did you see your mother today?" John would always ask. "Did she ask after me?"

Simon didn't like to lie, so he asked his mother to show some interest in John.

"Are you joking?" she said. "I understand he's your father and that you love him, but he did something wicked and I will never forgive him."

"That's not been proven," Simon said stubbornly. "Anyway, why can't you just ask how he is, even if you don't care, just so I can say you did?"

"Ridiculous," his mother said. But she did begin to ask after him, in deeply sarcastic tones, as soon as she'd kissed Simon hello, so she wouldn't forget.

As soon as they had finished eating, Simon escaped up to his room. He needed to think. How does a climate activist get started? Websites, social media. But anybody could do that. Inevitably, research on websites was ambushed by dreams of the talisman. Why, if he had a talisman he could fix the problem with one trip! Technology was key to transferring over to non-fossil fuel energies. Simon googled different climate solutions. He read about solar panels and carbon capture and storage. Many of these technologies had been developed or improved since he was born. Reliable websites stated that speed was one of the main barriers to the wide employment of these newer carbon capture technologies. Many of them posted designs on their website. If he had a talisman, he could go back and give the designs to a well-known climate scientist from 2009, thereby speeding up the discovery of these technologies by 13 years! If the world was heating up because there was too much CO_2 in the atmosphere, speeding up the discovery of ways to remove it must be key to solving the issue. Simon was sure of it. He printed off some designs and googled addresses for the top scientists of 2009. He could only find some of the cities where the scientists had lived and he had to find one that lived where he had at the age of two. He knew that he had been born in Edmonton, but his parents had moved for one year only when he was two, because his father had been transferred to the Vancouver office of his company to complete a specific project. Simon broadened his search to include climate activists and professors from 2009. He found an influential TV personality who was also an academic and climate activist, who had periodically been in Vancouver in 2009. Simon printed his address. Each night, he would go to sleep with daydreams chasing each other in his head.

∞ Usually when Simon got home from school Rakita would be cooking or gardening, depending on the weather. He explained his idea to her, and asked if he could borrow her talisman. It was one of the few times that Rakita had lost it.

"We are not allowed to change history, Simon. That's the most important island rule!" She dropped onto her knees, right on top of the seedlings she'd just planted. She buried her face in her mud-stained hands. "How can you be thinking like this after reading my story? Don't you remember what happened to me when I broke the rules?"

"But the leaders changed the rules because the climate crisis was important enough to throw everything they had at it," Simon said.

Rakita grabbed his shoulders and Simon tried to wiggle away. "Mum! You've got muck all over my shirt!"

"You're a boy. You're not a fucking leader."

Simon froze in surprise at the expletive.

"Do you understand? You must never, ever break the rules. You will never get a talisman if you break the rules. If I let you time travel again—and I'm not supposed to lend my talisman to others because it's mine, and each person's talisman works best for them. But if there was a good reason and I did, it would only be if you gave me your solemn promise that you would observe only, hidden from sight."

"All right Mum," Simon said gently.

She looked into his eyes for a moment, and let him go. Simon went to change his shirt; there was a hand mark on each shoulder.

But night after night alone in his room, Simon began to build a basis of doubt about whether his mother was a reliable guide in this matter. He remembered her angry swearing and terrified face as she stared into his eyes. What if his mother behaved out of character when she was emotional? Threatening his father with a knife, swearing violently when Simon presented a brilliant plan to help the climate crisis —her talisman was always at the centre of these outbursts.

She was emotional about her talisman, probably because she had lost it for so many years. But if she was emotional, then her judgment might not be sound. His idea was a great one. Advance carbon removal technology by 13 years, and there would be a lot less carbon in the atmosphere. The world would not be heating up so quickly. Simple math. And that was just the first trip. He could do it again and again, with different technologies and ideas and knowledge, until technology pre-empted the climate crisis. He had to approach his mother again.

He had to make her see. But if she was emotional, perhaps he wouldn't be able to make her see. Maybe he could write to the Leaders and get permission from them. But he'd have to ask his mother for the address, and what would he say if she asked him why he wanted it? Simon was terrible at lying; he always turned red.

He would turn and twist in his bed, wondering whether Rakita was stopping him from saving the world.

∞ One day school was dismissed in the morning due to an electrical issue that resulted in the school losing power. When Simon got home, he did not find his mother in the kitchen cooking, so he looked in the garden, but she wasn't there either. She was probably sleeping, since it was still morning. Simon poked his head into his parents' bedroom, curious as to where she slept during the day. Eventually, he found her sprawled across the sofa, fast asleep. She was lying with her head propped up on the side of the couch and she didn't look particularly comfortable. Simon was sure she usually slept elsewhere, and had fallen asleep here by accident. He approached and saw the glint of the talisman on her chest. The chain encircled her neck in the gap between her shoulders and where her head lay against the arm of the sofa, so Simon could pick it up gently without waking her. He searched for the mother bird returning to her nest, as he always did when he looked at the talisman. The light was dim by the couch, and Simon tried to turn the face of the talisman towards the window. His mother snored gently. Simon saw she was deeply asleep. If he just lifted her head very gently, he could draw the chain over her neck without waking her. Then he could take it over to the window and look at it properly, without bending awkwardly over his mother. Millimetre by millimetre, Simon slipped his hand under his mother's head and lifted it. Slowly, he drew the chain over her neck. If she woke, he would say that he just wanted to look at the talisman. He didn't let his brain think of any other possibility. It would not be a lie, because that was what he was doing.

But she didn't wake up.

Simon took the talisman over to the window and gazed at the mother bird and the chicks in the nest. The intricate details of the tree made it look three-dimensional.

Simon looked at his mother, who still gently snored, and slipped the chain of the talisman over his head as he went up to his room. The Leaders had changed the rules before, in order to avert climate catastrophe, and the deaths of millions of people. Simon was doing the same thing. If accelerating carbon-capture technology by 13 years solved the problem, wouldn't it be worth it? He retrieved the papers for the carbon capture and storage designs and the address for their destination. He put some money and a pen in his pocket, clasped the talisman and said, "I would like to go to 2009."

When the whoosh of air had subsided and the darkness had fallen away from his eyes, Simon looked up to find a toddler grinning at him from between the bars of its cot.

Simon smiled back, but he didn't want to linger with his Past-Self. He was very conscious of time, and wanted to complete his task and get back before his mother woke up. He slipped out of the room and froze as the gurgles from the cot escalated to whines. He turned back to the cot, and the toddler's anxious face morphed into grins again.

Simon turned again to leave, and again his Past-Self started to blubber. This time he ignored it and crept down the stairs. The whimpers behind him spiralled with each step until it was screaming. Simon froze on the last step as he heard his mother's voice approaching. "It's all right, Simon. I'm coming."

He sprang from the last step and dove into the first door on his right. It was a coat closet. He heard his mother's footsteps ascending the stairs and hardly dared to breathe. He wondered if she had seen him. Suddenly the plan didn't seem so good—he felt sick and he wasn't even out of the house yet. Who was he, to break the rules? Simon crouched among the coats, his heart hammering. As soon as the steps died away he was out the door and down the street, running as though the bullies were after him. But luck was with him; the bus he needed to catch was just pulling up as he pounded up to the bus stop. Sitting at the back, Simon took deep breaths until his heart stopped thumping. He caressed the talisman through his shirt, and smiled. He was doing it. And it felt great!

Luckily Simon had brought some money with him because he had to change buses once and then take a train and a ferry. But nothing broke down, nobody looked at him strangely, and with every turn of the wheels he drew nearer to his destination.

He had to walk the last bit, and he ran down the streets, pursued by images of his mother waking up and going ballistic on discovering the talisman was gone. When the house loomed before him, he almost ran past, he was so sure it couldn't be the right one. It was huge. Why would someone who understood the need to reduce consumption live in a house that demanded so much energy to heat? But the number was emblazoned across the open gate at the end of a tree-lined driveway. It was definitely the right house.

Simon rang the bell again and again. He had known the TV personality travelled a lot—another thing that puzzled him, if he understood the need to reduce his footprint—and that it would be a matter of luck to find him at home. But he had assumed the open gate meant the house was occupied. He rang again and the peals of the doorbell reverberated through the empty house. It didn't matter; he would slip the designs under the door and they would be found on the owner's return. Simon fished the pen out of his pocket and scribbled on one of the designs:

> You know that burning fossil fuels is overloading our atmosphere with CO_2, leading to rising temperatures. You know the very future of humankind is at risk if we don't reduce the CO_2 in our air. Because you know, I am entrusting these designs for cutting-edge carbon removal technology to you. These inventions enable us to extract the CO_2 from the air and store it, which will reduce the amount

of CO2 and mitigate the temperature rise. Please spread the word about this innovative technology to your wide circle of contacts in the government and science world. I am giving you the means to save humanity—please get the word out.

Simon didn't sign the note. He folded the papers and pushed them under the door. Then he grasped the talisman. "I wish I was 15."

He landed right by the couch and his mother was still sleeping. Simon couldn't believe his luck. He had been gone for several hours. If this wasn't a sign that the talisman approved of what he was doing, he didn't know what could be!

He crept up to his mother and tried to repeat the gentle, slow movements of the morning, lifting her head by infinitesimal degrees so he could slip the chain over her head. But her head had slipped down to rest on the seat of the couch and he had to lift it further. Rakita's eyes flew open as he placed the talisman on her chest. She gazed up at him startled, and her right hand groped automatically for the talisman, patting it in relief.

"What are you doing?" she asked.

"I was just looking at the talisman. I always search for the mother bird."

"Me too." Rakita looked at him for a second, patting her talisman. There was something in the look that prevented Simon from saying more. He wanted to tell her, but he couldn't right then, not with that odd look on her face.

"Is this where you usually sleep?"

"No, of course not. I thought I'd meditate for 15 minutes before preparing a chicken for dinner and I must have fallen asleep." Rakita looked at her watch and sat up abruptly. "I've overslept."

Simon followed her into the kitchen to help her prepare a quick meal. Rakita turned on the CBC to listen to the news while they worked, and again Simon couldn't find a time to tell her.

The salad was on the table and the omelette had just been flipped in the pan when they heard John's car drive up. His mother gave him a quick kiss and was gone.

Simon fished out his phone and googled current global temperatures and carbon capture deployment in Canada as he eased the omelette onto buttered toast. It was odd, but he couldn't find any evidence that his trip had made a difference in his current time. He was still reading as they sat down at the table.

"Put it away, Simon," his father intoned automatically. Usually, Simon accepted the family rule of no-screens-at-the-table, but these days they rarely had anything much to say to each other and Simon sometimes wished they could watch TV during dinner, like so many other families did. But today Simon had questions about the current state of the world. His father was in an unusually chatty mood, and took active part in the discussion. An uneasy feeling grew as it became clear that his father barely knew what carbon capture was. If it had been a major force in the fight against climate change, his father would have heard of it. Simon felt puzzled. Had the papers been lost somehow? He couldn't take the talisman again without telling his mother. He had planned to use the success of his first venture to persuade her to let him borrow it for additional transfers of knowledge back in time. But if his first trip hadn't worked she'd still refuse to give it to him. And even if he was willing to take it by stealth, what were the chances he'd find her sleeping on the couch again?

"How was Alley today?"

Simon assured him as they ate banana cake for dessert that he and his mother had talked quite a bit about him that day. Gratified by that elusive smile hovering around his father's lips, Simon exaggerated Rakita's interest, concocting questions about John's wellbeing. When John had wiped up the last crumbs of cake with his finger, praising its taste and texture, Simon decided to take advantage of his father's good humour. He had been anxious to broach the subject of his summer vacation for some time now, but it was difficult because he was worried about his father's reaction. He had to screw up his courage and overcome his reluctance and there was no time like the present.

"I'm thinking about going to the island this summer for a visit, Dad. You know, meet my grandparents and stuff."

"Have they given you a pendant?"

"No. We have to travel the normal way."

"We? Am I supposed to take you?" John said, with a tinge of belligerence.

"No, no. Mum will travel with me."

"I'm not letting you disappear into the blue with your mother, who hates my guts and would do anything to steal you from me."

Simon was surprised at the U-turn in his father's tone, which had switched from tender inquiry to hostility when Simon had mentioned going away. "That's not true, Dad. If that were the case, she'd be fighting for custody in court."

"Ahh, but she's selfish as well. She wants to live on her damned island. The courts won't allow her to do that."

Simon surreptitiously slipped Toby the last crust of bread, standing up at the same time. He didn't want to hear an attack on his mother, served up straight from his father's emotions, devoid of logic. In any case, the first step had been achieved—his father had been informed. He had weeks to get used to the idea, so Simon wasn't going to let his initial reaction upset him. "I want to live with you, Dad. I've told you that a dozen times. I'm going up to my room now."

"Don't expect me to pay for this!" John yelled after him.

CHAPTER NINE

AS THE SCHOOL year drew to its close, Simon got more and more anxious about how he'd be able to travel to the island. His father continued to react badly whenever the subject was mentioned, and although his mother assured him she was 'working on it,' Simon didn't know how. People didn't seem to make money on the island in the same way, although his mother had explained that they could usually get what they needed. Just days before they were due to leave, he expressed his anxiety again, and his mother waved an airy hand, assuring him that it was taken care of. When he asked if he should thank his father, she cryptically answered that that wasn't necessary, and made it clear the subject was closed. Simon concluded that his father had been true to his word, and his mother had found a way to finance the trip by herself.

On the very last day of school, he grabbed his father's arm as he strode out the door to go to work in the morning. "Give me a hug, Dad. You won't see me for a couple of months."

When Simon saw the face his father turned on him, any residual anger he'd felt over his father's refusal to fund this trip, evaporated. "You're not coming back, are you?"

Simon grabbed his father around the chest and held him tightly. "Are you crazy? I love you. You're my Dad."

"And she's your Mum."

"Dad, I'll be going to school here in the fall. I'll be living in this house with you. I promise on my honour. It's what I want, but even if I didn't, I told you that I haven't got permission to live on the island."

John nodded sadly, pinched his son's cheek, and left.

The school day dragged on interminably. Sandra was also morose, facing an entire summer without him. He had put three of her favourite chocolate bars in his lunch bag (it was much easier to buy junk now that his mother wasn't around to unpack the shopping) and he presented them to her with a flourish after she'd finished her peanut butter and jam sandwich. She brightened up a bit after that, and began to extract promises.

"Whatsapp me every day and give me the highlights?"

"Yes, if I can. I haven't even asked my mother if they have Internet, but they probably do; it's all over the world. They must have service, so I'll definitely text. And you have to text back."

"I won't have any highlights," Sandra said, with a return to moroseness.

Simon practically skipped out of school that day, despite the heaviness of his bag, carrying the last remnants of a years' worth of work. A shout stopped him before he reached the end of the school parking lot. "Simon, wait!"

He turned to see Sandra rushing after him. She skidded to a stop before him, gulping for breath.

"Aren't you going to miss your school bus? You know that you can't come over today," he said gently.

She moved closer, and his heart lurched as he realised what she was going to do. His own breath started to come fast, and he looked at her cupid lips, parted slightly, with a tiny stud winking below the fullness of the lower lip. Then she reached up and kissed him, and Simon felt the warmth of those lips against his, and his arms crept around her body and pulled her closer. Sandra drew back to look into his eyes, but he wanted more, more, and he lowered his head and brushed his lips against the warmth of hers, tentatively. His hands pressed against her back—he couldn't believe this was happening—and he pulled her closer so that she was pressed against him, straining her as close as he could, as though he would swallow her up. He sensed her own hands on his back, kneading and stroking. He knew that she could feel his desire; he didn't have to hide it anymore, because surely she must feel the same way, if she was kissing him like this? Then she pulled away and looked at him. Her face was flushed and her eyes looked darker. He wondered if he looked like that, too. He felt her moving away and he tried to pull her towards him again, but she lifted her hands and gave him a little push, and he knew it was over, though his whole body screamed, *Nnooooooo ...*

"That's so you don't forget me," Sandra said.

"Don't worry about that."

He watched her run back into the building and caught the bullies staring at him from the school doorway. He waved at them, his heart singing and a foolish grin plastered over his face. He couldn't care less what they thought, and to prove it he executed a gigantic, exuberant leap into the air, trying to click his heels. His heart was bursting with delight, and he cavorted home in seventh heaven.

Both Toby and his mother rushed down the driveway to meet him, his mother waving tickets in the air.

"You got them?" Simon asked, noticing the taxi parked outside the house.

"Yes, I have everything. Now hurry up, our first plane leaves in a couple of hours."

Simon exchanged his school back pack for a larger one, already packed to the brim with clothes. Then he fell on his knees to embrace Toby.

"Hurry up, Simon!" his mother called, while simultaneously telling the taxi driver: "Don't you dare turn on your engine again. What is the point of keeping your engine running when you're not moving?"

"It's hot," the taxi driver said. "I need the air conditioning."

"Isn't a little discomfort worth a little less pollution?"

Simon smiled into Toby's fur; his mother used to do this when he'd been younger, before she'd retreated into herself. 'Spreading awareness,' she called it, ignoring his embarrassment. "Bye Toby," he told the dog, who looked a little puzzled. He wasn't sure if it was a good thing that dogs couldn't anticipate the future, but he knew that Toby would miss him. He'd left a long To-Do list for his father, with "PLAY BALL EVERY DAY WHEN YOU GET HOME FROM WORK" in caps at the top, underlined twice. He suddenly felt sad, looking down on Toby's loving face.

"Come *on,* Simon."

He turned away and got into the taxi.

The journey took three days. Simon hadn't travelled much previously so, although there was one 13-hour flight which he found a bit long, on the whole he was delighted with everything. He enjoyed the plane food, binged on the in-house entertainment in a way he'd never be allowed to do at home, and texted Sandra. Meanwhile, Rakita did a lot of meditation (to calm herself), and writing in her diary (to ensure that the three days weren't a massive waste of time). She also spent a great deal of time talking to each and every person in her vicinity about the environment. Simon wanted to sink into his chair from embarrassment.

"You're on a friggin' plane talking to flight attendants about reducing plastic waste. You don't see the hypocrisy in that?"

"Language, Simon! Spreading awareness is vital. The more people speak out about the environment, the greater the impact. Do you remember when everyone used to smoke? I guess that was before your time, but they made smoking socially unacceptable by spreading awareness. Envision a day when it will be socially unacceptable to drive a fuel-powered car!"

"How is it *not* hypocritical, to yell at a taxi driver for leaving his engine running for two minutes, before we travel across the globe on a carbon-spewing plane?"

Rakita patted his knee. "Damn, you're asking good questions these days, Simon! Some activists say focussing on the negligible contribution of individuals is pointless, and instead we should focus our energies on the handful of individuals who produce one third of the world's greenhouse gas emissions, pouring billions into efforts to delay public realization that this catastrophe is going to destroy our lives. But I don't agree; each individual action might be negligible, but the collective action of the human race has make-or-break impact."

Simon tried to stretch his legs in the cramped space. "So why are we yelling at idling cars while travelling 13 hours in a plane?"

"It's all part of spreading awareness. If a few clients tell that taxi driver not to idle, then he'll probably stop because he doesn't want to piss off clients. Societal pressure."

Simon's eyes wandered back to his movie. "We shouldn't even be on a plane," he muttered.

"If people feel guilty for what they are doing, they'll end up doing even less. It's not what we do or don't do—it's looking at *everything* we do through the lens of the climate crisis."

"What does that even mean?" Simon wanted to return to his movie.

"It means we think about the energy we use in terms of its climatic impact—do I really need to use this energy, or not? I was desperate for you to see my island and meet my parents. If I decide not to take you because planes hurt the environment, I'd feel really bad. As an individual this sacrifice is negligible in terms of the greater good, so my pain isn't worth the cost in this case. People can't give up everything they love; instead they just need to think about everything they do, from the endless one-liner emails to 13-hour plane trips. Consciously making decisions about our energy consumption, instead of mindlessly consu—"

"OK, I get it, Mum!" Simon said, plugging his ears with headphones. But he smiled to himself. It was like his mother was a different person, chatting to everyone she met.

Simon especially loved the ferry, where he could walk around and explore. But the best part of the journey was the final boat ride to the island. He couldn't believe it when his mother just hopped into one of the boats tied to the wharf on the next-island-over and beckoned him to follow. "Who does this belong to?"

"The island."

"We don't have the keys."

Rakita reached under one of the flat, long cushions lining the outside benches and jingled a single key triumphantly in the air.

"But if you can find them, couldn't someone else find them, and steal them?"

"There are only a few hundred people on this island. Everybody knows everybody else, which is the best deterrent for would-be thieves."

"But there are thousands on your island, right?"

"Just over a million."

"How long will it take us to travel there?"

Simon continued to belt out question after question for the entire five-hour boat ride, desisting only as his mother wobbled to her feet and reached out her hand towards a weird, triangle-shaped rock jutting off the left side of a pile of rocks. This couldn't be their island, surely? His jaw dropped as his mother's hand seemed to disappear directly into the sky. Her fingers and thumb came repeatedly together, as though she was trying to grasp the air itself.

"What are you doing?"

"Shh," Rakita said. "I always get tense that I'm not going to be able to find it."

"Find what?" Simon asked. But then his mother's hand closed over air and she began to pull. A crack appeared in the air above the triangle rock, revealing the same sky beyond. What was going on?

The boat moved into this growing crack and Simon swivelled his head back and forth as they passed through the sky-curtain. Were they entering a magic realm? He couldn't see what was magic about it; it looked exactly the same as the other side. It was definitely the same place.

Simon didn't understand, and looked towards his mother for an explanation. She was still eyeballing the horizon. His eyes followed her gaze and he suddenly saw it. A distant island, that hadn't been there on the other side of the triangle rock. It was magic! Simon's excitement grew as they drew closer to the island. Huge offshore wind turbines towered over the tiny islets that dotted the sea around the main island.

Simon stared up at the structures with wide eyes. "Why are there so many wind turbines, Mum?"

"You'll see more on the island; they provide the energy we need to be self-sufficient. The entire island is carbon neutral. The wind and sun provide our electricity."

"All the energy for more than a million people? You don't use any oil or coal at all?"

"No, I told you we're completely carbon neutral. We don't guzzle energy like so many first world people do. We don't travel; we buy local, which means we don't eat food that's not in season. But we don't lack for anything and we don't pollute."

"So if the carbon we produce with fossil fuels is polluting our air and screwing up the climate, why don't we switch to turbines in North America?"

"Or solar. Or any renewable energy option. Because the people aren't demanding it. The goal is to help them see the need to demand."

They were drawing close to the shore now, and Simon could see vividly coloured structures spaced along the shore line. "Why do they paint their sheds such bright colours?"

"Isn't it pretty? But those aren't sheds, they're houses," Rakita said, manoeuvring the boat to a mooring on the quay. There were lots of boats moored there, also sporting some funky colours. Several of the boats reeked of fish. "We'll go straight to your grandparents' house. They are dying to see you."

"Why are the names on the boats in different languages?"

"The ethnicities of the island's people are as varied as the people of earth."

"What do you mean? Aren't you all the same race? Don't you all speak the same language on the island?"

"No, there are many different races. We share a common language, English, but many households speak their own language within their families."

Simon felt like the questions were going to burst out of his head. "Why are the houses so small?"

Rakita laughed. "I remember the first time I went to North America I was astounded by the size of everything: the cars, the houses, the roads."

Simon hoisted his backpack onto his shoulders and hopped off the boat. "This is your island," he said reverently, resisting the urge to touch the ground.

Rakita gathered her things and joined him on shore. "I never understood the advantage of a huge house. Why does anyone need more rooms than they'll actually use? How many rooms does a 3 or 4-person family really need? A smaller house uses much less energy."

"A bedroom each," Simon replied, his eyes swivelling left and right, drinking everything in. "At least two bathrooms."

"Why two?"

"Well, in case you are desperate and someone else is in the other one."

"Rubbish," Rakita said. "I can't recall a single time when you had to wait to use the bathroom. And even if you did, would it kill you to hold it in for two minutes?"

Simon giggled, and continued to suggest rooms that Rakita rejected, as they toiled up the dirt road from the wharf. He kept looking around for cars. "How are we going to get to your parents' place?"

"It's a half an hour walk, or we can catch a tram."

Simon preferred to walk the whole way, so he could really absorb his surroundings. He marvelled at the pretty little houses, the neat properties with their rows of fruit trees and large vegetable gardens. He gave a yelp of excitement when he saw the first animal enclosure. "Look Mum—pigs!"

"A lot of people have animals. I just got some new goats a few weeks ago."

Simon hadn't known his mother had animals, and the idea that he'd be amongst animals all summer made him happy. "But is everybody on the island farmers? Is that how the rest of the world should be living?"

"No, of course not. We have a couple of cities, and several 'real' farms which help to provide food to the cities. But small, self-sufficient holdings of a few acres is a wonderful model. Everybody produces a little more than they need, so they can trade the excess for things they don't produce. Nobody here is ignorant about where food comes from. Nobody misunderstands our utter dependence on nature, because they live their whole lives in a steel trap of a city, like so many in Canada and the US."

Simon wondered if goats could be trained to catch balls and pestered his mother for details about any other surprises that might be in store for him. He was over the moon to discover that she had a dog and chickens as well.

"And here we are; look Simon, those are your grandparents waiting outside for you."

Simon looked up, and saw an old couple standing outside a canary-coloured house with light brown windows. He felt suddenly shy, and hung back to let his mother lead the way. But his grandmother shuffled towards him, holding both arms wide, and he went forward into her embrace. When she pulled back to look at him, clasping his face in both her hands, he saw her eyes were wet.

His grandfather hugged him too. "He looks just like you, Rakita."

"My blue eyes are from my Dad," Simon offered shyly. It was strange to think of these people as his grandparents. He had visited his Dad's parents often, but these new grandparents seemed ancient, compared to them. They were tiny and wizened. The grandfather used a stick to get around and spoke loudly because he was deaf; the grandmother's lips trembled when she spoke.

They led them around to the back of the house and Simon saw what looked like a vast field stretching before him, filled with wonderful fruit trees, chickens pecking in their shade, bee hives lining the outer perimeter. In the shade of an oak tree close to the house, there was a long table laden with good things to eat. Simon's stomach grumbled and he realised how hungry he was.

"You must have been working all day," Rakita said.

"We got Joe to help us. Joe is the neighbour's son, and he does most of the work around here, now that we're getting old," his grandmother explained to Simon. "When you move here to live, perhaps you can take on that role."

Simon looked at his mother eagerly. Had something been decided? But she shook her head at him. "Nothing has changed."

Rakita filled up a plate for her mother, gesturing to Simon to help himself. He took a little bit of everything, even though he wasn't sure what some things were. He could see from his grandparents' shining eyes that they would be indulgent, and wouldn't insist he clean his plate. There were several different types of salads, fresh bread and cheeses; butter and honey. Bowls of fruit and plates of home-made cookies to be washed down by hot tea or a pitcher of ice-cold water packed with mint from the garden.

When his plate was full, Simon asked: "Why do the Leaders get to decide everything? If they've gathered a whole bunch of information in order to make a decision about me, why can't they share it with us? Even *our* politicians have to explain why they're doing stuff. It's called being accountable."

"I think there is a reason for their insistence that you stay in Canada. Perhaps they know something about your destiny that we don't. If that is the case, they aren't allowed to tell us. It's one of the island's rules."

Everything was so delicious, Simon ate and ate. The vegetables in the salad tasted like they had been picked from the vine or dug from the ground that same day—he knew the difference between fresh vegetables and store-bought vegetables from his mother's garden at home.

"Will I meet the Leaders?" he asked.

"Yes, they have asked to meet with you towards the end of August," Rakita replied.

They sat and chatted after the meal, drinking their endless cups of tea and gazing out over the orchard. Simon smiled at the familiar coziness of the tea-drinking ritual. He told his new family all about his home-life and his father and Toby. He told them a bit about how he'd been bullied at school and how miserable he used to feel, and how the talisman had already changed all of that, performing miracles in his life, even though he didn't even own one yet.

He pelted them with questions about the island, and learned that, apart from the wind turbines, there were heating systems which relied on miles of piping to supply heating and hot water from centralised biomass boilers, fuelled with locally grown straw. Houses that were outside the reach of these central systems had biomass boilers of their own. He asked about their education system, and their government. He asked about the animals, and learned more about their trading system.

"I get literally gallons of honey from my hives," his grandfather told him. "I trade it for all sorts of good things, including the flour that made those cookies you seem to be enjoying. Do you want to see my bees?"

Simon wanted to see the bees very much, but had once been stung by a bee and was a bit nervous. "Don't worry," his grandfather said. "Just make sure you stand to one side of the hive, so you're not in their way."

They crouched down next to the side of the hives and watched the busy bees congregate next to the opening in the hive. There was a little landing area just outside the opening and Simon watched in fascination as bees laden with pollen landed and sought the entrance, trooping past an endless cloud of bees heading out. His grandfather explained with pride the industrious example these insects set, working hard, each with its own role. He explained how they would do a little dance to describe the location of a rich source of nectar to the other bees.

"You sure do love bees," Simon said. "Will you show me how you extract the honey?"

"It's not the right time of year, but maybe by the end of the summer some of the hives will be ready for harvesting."

"Simon," Rakita called. "I'm exhausted. Let's go home and we'll see Mum and Dad again tomorrow."

They hugged good bye and took up their backpacks, setting off along the dirt road again. A bus passed them en route, and Rakita explained that cities and the more heavily populated areas were served by an electric tram system, while electric buses served the more rural areas. On long journeys, the bus might have to stop to recharge its battery, in which case another bus would be waiting to convey the passengers onwards without delay.

Simon was just beginning to feel rather tired, and that it had been a long day, when his mother gestured towards a little, sky-blue wooden house set back from the road, with a pretty flower garden in front. A huge German Shepherd rushed up to Rakita and raced around and around her legs, until she secured his collar and commanded him to sit. Then she introduced Ronny to Simon. The young dog wiggled with delight as Simon petted his head, marvelling at his size. "Who takes care of Ronny when you're with me?"

"I have my own 'Joe', whose name is Sam. His job is to check both morning and evening to see if I'm here or not. I wouldn't have gotten a dog, since I never know how long I'm going to be absent, but Sam's mother is allergic to dogs and he adores them, so the more I'm away, the happier he is."

She took Simon around the back of the house, and pointed out the goat enclosure, which plunged into the forest beyond the vegetable garden and the orchard. Simon looked yearningly towards it, so Rakita whipped up her failing energies and led him there, pointing out various fruit trees and listing what she had already managed to plant in the garden.

"You've done such a lot, Mum," Simon said.

"And I've only been here sporadically for a couple of months. I used to have a different house, but it was sold when I disappeared the first time. You see? I'm not lazy. You used to get angry with me and claim I never did anything. But it was because I wasn't happy, not because I was lazy." Rakita paused a moment before pushing open the goat enclosure. "I'm sorry I was so tired all the time. It can't have been much fun, having a mother like that."

None of that mattered any more, and Simon pushed into the enclosure as his mother called the goats. A large white one rushed towards Rakita in comic haste, her heavy milk bag swinging between her back legs as she ran, two little black and white twins frolicking behind her. Simon laughed and fell to his knees, inviting the little babies to climb on top of him. They snuffled at his face and pushed at him with their little heads, while the mother received her expected scratch from Rakita.

"They're so lovely," Simon said, giggling as the babies sampled his shirt. "How did you get them? Did you buy them?"

Rakita explained that her three goats were to be paid back with interest; she owed the next four kids born. Simon glanced in their shed, which had an overflowing hay rack and a bucket of water. The door of the shed opened to their large, fenced-in enclosure, which was mostly in the woods.

"Do they like the woods?"

"Yes," Rakita answered. "They like to browse and chew on the poor trees."

"Do all the holdings include forest?"

"You noticed that, did you? Yes, most people have around 5 acres of land, and half of it is supposed to be forest. Our goal is to live together with nature, so we try to preserve the habitat of all the other animals who share this island with us. Now I'm almost dropping with exhaustion, can we go in?"

Simon was anxious to see the inside of the little house, so he kissed his new friends good-bye and skipped in front of his mother towards the sky-blue house.

"You can go in if you like," she called after him. "It's not locked."

Simon eagerly pushed open the door and found himself in a snug room, divided by a rustic kitchen table and filled with paintings and windows. To his left was the kitchen, with herbs and pans hanging from the ceiling. On his right was a sitting area, with two La-Z-Boys and a sofa facing each other across a low table. The La-Z-Boys, he saw, could be swung around to face a television hung on the far wall behind them. Book shelves filled one of the other walls from floor to ceiling. Opposite where he stood in the entrance, a flight of stairs led to the second floor. He leapt up the stairs and discovered two bedrooms, with a bathroom between them. His mother had placed some books and sweets on his bed, and there were fresh flowers in a vase on his bedside table. More paintings and bookshelves adorned his walls. He rushed downstairs when he heard Rakita come in. "Mum, are these paintings all yours?"

"Yes. I used to love painting. It relaxes me. I'll have to take it up again."

"I love your house, Mum," Simon said, hugging her, while Ronny shook with excitement between them, controlling seemingly violent urges to jump on them.

They were too full to eat dinner, so they had more tea, and then Simon helped his mother with the evening chores, delighting in everything, from the goat-milking to locking up the chickens. The boy who helped out with the farm showed up and Rakita introduced him as Sam, and expressed the hope that he'd show Simon around the island. They made plans to meet up the next day, and finally Simon went to bed, gazing out his window into the branches of an oak tree. He felt absurdly happy.

The summer fell into a pattern of delight. Every morning Simon would help with the chores, and grew so adept at milking that he could empty Current-Nanny quicker than Rakita. After feeding the chickens and filling the various bird feeders around the property, Simon would gather eggs and fruit and head in with the milk to prepare breakfast. He got immense satisfaction out of eating such meals, created from ingredients gathered moments before from the richness of nature.

After breakfast he often went for long walks, exploring large tracts of the island on foot. He observed all the time: few people had cars, but the public transport ran efficiently and frequently, and went everywhere. Everything was reused: clothes were handed on until they began to disintegrate, when they were cut up into cloths for cleaning. Containers could be recycled, but many people hoarded them to fill them with products from their farms, like honey. Everything on the island was well-made, so if you bought a pair of shoes, or a tool, or a bucket, you expected it to last for years. It was a culture where the emphasis had shifted from money to the survival of the human race. Status symbols in the West—big houses, new cars, more junk—were Shame symbols here. Nobody bought the newest versions of devices, unless there was a feature they desperately needed. Societal pressure, which goaded people to buy more and more in the West, chastised excessive consumers here. Simply, there *was* no excess, and therefore much less waste. If you didn't finish the food on your plate, the animals got it, and if they didn't want it, then it was composted and the garden eventually got it. Nobody had more than two children. Few people ate beef, which was very expensive. There were no plastic bags in the shops, only good-quality cloth ones. Simon immediately noticed the dearth of one-use plastic products: there were no straws if you bought a drink, no plastic cutlery or cups. If you bought a coffee or a coke, you could either supply your own cup, or buy a reusable one, which tripled the cost of the coffee. Maybe it was because Rakita had brought him up with second-hand clothing and five-minute showers, but Simon couldn't pinpoint any negative impact these changes made on his life. They were no-brainers, once you were aware of the situation. Looking at energy consumption through an environmental lens became automatic. Reduce, reuse and recycle—in that order of importance—became second nature.

Simon wandered around, and talked to people, and absorbed.

Sometimes Sam came with him on his morning excursions, and showed him a private swimming spot that could only be accessed through a hole in the foliage. The water was clear and warm and Simon swam almost every day.

Sometimes his mother organized an outing; they went horse-riding (though Simon couldn't walk for several days afterwards) and kayaking. Rakita took him to the city, where they enjoyed the rare treat of eating in a restaurant (where, Simon noticed, all the food was grown locally).

Every afternoon Rakita imposed a 'quiet time', where she meditated and Simon read, or texted Sandra, who missed him and complained she wasn't doing a single thing, ever, although that was literally impossible. He texted mainly about his impressions of the island, and kept his horse-riding and swimming accounts to a minimum. Simon also texted his father, who insisted that both Toby and he were doing well, though his replies were short. Simon worried about him sometimes.

They often spent the evenings at the grandparents' house, with Rakita lugging ingredients so she could prepare the meal at their house, while Simon helped with the chores. His grandfather wasn't sure the honey would be ready to harvest by the time Simon left, so one day he lifted off the cover of the bee hive so Simon could see inside. "Why can't you leave the bloody bees alone," his grandmother had snapped uncharacteristically.

"She thinks it makes them unhappy when I bother them," his grandfather said, chuckling. "But I do it so carefully they barely notice. They don't have brains, you know."

Simon looked inside the hive and marvelled at the moving tide of bees clinging to the frame. "Lucky they're not claustrophobic," he said.

He grew a couple of inches, and became tanned. He turned sixteen.

Gently, the island chipped away the last remnants of the nugget of unhappiness nestling in Simon's heart since his parents had broken up. The feeling that the safety blanket of his home had been ripped from under him, slowly ebbed as he watched his mother in her native surroundings. She did everything with quiet joy. She greeted people with interest, not with the dull dislike she'd frequently displayed in Canada. He understood why losing the talisman had almost destroyed her. She had had to leave John, if she suspected him of this theft. John was a great father, and Simon loved him. There was no point in judging him for things Simon couldn't understand. He would survive with divorced parents. It would be OK.

As the wonderful summer reached its zenith and began to decline, he started to dread the upcoming 3-day trip back to his dreary, regular life. Why did he go have to go back? He loved the island, and had as much right to be here as anybody else. If Rakita hadn't suddenly announced that they were going to see the Leaders that week, he would have tried to take the initiative himself.

On the auspicious day, they walked together towards the modest grey brick building, where many of the island's decisions were hammered out. Simon had expected to sit in a chair opposite a row of Leaders, rather like an interrogation. Instead he found two youngish men and an older woman sitting comfortably on a couple of old sofas, drinking the ubiquitous tea. They gestured to Rakita and Simon to help themselves from the teapot, and continued to chat. Simon sat quietly, sipping his tea and eyeing the Leaders with surprise. He didn't know what he'd expected, but not these casual, normal-looking humans, sprawled over a sofa.

Eventually, one of the young men threw a smile in his direction. "Hello Simon, my name is Mohammed. This is Pierre. And Ji Su. Welcome. We wanted to meet you, just to get a sense of you, really. Can you talk to us a little? Tell us about your school, your interests?"

Simon had a few lines at the ready, developed over a summer of people asking him similar questions. When he had told them a bit about himself, he asked them: "Does your interest mean that you are considering giving me a pendant?"

"A talisman?" Mohammed said, smiling. "We like your directness, Simon. We think you would be a wonderful inhabitant for the island, but ..." There was a slight hesitation as Mohammed looked down at his hands, and Ji Su leapt into the breach.

"You can't have a talisman yet. We'd like you to stay where you are, leading a regular life, until you have finished school."

Simon opened his mouth to protest, but Ji Su pre-empted him. "You are not ready for a talisman yet."

"How can you know unless you give me one? I know that I become a climate activist. I see the climate crisis like an enemy that is going to decimate the human population. We have to stop using fossil fuels to survive, and the sooner we stop, the better our lives will be. This is a war against an enemy—the climate crisis—and I am ready to join the fight. Think how much more I could do with the aid of the talisman!"

Ji Su got slowly to her feet. "We know that you are not ready because you have already broken two of the most important rules of the island, without even possessing a talisman. Nobody breaks the island's rules. If you had grown up here and lived here, you would be banished."

Rakita looked at him. "What rules did you break?"

Simon couldn't speak. How did they know? Had his mother seen him?

"He stole your talisman to visit his two-year-old self," Ji Su said. "Then he travelled across town alone to deliver a package to a scientist from 2009. The package contained the design for various carbon removal technologies. Simon thought that accelerating the development of carbon removal technology would have a massive impact. If too much CO_2 was heating up the world, finding a way to remove it would fix the issue. Right, Simon?"

Simon tried to think why it wouldn't. It was hard to think with his mother staring at the side of his face.

"I thought it would help. I tried to think about it from all angles, because I know that's what you do with really important decisions. I couldn't see what harm it could do, and it might have done some good."

Simon wondered again why there hadn't seemed to be any difference in his own time.

"What you did was rash and stupid," Ji Su said, falling back into her seat. "Who do you think you are? You are 16 years old. A child. You don't know anything. *Never* break our rules again."

There was a short silence. Simon glanced at his mother. He didn't like the look on her face. It was the same look she had given his father. *When she found out he had stolen her talisman.*

Simon turned quickly back to the elders. They were all looking at him. Mohammed leaned forward. "Simon, I believe you can grow into your role. I believe you can mature enough to earn your talisman."

"You certainly aren't ready for one yet," Ji Su said.

Simon hoped he wasn't going to cry. That would really put the finishing touches on this awful day. He was 16. Practically grown-up! He must put crying behind him and be brave. He should remind them that he hadn't caused any harm; he had been trying to do good. Isn't that what they wanted from him? He wouldn't always succeed, but he'd only succeed if he tried. He opened his mouth, but his mother nudged him in the ribs so sharply he was shocked into silence. She thanked the Leaders and got to her feet.

"We are glad to have met you, Simon," they said, and got up one by one to shake his hand. Simon couldn't quite believe that the interview was ending. The one called Pierre hadn't uttered a word the entire time.

As soon as the door closed behind them, Simon turned to his mother. "Why didn't you let me speak?"

"Because you were going to argue with them, and that's not acceptable. They know what they're doing. Trust them. Ji Su is sometimes a little abrupt, that's all."

In his heart, Simon did trust them. So long as he would get a pendant, a talisman, at some point. So long as he could choose to live on this wonderful island in the nearest-possible future. But he still thought it unfair that things that concerned him weren't explained clearly. How was he supposed to know? He hadn't stolen his mother's talisman—he had borrowed it. He would need to memorize the rules, that was clear. He wouldn't break them again. It had just been ignorance. Everybody else his age had had a talisman for three years already. What possible reason could the Leaders have for denying him a talisman, especially when they as good as said that he could live here at some point? So why not now? He could visit his father every day, just like his mother visited him. His father would hardly know the difference.

Eventually, Simon realized his mother was more silent than usual.

"I didn't know it was forbidden to borrow talismans, Mum. I didn't steal it, obviously—you still have it, don't you?—I just borrowed it for one trip."

She turned that same face on him. The only face that John would ever see, for the rest of his life. "You know it was wrong. That's why you didn't tell me."

Those damn tears threatened again. "Mum, I'm sorry. Don't look at me like that. I would never steal anything. I only borrowed it. It's not ... like Dad."

Rakita heard the tears in his voice and stopped to give him a hug. They held each other close for several minutes and Simon felt he had been forgiven. The look on his mother's face had shocked him more than Ji Su's anger, and he felt shame. "I'll never do such a thing again," he told his mother, and they walked on.

When the little, sky-blue house rose into view, Simon took Rakita's arm. "Why didn't my plan work? How come speeding up the discovery of carbon removal technology didn't make an impact?"

"For two reasons. First, there's no silver bullet—no one technology is going to save us on its own. Global warming is caused by different human activities, and we need a multi-pronged approach to solving the problem. In other words, it's not enough to remove the carbon, we also have to stop producing it.

"I know, but no impact at all ..."

"Don't interrupt," Rakita said. "Second, lack of technology and knowledge isn't the problem. You don't need to help the scientists and engineers develop technology faster—we already have the technology to start switching to renewable energy. It's the people, Simon. People need to change their personal habits, especially in the West. It's already happening—school kids are striking, the price of renewables is plunging and we have a blueprint—the Paris Climate Accord. This is a time of global change."

"Mum, don't rant!"

Ronny came rushing out to greet them, coiling himself around their legs ecstatically. Rakita bent to scratch his ears, then continued into the house. "Even if each human only adds a single drop of water, it will still create a tsunami of change. Studies show that most people want their governments to fix the problem of climate change, even if that means sacrifice."

Simon enveloped the wriggling Ronny in a bear hug. "But?"

"But there's still a lot of people living their lives, business as usual. If we want to speed up change, we have to focus on people. Now what shall I make for dinner? Pizza, as a treat?"

∞ Over the last few days of his trip, Simon thought about how to change people. Whatever direction his thoughts took, they always circled back to the fact that he would achieve more with the help of a talisman. "I've been thinking a lot about what you said," he told Rakita. "That we need to influence people. I've been thinking about how to do it. I have to tell them the truth, but I also have to listen, to discover what's preventing them from hearing the truth."

They were preparing the dinner to take to the grandparents and Rakita was flushed from the heat of the stove. "That's great, Simon. One person at a time."

"Or I could access a whole bunch of people with social media like TikTok, Instagram, Facebook ..."

"Mm-hmm." Rakita was tired.

"But anyone could do that." Simon slashed more savagely at the vegetables he was cutting up for a salad. "Think how much more I could do with a talisman! If I could visit myself at different intervals of my life and learn ..."

"Well, you shouldn't have stolen it."

Simon looked wounded. "I didn't steal it. I thought we'd discussed that."

Rakita rubbed his arm on her way to the fridge. "Sorry, we have discussed it. But you're not getting a talisman, so drop it."

"Well, can I write the Leaders a letter or something? Explain how I want to use my talisman for good purpose?"

Rakita slammed the cheese on the table. "I don't know, Simon. I wish you'd stop badgering me."

"Badgering? I thought we were brain-storming."

"You might be brain-storming, but I'm feeling uncomfortable. It's against the rules to tell you."

Simon was flabbergasted. "What do you know?"

"Look, you're leaving tomorrow, and we're spending tonight with Grandpa and Grandma, who don't want to hear you whining about what you can't have, all right? Just leave it."

His mother's sharp tone of voice was so surprising that Simon did leave it, and enjoyed a quiet evening with his grandparents, whom he had grown to love. As he kissed them goodbye, and took his leave of the goats and Ronny the next morning, he recalled how sad he'd been to say goodbye to Toby. It felt like he lived in two places now, and would forever be saying goodbye to one or the other.

Rakita shouldered his second bag, which was full of good things from the island. For her three-day trip, she had only brought her hand-bag, which contained some facial cream, a toothbrush, and her nightie. Islanders travelled light. "We'll have to lie at customs," she said.

"Why?"

"You're not allowed to bring foodstuffs from other places, and certainly not things like my wonderful, unpasteurised goat cheese."

Simon tried not to pester his mother about what she knew, but during the three-day journey the questions kept circling in his head, giving him no rest. It was on one of the plane trips, where they usually sat side by side plugged into different worlds, that Rakita suddenly yanked out her ear buds.

"OK, Simon, since you won't stop nagging me about it."

"What are you talking about? I haven't even mentioned it."

"Ah-ha, you know exactly what I'm referring to, don't you? Your thoughts are driving me crazy!"

Simon giggled and half-turned in his seat to face Rakita. "Well?"

Rakita took his hand and stroked it absent-mindedly. "Before I lived with your father, I time-travelled to the future occasionally, and many others on the island time-travelled much more frequently. It's hard to describe the state of the world as we saw it, Simon. It was terrible. Do you know that we are currently experiencing the worst mass extinction period since the dinosaurs?"

Simon nodded, leaning forward to catch her every word.

"We saw terrible natural calamities, like rain storms that lasted for weeks. We saw a mass exodus from all coastal areas as they became submerged. We saw terrible wars break out as water and food became scarce. Because of what we'd seen, we didn't question for a second the Leaders' decision to allow us to travel for longer periods of time, in an attempt to educate humans before it was too late."

Simon jerked his hand from underneath his mother's grasp. She had already told him a bit about this: what was her point?

"All right, Mr. Impatient, I'll fast-forward until now. This summer, I visited my 80s again, for the first time since I went to live with your father."

"Why?" Simon said. "If I had a pend ... talisman, I'd visit the future every day."

Rakita laughed, imprisoning his hand again. "You forget that I've been visiting somewhere a lot more important than the future since I got my talisman back. I can only time-travel once a day, remember?

Anyway, I did visit the future this summer. And ... there has been a change. It wasn't the same future that I saw 17 years ago. Things were ... better."

Simon waited for a moment, returning his mother's intense look. Eventually, he said: "So?"

"So, we know that this is a critical time for the world. Right now. For the future to be different, there needs to be big changes *right now.*"

Simon continued to stare at his mother, while she nodded at him expectantly. She obviously felt that she was saying something very clear, but he hadn't a clue as to what this had to do with him. Eventually, Rakita noticed his bewildered expression.

"Simon," she said slowly. "I have gone into the future and seen a change. History has been changed. And that is exactly what the Leaders said when I told them I was pregnant with you. They said to me: 'History has been changed'."

Rakita looked directly into his eyes. "Simon? The thing that is going to change the future—it's you."

CHAPTER TEN

RAKITA LEFT SIMON to time travel back to the island as soon as they reached the end of their driveway, promising that she'd begin sleeping in the house again the following week, when Simon started school.

It was Sunday, and he could see his father's car in the driveway as he ran towards the house, his heart beating with anticipation. He flung open the door so quickly Toby didn't even have time to bark; as soon as he realised who it was he catapulted into Simon's arms. Simon sank towards the floor under his weight, laughing and allowing him to lick every inch of his face. Then someone was hugging him from above and he was laughing and embracing his father.

Finally, the trio broke apart and Simon got to his feet, regarding his father analytically. "Have you lost weight, Dad?"

"Perhaps. Now you're here we'll eat properly again. I've ordered Indian take-out for a treat tonight."

Simon didn't mention that take-out was one of those unnecessary luxuries that produced waste, and thanked his father.

Over dinner, he told his father about his summer in detail, saving the most important revelation until the end. "It's like I've just met the most advanced, brilliant society on earth, and they're looking at me and saying, it's all up to you, kid. I'm a bit frightened, to tell you the truth."

Simon watched his father carefully. He wasn't sure how to process what his mother had told him, it seemed so crazy, and he wanted to see if his father weighed in on the crazy side.

John spooned more curry sauce over his rice. "Sounds farfetched to me. Are you sure they're normal people, like us? Are they technologically advanced? Because it sounds to me like they're obsessed with the climate, as though all the other risks to society—such as nuclear weapons and AI—don't exist."

Simon looked at his father in exasperation. "They can see into the future, Dad. They *know* what's going to happen. Besides, why's AI a risk?"

John glanced at his son, recognizing the muted annoyance in his voice. "Once they manage to create a computer that can think better than we can, what's to stop it deciding that it wants to be top dog? Anyway, let's assume the island people are right; I expect the way in which you're destined to help will become apparent with time."

"So you're saying I should just wait, hoping some type of vision will appear at the right time? That could take years. There are things I could be doing right now."

John smiled at him. "You know how to save the world? I thought I knew that too, at your age."

Simon grimaced in irritation. "You forget, Dad, I have a few tricks you didn't have. I've already seen my future, or at least a bit of it. Don't get me wrong; I'm open to any information or advice that come my way. But I'm going to get started now."

"What does that mean?"

What did it mean? Simon hadn't been sure, either. He had spent the first few hours after the conversation with his mother floating about in a cloud of fantasies where crowds prostrated themselves before him—a knight in shining armour, Saviour of the World. But then the absurdity struck him. He had begun to expostulate with Rakita: the connection she and the Leaders had made between the changes in the future and his own birth were preposterous and unproven. He was a kid; what the hell was he supposed to do? How could he influence people?

"Perhaps you won't do anything other than what we've already been doing for a very long time," Rakita answered calmly. "You know the Pulitzer Prize?"

Simon nodded, wondering what she was going on about now.

"I often read prize-winning books. And I often read books that haven't won any prizes; books I find on the dusty shelves of a second-hand store, whose titles catch my eye. Often, those books by unknown authors are just as good as the big winners, even though nobody knows about them."

Simon picked at a hangnail, wondering if there was any point in his mother's ramblings.

"Many people on the island have been campaigning throughout the world for years. If a critical mass of the world's people can be educated to believe what we know, then change will happen. The secret is getting the message across, again and again, to every level of society: individuals, communities, right up to governments. Why are you destined to be more successful than us in this? Who knows? But don't let it go to your head." Rakita smiled and ruffled his hair. "Your book isn't any better than many others, even if it's destined to win the big prize."

Simon tried to understand what she was saying. "You mean there's no special role I have to play? I've just got to get the message out, like you've been doing all along?"

"That's certainly how I'd start, anyway. I can help."

So Simon knew exactly how to answer his father. "I've already made a list of the things that need to be communicated." Simon got up from the table, followed slavishly by Toby, who hadn't taken his eyes off him since he'd come through the door. He ruffled in his backpack and extracted a scribbler, placing it open to the left of his father's plate. "These are in order of importance."

John began to read out loud.

Needs: Government level
   1.) Carbon tax
   2.) Caps on company's emissions, with penalties
   3.) Boost investment in renewable energy sources
   4.) Curb deforestation

"I get the idea," John said, pushing the scribbler away. "You seem to be unaware that our government has already committed to investing in renewable resources, so your important communication is a little late."

"Our government talks the talk, but they're walking the walk like laggards. This needs to happen *now*. But it's only going to happen if their citizens make some noise. Don't you want to read the rest? That's just what we need to petition the government about; look at this page, these are for individuals." When John didn't raise his eyes from his plate, Simon read:

"One. Educate people about their personal emissions and how they will impact their children. Two ..."

"Simon, it isn't very interesting to hear lists read out. I get the idea. How are you going to do this, exactly? Don't you know there are millions of Canadians and Americans all lobbying for these exact things? Scientists, nature conservationists, educators. Many countries in the world have signed the Paris Climate Agreement to try to keep the temperature from rising more than 2°. It's ridiculous to think you have a special role to play. It's being done already!"

Simon looked down at his scribbler, struggling to keep the surprise at his father's reaction off his face. "Mum told me to think of it like a war, Dad, and our side needs as many soldiers as it can get. I'm just another soldier, like the scientists and educators. We are fighting the only real war that matters—the war against the climate crisis."

"So that matters more than the wars in the Middle East, does it? And all the other, multiple problems in the world?"

"What do you mean? This is my life we're talking about. My

RIGHT to breathe clean air and drink clean water. I shouldn't have to be figuring out how to convince people. It should be a given. What the fuck is wrong with people?"

"Don't use language like that, Simon! Do you think it strengthens your argument?"

Simon took a deep breath. "Dad, we're heading towards self-extinction, while people spend billions making sure fossil fuel consumption continues because they make money from it. Many more are ignorant about how vital this issue is. The only way to make this happen is by educating as many people as possible." Simon made a dismissive wave of his hand, confident of the research he had done. "Of course, I'll continue to make a lot of noise at the government level—like protests and petitions."

John gave a bark of laughter and pushed back his chair to stand up. "Seriously? Let's say you educate every single Canadian and they vote for a government that supports all the actions on your little list, but China says screw that, our billion plus people are going to continue using coal. So we're dead anyway, according to you and your mother."

"Me and Mum and every mainstream scientist," Simon snapped at his father, because he didn't really know how to answer the question. What his father had said made sense. He felt irritated; if he couldn't convince his father, then what chance did he have of convincing the world?

His father was just standing there, as though he wasn't sure what to do, now he'd stood up.

Simon's irritation vanished in compassion. "Do you want to go for a walk with Toby, Dad?"

They set out into the warm, soft air of a summer evening. Toby ran free beside them; he never strayed far and Simon could always find a piece of garbage, like a one-use coffee cup, to scoop up poo, although he was a very routine-based dog and usually retired discreetly to do his poo right after breakfast every day. Simon kept noticing differences between his subdivision and the island: he stiffened in irritation as a man stopped to chat with a neighbour, leaving his car running throughout the conversation. This man wasn't wicked; he was just ignorant. Simon was sure that the key lay in education. "Do you want to hear a few of my action items, Dad? I'll start by setting up a website, and I have to blog, and post YouTube videos. Use social media like TikTok and Facebook. I've already filmed some stuff on the island."

"Will you mention your father's profession, on this website of yours?"

At some point Simon wanted to broach the subject of his father leaving his current work, but he thought he'd wait for a better mood. He linked his arm through his father's, determined not to feel deflated by his negative attitude. Determined not to feel bad because he was here, and not on the island. Guilt pumped through his body, but he smiled up at his father. "You know a lot of people in high places, Dad. I hope you're going to help me drop information into the right ears. Together, right?"

"So long as the information doesn't hurt anybody's pocket, son."

Again, his father's sad face diluted Simon's irritation. He hugged his arm.

"I miss her." John spoke so quietly that Simon wasn't sure he'd spoken at all. He glanced up. His father's eyes were trained on the ground. "Being with her made me feel that I was connected to decency. She was ... good. I felt good when I was with her."

Simon wasn't sure what to say. He squeezed his father's arm and waited. When no more was forthcoming, he pulled his arm from his father's and ran ahead a little with Toby, who danced along on the edge of the grass bordering the sidewalk, one eye trained on Simon at all times.

"Hey," shouted a heavily tattooed man mowing his lawn. "Put your dog on a leash."

Simon ran back to his father and took refuge by his side. John completely ignored the man. "You have no idea how hard it is to educate people, Simon. Your task is impossible."

Simon wasn't sure why his father had to be such a downer. For the first time in his life he was glad he was going to school tomorrow.

∞ The next day Simon dressed more carefully than usual, attributing the butterflies in his stomach to the fact that he hadn't slept well; Toby had pressed against his back so closely that Simon could barely turn over all night. "It's not because of Sandra," he informed his reflection severely, pressing down a black curl that refused to stay in place.

Can't wait to see u, Sandra had texted him the previous evening. But although they had communicated all summer, it was going to be weird seeing her again. Every time he thought of their last meeting, the blood rushed to his face.

She wasn't there when he got to school, so he sat quietly in his seat until the first class started. The announcements at the start of each day informed him that the number 67 bus—Sandra's bus—was running late. When she eventually arrived, she waved a languid hand in his direction and he began to feel a bit silly about his excitement.

"Are you going to eat in the library?" he asked her uncertainly at lunchtime.

"Of course," she said, giving him a strange look.

She chatted about her summer and consumed her peanut butter and jam sandwich in such a normal way, that Simon felt quite embarrassed about his previous nerves. Perhaps what had happened at their last meeting hadn't meant much to her. Perhaps she'd already forgotten it.

Simon began to tell her about his plans, and was gratified by her instant, intense interest. "This is a big job, Simon. You can't do this all alone. If your Dad drives me home, I can come over and help you."

This was way better than his father's reaction! Simon felt cheered immediately, and texted his father to ask if Sandra could come over that very day.

And so, just like on the island, life fell into a routine. Simon and Sandra would work from the moment they got to his house until his father drove Sandra home, just stopping long enough to grab a snack. Toby's ball-throwing activities were reduced to a half-hour slot before bedtime, by which time Simon was often so tired he couldn't see the print on the computer to work anymore. They researched endlessly, reading copious articles on the best environmental sites. They created a website and argued ferociously over the name, eventually settling on Sandra's choice, 'Go To Bat for Nature', mostly because Simon didn't want to waste any more time arguing, even though he was convinced nobody would ever find such an obscure name with Google. He began to write a blog called (after much more argument) *A million and one easy ways to reduce your energy consumption*. Each blog began with a cartoon, injected with a bit of black humour to boost interest: 'How to enjoy five-minute showers' included a cartoon depicting a person revelling in a shower, with a 'Five Minutes' sign over his head; the next panel showed his grandchild showering fifty years later. The following panel showed someone showering with a 'Fifteen Minutes' sign above their heads, followed by a filthy grandchild standing under a dry shower, because there was no more water.

"Seriously?" Sandra said. "I'm not taking five-minute showers. I love my long, hot showers."

"So take a long, hot shower once a week. You'll enjoy it twice as much if it's a treat. Plus, shorter showers are healthier ..."

"Seriously? Once a week? You're insane. Plus, you repeat everything ten times. You're like a friggin' parrot. It's crazy to think showers are gonna make any difference."

"It's not the showers per se, Sandra. It's looking at everything we do through the lens of this crisis. We need to stop consuming mindlessly. If buying something new or going for an ATV ride or eating meat makes me happy, I should do it without guilt. So long as I think about it, ask myself if I really need it. So long as I'm not doing it as often as I did before I started thinking about it. If you love your hot showers then take them—just not every time."

"So if everybody stops consuming so much ..."

"... emissions will plummet. Pretty much everything we consume—from our new iPhone to our social media—exist because of fossil fuels."

"Jeez, you want me to think for ten minutes every time I write an email? It's boring."

"Eating rations during the Second World War was probably boring too, but people did it happily because they felt they were fighting for something worthwhile. I'd say the life of your kids is pretty worthwhile, wouldn't you?"

"Ain't having no kids," Sandra muttered.

Simon hunched closer to the computer, trying to focus on what he was writing. Suddenly, he felt her hands on his shoulders and froze.

"Relax," she said, kneading his shoulders airily for a minute or two before flicking his ear and turning away. Then Simon did relax, sighing and chastising himself inwardly. He really had to stop freezing like a deer in headlights every time Sandra touched him. She had never referred to the time she'd kissed him. She had been sad he'd been going away and it was her way of saying, 'don't forget me'. But she didn't feel the same way about him that he felt about her, otherwise she'd have given some sign. Just as well, who had time for that with all this work to do?

Simon's home page included tips like, "What you can do in your home" and "What you can do to influence your government". He linked to environmental articles and videos on his website; often he summarized the content in his own words so his readers could get the gist without reading the whole article. He used Facebook, Twitter, Instagram and other platforms to spread the word. He joined Avaaz and began to circulate petitions, starting with his own province (Support mandatory recycling laws!) and creeping up to the national level (Persuade the Prime Minister to Keep his Environmental Election Promises!). He wrote to his mayor, then the Premier of the province, asking for their support with specific projects. He corresponded with other environmentalists, responded to other people's posts, and wrote to the comments section of newspapers and magazines. He contacted celebrities that he knew were pro-environment, and asked them to endorse him. People began to visit his website, and follow him on Facebook.

Sometimes his father made him feel down, and he was grateful for Sandra's passionate support (in everything except the issue of shower-length). But it was his mother who really bolstered his determination and resolve. Simon probed her brains for everything, from next steps, to clarification of things he didn't understand. They usually walked to the edge of the garden with their teacups in hand, so Sandra could climb her favourite oak tree and vape as they talked. One of the first subjects Simon broached was John's comments about the uselessness of one country's efforts in the face of world pollution.

"Let me tell you a parable, Simon. Once upon a time there was a terrible storm, which washed millions of starfish onto the beach, where they lay dying."

"Millions?" inserted Sandra, who had linked her legs over a low branch and swung head-down, listening.

"Yes millions. Never interrupt a story, Sandra. This little girl visited the beach and saw the starfish. She felt so sorry for them, she stood on the beach and picked them up, one after the other, and threw them back into the sea. A man was watching her do this, and he laughed at her, saying, 'What is the point of doing that? There are millions of dying starfish here. It makes no difference, throwing a few back.'

"The little girl picked another one up and held it high in the air. 'To this one, it makes a difference,' she said, and threw it as far as she could into the sea."

There was silence for a minute or two.

"I understand," Simon said finally. "Now I know how to answer Dad."

Rakita glanced up the tree trunk towards Sandra. "You know, I hate standing up while I'm drinking tea. Can we …"

"I'll bring a couple of chairs," Simon said quickly, before his mother decided to separate from Sandra. "It'll be nice, sitting here under the shade of the oak."

"While Sandra drops bits of bark on our heads."

Simon brought the chairs, and they sat. "Good news, Mum," Simon said. "I've been invited to speak on our local radio show."

Rakita gave a whoop of joy. "Wow Simon! You really are doing well, getting the word out. Do you think it's because you're a kid?"

"Two kids!" Sandra shouted from the top of the tree.

Rakita grinned. "Well, we'd better prep you then."

Rakita swivelled her chair around so she was sitting at right angles to Simon, like she imagined they'd do in radio. Toby sat in front of them, gazing unblinkingly. "Just where the cameraman might stand," Rakita said.

"There's no camera for radio," Sandra said.

"Whatever," Rakita said, not really having any idea how radio worked. "So Simon, tell us a little bit about yourself. How old are you?" She began easily, soon moving on to more difficult questions, like, "How did you become so interested in the environment?" and, "How is the public responding?" She helped Simon to focus on the nitty-gritty and curb his more long-winded answers. After she had pelted him with questions for half an hour, Rakita leaned back in her chair, smiling. "You did great, Simon. So I'm going to ask you one more question: what are you trying to achieve?"

Simon thought for a minute. "Raise awareness."

"In general? Do you have a specific goal?"

"I would like to replace all fossil fuel use with alternative sources of energy. Is that the right answer, Mum? Because there are so many things I'm trying to do! I also want individual people to understand that saying no to that one-use coffee cup, or that straw, or that plastic bag, actually does matter. The more people do it, the more it'll matter, and if everybody does it, it'll make a huge difference, right?"

"Like it made a difference to that one starfish," Sandra chimed in.

Simon beamed at her. "Exactly. But do I need to focus more effort on the government level, Mum? Because more starfish will benefit?"

Rakita threw back her head and drained her tea, at the same time that John's car turned into the driveway. She rose to her feet. "I'm going to leave you with something to mull over. You're both doing a great job spreading a wide net, but I think there is one, crucial issue that you need to focus on more than any other. Right now, BigOilGramby is using all its resources and power to lobby for a new pipeline. A huge, oil line running through the habitats of hundreds of species, transporting a product whose extraction and use hurts the earth. And your father is a major player in that company, Simon."

Rakita sprinted away suddenly, just as John got out of his car and turned his eyes towards them. Simon didn't even have time to say goodbye.

CHAPTER ELEVEN

SIMON'S RADIO INTERVIEW was scheduled to happen early in the morning, before school. Simon was so nervous before the interview that he couldn't eat.

"It's just the local radio," his father told him. "If you run to school faster than the average kid you get invited to speak on the local radio."

As though that made any difference! Simon felt his stomach churn, as he stirred his porridge around and around his bowl. Normally porridge was his favourite comfort food, warm cereal with a splash of milk and a dribble of brown sugar. Now it looked like barf.

All the way in the car, and later sitting in the waiting room, Simon rehearsed the practiced answers in his head, praying that they wouldn't ask completely different questions. Speakers played the radio station for the occupants of the waiting room; Simon practically leapt out of his skin when he heard his own name, announcing he'd be on next.

"You'll be fine," his father assured him, as the receptionist beckoned Simon out of the waiting room. "I'll be right here, listening."

Instead of sitting at right angles with his interviewer, Simon was placed in a chair on the other side of a glass window from the radio host, who was currently belting out the news headlines in a cheery, professional voice. Simon's stomach curdled as he realised his mother had been wrong about the set-up, and wondered if she had been wrong about the types of questions he would be asked as well. Simon took deep breaths to try and calm himself. After the news there were some ads, and the radio host came out from behind the glass window and introduced himself as Bill, though Simon already knew that. "So a couple of tips, Simon," Bill said. "Speak slowly, and take a few seconds to think about what you want to say. I'll start off introducing you, and giving a brief overview of some of the things you've been doing in the community. Then I'll probably ask you what got you so interested in the environment, what your goals are, things like that."

Simon felt a great whoosh of relief, and he blessed his mother silently. Bill reappeared behind the glass, and gave Simon a thumbs-up as he began the introductions. Then the questions started, and Simon reeled off a list of the projects he'd been working on, remembering to speak slowly, never taking his eyes off Bill, who smiled encouragingly through the glass.

After several questions, Simon's confidence began to increase; he leant back in his chair as Bill lobbed another question his way. "My goodness Simon, it sounds like you've been a busy boy. The environment is a complicated subject, and your hands are dabbling in several pies, but would you say you have one, special goal that you'd like to achieve?"

It came out of Simon's mouth before he'd really thought about it. "Yes. I'm going to stop the new pipeline that BigOilGramby wants to build."

Bill laughed. "You're taking on a pretty big company there son, but it's not BigOilGramby who decides whether that pipeline will be built or not. It's slated to run through several provinces, so it's a federal matter. Do you think the Prime Minister of Canada will listen to you?"

Simon swallowed. These were questions he hadn't rehearsed. *Think, think,* he told himself, *take your time*. But he couldn't think. "I … I don't know," he mumbled. His confidence plummeting, he waited anxiously for the next question. But Bill only asked if he was working alone, or if someone was helping him. He listed all the people who had endorsed him, or supported him in other ways, and of course named his mother and Sandra.

"What about your father?" Bill asked.

Even if he hadn't been hyper-aware that John was sitting in the next room, listening, Simon could hardly have said that his father's main contribution had been relentless negativity. His voice faltered for the second time. "I ... live with my father. He drove me here." Simon nodded vigorously at Bill, so he'd realize that was all he had to say.

"I see what you're saying, Simon. Your father basically enables everything you do; am I right or am I right?"

He was hideously wrong, but Simon gave an ambivalent giggle.

"But your father works for BigOilGramby. How does he feel about the pipeline?"

Simon was beginning to feel like he was in a nightmare that wouldn't end. It was only supposed to be a ten-minute interview—how much longer could it go on? Should he say he hadn't discussed it with his father? His brain raced, desperate to answer before the pause became evident to listeners. Then, a brainwave. "You'd have to ask him."

"Well, I wish you the best of luck in all your endeavours, Simon. You're a pretty special kid and I'm sure that both your parents are very proud of you." Bill told listeners how they could donate to Simon's causes as Simon removed his headphones, suddenly exhausted. When the ads started Bill came out to thank him and wish him luck. "This your first radio interview, son?"

Simon nodded.

"You did a great job. You sounded earnest and genuine and you spoke really well. Hell, you've even convinced *me* to give you a donation. Good luck!"

Simon tottered out to the waiting room, anxious to hear what his father had thought. John was standing by the door, holding it open already. Perhaps he was late for work.

"What did you think, Dad?" he asked as they exited the building.

"What the hell do you mean by bringing in the name of my

company? Was this your mother's idea? Do you know how embarrassing this will be for me if any of my colleagues heard you? I am the
Executive Vice President at BigOilGramby, and my son is on the radio
chirping about how his main goal is to stop our Number One project."

Perhaps it was because he'd been so tense before the interview and
now felt exhausted and ravenous. Perhaps it was because he suddenly
realised how much he wanted his father to support him as he'd once
done, and the pity that excused his father's changed behaviour was
drying up. But suddenly, Simon was very angry.

"Do you know how embarrassing it is for me to have a father who
works for an oil company? Shame on you."

John stood stock still. "How dare you."

"Mum and I don't call people who ignore this crisis Climate
Deniers. We call them Climate Ignoramuses—only blind ignorance
and ... and ... stupidity ..." Simon felt anger rise up in his throat and
choke him.

"You're the one who is ignorant," his father said, slamming the car
door shut. "Have you ever thought about the boost to the economy that
such a pipeline would bring? The people it would employ, the lives it
would help?"

Simon remembered that to be wise, you had to listen to every
perspective. So he swallowed his anger and listened carefully as John
detailed all the potential benefits of a pipeline such as this. "Do you
think it's better for the environment to transport oil from the Middle
East? People need oil. It's better for the environment—and our economy—if it's local oil." By the time John had finished, they were half-way
to the school.

"OK Dad, I understand that our country would be richer as a result of the pipeline, and that the extra money could buy lots of great
things that our city needs. I get that Dad, I really do. But if we know
that burning fossil fuel is destroying our world, then how can we continue to do that, no matter what the short-term benefits? We have to
abandon oil, local or otherwise. It makes no sense to produce more."

"It's a balance, Simon. Many people with a lot more knowledge than you have weighed the pros and cons of these decisions very carefully."

"And they've come to the conclusion that to enrich a few people now is more important than the survival of the entire human race?"

His father laughed and reached over to muss Simon's hair, a gesture which Simon found excruciatingly irritating. "How you exaggerate! You must try to avoid using such extreme language, Simon—it doesn't strengthen your point."

"You do understand, Dad, that Mum can travel to the future? I can assure you, that the world in 2050 will be a lot less pleasant than the world we know now. Hotter, drier, extreme weather ..."

"Yeah, you've told me this, Simon. Even if I believed your mother could time travel, it's not like I can use that as proof to persuade my colleagues to abandon the pipeline, is it?"

The parking lot in front of the school loomed ahead of them, to Simon's relief. "You can tell your colleagues to listen to the scientists. That's how most of us learn about the world we live in."

John parked, and switched off the engine, leaning back in his seat and smiling at his son. "Some scientists say that the activity of humans has very little impact on the earth."

Simon felt his heart constrict with pain. He had always loved and admired his father. He wanted so very, very much to continue. "The vast majority of scientists say that humans are causing climate change, Dad. Please. No rational, thinking human being could claim that humans aren't impacting global warming. No rational human could claim that making money was more important than preserving the earth we depend on. Maybe your anger about Mum is making you emotional. If that's the case, let's not discuss this subject, because I don't want to waste time having irrational conversations. I have a job to do, and I will do everything I can to stop the pipeline, with or without your help." And Simon twisted open the car door and slipped out.

∞ As soon as he'd sat down at his desk, his phone beeped with a message from Sandra: *How was it?*

Lunch, he texted back. He felt too upset from the conversation with his father to text about the interview. Plus, it was over an hour to lunch, and his stomach was rumbling so loudly he was surprised the whole class couldn't hear it.

An hour of math calculations calmed him somewhat, and after he'd devoured everything in his lunch box and was poking through the remaining contents in Sandra's, he felt composed enough to tell her about the radio interview, although he didn't mention the argument with his father. "I'd like to focus on the pipeline," Simon said, "so all our other projects will be put on a back burner."

"What, you mean like our petition for the Premier to force fossil fuel producers to pay higher carbon taxes? Why's that less important than the pipeline?"

Simon had to smile. Environmental terminology peppered Sandra's speech so heavily these days, it was almost like she'd learned a different language. "It's all important; but we don't want to spread ourselves too thin. Better to focus on one or two main goals at a time."

Sandra leaned forward and tapped him with a food container that had held cookies up until a few moments ago. The saran wrap that had once swathed her food had been replaced with reusable Tupperware. "D'ya expect me to agree with every change in direction?"

Simon looked at her. She wore that mischievous smile which he never completely understood. "I guess, yeah. Unless you have a good reason why not?"

She tapped his arm again, playfully. "Even when I do have a good reason, you still try'n railroad me into doin' what you want."

"Like when?"

"Like with the showers. I've told you how much I love long showers and you still go on and on about it, as though it makes any friggin' difference ..."

"Don't forget the little girl and the starfish. Each short shower is another starfish saved."

Sandra stood up and bent over him, her face inches away. Simon looked at her as though he wanted to memorize every feature. She was wearing a t-shirt with a V-neck. Studs glinted from her ears and nose. "Screw the little girl and the starfish. I want long showers, and it don't make no difference to the earth if I have them."

"Says you and the world. Everybody thinks they, personally, deserve the long showers, the extra pair of shoes, the convenient plastic—especially in the West, where most people lack for nothing. I guess that's just the way it goes, the more you have, the more spoiled you get, the less you appreciate, the less happy you are, the more you think you deserve. Vicious circle. We're so entitled."

Sandra shook her hair in his face. "Well sorreee ... anyways, I can't stand in the shower no more, enjoying the heat; I feel too guilty. You've totally ruined showers for me, dude."

Simon laughed and gathered up his lunch things. Sandra always made him feel better.

∞ When Simon got home that day he found Rakita in the kitchen frying up a mixture of veggies and noodles that she would douse with soy sauce and dub 'Chinese food'. Simon perched on a stool and cut up whatever veggies she handed him, recounting the story of the interview for the second time that day. Then he told her about the argument with his father.

"Damn," Rakita said. "We need him to help you get a meeting with Premier Smith."

Simon didn't answer and after a minute Rakita came over and gave him a hug. "Your father is a good man who loves you very much," she said. "He's just miserable right now. It'll get better."

"But I want him to support me because it's the right thing to do. Why isn't he being rational? I don't want a stupid father."

"Hush now; he's not stupid. He's just ... sad. Emotional. Remember? Nobody can be emotional and rational at the same time. He'll come around. Is there a reason you're eating more broccoli than you're slicing?"

Simon giggled. "I'm starving. I missed breakfast and I've been starving all day."

"Well let's take some tea and cookies outside and chat some more. Toby is dying to go out."

As soon as they were sitting comfortably ("Thank God we don't have to stand under that bloody tree to drink our tea," Rakita muttered) and Toby had chased the ball three times and was content to gnaw it quietly in the shade for a time, Rakita began to give him contact numbers for First Nation chiefs. "You don't have to persuade them to your side, they're already on your side," she told Simon. "They've had experience campaigning against these pipelines already, and they can give you a lot of advice and support."

"But they don't know who I am. Will they help anybody who asks?"

"Anybody who is doing the type of work you're doing. Perhaps many of them possess our foresight, even without our ability to go into the future. They can help you understand the impact of the pipeline on the natural world."

Simon threw the ball for Toby again. "How come they understand the natural world?"

"I don't know much about their culture, but before the white settlers got here, their lives were intertwined with nature and their culture was steeped in the natural world. I wonder what it must have been like for them, living from nature, respecting and appreciating everything nature gave them, and then the rapacious white man arrives, greedily grabbing everything nature supplies without thanks, without thinking in terms of nature's ability to renew. Like the decimation of millions of buffalo; here today, gone tomorrow. Fast forward a couple of hundred years, and we are still rapacious, still destroying the earth to line our pockets. Only this time, we're not talking about a species like the buffalo. The world itself might not be able to renew."

Simon stood up and threw the ball again for Toby, harder than strictly necessary. The situation was clear. How could his father not see it?

CHAPTER TWELVE

SIMON AND SANDRA spent the next few weeks working doggedly towards their goal. The meeting with the First Nation resulted in a website that was much more aggressive in its approach than anything Simon had done on his own. The main page was dominated by a clickable green button entitled 'Tell Premier Smith to Stop BigOilGramby Pipeline'. Once people clicked on that, they were brought to another page which asked them to go further: 'Click on the name of your bank or financial institution below to discover if it supports the BigOil-Gramby Pipeline'. If their bank was guilty, the website encouraged the users to withdraw their monies from said bank: 'They won't listen to morality, but they listen to money. Take a stand and protect your children's future!'

Simon had been dubious about how many people would be willing to change their financial institutions based on whether they supported the pipeline, but as he saw the numbers of people adding their names to the petition creep up, he had to admit that the strong language and demand for action was getting results. There was also a place on the website where people could leave messages, and he was deeply moved by the level of support in his community.

Simon didn't stop there. He stood outside BigOilGramby and handed out pamphlets to employees and passers-by alike.

"How come this feels so déjà vu?" John joked when he saw Simon. They had achieved an uneasy truce, mostly by avoiding the subject. Simon wasn't happy with this—he'd always communicated openly with both parents—but at least they weren't arguing. He knew, at some point, he'd have to ask his father for help in setting up a meeting with Premier Smith. He'd already written to the Premier, and received a generic reply. Rakita explained that he should continue to write/email/ tweet every week, but she warned him that it probably wouldn't achieve a positive result. "You have to have an 'in' to obtain an interview with the Premier, and John is our 'in'."

"How does one get to be 'in'?" Simon inquired.

"You golf!" Rakita said.

Simon didn't have time to learn golf, so one evening he grabbed the bull by the horns during dinner. "Dad, I really need to meet with Premier Smith, and I was wondering if you could help me set it up."

His father stopped slurping the vegetable soup Rakita had left them and looked at his son incredulously. "You want me to set up a meeting so you can persuade our Premier to stop a pipeline that I support? Did I get that right?"

Simon rolled his eyes at Toby under the table. "You don't support it, Dad, your company supports it. You parted ways with your colleagues years ago. You live differently from them; you have one house, one electric car ..."

"I don't need an inventory of my belongings, Simon," John said. "I changed my lifestyle to accommodate your mother. What's that got to do with the current situation? I have ..."

It was Simon's turn to interrupt. "You might have made those changes for Mum, but since you got rid of your summer cottage and your boat your life has been simpler and happier, hasn't it?"

John laughed bitterly. "Yes, your mother certainly has made me happier."

"The point is, Dad, instead of feeling guilty because you have so much ..."

"I didn't feel guilty. I worked hard for everything I had." John threw his spoon into his empty bowl with a clatter. "Thousands of my employees are dependent on that pipeline for their employment. Most of them have families. You should feel thankful I'm not obstructing you, but help you? Forget it."

John got up and marched out the door, but Simon rushed after him and yelled up the stairs at his retreating back. "You're destroying my future! Mine—your son's! What word don't you understand?"

His father's silence enraged Simon further and he screamed up the stairs, "If you care about your employees more than your son, they'll surely thank you for the money in their pockets when they're wearing masks to breathe! They'll thank you when rising waters flood their homes and threaten their food supply! They'll ..." Simon only shut up when he heard the door of his father's room slam.

He bent to hug Toby, breathing deeply to calm his anger.

∞ A week later Simon was invited to do another radio interview, and felt that he spoke much better; certainly he was less nervous the second time around. Then he was invited to speak on TV, and his nerves shot through the roof again.

"It's just the same as radio," Rakita assured him. "Just forget there's a camera."

"Have you ever been on TV?" Simon demanded.

Rakita hadn't. "Don't worry, you can rattle off environmental facts like a pro."

"No, Mum. Environmental facts put people to sleep. I need to look right at the camera and say: 'Do you love your children?'"

"Yes," Rakita said. "Brilliant. They have to hear words that convey the truth, as it pertains to them."

"I hate public speaking," Simon said. "I'm no actor."

"Then don't act," Rakita said. "Just speak your truth."

∞ On the day of the TV interview breakfast went untouched again, and Simon only started to calm down when the questions started rolling. Unlike the radio, he was sitting at right angles to the TV host, just like during his practices with Rakita. The only thing that was really difficult was the camera. Simon was aware of its presence at all times, and had to make a conscious effort not to look towards it. Until the right time.

He had wrestled with when to turn his head and look directly at the camera. The right time to ask, "Do you love your children?"

But when then questions started rolling, he knew. He injected it into every answer.

What did he want to achieve? He wanted to ensure clean air for him and his children. He looked at the camera. "And for your children as well."

"And how do you want to ensure clean air for you and others, Simon?"

"I want people to look at everything they do through the lens of this crisis. Our air is in danger. Please travel less. Eat less meat. Retrofit your houses—there are good governmental rebates. Buy an electric car if you can." Simon looked at the camera. "So that your children will be able to breathe outside, every day. Curb your consumerism now, to grant them that one, basic right."

His eyes were full of tears. And he wasn't acting.

∞ A couple of days after the TV interview, he was invited to meet with Premier Smith. Apparently Rakita was wrong. You didn't necessarily need to play golf to meet a Premier. A bit of media attention would do the trick as well.

∞ *Tell me tell me tell me,* texted Sandra as soon as Simon arrived at school after his meeting with Premier Smith.

Lunch, Simon texted back, but he looked over and gave her a thumbs up, grinning like a lunatic. He had been worried the Premier would be like his father, condescending and resistant, but it had felt more like a chat between friends. From the first warm handshake he'd started to grin, and hadn't stopped. Sandra beamed back at him from the other side of the classroom.

When lunch rolled around Simon started to head towards the library, as usual, but Sandra pulled at his arm. "Let's eat outside."

Simon nodded, and followed her out the back doors and across the soccer fields to the woods beyond. When Sandra plunged into the trees he called: "Are we stopping sometime, or do you want to keep walking all of lunch?"

"I've found a special place. You'll see." Sandra led him to a thick copse of trees, then dropped on her knees and wiggled through a gap between their trunks. Simon sighed in resignation and followed her. The tree trunks, which had looked so thickly clustered from the out-side, hid a bare patch of land covered in pine needles.

"Isn't this great? It's totally private."

"That's important," Simon said, sitting down and leaning his back against a tree, "because so many people are walking around just out-side."

"Very funny. Now tell me about the interview."

Simon pulled out his chicken sandwich and took a bite. "The Premier was so easy-going, it was almost like talking to you. I'd ex-pected him to talk about the economy and stuff, but he more or less said he'd been looking for ways to make our beautiful province green-er and building new pipelines didn't jive with that vision."

"He said 'jive'?"

Simon had already wolfed down his sandwich and was chomping his way through an apple. "Mm-hmm. Something like that. Sandra, at the end he more or less said he was going to oppose the pipeline. Can you believe it's going to be so easy? Pinch me."

Sandra leaned forward and pinched him so hard he leapt to his feet and swore at her. She patted the pine needles invitingly. "Sit down. You *told* me to pinch you. So are we done then? With the pipeline project?"

Simon sat down, rubbing his arm gingerly. "The fact that Premier Smith is on board is a huge step, but the pipeline has federal approval. Once that's revoked, we're finished with this project. You got anything else to eat?"

"You're always starving on interview days. You can have my leftovers when I'm done. We're never gonna get federal support."

Simon tried not to watch as the chips travelled one by one into Sandra's mouth. "We'll change our website message to focus on our PM, and I'll re-direct my daily tweets to him. Premier Smith will probably talk to him, as well. Are you going to eat every last chip?"

Sandra sighed and threw him the chip bag, followed by her entire lunch bag. "It's not like I can eat with you staring at me like that."

"Sorry," Simon said unrepentantly, and tipped the chip bag into his mouth to catch the last few fragments.

Sandra lay back on the pine needles and took out her vape, blowing smoke rings into the air. She watched Simon devour the rest of her crackers, and stick his fingers into the sandwich container to wipe off the peanut butter clinging to the side. "For God's sakes," she said, closing her eyes, "it's like you haven't eaten for months." Simon ignored her and continued to rummage for crumbs. "Didn't you say something about your father knowing someone who knows the Prime Minister?"

Simon finally decided there wasn't a single speck of food left to eat, and leant back on his hands, surveying Sandra freely, since her eyes were closed. He looked at the white column of her neck sliding into the blackness of her t-shirt. He saw the tips of the tail feathers of what he knew was a peacock tattoo edging along her shoulder.

"Do you want to kiss me?" Sandra said from her supine position.

Simon almost gasped, he was so shocked. His first instinct was to say 'no', but that sounded so ... ungallant. Besides, it wasn't the truth. "Sometimes," he said.

"Well, you never show it."

Simon was astounded. How was he supposed to *show* it? She'd kill him if he showed any such thing.

Sandra rolled over on her side and opened her eyes, slipping her vape into her pocket. She had that indecipherable, mischievous look on her face again. "Let's go out on a date."

"What?"

"A date. Tomorrow's Friday. You arrange everything." Sandra stood up and turned around so her back was towards him. "We should head back. Can you brush off the pine needles?"

Simon's hand trembled as he approached her, and he brushed with such vigour that Sandra was propelled forward. She laughed, and turned towards him. "This is how you brush," she murmured, and he felt her hand at his back, snaking its way lazily down his spine. His whole body felt like it was blushing with pleasure and embarrassment at the same time. He couldn't move or speak.

"Am I brushing it all off?" Sandra's voice was very close to his ear. "Yes," he whispered, and turned his head infinitesimally towards her. He yearned to kiss her, but Sandra being Sandra, she could just as easily punch him as melt into his arms. It was so difficult to know what to do. He'd hate for her to think that he wasn't interested because he didn't 'show it'. On the other hand, he would die if she rejected him! Her cupid lips were so near his own, as her hand leisurely traversed his back. Slowly, he lifted his own hand and touched the firm flesh of her cheek. Instantly, she moved away, bending to grab her bag and slipping through the gap in the trees without looking at him. Startled, he followed her; she was walking so fast he had to run to keep up.

"You mad?" he asked.

"What for? We can have a bite to eat tomorrow and then see a movie. Pick me up at 7." And she was through the doors of the school and marching towards the classroom before he could gather his thoughts. How strange girls were! Or Sandra, at least. Maybe he should tell her how he longed to kiss her, to caress her, but he didn't know how she'd react. But she'd asked him out on a date. She hadn't said, let's hang out tomorrow. She'd said the word 'date'. She must like him, mustn't she?

∞ When Simon got home he told his mum about his meeting with Premier Smith.

"That's fantastic, Simon. You should phone Chief Tomah and let him know as well; he's helped you so much and this is a major achievement."

But the Chief interrupted Simon in the middle of his first sentence. "Yes, yes, Premier Smith will block the pipeline if he can. Did he say anything about using his influence to pressure neighbour provinces?"

Simon paused. "How did you know he'd be on our side?"

"Me and the Premier go way back. There was a time when jobs were more important to him than the environment. But his son was travelling in Peru when that terrible downpour happened. Caused by high ocean temperatures. Remember?"

Simon didn't.

"Anyway, Smith's son drowned in the flooding. Now the Premier understands what's important."

Simon was silent with shock. After a minute the Chief asked: "Anything else?"

"That's terrible."

"How many plagues did God have to throw at Pharaoh before he released the Jews from slavery?" the Chief said. "Do you think I wouldn't sacrifice my first born if I thought it would save our species? Let fire and flood wipe out our entire country, if it'll bring the rest of the world to its senses!"

Simon held the phone away from his ear as the Chief's voice climbed an octave. Finally the torrent of words eased to a trickle and they exchanged polite goodbyes.

"Whew, what a nut."

"Depends on your point of view," Rakita replied. "China used to call climate change a hoax, until its health bills shot up from heat waves that killed thousands of people. Now the cost of implementing green technology doesn't seem so expensive."

"What are you saying?" Simon said. "That terrible human suffering is necessary to change people's minds? The Chief said he'd sacrifice his first born—would you sacrifice me?"

Toby barked as John's car pulled up outside the house. "Would I sacrifice you to save the world? Ooh, I love philosophical questions like that. Shame we don't have time to discuss it." And Rakita disappeared in the direction of the stairs.

CHAPTER THIRTEEN

THE NEXT DAY Simon discovered that dates and interviews had something in common: they both prevented him from eating breakfast. John blew through the kitchen like a tornado, shoving bits of food into his briefcase and pouring coffee into his portable cup. His alarm hadn't gone off and he was running late, but he noticed his son's listless picking. "What is it with you and breakfasts lately? It's the most important meal of the day."

Simon had to smile to himself. Although his father had figuratively turned his back on 'Alley's crazes' since her desertion, his life was sprinkled with her nuances. She had always pushed him to bring food from home, instead of eating out while he was at work, and she'd always insisted on breakfast. He debated whether to tell his father about his current predicament, reflecting that it was, at least, a non-confrontational subject. John's face relaxed into a smile as he listened. "I was wondering when something would surface between you two. I can feel the sparks shooting in all directions when you're together."

"You can *not*!" Simon said, his face crimson. "I don't even think I want to go on a date with her. It'll screw up our friendship."

"Why should it? Your relationship is just developing in a different direction, that's all. Apart from unfounded fears, is there anything real bothering you?"

"What shall I do with her?" Simon blurted out.

"That young lady has clear ideas of her own. Didn't you say dinner and a movie? Let's look up movies, shall we? And then restaurants close to the movie theatre."

Simon relaxed against the arm of John's chair as he googled movies on his device, grateful that his father was taking this time with him, even though he was late for work. There were several movie options—he'd let Sandra choose—and an Italian restaurant a block away. "Can we google what bus takes us there?"

"You can't go on a date in a bus," his father said. "I'll drive you, and you can get a cab back." John stood up, casually throwing some money on the table, and left the house.

Their electric car was powered by solar panels, but Simon knew his mother wouldn't like him driving back in a cab when a bus was available. But the idea of being driven effortlessly calmed his rioting nerves. *Just this once*, he promised himself, *like indulging in the occasional 10-minute shower after a month of five-minute showers, as a treat that you'll really appreciate.*

He was nervous about whether they'd be able to interact normally during the day, with the rare intimacy of yesterday still lingering and the date looming ... but Sandra took control of that, as she did of most things. She barely talked to him all day, and informed him at lunch that she was going to play some soccer with her girlfriends. "I gotta have other friends, you know. Or what'll I do in the summer when you piss off to your island?"

So he ate in the library by himself, agonizing over what they'd talk about that evening. He idly scrolled through his texts, and then logged onto the website to see how many people had signed up since yesterday, and to check his messages.

Then he saw it. No name. No greeting. Just the words:

Stop your campaign or we'll stop you.

And another:

We need the pipeline! Stupid kids who don't know any better should wizen up.

And another:

Why are you doing this? The pipeline will feed my family.

And:

If the pipeline goes down, you're going down with it.

And:

Stop Your Campaign Or Die.

And others. There were so many. Words pulsating violence. Hatred spewing off the screen.

Or worse than hatred: *My son is disabled. The pipeline will pay for his drugs. Please stop.* Simon felt sick. He slammed his screen shut and sat back in the chair, chafing his stomach to ease the sudden nausea that had sprouted there.

"Are you OK?" the librarian asked.

Simon nodded, staring at his closed screen. So many angry people. Angry with him. He realised he'd been coasting along in a dream, thinking what he was doing was so great and right that anybody reasonable would be on his side. He should have listened more carefully to his father. He was ignorant of other perspectives.

He shuddered; he didn't want to open up his screen again. Ever. He took it gingerly under his arm, as though it were a dangerous beast, and slunk back to the classroom.

Simon couldn't focus. Instead of the actual text, he saw the words in his mind: *You want trouble? Keep it up.* Or: *I've been unemployed for three years. Don't destroy my current livelihood.*

A pair of fingers snapped under his nose. "Hey dreamy-head, don't forget, 7 o'clock."

Simon nodded abstractedly, surprised to discover the strident peal of the end-of-day bell hadn't pierced his fog of anxiety. He ran home, anxious to talk to his mother about it, and found her rushing around the kitchen preparing her quickest meal, spaghetti. Toby kept following her around, plonking himself down on her feet every time she was still, sniffing the air ecstatically.

"Are you in a rush for some reason?" Simon asked.

"Your father left a message on the answering machine saying he'd be home early, so we don't have a lot of time. I'm glad he's the type of man who always announces his arrival. What do you think he'd do if he discovered I was sleeping here all day?" Rakita bent over with a sudden laugh, and then straightened with a frown just as sudden. "Why didn't you tell me about your date?"

Simon shrugged. "It's just Sandra."

"Good thing, because you're too bloody young for a real date."

Simon wasn't sure what a 'real date' might be, if a movie and dinner didn't meet the bill, but he had something more important to communicate to his mother. "Can we take some tea out into the garden?"

"We don't have time, Simon." So he had to prop his device against the cutting board as she chopped onions, garlic and coriander for the pasta sauce. He read the messages out to her in a slow, sonorous voice, as though he were delivering a script on stage. The assumed voice helped to distance him from the pain of the messages. Rakita listened in silence until he had finished, and still the silence stretched on.

Simon was leaning forward, tensely waiting her verdict as she scraped the spices into the bubbling oil and added salt and pepper before handing him the spatula. "Mix it all together with the other veggies."

"O ... kay."

Simon mixed and waited. His mother put pasta in a pot to boil. "Check the pasta every few minutes; you'll know when it's done."

"What, you're leaving?"

"I'm preparing for a quick get-away. Who knows what 'early' means? He could be home any minute."

"But I need you to help me."

"With what, Simon?" Rakita started to take off her apron.

"What am I supposed to do about all those messages?"

Rakita stood beside him and brushed his hair away from his eyes. "You're so young, Simon. Too young, perhaps. This is hard for you. I'll tell you what I'm going to do. I'm going to march right up to the Leaders and demand that they give you a talisman. If you have one of those, you can always escape danger, in any situation. That's what I'm going to do, Simon."

Simon felt close to tears. "But, Mum, all those people hate me! What am I going to do about that?"

"My dear boy, look at me." Rakita gently took his face in both her hands and turned it towards her. "If you discovered that a million people would be pushed under the poverty line if the pipeline fell through, would it make a difference?"

"Wouldn't it?"

"No. A billion wouldn't make a difference. The world has *got* to use other sources of energy—renewable, non-polluting ones."

"Yes?" Simon asked, hoping his mother would come to the point soon.

"There will be lots of employment in the new energy industries, Simon. These people will be fine."

"Really?"

"Of course. People depend on energy and there will always be jobs in the energy sector. But people don't like change. They want what they know, and they only know oil. If you're a shaker and a mover, lots of people will hate you. You mustn't let them affect you."

"What if they try to hurt me?"

"I don't think that's likely. Only an animal would hurt a child, and these are just frightened people, not wicked ones. Meanwhile, I told you I'd talk to the Leaders about a talisman."

Toby started to bark and rushed towards the door. Rakita pecked Simon on the cheek and wished him a pleasant evening with Sandra, and left.

Simon decided not to tell his father about the texts. John might easily go into panic mode and demand that Simon stop his campaign immediately, and at that moment Simon didn't feel strong enough to fight with him. Instead, he took Toby out for a ball-dominated walk, and then sequestered himself upstairs to prepare. First he had a five-minute shower, brushing his hair carefully afterwards and hoping it would fall nicely across his forehead as it dried. He brushed his teeth, and chose a blue turtleneck that accentuated his eyes, and a pair of jeans.

He was ready half an hour before it was time to go, and sat impatiently by the door with his knapsack, his stomach rumbling its objections.

"You look great," his father said as they drove to Sandra's house, "but why lug around a knapsack? Put your wallet in a pocket."

"It's not just for my wallet, Dad. There's metal straws because Sandra likes to drink from a straw and Tupperware, in case we don't finish our meals and want to take them home."

"Who the hell brings Tupperware to a restaurant?"

"Anyone who wants to reduce plastic."

John was silent for a few moments. "I bet Alley's pasta is better than anything you'll eat in the restaurant tonight."

"You always said Mum couldn't cook."

"She never used to, but the meals she's been making lately have been great."

Simon nodded absentmindedly, breathing through his mouth so he couldn't smell his father's breath. He'd make sure not to eat anything with garlic unless Sandra did too. When they arrived at her house, Simon told his father to beep the horn to let her know they were waiting.

"It's a date, Simon," his father said. "You have to go up to the house."

Simon gulped and shot out the door. He should have googled how to behave on a date. He knocked and peered forward nervously as the door opened, but he didn't see anyone until he dropped his eyes. A very small version of Sandra was clinging to the edge of the door, grinning up at him maniacally. Then there was a cough and he lifted his eyes again to perceive Sandra, descending the staircase one step at a time. She was wearing a long, summery dress scattered with flowers. A matching scarf encircled her head, and she had lipstick on. Simon had never seen her look quite like this. Realising her slow descent required a response, he began to clap.

"Oh, do shut up," Sandra said, sweeping past him. A little bit of nervousness sloughed off and washed away. She was obviously going to act like the old Sandra, even if she didn't look like her.

Aware of the need to act like a date, he started to ask where she'd like to sit, but she was sliding into the front seat beside John before the words were out of his mouth. Simon was surprised by their easy chatter —his father seemed more comfortable with Sandra than Rakita was— but then he recalled that his father drove Sandra home several nights a week. He watched to see whether Sandra would start breathing through her mouth, but she didn't.

John dropped them off in front of the restaurant and Simon felt some of his nervousness return as the car retreated. "Mm," Sandra said, taking his arm as though it were the most natural thing in the world. "I love Italian."

They ordered cokes and lasagna and pizza, and Simon showed Sandra the messages he had received on the website. Some creative cursing exited her mouth before he kicked her sharply under the table, reminding her that they were in a public place.

"Sorry. But people like that get on my friggin' tits. Why're they only writing to you, anyway? You should let me do an interview or two, so they'd know there's lots of us."

Simon wisely didn't divulge his opinion about that.

"Let's write back something bad, tell them to bring it on! We'll take on those nasty little shi ..."

"Quiet!" Simon said, glancing around at the other diners. None of them appeared to have noticed her. He leant over the table and told her, sotto voce, what his mother had said.

"What did your father say?"

"I didn't tell him."

When the bill came Simon paid, reflecting that the hardest part of the evening was over, and it hadn't been very hard at all. They'd talked as they'd always talked, naturally and easily. He'd been silly to worry about it. Nevertheless, he was glad the meal was over. Now all they had to do was watch a movie together. Piece of cake.

They bought a huge bag of popcorn to share, which Sandra loaded with fake butter. Simon was stuffed with lasagna, but somehow the bag emptied slowly as the film progressed, balancing precariously between them. It was hard to concentrate on the film. Sandra's leg rested naturally against his, and he was so aware of the length of calf leaning casually against his own that he could barely breathe. He was thankful for the presence of the popcorn, which occupied his arm and removed any worries about whether he was expected to hold her hand. Instead, he began to worry about whether he should kiss her at the end of the evening. He couldn't let her control every intimacy; worst case scenario she'd reject him, but at least she wouldn't think he was a wimp. Maybe he should preface the kiss by telling her that he was terrified her reaction would be to punch him. She'd probably laugh. Yes, that's what he'd do. Simon began to make up pre-kiss speeches in his head, glancing sideways at Sandra's profile. She seemed engrossed by the movie: her lips were parted slightly, a cupid's mouth, with a distinct heart shape in the middle of the upper lip. Yes, he definitely wanted to kiss her. But what if she did something unpredictable? He didn't want to feel embarrassed to see her on Monday at school. Or what if she really liked it and started wanting to be smoochy all the time? Wouldn't that ruin their friendship? Anyway, it was stupid to worry so much. He really only had to make a decision before they parted for the night.

Simon had no idea what the movie was about, but Sandra's occasional chuckle reassured him. Her leg was warm. He felt happy. He let his thigh relax against hers. If only the movie would go on forever.

But all things come to an end and Simon found himself blinking at the credits as Sandra's thigh leapt away from his own and she was standing up, brushing popcorn off her dress. She chattered about the movie as they exited the cinema, loving the plot, dissing the rotten acting of the main heroine, whom they'd obviously chosen for looks alone. "Did you like the movie, Simon?"

"Yeah, it was great." Simon looked up and down the street for a cab. He'd seen people wave down cabs in movies and held his hand at the ready.

"What bit didja like most?"

"Dunno. All of it."

"Did you even watch it?"

"Sure, I did."

"Why didn't you watch the movie, Simon?" And Simon turned his head and saw the familiar mischievous glint, and her cupid's bow. Should he kiss her now?

"Hey, it's that kid."

Simon's eyes turned slowly away from the cupid's bow and looked up into a pair of hairy nostrils. It took him a second to register that the guy was talking to him, despite his proximity. He didn't know him.

"Who do you think you are?"

Simon looked above the hairy nostrils into a pair of blood-shot eyes. The man was in his fifties, a t-shirt fit snugly over his paunch and a bottle of beer dangled from his hand. Beside him, a smaller man with a thin, sharp face hovered, his narrow eyes peering with dislike.

"Are you listening to me?"

"Yes," Simon said.

"So listen good. Back off the pipeline, you got me?" The man lifted a hairy finger and poked it into Simon's shoulder. "You're a stupid kid and you don't know what you're doing. A lot of people's lives depend on that pipeline. If you keep up this shit, you'll be sorry."

Simon nodded vigorously. He was paralysed with fear. He couldn't believe that two men could threaten kids in public like this, without someone stopping to investigate. There were plenty of people walking along the sidewalk on either side of them. Would they intervene if the man hit him? The best thing was to agree with everything the man said and get away from him as quickly as possible.

"You should look up the meaning of the word 'depend'," Sandra said. "Our lives depend on the environment; nobody's life depends on the pipeline. Too bad that people will lose their jobs, but oil jobs are gonna get pretty dicey from now on, so anyone with an ounce of brains would be looking for different work anyways."

Simon's heart sank as he watched a mottled red blazon across Hairy Nostril's cheeks. "Listen, you stupid bitch, we got jobs. There ain't no other jobs that pay like this. Who the hell are you, anyway?"

"I'm a stupid bitch, apparently. Let's go, Simon. If he thinks his job is more important than the environment, what's the point of talking?"

Sandra's words penetrated the thick fog of fear clouding Simon's brain. Perhaps this man simply didn't know the facts? Perhaps, if Simon explained, the man would understand better why Simon was doing what he was doing, and not take it so personally. So ... crazily. They were *adults,* after all. Not like the stupid bullies at school. "Listen to me," he said gently, "I hear your pain. I understand that nothing is more important than your own wellbeing, and that of your kids. And you know what? You're absolutely right. We'd do anything to help our family. But if we continue using fossil fuels, we are destroying the lives of our children, and our children's children. Wars, famine, lack of water ..."

"Shut up," Hairy Nostrils said with a snarl.

"Yeah, Simon," Sandra said, smiling up at him. "I'm surprised he let you go on so long. 'I feel your pain?' Seriously?"

Simon saw Hairy Nostril's hand rise and for a second of dread he thought he was going to hit Sandra. He'd have to protect her (as though that were possible, against two grown men) and then he'd be hit as well. But Hairy Nostril's hand seized a hunk of Simon's sweater and pulled him closer. "This ain't a joke. And it ain't a request, neither.

I'm telling you, drop your campaign right away, or we'll break every bone in your body." A blast of beery breath hit Simon's face and he wanted to retch.

Ratface spoke for the first time. "He's a chicken, letting a girl do his dirty work."

"What dirty work?" Simon said, praying his voice wasn't as weak as it sounded to him. "I'm sorry about your situation, but the whole human race is doomed if we don't stop burning fossil fuels. Every person has to follow their own path, don't they?"

Hairy Nostrils gave him a shove that sent him crashing backwards onto the pavement. In an instant Sandra was beside him, her arm around his shoulders as she tried to propel him upwards again, but Simon was so shocked he couldn't move.

"The little boy wants to follow his own path," Ratface said with a snicker.

Sandra leapt to her feet. "Stop it, you stupid animals."

"That ain't nothing," Hairy Nostrils shouted. "We'll kill you unless you take down your website and stop the campaign. Do you get it? We know where you live. We'll kill you."

Simon looked around in a daze. There was a crowd surrounding them. Not a single person was moving, or saying anything. They were just standing there, gawping. He looked back towards the men and with a great whoosh of relief, he saw that they were moving away. The crowd parted to let them through, but Ratface turned back and pointed at him. "We know where you live."

There was silence for a minute or two as the men receded from view, and then the crowd converged on them and voices swirled around their bent heads. Someone dropped to their knees beside Simon.

"Are you OK?"

"What brutes. Did they hurt you?"

"I've seen that kid before. He's been on TV, trying to stop the pipeline."

"You're too young to get involved with this type of thing. You should back off, like he told you."

"Do you want us to call a doctor?"

"You're really pissing people off. I'd stop while I was ahead, kid."

"Can we do anything for you?"

"A taxi," Sandra said, pulling Simon by his turtleneck until he rose unsteadily to his feet.

Within minutes, they were sitting inside a cab. Simon held out his shaking hands. He couldn't stop trembling. Sandra slid over the seat and put her arms around him. "It's all right, Simon. It'll be OK."

"Will it be OK if I stop the campaign, or if I continue?"

"You can't stop."

"Sure I can."

Sandra looked at him for a moment. Then she patted his knee. "We'll talk about this at school on Monday. Hey, I couldn't believe how all them people just stood around while they was beating you up."

"It's called the bystander effect. I've read about it."

"What, people are too chicken to do anything?"

Simon felt tired and sore all over. He leaned his head against the back of the seat, hoping Sandra would get the message that he didn't really want to talk. "No. People tend to intervene more when they're alone than when they're in a crowd, so it's not fear. It's more like copying what others are doing. If nobody else is interfering, then maybe I shouldn't either."

Sandra had plenty of choice words to say about that, but Simon kept his eyes closed until the cab pulled up at her house. Sandra patted his hand as she got out of the car. "It'll be OK, Simon," she repeated.

When Simon got to his own house Toby bounded towards him, tail fluttering madly. Simon could almost see his ecstatic look change to concern as he got nearer and marvelled—not for the first time—about Toby's astute instincts.

He stumbled through the front door and met his father's expectant grin with tears. Simon told him what had happened in as few words as possible, while he brushed his teeth and got into his pyjamas. John didn't say much, though his face took on a grim expression. "Are you in any pain? Would you like some Tylenol?" he asked.

"No. I just want to sleep."

John gave him a brief hug and Simon climbed into bed. Toby snuggled next to him, as close as he could get. Simon held out his hands and looked at them. Still, they trembled. He didn't want to think about what had happened. Or what he was going to do. He would talk to his mother on Monday. He wished she was here right now. New tears slid down the sides of his cheeks into his pillow. A warm tongue licked them away. His mother would have made him some warm milk and plumped his pillows. His dad was great, but only a Mum knew how to pamper when you felt really rotten.

Just as he was drifting off to sleep, Simon realised that the incident had driven his anxiety over the kiss completely from his mind.

CHAPTER FOURTEEN

SIMON SPENT THE rest of the weekend close to home, throwing balls for Toby and trying not to think too much about what had happened, except that backfired and he spent huge chunks of the weekend obsessing about it.

He had assumed adulthood was a different world from childhood: a more civilised, logical world. A world in which violent, inexplicable behaviour was rare, and if it happened, there were societal mechanisms in place to deal with the perpetrators. But society had stood by and gawped while adults had threatened him. Simon's whole worldview had come crashing down and he felt insecure and anxious.

Did he want to continue with his mission? It was important. He believed in it. But he was getting life threats, it was so crazy! Surely even the island Leaders wouldn't want to put his life at risk? It would be totally unfair for them even to ask that. They never put their own lives at risk. They had their talismans to whisk them away from danger.

He wanted to talk to his mother, but he knew she wouldn't come until Monday, when John returned to work. His father treated him with gentle affection all weekend; they ate dinner together and watched a movie in the evening, but they didn't discuss what had happened. Simon thought his father would bring it up and when he didn't—other than to ask him solicitously if he was OK—Simon followed his lead. Sandra only texted him once, also to ask how he was doing. *Fine,* he replied.

And that was it. The weekend had never seemed so long.

He wanted his mother.

It was a relief when Monday rolled around. His father looked grim when he came down to pour coffee into a travel cup and grab a piece of toast. Before he left for work, he propped an envelope between the salt and pepper shakers. The name "Alley" was written in block letters on the front.

"What's that for?" Simon asked.

"I want to talk to your mother."

That makes two of us, Simon thought. "What about?"

"What do you think?" And his father strode through the door without glancing back.

Simon was relieved. His parents cared. They would join forces to protect him, as parents should.

∞ If his father's weekend-long silence had been unhelpful, the fact that Sandra spent most of Monday rehashing and dwelling on the event was even worse. She raked over every detail during lunch, embellishing and analysing. He realised she was excited by the whole thing, was even relishing it, in retrospect. "Could you just shut up about it?" he'd eventually said. Then she'd been affronted and gone off in a huff, only to return five minutes later. He'd refused to acknowledge her return, keeping his eyes trained on his book, but when he felt her hands on her shoulders the usual crazy jolt ricocheted throughout his body.

"Simon," she whispered, her lips so close that his hair trembled with her breath.

"What?"

"Let's go out again this Friday."

"Yeah, right."

She blew gently against his ear and he could feel his entire neck blush.

"C'mon Simon. We can't let them bullies freak us out. We'll come prepared this time ..."

Simon twisted his head to stare at her in disbelief, blushing neck forgotten, as she outlined her plan to attach a baseball bat to her back with a belt, under her coat. Finally, he interrupted her in mid-flow. "I love your ingenuity, but save it for a better cause. There's no way I'm going downtown again. Ever."

"Awww, Si," Sandra simpered, perching precariously on the edge of the table and leaning against his knee. "We gotta face our demons. Nothin' happened, really. Don'tcha wanna go out with me again?"

He had to smile at her leering face as she batted her eyelashes furiously. "Sure I do. Sometime."

"Your best friend's inviting you on a date and you're refusin' her?"

"I could make you a meal and we could watch a movie at my house. Dad would give us privacy. It'd be just as nice and a lot cheaper."

"It's not the same," Sandra said with a pout, collapsing in a nearby chair and folding her arms crossly. "I'm at your house every friggin' day anyway, how's that a date? D'ya think I'm gonna dress so pretty just to go to your house?"

Simon shrugged and tried to focus on his book. The silence lengthened as he battled the desire to glance up to see what Sandra was doing. He read the same two lines about fifty times and was just about to risk a peek when her hand slammed down on top of the page.

"I got it!" she announced.

"I'm glad you finally get it."

She leaned over, pushing her face within an inch of his. "We won't go downtown."

"Correct."

"We'll go the opposite direction, into the country."

"Good movies showing in the country, are there?"

Sandra waved her finger playfully under his nose. "Funny boy. There's Fred's Bistro in Woodsville, that's a decent restaurant."

"That's the only restaurant." Even as Simon scoffed, he considered the idea. Woodsville was a small town of about 300 people with one main street, 20 minutes from their suburb in the opposite direction than the city. Fewer people in the country. Probably nobody would know him. Even if they did, everyone knew that cities were way more violent than the country.

"So? It's still good; got the best nachos I've ever had. They load it with stuff."

"When were you there?"

"We go every summer. While you're pissin' about swimming and milking goats we have a couple trips to stupid Woodsville to swim in the lake and eat at Fred's."

"Maybe," Simon said.

Sandra threw herself against him and wrapped her arms around him so precipitately that his chair toppled backwards and they lay in a heap on the ground, laughing helplessly. The librarian wasn't amused, and banned them from the library for the rest of the day.

∞ When Simon got home Rakita was waiting for him, holding John's note in her hand, pale with anxiety. Her palpable tension surprised him for a minute, and he realised how profoundly Sandra's approach to the incident had impacted his own. He had spent the weekend drenched in anxiety, probably looking much like his mother did now. But Sandra's attitude had shifted his own, and the incident seemed like an isolated, crazy, unpleasantness. Nevertheless, Simon hugged his mother in relief. She wouldn't let him speak until they were sitting in their favourite chairs with a pot of tea between them. Then she made him tell her every detail, slowly, while she listened intently. Toby sat between them, gazing at their faces and ignoring his ball, as though he sensed the significance of their conversation.

There was a short silence when Simon had finished. Rakita sipped her tea. "I am so sorry this is happening to you, Simon. I did talk to the Leaders about your talisman."

"Are they giving me one?"

She shook her head.

"They want me to do all this stuff, I'm supposed to play this big role to help save the world, and they won't lift a finger to keep me safe? Can you explain the logic of that, Mum?"

"I'm not sure, Simon, but I can hazard a guess. When kids your age get their talismans, it often takes over their lives for a while. It opens up so many new possibilities and it's so exciting. I guess the Leaders think you're doing a fine job, and they view the talisman as an unnecessary distraction at this point in your life. They didn't think there was any real danger, but I will certainly go back to them with this new information."

Simon stared at his mother anxiously. She put her hand over his. "Try not to worry so much."

"This is awful, Mum. I hardly dare go on my website, I'm so freaked out by the messages."

Rakita sighed. "This is a complex situation and we have to think about it carefully from all angles. Meanwhile, you need to keep calm and continue your work ..."

Simon raised incredulous eyes and she hurried on, "... your work will take your mind off worrying. You know you're doing the right thing, don't you Simon? Change is hard and people get really scared when they think their livelihood is threatened. They're bashing back, it's bound to happen, but it doesn't change a thing. This is a crisis and we have to do everything we can. Do you still agree with this?"

Simon nodded without hesitation. His certainty surprised him; he remembered how his days used to revolve around how to thwart the bullies at school. This time, he wasn't reacting to something being done to him—this time, he was the one pulling the strings and making the decisions. It was different, and it was all because of the talisman. So much had changed since it had come into his life—even though he didn't actually have one!

"Would it help if you didn't read the nasty messages?"

"I have to," he replied in a small voice.

"Then can I ask you not to read them alone? Only with me or with Sandra?"

Simon thought of Sandra's energy, her fearlessness; she would read them differently, he was sure, and help him to see them differently in the process. He nodded again.

Rakita patted his hand. "Good. Now your father is coming. Go upstairs and do your homework; it's best I talk to him alone."

"Why?"

Rakita looked at him intently. "He doesn't see how important this is, does he? Naturally he's going to be worried and want you to quit. I don't want him to weaken your resolve."

Simon wasn't sure what he wanted, but he did as his mother requested.

As the week chugged along, Simon's certainty that he must continue grew. They began their after-school workday with a cup of tea under the oak, while Sandra read out all the messages on the website, lingering on the positive messages, zooming through the sad ones so quickly Simon could barely register their content, and acting out the nasty messages, adopting a variety of funny voices to reduce their impact. "You deserve to diiiieeee," she wailed in a high falsetto, wielding an imaginary hang rope to lynch him with. This strategy seemed to work; Rakita and Simon were often in stitches by the end of the messages. "You should be an actress," Rakita said, gasping with laughter. Simon felt quite proud of Sandra.

Friday rolled around and Simon didn't contradict Sandra's assumption that they had a date. This time, he insisted on taking the bus.

"It only goes to Woodsville once an hour," John had complained, until Simon had promised to get a taxi home if the timing didn't work out, though he had no intention of doing that if he could avoid it.

"You don't mind taking the bus, do you?" he asked Sandra, who was dressed in her usual jeans, though she'd donned a turquoise sweater with matching studs in her ears and nose.

"It'd be fancier in a taxi," she said.

"Thinking about every choice through the lens of the climate crisis isn't fun, but it's worth it, no? To minimize our impact as much as we can so we can *breathe* later on ..."

"Shut up Simon, we're on a date for God's sake, give it a rest," Sandra said.

"Bus today, breathe tomorrow. Doesn't sound so bad, suddenly, does it?"

Sandra pinched his leg viciously, and he shut up.

The dinner was actually pretty good. They started with a plate of nachos, which lived up to its promise and arrived smothered with every imaginable topping. Unfortunately, the nachos filled them up so much that they couldn't finish their main courses, even though both Simon's veggie burger and Sandra's pasta were delicious.

"We'll take it home," Sandra said, raising her arm to call the waiter.

"Wait," Simon said, and opened his knapsack to produce a plastic container. "They can put the food in that."

Sandra stared at him. "That's weird."

"It saves using an additional plastic container from the restaurant, doesn't it?"

Sandra gave an impatient shrug and Simon smiled. He knew she ridiculed him and then went home and forced her whole family to copy him.

"What're ya smiling for?"

"Remember our argument about energy? You thought we could just unplug from fossil fuels and plug into renewable energy sources and carry on, business as usual. But I was saying we had to reduce our energy use, because solar and wind turbines don't give us the same energy return ..."

Sandra flicked a crumb off the table at him. "Nobody's ever goin' to like you if you blather on all the friggin' time about this crap."

Simon looked pointedly at her watch, which she'd bought—along with other things like solar-powered lights—after he'd explained that it wasn't enough to switch to renewables; humans had to *reduce* their energy consumption. She'd been so mad when he pointed out that even computer use had to be examined under the climate crisis lens. "Isn't there ANYTHING I can do without feeling guilty?" she'd screamed at him.

"Don't feel guilty about anything, just think about what you're doing," he'd replied.

So he grinned at her over the table. "You called me a 'frigging PARROT' when I told you to cut down mindless computer use. Your favourite insult." He reached out and pulled her back to her seat as she scrambled ungracefully out of her chair.

She whacked his hand away. "If we have to sit on that stinking bus for an hour I wanna go now."

"We have 20 minutes until it comes; it's cold outside."

Sandra rummaged in her purse and held up a vape triumphantly. "I want my after-dinner smoke."

Simon stared at her in disbelief. "What is the point …"

"Piss off, Parrot," Sandra snapped and lurched out of her seat. Simon followed her resignedly out the door.

They stood shivering under the roof of the bus shelter while Simon admired her smoke rings and thought about how to retrieve an element of romance. Telling her it was illegal to smoke under the bus shelter probably wouldn't do the trick; in any case they were alone on the side of a narrow stretch of road.

Finally headlights appeared and Simon strained his eyes in the dark, hoping it was the bus. But it was a beat-up old car, careening along the road at breakneck speed. Simon caught a glimpse of four young faces turned in their direction before it shot by, closely followed by another, and then another. A whole convoy of cars seemed to be racing by, filled with screaming, laughing teenagers. The fourth car slowed down as it passed so the occupants could stare at them. Simon could see beer bottles and cigarettes changing hands. "That's so dangerous," he muttered.

"Lighten up," Sandra replied, raising her vape in a toast as they passed.

"Where are they all going, anyway?" Simon asked as the fifth car slowed to stare.

"Joy-riding, prob'ly. Having fun, like normal people. Not like you."

Simon felt hurt. She seemed to be implying that their evening hadn't been fun. "Stupid, mindless people. Not even going anywhere, just spewing poison into the atmosphere for no reason."

"I know everything you're gonna say before you say it, Parrot. It's so friggin' boring."

Simon felt bad. Why didn't the evening feel like a success? Where had he gone wrong? Was he talking too much about the environment and becoming a bore? He strove to think what to say to make things better, wracking his brains for a joke. "Knock, knock," he started, but then he saw another string of cars heading their way from the opposite direction and irritation swamped him again. He couldn't help it; the inability of the human race to modify their behaviour to save themselves was beyond his comprehension. The first car skidded to a stop opposite them. Four teenagers got out, looking right at him. The next car stopped behind it and the half-drunk occupants spilled onto the road, marching across without looking in either direction. Simon glanced at Sandra nervously; she was still pulling on her vape, squinting at the newcomers through a screen of smoke. Two more cars stopped; within minutes about 14 kids surrounded them. Fear blossomed in Simon's chest and knocked against his ribs, like a bird beating its wings fruitlessly against the bars of a cage. The teens were totally silent, staring right at Simon. Why weren't they saying anything? He didn't dare glance at Sandra. He didn't even dare to swallow, although saliva was building at the back of his throat. He didn't dare glance at his watch to see how much longer until the bus came. If it came on time. Please make it come on time. He stared up into the eyes of the boy directly in front of him, a big lad with unkempt black hair and dark, unsmiling eyes. The silence seemed to stretch on forever.

"Hey," Sandra said eventually. If Simon hadn't been so frightened, he would have smiled. The big boy totally ignored her. Simon hoped she wouldn't do something stupid, like ask if he was deaf or something. Typical Sandra, but any comment might be fatal. If they kept staring like this long enough, the bus would come. He just needed to hold the big kid's eyes as long as possible.

The boy's eyes moved. They scanned up and down Simon's body with an air of contempt and swivelled to the girl standing next to him. Simon allowed his own eyes to turn in unison, almost in relief. The girl had a huge pony tail sprouting from the top of her head, and her thick brown hair flowed over her shoulders. She had slathered makeup on an otherwise attractive face; Simon noted that she seemed to have removed her eyebrows and replaced them with a thick pencil wedge. She chewed gum rigorously and incessantly.

"This him?" the boy asked.

She nodded, without pausing her mastication.

The bird of fear in Simon's chest flung itself violently against the bars of his ribcage.

The boy's eyes veered slowly back to Simon and he took a step forward, so close that Simon felt his breath on his face. It made him feel slightly sick. It made the bird retch.

"Ya like fucking up people's lives, asshole?" the boy asked.

Simon's mouth was so dry his voice came out in a croak. "What do you mean?"

Without warning, the boy's arm shot out and shoved Simon, who bashed against the back wall of the bus shelter and rebounded against the boy's arm, which promptly shoved him again. He was more prepared this time and stayed plastered against the wall. The bird crouched down in his stomach, praying that the bus would come.

"Hey!" Sandra shouted.

"Shut the fuck up," Eyebrows said, "unless you want some too."

Be brave, Simon thought to himself. *Don't piss your pants. In five minutes this'll be over.*

They made a half-circle around him, cutting Sandra out. She squawked in indignation and from the periphery of his vision he saw a scuffle break out, but he couldn't turn to look or focus on anything except keeping upright, because they started to shove him from one to another, like he was a ball in some convoluted gym game at school. His head jerked as they propelled him back and forth, his whole mind focussed on keeping on his feet, as though his life depended on it, as indeed it might. Fear seemed to disappear, replaced by the instinct to survive. Then a fist crashed into his face and pain detonated in his brain and there was blood in his mouth and he couldn't see and there were more fists but no more pain, bizarrely, his mind wasn't working, it seemed to be frozen like the bird in his chest, and there was blood in his eyes and he couldn't see anything and didn't know where the punches were coming from and couldn't brace against them and so he went down, banging hard into the freezing, unyielding sidewalk until he curled up like a newborn infant, protecting his head and his chest from the punches and kicks, and the bars of his ribcage broke open and the bird flew from its endangered prison and perched on the roof of the bus shelter above their heads, and Simon could see his foetus-form below, hemmed in by flailing bodies, how small and insignificant it looked, wrapped like a tight package with its arms in front of the face and around the head and from somewhere far off he heard police sirens and Sandra shouting but he couldn't make out the words and then the bird fell asleep and he saw no more and heard no more and knew no more.

CHAPTER FIFTEEN

SIMON WAS IN bed. Toby snuggled so close to one side that he was practically on top of him and his mother lay smack-dab against him on the other side, an arm thrown over her face. There were books and sweets scattered over his night table and a tray with the remains of his breakfast on the floor beside his bed. After he'd been discharged from the hospital with broken ribs, a broken nose and a fractured arm, he'd been treated like royalty. He'd yearned for his mother all weekend, even though his father had pampered and spoiled. There had been no way to contact her and his father had initially refused to go to work on Monday morning. Of course, John had no idea what Rakita's habits were. He didn't know that she slept in the vicinity during the day in order to be there every afternoon for her son. Simon assured him she would be there to look after him during the day and promised he would phone the minute Rakita arrived, but John still hesitated, because Simon wouldn't reveal why he was so sure Rakita would show up. Simon sensed his mother wouldn't want John to know she was there all day. It was only when Simon threatened to rise from his sickbed to manhandle his father out the door, that John reluctantly departed. Within ten minutes Rakita had arrived and Simon told her the whole story as she sat and wept. Then she held him for a long time, hugging him as if she was adrift in the open sea and he was a life-raft.

"What kind of mother am I, Simon? This can never happen again."

Simon giggled. For some inexplicable reason, even though this incident had been so violent, he didn't *feel* as fearful as the first time. It was almost as if he'd been terrified by the idea of being beaten up, but now he'd experienced the reality it wasn't so frightening. He wondered constantly at the absence of actual pain during the beating, so blessed but unappreciated at the time, because all his instincts had been on survival and the lack of pain hadn't registered. Of course there had been pain afterwards, but the doctors had been generous with pain-killers and his father's attention—especially in the form of edible treats and unlimited screen time—did much to alleviate the physical discomfort.

"How could I not have sensed you were in trouble? I can't believe I wasn't there for you."

"Mum, we're practically in the middle of the 21st century. Communication isn't a problem. Just get a cell phone like everyone else!"

"I'll buy a phone today," Rakita said. "You're right, it's luddite and stupid, especially when you're doing dangerous work. I can't just disappear every weekend! So if I have to go shopping anyway ..." The spasm of revulsion that involuntarily crossed her face amused Simon greatly, "... I'd like to get something for Sandra. Sounds like she saved the day."

Sandra had regaled him with the story of her 'saviour' status twice that weekend already, although she called it 'saving his ass'. The second telling contained considerably more details of courage and quick-thinking than the first telling, and Simon wasn't entirely sure what was fact and what was embellishment, but she had apparently fought valiantly at his side until he went down, whereupon she abandoned the fight—stifling all her natural instincts to do so—and fled to dial 911.

"She'd be pleased," Simon told his mother. He suddenly remembered the folded note John had left for his mother with the word "Alley" scrawled across it the week before, and asked his mother about it.

She produced the note from her pocket and Simon unfolded it and read: 'I am sure Simon will tell you what happened, if he hasn't already. Life threats and violence are serious. We need to talk.' That was all.

An almost imperceptible tightening rippled across Rakita's shoulders as she nodded and took the note, shoving it back in her pocket. "I had been planning to talk to your father today in any case."

Simon didn't ask why she'd waited a week. "Did you see the Leaders about giving me a talisman?" he whispered.

"Yes."

Simon could see from her face that no talisman was forthcoming. The image of Hairy Nostrils and Ratface danced across his vision and a smidgen of fear returned. "Why?"

"They are worried that the magic of the talisman will consume you, even more than most kids when they first receive it, because you didn't grow up with it."

"So they'd rather put me in danger, than risk me slacking off ..."

Rakita grasped both his hands and shook them. "Simon, they *know* nothing terrible happens to you, right? They know you're going to be all right. Do you think I wouldn't give you my own talisman this minute, if I thought your life was at risk?"

"They can't see *inside* my head, can they? Maybe I'll be psychologically damaged ..."

"I know this is hard. So much to ask from such a young person. I wish this burden hadn't fallen on you. But it has." Rakita kissed his hands, one by one. "Your father will also object and we'll have a long talk about this tonight. During the day, I want you to think about things very carefully. Of course it is your choice, and I will support you in whatever choice you make. Remember that, Simon. You decide." Rakita got to her feet. "Now I'm going to prepare a smoothie."

∞ After a delicious fruit smoothie, Rakita tried to wash those bits of him that weren't covered in plaster. "I'm not an invalid, Mum. I can totally wash myself," he said, embarrassed. "Isn't this your time for sleeping? Aren't you tired?"

In truth, he was rather interested to find out where she slept. He'd imagined her sleeping in the bedroom, in her bed opposite the antique wardrobe, but he didn't actually know.

"I have to buy the cell phone."

"Aren't you tired?"

"I can't go shopping and take care of you and sleep simultaneously, can I?"

"I don't really need anything. Dad's given me unlimited screen time while I'm sick."

Simon half-expected furious objections, but none were forthcoming.

At last his mother agreed to buy a cell phone in the evening, after she had talked with John. "Perhaps he'll even have an old one that he doesn't need anymore," she said, her face lighting up. "I will catch a couple of hours sleep, if you're sure you don't need me."

"Ok, Mum. Will I be able to reach you if I need you?" he asked, dying to know where she was headed.

She looked at him in surprise. "I thought you knew. I've made a little nest for myself in the basement of John's workshop."

Simon's face blanched. "No! In that horrible place with all the spiders?"

"I like spiders," Rakita said, laughing. She put the landline phone by his bed, borrowed his cell in case he needed to contact her, and disappeared.

∞ In the late afternoon Rakita brought Simon some lunch, and announced she was going downstairs to make supper. Simon had just finished his book and was sick of video games and decided he needed a change of scenery, though he was wise enough not to enlighten Rakita. Intermittently throughout the day, he'd tried to think about what he *wanted*, but it seemed to change from moment to moment. He loved the excitement and purpose of his new life. Now that he understood the climate crisis more deeply, he realised that inaction might well lead to despair. Doing something created hope. He *knew* he was doing the right thing. The world *had* to stop burning fossil fuels, so stopping new pipelines was a no-brainer. The very survival of the human race might depend on it. But ... he remembered the fury on the faces of Ratface and Hairy Nostrils. It had been horrible.

He didn't know what to do.

But he knew he'd go mad if he didn't get out of this bed. Even Toby had abandoned him from boredom.

Simon waited until he was sure Rakita would be immersed in cooking, and then quietly slid off the bed. Moving was painful, but if he walked slowly and carefully it was manageable. It was surprising how weak he felt. Hobbling downstairs, he slipped into a chair at the kitchen table so quietly that Rakita, busily cutting veggies for chicken soup, didn't hear him. When she turned around she shrieked in surprise, immediately launching a heated argument about the need to rest to heal. But just like possession is nine-tenths of the law, so the fact that he was already downstairs weakened her argument that he shouldn't be out of bed. In the end she compromised by hemming him in with cushions and covering him with a blanket. They chatted companionably until Toby gave a short bark and ran towards the doorway. A minute later John's car pulled into the drive. Rakita rushed about, preparing the indispensable tea and reducing the heat on the boiling veggies and chicken to let it simmer. Simon noticed that her hands were trembling.

When John came in they were both sitting at the kitchen table, hands folded before them, like obedient children at school. Toby laid his head on Simon's lap under the table, his gaze riveted upwards. John stood beside Rakita's chair, staring down at her face. "You look well," he finally said.

"Thank you. Why don't you take a seat so we can talk? The tea is ready."

"Let me hug you."

Rakita looked down at her folded hands, silently.

"You know I am in pain," John said. "You've condemned me to misery for the rest of my life. Let me hold you. Let me be happy for a few minutes."

Rakita got up without a word and they embraced. After a minute Simon saw his mother try to move away, but John gathered her closer, straining her against his breast, and she put her arms around his neck and hugged him back. They hugged for a long time and Simon had to turn his head away, because he saw in his father's rigid, ecstatic form the same feeling he had when he held Sandra.

Eventually, with infinite tenderness, Rakita extricated herself from John's arms. They sat down and took their mugs of tea, and began to talk. Simon leaned back and listened to the conversation go back and forth. His father's doubts and worries, his mother's attempts to explain the role that her people felt Simon had to play. "It's not a question of doing this or not, John. You do understand that we can see into the future? We're not making things up. Simon has to do this."

Simon knitted his brows. He didn't have to do anything. It was his choice.

"It's ridiculous, attaching so much importance to one kid just because he's ... an aberration, or whatever. How does that make sense?"

"You're right; maybe he's just a kid and this is a massive, unfair burden. So what? If he's making any difference at all—and I think we both have to agree that he is—then he's got to continue. We've got to throw everything we can at this, John. It's like a war; except if we lose, everybody loses."

"This is his life we're talking about! The life of our son!"

Simon looked from one parent to the other. He realized he was feeling fear.

"It's not his life, John. I can assure you that our son lives to a good, old age ..."

"How do I know that you're not a fanatic, sacrificing my kid ..."

As John spoke, Simon jumped to his feet and stared at his mother.

He'd had enough of his parents quibbling. He had a voice too. "This is my choice and I'm trying to listen to both of you. Mother, are you saying I just continue on as though nothing has happened?"

"Yes," Rakita said, "and no. We're aware of this now. We're going to make sure nothing happens to you."

"They know where I live," Simon said, and his voice sounded high and strange. "How are you going to protect me, exactly? You haven't even managed to get me a talisman."

"I know you're frightened—"

"You don't know what I feel."

Simon felt like crying and was annoyed by his own weakness. He sank back into his chair. "You're right. I am so frightened, Mum."

"Oh, Simon." She got up and leaned over his chair to hug him. "I won't let anything terrible happen to you."

"Something terrible already has!"

"I know, but now we realise the threat we can deal with it. No more traipsing about at nighttime, for example. No more …"

Simon took a deep breath as his mother listed safety precautions. These were his parents. They were on his side. They were rational, thinking humans, not like those idiots that seemed to rule the streets on Fridays, both in town and in the country. This thought gave him a surge of hope. He only needed to communicate clearly and they would understand; then maybe they could guide him to the right decision. "Yes, I'm frightened. Those adults last week behaved just like the bullies at school, and I didn't know that could happen. It changed things for me. I know now that there are no dividing lines between adult and child, black or white, man or woman. The only dividing line is between people who think, and people who don't. But Mum, are there more thinkers than idiots in the world?"

"We have to believe that most people are rational, only they are ignorant about the extent of the danger, because they can't see into the future like we can."

Simon looked towards his father. "Do you think so too, Dad? Rational ignoramuses are the majority?"

"No. Clearly, from the state of the world, most people are *not* rational."

Rakita threw her hands in the air. "Great. You're right, people are all idiots. So let's give up, because what's the point?"

John put his hand over hers. "We are already seeing increases in storms, wildfires, and floods. The environment itself will convince the idiots and the whole world will join forces to fight this crisis, just like they did with COVID." He squeezed her hand as she opened her mouth to expostulate. "Together with increased knowledge, spread by people like you."

"If you really think that, why don't you spread the word a bit yourself?" Simon asked.

"Yes, yes," John mumbled, gazing into his wife's face. "If Alley will stay with me, I will do anything to support your cause."

Rakita flushed with a mixture of annoyance and pity. "Support cannot be offered for reasons like that. Try to think rationally John, and show your son which side of the dividing line you're on, despite your strong emotions for me. What if everybody's support was dependent on the actions of somebody else?"

"Like the bystander effect," Simon said. "But even if it is the behaviour of others that makes people act, rather than their own rationale, it still boils down to spreading awareness to a critical mass."

Rakita sat back in her seat and began to stretch her arms across her chest. "Yes darling, it boils down to the fact that you must continue."

A brand new idea sprouted in Simon's mind. "So if my aim is to help the critical mass to understand this issue, I don't have to campaign on the website about the pipeline. My website needs to focus on logic. I need to produce articles filled with verifiable facts that paint a picture of the future."

There was a short silence, as Simon gazed around the table with shining eyes, galvanized by this wonderful new idea. He'd avoid violence, while still fighting the good fight! It was perfect!

"You can fill your website with the most rational, persuasive pieces, but it won't get you on the news," Rakita said. "Only controversy at the local level gets you on the news. And if you're not on the news, nobody is going to read your wonderful pieces, darling."

Simon banged his mug on the table. Luckily it was almost empty. "So you're saying the only way I can fight this fight is to piss people off? Great. The First Nation want to organize a rally against the pipeline. I was going to tell them that I didn't want to be involved, but instead I'll just leap into the thick of it, right? And if anything goes wrong, you can always console yourself with the fact that you *tried* to get me a talisman."

Rakita reached for his hand across the table, but he pulled away. She sighed. "Like I said, we are going to do things more carefully now. You can help to organize the rally and spread the word, but I don't think you should hold a prominent role at the rally itself. Don't agree to speak. If you decide to attend, you should wear a disguise. As for the talisman, I'm working on it."

Simon glanced at his father. Now would be the time for him to voice his many reservations about the cause. But John continued to drink in his mother's face, as though she sported a halo.

"I'm frightened!" he yelled at them.

Rakita came around the table and tried to hold him, but again he pulled away. "I'm so sorry Simon, but this is the biggest enemy the world has ever seen. We need as many soldiers as we can get, to fight it."

"Child soldiers?"

"Yes, every child should know what they can do as individuals."

"And risk their lives?"

"No. But you're not every child, Simon."

"My own mother is telling me to risk my life?"

"I will give you another tidbit of information, even though I'm not supposed to. Listen carefully." Rakita leaned over to look directly in his eyes. "For all time-travellers, the future remained bleak until a certain Thursday last year, after which there was a sudden change in what they saw in the future. I told you I also saw a change. You know what happened on that day?"

Simon strived for utter sarcasm. "Sure, just let me know which Thursday you mean. I remember every Thursday from last year, miraculously ..."

Rakita interrupted him. "That Thursday was the day you first time-travelled, by mistake, because you wanted to be older so you wouldn't be bullied anymore." She paused for effect, but Simon just gaped at her. "Do you understand?"

For a second, Simon caught a glimmer of something. But how? It was impossible. "I'm not brave or strong," he said, thinking of Sandra. "I don't know what I'm supposed to do."

"Just what you're doing," Rakita said, holding her arms wide. "Just what you're doing, my darling."

And this time, he let her enfold him in her arms.

∞ For a few days, Simon was besieged by waves of resentment, anger and fear, which poured over his mother during every visit. Rakita maintained a no-nonsense, calm attitude throughout his tirades, even when his negativity was so overpowering that even Sandra couldn't embellish.

But it was uncertainty at the root of the fear. "I'm just an ordinary kid. I can't do this."

"What, chop veggies?" quipped Sandra. They were perched on stools in the kitchen, preparing a salad while Rakita cooked rice and beans by the stove.

But Simon wasn't in the mood for humour. "No. Die."

Sandra peered at him. "You don't look dead to me."

"No, they just smashed up my body this time. Lucky me."

Rakita left the stove and stood before Simon, looking intently into his face. "Do you have any idea how much you've grown since you discovered the talisman?"

Simon looked at her in surprise. "What do you mean?"

"Before the talisman, your main preoccupation was how to escape the bullies. Now, you are preoccupied with how to contribute to the fight against the climate crisis. You are not reacting to a problem, you are creating a solution, even though that creates other problems. You are in control. Don't you see the difference?"

Simon remembered thinking the exact same thing himself.

"Yeah, you have changed." Now it was Sandra's turn. "You ain't so scared all the time. I was pretty impressed by how you stood up to them fighters. You looked them right in the eye."

But he had been scared! Yet, at the same time, he hadn't been overwhelmed by his fear. It was almost like he'd been detached from his fear, watching it from above, like a little bird.

It was almost as if he'd been terrified by the idea of being beaten up, but now he'd experienced the reality it wasn't so frightening.

Was this because of the talisman?

Rakita was slipping the chain of the talisman over her head. She held it out to him. "I think you need a little talisman-boost right now. You're feeling dispirited and uncertain. Take a little trip; see if it makes you feel better."

Simon lifted his hand to grasp the talisman but his mother didn't let go of the chain. "If you could choose what you were going to get from this trip, what would it be?"

Simon looked at the engraving of the tree. His eyes sought the mother bird returning to her babies. He thought of how fearful he still was, despite what his mother and Sandra said. How hard it was to continue, sometimes. "I guess I'd want to see something that would help me to move forward," he said.

His mother nodded and released the chain. The weight of the talisman felt pleasant in the palm of his hand. His heart started to beat in excitement. He was going to time travel!

∞ Rakita tripped off towards the workshop as soon as the food was done, and John returned a few minutes later. He drove Sandra home and then they ate. Simon was on tenterhooks to finish the meal and disappear into his room. What year should he choose? Maybe he should just hold the talisman and focus. Perhaps he would sense what year to choose.

"You're preoccupied today," his father said.

Simon smiled as he gathered up the plates. "I'm feeling better about stuff."

"I hope that doesn't mean you're going to continue this foolhardy work. Next time they might kill you!"

This was so close to what Simon felt in his worst moments that he winced. As soon as he could, he escaped into his room. Toby plastered himself to his heels; he hoped the mutt wouldn't bark when he disappeared.

Simon drew the chain over his neck and lay on his bed, holding the talisman in his hand. He emptied his mind of all thoughts, focussing intently on the feel of the round, metal disc in his hand. Tracing every branch of that crazy apple tree with his eyes.

I wish I was 30.

∞ Simon was behind a curtain on a balcony, overlooking a crowd so vast that it spread like a rippling sea as far as the eye could see. He could hear voices on the other side of the curtain. He listened to their conversation, assuming one of the voices would be his 30-year old self. But he couldn't hear his own voice.

"Je-sus. Look at all those people. There's never been a protest this big in the whole history of Canada. How many do you thinks down there, Mary?"

Yes, Simon could see it was a protest now; many of the people held signs. He looked down and squinted. CHANGE NOW, read one. NO MORE DELAY.

"Too many for the police to control, that's for sure."

Why couldn't he hear himself? Wasn't he always supposed to land near his present-day self when he time travelled? Simon tried to peek through the curtain. A middle-aged, overweight couple leaned over the balcony rails, gawking at the crowd below.

"I hope the police are OK. We should phone your brother." The man took a long drink from a bottle of beer in his hand.

The woman fished an iPhone out of her pocket and poked it with her finger. "Bill? What's going on down there? Are you OK?"

She swivelled the phone away from her mouth and whispered to her beer-swigging partner, "Bill says with so many people they just gotta watch. Nothing they can do, if the crowd decides to go crazy. But he says they're not violent."

The woman spoke into the iPhone. "I know you gotta go. Stay safe."

The man burped. "The PM can't ignore this. Looks like Simon Scendel is going to get his way, finally."

Simon jumped when he heard his name. What did they mean, he was going to 'get his way, finally'? He looked at the crowd below more intently, reading the signs. 100% RENEWABLES TODAY. HIGHER CARBON TAXES. TIME HAS RUN OUT.

Where was he? 2037. It looked like they were protesting that change was taking too long.

"You can't be protesting when the government is doing what it promised," the woman said. "They promised to complete the switchover from oil to renewables by 2050, and they're sticking to that."

The man took a swig from the bottle of beer that dangled from his hand. "The protesters want to speed up the process. They say the quality of life for the next generation depends on how quick we stop polluting."

Simon frowned. It was true; every reduction in green house gas reductions had a direct impact on the temperature, which had a direct impact on air quality—not to mention sea level rise, fires, droughts, food supplies and climate refugee numbers. Everything that would plague his middle age and the lives of his children. It was a no-brainer to invest everything in the transition away from polluting sources of energy and time was of the essence. Simon gazed down at the massive crowd. It looked like a lot of people wanted the government to move more quickly.

"Can you see Simon Scendel?" the woman asked.

"He's probably at the front, directing the whole thing."

Simon peered towards the front of the crowd. He wasn't sure the beginning was in sight—the crowd surged as far as the eye could see in every direction. Suddenly a voice rang out from loudspeakers placed in strategic positions along the length of the crowd.

His voice.

"Friends, we are gathered here together to insist that our government listens to our plea for Change Now. Nature is angry. Time has run out. I want my children to have reasonable lives. Do you want the same?"

A cry undulated amongst the crowd. Yes, they wanted the same.

"We are going to march on Parliament Hill and demand Change Now, for the sake of our children. We are willing to cut down our meat intake, our air travel, our consumerism. We will retrofit our houses and save for electric cars. But our government must do its bit. Invest in efficient buildings and transport—now. Make big polluters pay high carbon taxes to fund investment in carbon renewal technologies—now!"

The crowd screamed its approbation and moved further down the street. He was in Ottawa, and they were marching on Parliament Hill. Simon felt energy and excitement course through his veins. There was something so thrilling, so powerful, about a huge crowd.

"How'd he get this many people to follow him?" the man asked.

"He believes it so strong. He got beaten up again and again, but he just kept on going, even when he was a kid. Like that movie we seen when we was young."

"Yeah." The man reached to the floor and came up with a fistful of chips. Simon saw there were several bowls of different types of chips on the floor. "What movie?"

"The one about that Indian guy, Gandhi. Remember? It's like they both believe in what they're doing so much, they don't care about their own bodies," the woman said.

Simon looked down. One look at this sea of people and the government would know their chances of re-election depended on what they did today. The talisman had brought him to a crucial period in the history of the fight against the climate crisis. This choice couldn't be random, surely? The talisman had shown him this to give him the courage to continue.

The crowd below moved in the direction of Parliament Hill, waving their signs and chanting. They were following him, Simon Scendel. There were too many people for the police to stop. They would pour over Parliament Hill like a tsunami and the PM would listen, because he had no choice.

CHAPTER SIXTEEN

SIMON FELT REJUVENATED by his experience. When Rakita popped through the door after his father had left for work, he flung his arms around her, in spontaneous gratitude for giving him the talisman. His mother asked no questions, but she smiled. Simon knew she loved him with all her heart; if she wasn't nervous about something bad happening to him, he shouldn't be.

So he threw himself into the organization of the rally without any residual doubts. He was spreading the word and—now he knew—the people would respond. If he could convince one person a day to join the fight against climate change, that day was worth living. Day by day. It might seem that everybody was against him, but he had seen the hordes who would rally around him in the future, and he knew change was like a rolling snowball, gathering speed as it sped down the hill. And right now the snowball was trundling past the pipeline issue.

With Sandra's help, Simon immersed himself in launching the rally; they contacted as many people as they could every day, encouraging them to attend from every available avenue: the website, social media like Facebook and twitter, the radio, TV and the papers. The main message was, 'We've Persuaded the Premier, now let's Persuade the Prime Minister.' Secondary messages motivated and empowered: 'Show the Prime Minister the Popular Choice! Come to the Rally!'

"What type of argument is that?" Simon criticized to his mother. "Come to the rally because your leader makes choices based on his chances of re-election, rather than caring about doing the right thing? If our leader is making irrational choices, are you sure that the majority of people are rational?"

Rakita laughed. "I think it's a moot point; what we need to do doesn't depend on finding out the truth about humans, thank goodness. And don't judge—remember we get mixed-up messages about the relationship between popularity and status from an early age. Even rational people can get confused. Don't you remember that Christmas carol *Rudolf the Red-nosed reindeer?* They never let him join in any reindeer games until Santa chose him to lead the sleigh, and then they all loved him because he was famous. What type of message is that sending to children?"

Simon wasn't sure about his mother's point, but he refrained from asking for clarification. The very subject of Christmas often produced a flood of fury at the obscene consumerism and the mountains of plastic it produced. His mother never seemed to understand the importance of tailoring her message so that people would hear it. There was no point flipping over Christmas—people just switched off if they thought you were totally crazy. *Nobody* was going to give up Christmas. But they might give up meat once a week or cut down their travel, if they could be convinced that doing so would make a real difference to their children.

He asked his mother if he could see the movie *Gandhi*, which was on Netflix. He felt embarrassed to tell his mother why, in case this Gandhi fellow was incredibly famous and it would sound like boasting.

Sandra was a different story, however. One day when she'd guilelessly said, "It's interestin' that I'm more brave than you. Do you think people is born with a certain amount of bravery?" he had suddenly lost his rectitude about boasting. Sandra insisted on seeing the movie with him, though she "… didn't usually go in for movies about Indians and stuff."

They chose a rainy afternoon because Rakita wanted to see it too. She made a huge bowl of buttery popcorn which they washed down with water. Sandra sat beside Simon on the couch with the popcorn balancing between them. As the movie progressed her knee pressed ever more firmly against his, and distracted him so much that he began to think he'd have to watch the movie again.

But mostly, they were mesmerized. Gandhi was inspiring and Simon felt awed that he had been compared to him. He did have a vital goal, like Gandhi. He knew it and was prepared to devote his life to it, so that he would have a life, when he was old.

But he wasn't brave. Not like Gandhi.

∞ The approach of the day of the rally generated another spurt of media attention. Interview days no longer destroyed his appetite, but Simon often felt tired. Sometimes life didn't seem very *fun*. Sometimes, he dreamed of being a normal kid again, spending hours meandering around the garden or playing video games, without any particular agenda. On the plus side, the fear that the talisman had dispersed did not return. Unpleasant messages still popped up regularly on his website, but he was working too hard to spread the word about the rally for fear to enter his head.

The day of the rally Simon kept looking around for his mother. Despite the fact that it was a Saturday, he was sure she'd show up to support him. "Support you in what?" Sandra asked, having arrived uninvited for breakfast. "It's not like you're doing anything. We're just gonna hang out on the outskirts of the crowd."

John and Simon had been frying up some eggs and tomatoes when she'd poked her head around the kitchen door.

"Do you mind Sandra showing up like this?" Simon had whispered.

John had laughed. "She's practically one of the family by now."

Of course Simon didn't ask his father to accompany them. Simon felt that John's initial resistance had dissipated, but his father still supported the people working under him. Simon didn't understand this, and he would have liked to talk to his father about it, because there must be something he wasn't getting. After all, his father was obviously one of the thinking, rational humans. But perhaps this issue was somehow tied up with his mother leaving, in which case it was emotional baggage that was best left alone. For now, at least.

Remembering his mother's advice to disguise himself, Simon wore a baseball hat and sun glasses. "Gosh, nobody'd recognize you now," Sandra said sarcastically, but he noticed that she covered her own orange tresses with a baseball cap as well.

They spent the time after breakfast creating a sturdy poster which read: 'Let our children live'. Simon didn't think the heading was very strong, but after an hour of arguing with Sandra about different options he didn't care any longer. They grabbed their sign and headed for the bus.

When they got to the main square of the city and saw all the people milling about, Simon began to feel quite excited. It seemed as though his cap and glasses had indeed rendered him invisible, and it was wonderful to be able to lift his sign and shout slogans along with the rest of the crowd, without attracting any particular notice. Simon realized how deeply sick he was of all the attention. He just wanted to be left alone. He began to smile, happy in his invisibility. More and more people trickled into the square, as inspirational speeches were belted out from the stage at the edge of the area, until it felt like the entire square was filled with people, all waving signs and joining in. Simon felt a wave of solidarity and happiness. "Isn't this wonderful?" he shouted to Sandra.

"We helped create this!"

"Surely they'll stop the pipeline now, there must be thousands of people here!"

Sandra giggled and hoisted their sign higher into the air.

At 2 p.m. precisely the rally began to move in an endless, snaking line out of the square in the direction of the intended site for the construction of the pipeline. Simon and Sandra mingled with the crowd, holding their sign between them. The First Nation Leader at the front of the line turned around to encourage the crowd through his megaphone: "They assure us the pipeline won't leak, but there are only two types of pipelines!"

Thousands of voices rose in a roar: "Those that leak, and those that are gonna leak!" The crowd took up the chant, bellowing it along the multi-coloured procession: "Those that leak, those that are gonna leak!"

Simon couldn't stop smiling as he shouted along with the rest; it felt so great to be part of something so big. Not just part of it, but an instigator! A mover and a shaker. As they drew closer to the intended construction site, Sandra nudged him in the ribs, gesturing with her eyes towards the opposite side of the road. Another group of people were strung along the road, holding their own signs; different ones, saying things like, 'Oil = Strong Economy' and 'Pipelines Feed Families'.

"I noticed them a ways back," Sandra said in his ear. "I thought it was just some stragglers, but there's more and more of them. They must've organized their own protest. Or counter-protest. Whatever."

The other group seemed to be shouting and yelling, unlike Simon's group, which had been progressing in an organized manner, chanting in a unified way. Simon looked from face to face. They were angry. He tensed as one of the people across the road ran into the middle, curses and antagonism spewing from his mouth. "We should get out of here," he murmured to Sandra.

"No way, it's just getting good."

Several more men joined the one in the middle, and they danced closer to the line of protesters, shouting abuse. Suddenly, a column of policemen marched down the middle of the road, between the two groups. Simon gaped at their plastic shields and batons, gripped tightly in their hands, ready to use. Some had dogs, straining at the leashes. Their very presence seemed to increase the feeling of potential violence in the air. "I want to go," Simon repeated to Sandra, yanking his side of the sign downwards so it tilted like a boozer.

"Nothing bad can happen now, the police are here," Sandra said sarcastically. They watched as the policemen drove the angry young men in the middle of the road back to their own side, although the men continued to shout. Simon looked up and down his own line of protesters. They weren't responding in any way to the sudden materialisation of a crowd of antagonists. They were still chanting with the same gusto. Simon felt thankful for their civility. This was how adults were *supposed* to behave. He turned his eyes back to the line of police, now firmly ensconced like a long rope down the middle of the road, between the two groups. Maybe it was going to be all right. He allowed Sandra to tug their sign back into the air, his eyes trained on the policemen, and the angry mob beyond.

Then he saw someone he knew, sauntering down the middle of the road right beside the line of police. "Sandra!" he hissed, pointing.

"What?"

"That's the CEO of BigOilGramby. The top dog. My Dad's boss."

Sandra bobbed her head in excitement, trying to see over the heads of the crowd. "What's he doing here?"

The CEO was walking slowly along the road, looking carefully, almost menacingly, at the faces of the protesters. He didn't glance towards the raging group on the other side; his eyes were fixed on the line of anti-pipeline protesters, looking into each face. Simon ducked his head. "He knows me," he whispered to Sandra. "We should go."

"I wonder who he's looking for?" Sandra said, marching forward determinedly and staring boldly. "Traitors? People he knows and can threaten?"

Simon kept his face turned towards her, facing away from the CEO, fearful of recognition. Sandra's face was bright with interest and excitement. *With courage*, Simon thought admiringly, but just as that thought popped into his head, Sandra's face crumpled without warning. Her eyes radiated fear and she dropped her head.

Simon didn't dare to move; he kept his face down, bent towards her. "What is it? What happened?" Visions of dogs ripping out throats and batons smashing down on flesh swarmed his head. Sandra peeked over an edge of the sign. "Wait, don't look now ... OK, now. Look. Behind the Boss."

Simon edged half an eye over the corner of the sign, which he had pulled over his face. His half-eye searched out the CEO, and with a shock discovered that he was almost parallel to Simon, his own eyes rummaging through the crowd. Simon wrenched his head back towards Sandra and closed his eyes, counting slowly to 10 until he was sure the CEO was past him. Then, still shielding his face with the sign, he peeked again. Just behind the CEO there were two men, also scanning the crowd keenly. They were freshly shaved and suited, but Simon recognized them instantly.

Hairy Nostrils and Ratface.

Simon could barely breathe. He inched his head around until he met Sandra's eyes. "You still want to stay?"

"We'll miss the best part."

"I'm going. Do what you want."

Simon dropped his side of the sign and turned in the opposite direction from the goons, pushing his way through the people. Before he'd gone ten yards he knew that Sandra was behind him, mumbling discontentedly under her breath. As soon as he got to the edges of the crowd he broke into a run, and didn't stop until he'd put several blocks between himself and the danger. He put his hands on his knees and bent over, trying to catch his breath.

After a minute or two Sandra skidded to a stop beside him, red with running and rage. "Were you just gonna run off without me? What the hell! Didn't you hear me screaming at you to slow down?"

Simon didn't answer; he took deep breaths, trying to calm his racing heart, the thoughts that ricocheted through his brain.

"What, you mad at me or something?" Sandra asked.

"No, I'm just thinking."

"Can we walk towards the bus stop while you think?"

They started off again, more slowly this time. Simon tried to organise his thoughts. "I've thought of a new angle on my rational versus emotional theory."

"Great. I didn't get the first angle, but go ahead."

"I thought it was only fools whose actions were motivated by emotion rather than logic."

"I thought you said everybody was, sometimes?"

"Yeah, but fools don't realise when emotion is controlling them. If you're a rational thinker, then you recognize your emotional triggers. Got it?"

"Talking to you is worse than reading a book."

"But it's not just fools. Power and wealth also corrupt the ability to see things rationally, just the same as stupidity. That CEO guy isn't dumb, but he's just as blinded by his wealth as if he were."

"Here's the bus stop. If I let you hold my hand will you shut up about your new angle?"

Simon stopped abruptly. "Even if you want to live like a decent person, it's really hard to pinpoint when your emotions are controlling you."

Sandra took his hand and squeezed it. "Simon," she whispered.

"But I have been lucky enough to pinpoint it now. Fear is controlling me. Fear made me run away. I need to go back."

"You must be friggin' jokin' me," Sandra said. Then she smiled. She moved a little closer and batted her eyes furiously. "Simon," she said again, in quite a different tone.

Simon began striding back towards the protesters, tugging Sandra after him. "We have to go back!"

Sandra heaved herself backwards, yanking him to a stop. "Simon, we're not going back there. No way. Give me a kiss."

Simon looked at her. Then he clasped her in his arms and kissed her passionately.

He reared his head back to look at her.

"Wow, Simon."

He released her and then he was off, pounding back the way they had come with Sandra's voice blaring after him. She pursued him, but Simon was a fast runner and her cries receded before he reached the outskirts of the crowd, which had now reached the intended site for the construction of the pipeline.

They had set up a stage on the edge of the construction site, and a group of people stood on it, taking turns to belt out speeches and lead chants.

Simon pushed his way to the side of the stage and waited until the current speech was over. As the speaker replaced the mic, he clambered onto the stage, but someone else had already launched into a chant by the time he reached the centre.

Simon nodded at a couple of people on the stage whom he knew and took the mic, holding his hand up, palm outwards, towards the crowd. Gradually, the chant stopped.

"My friends," Simon said. "We're heading towards self-extinction, while people making millions from fossil fuel spend millions to spread disinformation—so we keep using it."

A murmur of applause rippled through the crowd.

"Others are ignorant. The Rich, the Stupid, and the Economy—surely that's the title of a book."

There was a rise of laughter, but only on one side of the square. Simon's eyes swept the crowd for signs of Ratface and Hairy Nostrils. "This is the reason the government isn't committed to our fight against the climate crisis. To our fight for the right to clean water and fresh air in 2050!"

Indignant noises came from the crowd. Simon's searching eyes dropped to the people nearest him, and he almost started when he saw Ratface and Hairy Nostrils. They were right by the stage, and they were looking intently at him.

Simon tore his eyes away and looked back at the crowd. To live a worthwhile life, he had to pursue his goal. His goal was his right to clean air. He would continue, even if his life was in peril, because his life would be in peril if he didn't. Simon lifted his chin. "This government wants to be re-elected. They look at all the rich supporters who will stop supporting them if the pipeline falls through. They look at the millions of potential voters who would lose their jobs. Well, I'm looking at this sea of people and I'm thinking we have the power to change their minds!"

One side erupted in cheers. Expletives and shouts came from the other side, but Simon barely heard them. "YOU are changing their minds! By being here. You are telling the government that you demand clean air too!"

The crowd cheered. Simon looked over the sea of faces and focussed on the tide of angry faces on his left. "We are all in this together. We sink or swim together. Please. Your children have the right to breathe fresh air."

Simon climbed down from the stage with his back erect.

Someone on the stage started a new chant:

"Aren't you aware?

You're taking our air!"

The only angry face waiting for him at the bottom of the stage was Sandra's, red and hot. "I'm gonna kill you for runnin' off like that," she said, grabbing his arm.

Simon allowed himself to be steered away.

Sandra laid her head on his arm. "I'm kinda proud of you though," she said. "Gandhi."

CHAPTER SEVENTEEN

THE RALLY SEEMED to spark a huge wave of activity on both sides of the equation. The media was filled with passionate explanations and harangues from various perspectives, and jubilantly published every detail of the events spreading like chicken pox throughout the community and beyond. Especially when the events weren't peaceful. Organizations in other provinces took up the hue and cry, venting their opinions as though their own families' lives were at stake. Finally, both Rakita and John were in agreement: Simon had done enough in terms of the pipeline, and should quietly withdraw from the issue. What a relief! The whole pipeline issue left a sour taste in Simon's mouth, which had germinated with John's attitude (the pipeline was still never mentioned between them) and blossomed with the goon incident. When Rakita gave him the OK to abandon further efforts, his heart lightened.

"That doesn't mean you're taking a break," Rakita reminded him. "This isn't even the tip of the iceberg."

"I know Mum," Simon replied, busy posting informative articles which he loved researching and writing, and refusing interviews with relief. The truth was, he wasn't sure what to do next. He had lost interest so completely in the pipeline that he didn't even follow the news on what was happening with it, although Sandra kept him up to date,

relating the juicier events with a relish that both repelled and fasci-
nated. "It's getting worse," she kept saying with approval. "The pro-
pipeliners are going nuts—didja hear about that guy that got beaten
up? What's betting our goons are behind it?"

We know where you live. Simon shuddered.

Rakita also followed the increasing violence with an anguished
eye. "This is what happens when emotions trump logic, Simon. People
are reduced to animalistic behaviour."

"Yeah, but why's our side acting badly? Aren't they the rational
ones?"

Rakita took his hand. "Welcome to the human race. Every conflict
consists of action and counter-action, with each side claiming the other's action came first, while their action was just self-defence. It gets
pretty boring and repetitive, after a while."

"So the non-thinkers do outflank the thinkers?"

"Sometimes it seems that way. But in another way, the world is
getting better all the time. Human beings have never enjoyed such a
high standard of living, or expected to live so long."

Simon snatched his hand away. "And what are we doing with these
advantages? We're just getting greedier and more selfish."

"Oh my dear, you aren't having enough fun. I'm glad summer is
around the corner, you need a quiet interval of swimming and nature."

Simon shrugged irritably. "You want me to have fun when the
world is falling to pieces?"

"Give me a hug."

Simon looked pointedly at the talisman as he approached for a
hug. It would be easy enough for his mother to give him some fun. He
still dreamt constantly of what he could do with the talisman, despite
the chastening experience of the Leaders' anger. He had made a list of
all the Island's rules and pinned it above his bed. He would never break
another rule, but he needed to time travel. He needed help to know what
to do next. How much he could learn and understand from his own

life! He'd be a 16-year-old as wise as an 80-year-old. Instead of being forced to take mini-steps. Stuff any other kid could do just as well.

"Mum, I think it would really help if I could time travel."

Rakita released him and turned to measure the flour for the cookies she was making.

After a minute or two, Simon said, "I need a bit of inspiration. I'm stuck. I'm not sure what to do next. Time travel might help, like it did last time. It gave me the courage to go back and stand on that stage and make a speech to the protesters of both sides. This issue has dominated the news ever since. I know there's a terrible, violent side to that, but it also means that the climate crisis is dominating the news. As it needs to do, every minute."

Rakita added baking powder to the flour. She still didn't speak.

"I would only go for ten minutes. I will observe for ten minutes and come right back."

Rakita began to beat sugar and butter with a wooden spoon. "Do you think time travel might lighten your mood?"

Simon's heart began to thump with excitement. "I am certain of it."

Rakita added eggs and continued to beat. "Let's think about the purpose of this time travel for a minute."

Simon knew that his mother believed that her talisman landed her in random spots within the years she had chosen. But Simon's trip on the balcony had given him the strength to continue to fight. Of all the hundreds of thousands of moments in a year, the talisman had taken him to the very moment that would enable him to see the human race in action, hell bent on their right—or their children's right—to breathe clean air in 2050. And he had helped to galvanize this human surge. He wasn't so sure that the talismans didn't pick strategic times, ones that could help you on your life's journey. Maybe his talisman did that, because he believed it. Maybe his mother's talisman was random, because she believed that. Maybe the talisman was whatever you needed it to be.

"The talisman will tell me where to go," he said.

"OK," Rakita said carefully. "But you choose the year. If you know your purpose, you'll know your year."

"If I hold the talisman and focus on the mother bird, the talisman will tell me my year, too." Simon clasped his hands together. "Thank you so much for lending it to me, Mum."

Rakita turned to open the fridge door so she could ignore his outstretched hand. "In what way do you hope this trip might help you on your journey?"

Simon tried to think. What did he want to know? "How to influence people?"

Rakita nodded. "You probably want to visit the future then." She turned and looked at him. "To influence people, you have to listen to them, and understand what is important to them. Then respond to that. For example, if they work in fossil fuels you could talk about how much they love their children, and why they think they'll be breathing clean air if they aren't willing to retrain for different work. If they're ..."

"Please Mum, you're starting to rant."

Rakita smiled. "The first time I talked to your father he asked, 'Are you always this preachy?' I guess I do have a tendency to blather." She held out the talisman. "Remember, you want to learn how to influence people. Good luck."

Simon turned to race to his room.

∞ Simon lay on his bed and held the talisman above his face, emptying his mind and focusing wholly on the gnarly branches of the tree. It would be helpful to see what he was doing in a couple of years. That could easily tie into what he should be doing now. Simon closed his hand around the talisman. "2024."

∞ He was standing in a corridor leading to a room where voices vied with the TV. Simon glanced behind him, then edged forward, flattening himself against the wall as one eye slid around the corner to peer into the room. It wasn't a room. It was an open space with a couch and TV nearest to him, and a kitchen up against the far wall. A dining room spanned the two areas. There was cat-sick on the floor and several overflowing ashtrays, and the air was laden with different odours. Future-Him was standing awkwardly beside Sandra as she argued with her mother. Several smaller Sandras were dotted around the kitchen. There didn't appear to be any boys. The second smallest Sandra was beaming up at Future-Him.

"This is the third time this week I'm putting the kids to bed. I want some fucking payment," Sandra yelled.

"Don't you swear in my fucking house," her mother yelled right back.

The smallest Sandra was holding onto her mother's legs, howling. A dog wrestled with a cat on the floor. The mutt looked like a cross between a spaniel and a poodle; the cat batted at its face and was unmerciful with its long, soft ears. The dog mouthed the cat in pretend bites. The cat, dangling off an ear with embedded claws, lifted its feet up and swung to and fro. The dog yelped and shifted to its back, grabbing the cat with both paws and imprisoning it on the ground. Simon stifled a giggle, and glanced at his 18-year-old face. He was gawping at the blaring TV. A fat man in an undershirt slouched before it, slogging from a beer bottle.

Simon's eyes were drawn irresistibly to the TV. He hadn't watched much TV growing up, and he found it mesmerizing (and apparently still did at 18). It was a wrestling match. Simon gaped at the fat, weirdly dressed men taking turns throwing each other about.

"Why should I look after your kids so you can go and get drunk?" Sandra shouted.

Little Sandra still grinned up at Future-Him maniacally. He couldn't believe this was Sandra's family. It put her in a whole different light. She probably hung out with him, because he was quiet and gentle, just like he hung out with her because she was lively and full of energy. The room vibrated with energy—he had never been in such vigorous chaos.

"Dinner!" Sandra's mother yelled.

Everybody filed over to the table. Older-Simon sat between Sandra and littler Sandra, who didn't remove her adoring beam for one instant, while the two middle Sandras served chicken nuggets and fries with the mother's help. Simon wondered where the vegetables were.

"You kids still doing that climate stuff?" the father asked him.

"Of course."

"Why, of course?" the father asked belligerently.

"Because I want to be on the right side of history."

"You're so full of shit."

"How so?" Older-Simon asked, with the weary look of someone who had had this conversation before.

The father waved his fork in his face. "Fossil fuels ain't the problem. The problem's the rich bastards that want to get richer while we get poorer."

"The way the rich live is despicable," Older-Simon said, "and I have launched a website that calculates the footprint of the rich and famous. It praises those who are making changes and publicly shames those with disgusting footprints. But being on the right side of history isn't about criticizing others; it's how you make a thousand personal choices a day. I choose to make every one of those choices through the lens of the climate crisis. That, for me, is a worthwhile l—"

The fork crashed down on the table. "That's what's bull shit. There's no global warming. And if there is, it's happening coz the world cools off during ice ages and then heats up again, and that's the way it is. But it ain't gonna be in our lifetime, that's for sure. Not for hundreds of years."

Simon remembered the 10-minute deadline and glanced at his watch. He had three more minutes.

"So you know more than 97% of the world's scientists, who say humans are causing the crisis and we have to change—"

"Don't you be rude to me, you little snot. I'm telling you it ain't true. It's a fucking government hoax." The father glared at him. "You think you better than me?"

Older-Simon speared some chips and chewed them. "I think I'm living a more worthwhile life than you, at the moment. But I'm sure you'll come around, especially when all your daughters follow in Sandra's brave footsteps."

Simon was impressed; it looked like he'd have no fear in two years. Was that what the talisman was telling him? Be brave? But he knew that already.

Sandra's father had risen to his feet and was looming over Simon. "You turning them against me?"

Older-Simon wiped a bit of spittle off his cheek and looked into the older man's face calmly.

Sandra and her mother had also risen to their feet. Sandra held a phone in her hand. "Go ahead Dad, punch him. He won't touch you back. That's why they call him Gandhi on social media. They're going to love this. Probably get a million views."

"No, Daddy, no!" cried Little Sandra, whose grin had fled as she grabbed her father's waist in a desperate bear hug.

Simon realized with a jerk that 11 minutes had passed. He clasped the talisman to return to 2022.

His mother was bending over, slipping a tray of cookies into the oven.

She stood up and smiled at him. "Did you learn something about how to influence people?"

Simon frowned. "I was having dinner with Sandra's family. They're very different from us. Right wing, poor."

"Ooh, interesting," Rakita said, leaning over the counter. "What makes you say that?"

"Small, dirty house, father drinking beer and watching wrestling on TV and violently expounding ignorant views about the climate. Animals and kids all over the place. We ate chicken nuggets and fries. Nothing else."

"So did you find a common thread?"

"Not really. That's the extreme right part. He was talking about conspiracy theories. They're like, crazy. If they don't believe it's real, they don't believe their children won't be able to breathe clean air in 2050. So, no common thread."

"Hmm. You'll have to think about it some more." Rakita held out her hand for the talisman.

"Mum, I'm not tired at all. Actually, I feel energized. Can I have one more, ten-minute trip? Just ten more minutes? I didn't understand what the talisman was trying to show me and it might show me something else. I'll get it this time, I'm sure I will. Please, Mum. I won't ask again for a long time. I'll be too busy doing what the talisman shows me."

Rakita's hand hovered in the air. "I can't believe you put such blind faith in the talisman. Don't you remember how you suffered when I couldn't get back to you for a week? What was the purpose of that suffering, do you think?" Her hand dropped to her side. "But you did come back promptly after ten minutes."

"I'll only be ten more minutes."

"Aren't you tired?"

Simon did feel tired, but either he'd be able to do it, or not. He shook his head.

"Okay."

This time, when Simon clasped the talisman in his hands, he felt that he should go further along his timeline. Maybe just before the big rally in 2037. He closed his eyes: "2035."

He was crouching behind a bookcase, wedged uncomfortably between a footstool dripping with papers and a cabinet behind him.

Future-him was sitting on the edge of a sofa beside several teetering piles of books.

Reclining in an easy chair opposite was an old woman he didn't know.

"A universal wage is key—it's the logical next step in human evolution. I think I'll go to Washington to attend the demonstration next week. Should be huge."

Future-him balanced a coffee cup on a book. "How can you keep flying when you know you're spewing poison into the atmosphere?"

The old woman raised herself higher in the armchair. Simon could see she was annoyed. "It's for a good cause. Whether I fly or not makes no difference to anything. It's the big corporations that need to stop spewing poison. It's China."

"That's true, and they will do it when the global movement for change forces them to." Future-him shifted in his seat. He didn't look particularly comfortable, unable to lean back because a cat was lying behind him. The whole room was full of stuff, with little pathways carved out so you could walk from one pile to the next. Simon realised the woman was a hoarder. "The global movement is made up of people, each one of whom must also change their individual ways. It will only work when we all do it. The quicker people do it, the cleaner the air will be in a few decades."

Simon glanced at his watch. Four minutes left.

"What is the point of limiting my lifestyle in my last few years when the big corporations and China are still polluting as though there's no tomorrow? It would make me miserable, and it wouldn't make the slightest difference to overall emissions."

"On the contrary," Future-Him said, and again, his voice sounded as though he'd said the same thing many times before. "Collective humanity is the greatest polluter of all—it matters what we decide to do as individuals. You are an educated woman. You know the science. Why haven't you modified your lifestyle to reduce your emissions? How can you live so selfishly?"

The old woman was practically hissing. "I know my science, my little friend. I've done a lot of research and it's too late. We're already screwed. There's already enough CO_2 in the atmosphere to heat up the earth, and what one little old woman does is completely irrelevant."

"The scientists are telling us we have a window of time. Why don't you believe them? It sounds like you're justifying your own selfish behaviour, to me. You should be allowed to travel in your last few years—even if the next generation will never experience travel—because it's too late."

"Why do you always berate me? I won't have you around if you lecture me. I'm an old woman."

Simon just had time to hear Future-Him's answer before he left, spoken in the same courteous tone he had used with Sandra's Dad. "That would be my loss."

∞ The smell of baking cookies was wafting through the house.

"Well?" his mother asked.

Simon felt truly exhausted now. He tottered over to a chair and sat down.

"I think I know what to do," he said slowly.

Rakita came over to him and took the talisman, slipping it over her own neck.

"What?"

Simon yawned. "I think the talisman took me to meet two people on opposite sides politically, with whom I'd had many conversations. There's too many on the right who think climate change isn't real, and there's too many on the left who think that it's too late."

Rakita grabbed an oven mitt and put the pan of cookies on the counter.

"Yes?"

Simon could hardly keep his eyes open. "On both sides, it comes from self-serving ignorance. The world's scientists are saying that we can do this but we have to do it now. And the response of the world has been incredible. We made a roadmap—the Paris Climate Accords —and there is an explosion in renewables and ..."

"I know all this, Simon. Now who's ranting?"

Simon smiled and closed his eyes. The next thing he knew his mother was prodding him with a plate bearing two cookies. She put a glass of milk in his hand.

"You were sleeping. I'm amazed you were able to do two trips in one day. Most people can't. But you must be exhausted. Eat these and go to bed."

Simon was happy to comply. The still-warm cookies were delicious. "I have to find a way to pierce that self-serving ignorance. I will tell them that they have to decide whether they want to be part of the problem or part of the solution. I'll tell them that their kids will curse them, or bless them, according to what they decide today."

"Nice message," Rakita said. "Warm and fuzzy."

Simon kissed her and went up to his room. He was asleep before his head hit the pillow.

CHAPTER EIGHTEEN

AS SOON AS Simon woke up next morning he googled how to influence people. He read about how he must listen and understand what barriers were preventing them from joining the right side of the war. *Appeal to their nobler motives. Talk about mistakes you made. Offer a challenge.*

It became clear that telling them that their kids would curse them wouldn't work. If they liked him, they'd be more likely to listen.

He read political canvassing scripts on how to engage people and spread awareness.

Political canvassing can deliver voter awareness and action.

When he came home from school that day he took his bike and told his mother he was riding up the street, knocking on doors, just to chat. To listen. To find a common thread.

Rakita and Toby trotted after him down the drive. "Don't you want to practice what you're going to say?"

"I'm going to listen. Then it will come to me."

Both Rakita and Toby panted behind him. "Don't you need to do any research about the people you are engaging with?"

Simon stopped his bike and looked back. "Mum, I'm starting with my own neighbourhood. I know the people."

The people in his neighbourhood were middle-class and about

one-half were Caucasian. The rest was a mixture of immigrants and Canadian ethnic minorities. The majority went on trips every summer and drove large SUVs. Their driveways boasted monstrous camping trailers and their lawns were immaculately mowed. Why were they ignoring the climate crisis?

∞ "Hello, my name is Simon Scendel and I go to the local school. I would like to talk to you for three minutes." Simon held up a timer.

Once they had established that he wasn't selling anything, he asked them what their top three concerns were.

He was surprised at how often the climate change was in the top three. Those were the easy ones. Many said they felt that what they did made no difference. Simon, politely and earnestly, told them that human activity was causing the climate crisis, and human action could stop it.

He sometimes had tears in his eyes, but he never let their eyes glaze over. He'd gesture towards their house-on-wheels. "I love camping. Where do you camp?"

They always waxed enthusiastic when describing their trips. Nature was often a common thread. Their children's right to enjoy it too.

The timer was usually ignored.

But it didn't always go like that. Many doors remained firmly closed.

Some people refused to engage, waiting for Simon to finish and answering his open questions as shortly as possible. A few became angry, and said they didn't give a fuck about the climate crisis. The introverted Simon was exhausted after ten houses, but he kept going until dusk.

Rakita was gone by the time he got home and his father was waiting anxiously by the door. He ushered Simon into the kitchen, where plates of frittata waited for them on the table.

He told his father about his adventures of the afternoon.

"I'm going to knock on every door, family by family, listening to their concerns. Maybe adding a concern or two they hadn't been aware of—like the fact that their kids won't have fresh air to breathe if they keep travelling three times a year. Could they maybe cut it down by one trip?"

"What made you decide to do this?" his father asked.

Simon didn't want to tell him about his two time travel trips. "Going from door to door is proven to be effective. I'm like a politician, Dad. I'm canvassing for support for the war against climate change."

His father pushed away his plate and stood up. "As long as it doesn't affect your school work."

∞ Now, most of Simon's time was spent outdoors, instead of in front of the computer. He thought that was fitting. Sandra often joined him and they moved through the neighbourhood twice as fast, and transferred to the next one. The local media got wind of his efforts and a subdued burst of interviews followed. A TV crew followed them for an entire afternoon.

Soon they had to switch their bikes for buses to reach new territory. Simon researched the kind of people who lived in each new place so he could strike the right chord. If they were religious, he'd talk about saving God's earth. If they worked in oil—and many of them did—he'd acknowledge the role oil and gas had played in local livelihoods. He talked about a childhood accident where he would have died without the medical technology enabled by fossil fuels.

"But we didn't know how fossil fuels harmed our world, and now we do," he'd say. "My generation has the right to breathe clean air." He used words like 'diversification' rather than 'transition', once he saw it was better received. He focused on future opportunities, rather than the past. Religious people, new immigrants, visible minorities, free trade lovers—they were all humans and it was possible to find a common thread.

You had to listen. You had to actually hear them.

∞ One day when they were walking along a street knocking on doors, a young man approached them and proffered a brochure. Simon read a call to attend a protest on Saturday, to protect some old growth forests from being cut down.

"Those trees happen to be on the intended route of the pipeline," the young man said. "So I thought you might be interested."

Simon looked more closely at him, but he didn't know him. That was happening more and more often these days.

"It wouldn't matter where they were," he said. "The pipeline isn't more important than trees. It's all part of the same fight. I will come."

As they walked onwards Sandra said, "I need a goddamn day off."

Simon researched the old tree growth protest and read that some people planned to protest by marching with placards, while others were going to chain themselves to the trunks of the trees.

Need u to chain me, he texted Sandra, knowing that would draw her. Sandra had got her license as soon as she could after turning 16, and on weekends she sometimes had access to her parents' run-down Ford. The site was in the middle of nowhere, and it took them over an hour to get there. Simon made Sandra drive at 95 km/hour, because he said that was the best speed in terms of emissions. Then he made her put the car in neutral on hills, then he wished aloud she had an electric car and by the time they got to the protest site they were arguing furiously.

Sandra got out of the car and stomped off, although there were only a handful of people there so she didn't have far to go. Simon ignored her and went to chat to a few of the protesters, who explained "the ropes". Some of them were 'day' protesters, marching with placards and supporting any other protesters that showed up. Others were chaining themselves to trees, and Simon saw there were people among the trees he hadn't noticed earlier, hammering nails into planks to construct platforms, which they secured as high as they could to the trunks with the aid of ladders. "How long will they stay up there?" Simon asked, thinking in his head 'we'.

"As long as it takes."

"What does that mean?"

"The Forestry Company logging these lands is applying for an injunction to have us forcibly removed so they can do the work they were commissioned by the government to do—cut down these trees. If they get the injunction, the police will come and make us leave and we'll show up in court and speak about the wisdom of destroying more wildlife habitat during a time of massive extinction, and the fact that we need our trees as carbon sinks. We might get criminal records, but we'll also get some media attention and people will hear of it. Maybe something good will come out of it."

Simon nodded. "You're spreading the word, and that's something really good. I've brought a chain. Shall I build a platform?"

They looked at him with respect. "You're awfully young. Are you sure you want a criminal record? It's not easy to stay in a tree for a long period of time."

Simon smiled and started to gather planks. After a time, Sandra cooled down and came up behind him as he nailed two planks together and batted him on the bottom. "Let's choose a tree."

"Let's get the platform built first."

"No, you idiot. First you choose the tree. That's a very important decision. Then you build the platform for that tree."

Simon liked the idea, and drifted to the edge of the copse of trees, as far away as he could from the others.

He stopped before each tree and really looked at it. They were so beautiful.

"Found it," Sandra called after precisely two minutes. She was standing smack-dab in the middle of the grove.

"No, over here on the edge," Simon called.

"No way. You need to be in the centre of the action. Besides, this one has a face."

Simon didn't want to yell out his preference for privacy across the intervening trees, so he stalked over to her rather crossly. "I don't want to be in the middle," he hissed. "I want to be by myself."

Sandra turned to look at him with raised eyebrows. "Listen, Gandhi, how are you going to inspire people way off by your lonesome?"

"Don't call me that."

Sandra took his arm. "Just look, Simon. Really look. It's one of the tallest trees. You can see the whole enclosure from this tree—a 180-degree view. Plus it's got a face. Do you see it?"

Simon couldn't.

"Squint your eyes."

The tree went blurry.

"Geez, are you blind? Don't you see those two holes about two-thirds of the way up the trunk? Those are the eyes."

And suddenly Simon did see, and below the eyes was a crack that tilted up at one corner like a lop-sided smile. The tree seemed to be looking at him benignly.

"You need to listen to me about this stuff," Sandra said. "You wanna influence people, right? Well, here's people."

"That's preaching to the converted," Simon said. "But whatever, this tree likes me."

"That's more like it," Sandra said. "It's called Gandhi."

"Will you stop?"

"Not you, pea-brain. The tree. I already named it."

Simon looked at the tree. It was a tower of strength, with a face of compassion. It was a Gandhi.

By the late afternoon they had a basic platform erected about 15 feet up the gnarly old oak tree. His teammates—his fellow soldiers, as Simon thought of them—supplied them with tea and food throughout the day. Towards evening, Sandra went home and Simon called his father to bring a sleeping bag, water, food and some other necessary stuff like toothpaste and utensils.

"Does your mother know you are doing this?" John asked.

"I'll tell her on Monday when she comes."

He felt happy lying in his sleeping bag on his platform and staring at the stars. When he was lying down the leaves of the tree hid him from view and he was enclosed in a green bower.

Simon slept deeply and felt refreshed when he woke up. He relieved himself in the bucket provided for that purpose—although he would go down to the ground for #2—and read until some people shouted at him to catch a rope which was attached to a bucket containing breakfast. Simon climbed down a little way to receive it, and carried the thermos and sandwich packet back to his platform. He felt like a squirrel.

Sandra arrived in the early afternoon and joined the other protesters marching around the chained tree huggers in a huge circle. She came over to chat to him. "How you doin'?"

Simon peered at her over the edge of his platform. "So far so good. You should have come out with my father, it's a shame to drive this distance twice."

"Frig, don't you ever give it a rest?"

"No, never. Coordinate with him next time you come. These trees can't absorb all the CO_2 we produce. There's no point spewing out hours of poison to protect them, especially when you don't have to."

"Ok, I'm done here," Sandra snapped and marched off with her placard.

"You have to start thinking like that for everything you do," Simon yelled after her. "Do I have to use this energy? Is there a way to avoid it? Our electric car is charged by the solar panel system in our backyard, so there's no impact on the environment to get here. Basic thinking is all I'm asking, Sandra."

She had broken out into loud song long before he'd ended this speech, while Simon shouted over her.

When the ruckus had died down, a fellow a couple of trees down called over to say that he also thought of everything he did through the lens of its impact on the climate, and he and Simon struck up a conversation.

Sandra didn't come back until Simon's father arrived, when she sidled over to see if he'd brought anything good to eat. He had, and Simon slipped down from his tree to join them on a blanket in its shade. They shared a wonderful picnic of chicken salad sandwiches, boiled eggs, fruit and cookies.

"What're you gonna do about school?" Sandra asked Simon.

"I'm going to stay here for as long as I can."

"I think you should go to school," John said.

"This isn't a weekend job, Dad. We leave, the loggers move in. Bye-bye trees. Our presence here is preventing these trees from being cut down."

John ran his hands through his hair. "You never listen to a thing I say anymore. Maybe you'll listen to your mother."

Sandra slipped her arm through John's. "Never mind, Mr. Scendel," she said. "He never listens to me neither."

∞ Simon had been worried about boredom, but he wasn't bored for a moment. He and his fellow tree huggers belted out chants with the protesters marching below and people would often chat with him. The day was pleasantly punctuated with tea snacks and meals. He examined Gandhi, and discovered a hole in her trunk just above his head, hidden under a cluster of leaves. Inside was a perfect shelf for his telephone, ear plugs, and toothbrush. Beyond the shelf, the hole went deeper and a squirrel lived there. At first, the squirrel scolded Simon raucously, flicking its tail and beating its back feet in fury, but shared meals eventually tamed him.

Simon also had his books and phone, with its music and videos, which he had downloaded beforehand because there was no bandwidth in the forest. When he needed it charged, he'd hand it down in a bucket and it would be returned some time later. He felt like he was being looked after like a king. For the first time in months, Simon was able to relax, gazing at the stars all evening, nestled in the powerful arms of Gandhi. He felt pleasantly alone, yet among comrades at the same time.

∞ On Monday he phoned his mother, once he was sure John would have left for work. He had thought she'd be pleased with his decision to chain himself to a tree, but something about the idea bothered her.

"If you spread yourself too thin you won't influence anything," she said. "That's why I told you to focus on one thing."

"These trees are being cut down to make way for the pipeline, Mum. I am focussing on one thing."

"You're not focussing on the pipeline anymore, you're focussing on people." Rakita's voice was a mixture of irritation and anxiety. "This kind of radical action turns people off."

Mum's worried I'll get hurt again, Simon thought. *How can I show her that it's going to be OK?*

Simon stroked Gandhi's rough bark. He was getting rather fond of the tree. "I am making people aware, Mum. I am stating that I am willing to do anything to wake people up."

"You don't have to anger people."

The difference between the coarse bark and Gandhi's silky leaves was amazing. "Mum, it doesn't matter what happens to me. If I thought that my death would bring about a change in the lifstyle habits of a critical mass of people, I'd give my life. Who wouldn't give their one, insignificant life, to save the world?"

Rakita's voice was low. "Most people wouldn't, Simon. You are special."

Simon laughed. "Said every mother to every child."

"Please don't take risks, or I'll make you come down."

"You can't make me," Simon said gently.

∞ As the week crawled by, Simon was touched to discover that his parents had come together to support him. Every afternoon after she'd had a sleep, Rakita would travel by bus to John's parking spot at work, visit Simon, and leave the car there in the evening before John finished work. His father would visit him late evening, and they had dinner together, just as usual. Rain came and they erected a tarp over the platform together.

The rainy day wasn't too bad—Simon had an umbrella for when

he needed to descend for #2—but he was glad there wasn't much rain in the forecast.

Rakita usually appeared with a bucket and rope. She would try to throw the rope up to Simon, but she didn't have the strength to fling it far enough for him to catch it, even though he descended several branches. He'd end up climbing down and sitting with her at Gandhi's base. The bucket would be crammed with good things; twice it arrived full of wrapped presents. Simon was truly grateful, especially since he knew she didn't really like him being there. He spaced out the opening of the packages. Each one contained his favourite treats, like Doritos and sour keys.

The media turned up and interviewed several people, including Simon, who was the youngest tree hugger in the group. Two days later a whole convoy of cars showed up and disgorged a bunch of kids from surrounding communities. They quickly claimed their own trees and gleefully chained each other to their hastily constructed platforms. At first Simon was bemused by this influx of new support, but the communication system they had set up (bellowing from tree to tree) soon informed him that they all thought it was a great idea to be featured on the news as a hero, while missing school at the same time.

Simon hadn't thought he might be seen as a hero for clinging to a tree. It was a new experience for him.

There was a girl about Simon's age in the tree next to him.

"You know what we are fighting for?" he called over to her.

"Sure. We're saving the trees."

"We're fighting for the right to breathe clean air and drink clean water when we're older."

The next day Simon climbed down from his tree so he could walk around and talk to everyone.

He called up tree after tree. "We're fighting for clean air. It's our right."

"It's our right," they shouted back, in growing anger.

At night, Simon climbed back into his tree to sleep in his leafy, green bower.

More kids arrived the next day, armed with chains and sleeping bags. More platforms went up. Simon saw some people from his school. They nodded and smiled at each other. Sandra turned up most afternoons, often hitching a ride with Simon's mother or father, but she had too many chores to stay overnight.

Simon continued to climb down from his tree and made a point of chatting with every person in the grove. Gradually, Simon felt a change. From a bunch of kids going on a lark to miss school, they became incensed about their own futures. Most of them would only be in their middle years in 2050. They would have their own kids. It was their right to breathe fresh air and drink clean water! The world had to do whatever it took to make sure they'd have those basic rights. Now.

More kids came every day; kids as young as 12 chained themselves to trees. The ranks of the marchers swelled too, and on weekends a veritable army trudged solemnly around the tree huggers' grove. Kids as young as six marched with signs that said things like: "I want a future."

The more kids that came, the more media attention they got. The idea of children chaining themselves to trees and missing school made a great story. So many people brought food that Rakita and John, who visited separately every day, only had to supply treats. Simon got so much food he began to feed the many other inhabitants of Gandhi's generous branches. Birds and squirrels sat on the edge of his platform and gorged.

The mill workers and tree fellers, deprived of work while they waited for the trees, were furious at the illegal delay. They staged their own protests, clashing with the protesters from the other side and shouting insults at the tree huggers. Police showed up to keep the peace.

Every day, Simon continued to climb down from his tree and talk. He chatted to the marchers and to the tree huggers and to the people who visited. He even tried to talk to the mill workers and tree fellers. He wanted to understand why so many people refused to join the fight in this climate emergency. He wanted to rouse the kids to future action. He wanted to challenge the adult protesters with inquiries about their personal consumption habits. He talked passionately of their shared future—the difference between clamping down on emissions now and ... not. The kids would get excited and angry, and animated discussions would ensue, especially when the workers were absent.

∞ Inevitably, the news came that an injunction was served against them, and the police arrived to remove them. Many of the tree huggers began to pack their stuff, but others picked up their chains and began wrapping themselves to their trees, while other protesters swarmed up the trees to help. Simon was the only kid who chose to remain in his tree. He felt all around Gandhi's trunk, which was the size of a water barrel. He knew that the least knobbly side was on the other side of the trunk from the platform. When a helper climbed up to help him, Simon swung to the other side of Gandhi's trunk, clinging like a limpet as the volunteer fastened them together until Simon's body was criss-crossed with chains and he could relax against Gandhi's rough bark.

"We're reminding everyone that you risk getting a criminal record for this action."

Simon nodded and the volunteer descended, taking the ladder with him.

Simon hung there, trying to relax. He liked the feeling of hugging Gandhi, their two hearts beating against each other.

The ones who had decided to leave voluntarily went home to await the court hearing. The area thinned out. The police started removing people from their trees by force. Simon closed his eyes and focussed on Gandhi's rough skin against his own. There were sounds of a scuffle and someone cried out. Simon began to sing, "Gandhi, Gandhi, you're my beautiful tree. It doesn't matter what they do to me. We're all just irrelevant cogs, you see. But every cog has a legacy. To live a worthwhile life, or not to be."

"Come on, kid. It's time to get down now." A gigantic police officer was standing below him.

"Sorry," Simon said. "We have to stop cutting down trees. We have to stop consuming so much. We have to do it now."

The policeman got a ladder and climbed up to the platform. A second policeman followed him.

"Come on kid, party's over."

"Does this look like a party to you?" Simon said, wrapping his arms more securely around the tree even as one officer took a pair of wire cutters and began to crack through the links of his chain. The other one read out his rights and told him why he was being detained, and that he could get legal advice from a lawyer.

Simon interrupted him. "Don't you believe what the global community of scientists are telling us? We are causing the climate emergency. We need to stop. Don't you want your kids to breathe?"

One of the policemen unwrapped the chain while the other unwrapped Simon's arms. Simon clasped Gandhi hard with his legs. "I'm fighting for the right to breathe for the rest of my life. I am fighting for your children."

"You're starting to get on my nerves, kid," the first police officer said, and jerked Simon's leg roughly. He gave a cry, more in surprise than anything else.

"Police brutality," someone yelled from below.

Simon peered down and saw a little crowd surrounding Gandhi's base. Several were filming with their cameras. The officers tried to pry him loose again, one holding Simon by his arms while the other tried to unwrap his legs. It was difficult to unwrap two legs from different directions at the same time. Simon was squirming like an eel and kicking. The officer lost patience and shoved one of Simon's legs out so far to the side that he cried out again.

"Why don't you taser him?" a sarcastic voice from below suggested.

"Yeah," another voice called out. "A kid clinging to a tree should be tortured."

A chorus of "He's just a kid" and "Shame" rippled around the base of the tree.

Simon wished his mother was there. Suddenly, the officers released his limbs and went into a huddle at the edge of the platform. Simon overheard words like, "just a kid" and "different procedure".

One approached Simon. "We're coming back tomorrow. You will be removed from this tree tomorrow, do you hear?"

Simon didn't answer, but he pressed his heart closer to Gandhi's hard bark.

Once the police had left, carting the other resistant tree huggers off in their police vans, Simon shrugged off his broken chains and collapsed onto his sleeping bag. He felt exhausted. One person brought him something to eat and another brought a new chain, taking away the broken links of the old one. People began to trickle away.

Simon was delighted to hear his mother's voice call up to him some time later.

He didn't want to leave his tree, and managed to convince Rakita to fetch a ladder and join him on his platform. She sat beside him and laid out all the good things she had brought to eat, as he relayed the events of the day.

He sat with his back against Gandhi, his pillow protecting him from the worst knobs, and devoured boiled eggs and fresh buttered bread with cheese, tomatoes and olives. He was ravenous. As he came to the end of his account, he saw his mother wasn't eating anything. "Aren't you hungry?"

"I feel like I don't know you. When did you get so brave?"

Simon smiled and took a long drink of water.

"But now it's time to come home."

Simon shook his head. "I'm not coming home, Mum."

"Don't be ridiculous. You can't stay here alone. Simon, you've done such a great job. You transformed every kid here into a climate activist!

You need to continue this work. It's not going to save the world if you die tonight. It'll cause a little flare in the news for a few days, and then people will forget. You need to stay safe."

Simon thought for a moment. "I don't think my life is at risk," he said slowly. "And I do think that staying here is making a much bigger statement than slinking home. So I'm staying, Mum."

"Come home for tonight. Please, Simon. You can't stay here alone. I can't stand it, Simon. Don't you care about the suffering you are causing me?" There was a catch in Rakita' voice.

Simon put a hand on her arm. "I can't bear that I'm causing you suffering, Mum. But I have to do what I have to do."

Rakita took a tissue out of her pocket and blew her nose furiously, but she didn't say anything else.

Everyone trickled away towards dusk, and Rakita stood up and gathered up what she'd brought. "You can't stay out here on your own, something might happen to you. I'll bring a sleeping bag for myself. I'll be back in a couple of hours."

Simon felt relief. "What about Dad?"

"I'll text him to take the public transit home today. Don't you want to come with me to get the sleeping bag? Stretch your legs?"

Simon had been talked at and photographed all day. He was tired. A couple of hours alone sounded pretty good to him. He said he'd stay.

Some time after his mother had left—Simon found it hard to keep track of time up in the tree—he heard rustling in the silence of the forest. He thought it might be a deer, and moved to the edge of his platform to look. What he saw made his heart tremble in his chest. Men were converging on his tree from every angle. He recognised a couple of them. They were mill workers and tree fellers. He took deep breaths to calm himself and got slowly to his feet. He phoned his mother and told her what was happening. Several men were dragging ladders towards Simon's tree.

"I'll phone the police. They'll be right there," Rakita said in a voice laced with controlled panic.

Simon closed his eyes for a second. *Be brave*, he thought. *It's just a few moments. I'm doing this for the greater good.* He lifted his phone and began to film them, delivering a loud commentary at the same time. "You can see the workers are carrying batons and wire cutters. Perhaps some of them have knives and guns. Around twenty armed men against one kid." Simon turned the phone on himself. "Me."

The first ladder banged against his platform and Simon left the edge of the platform to shove his phone into the hole in Gandhi's trunk. Another ladder clanged against his platform. He rushed over to the first ladder and peered down. The man was almost there. Simon grabbed the rungs of the ladder and threw it away from his platform as hard as he could. The ladder fell backwards and the man cried out, but Simon didn't wait to see what had happened to him. He jumped to the other side and shoved the end of the other ladder off the platform. He did wonder, for a moment, if his behaviour was strictly non-violent in a true Gandhi-like spirit, but he told himself that he wouldn't lift a hand against them, when they got to him. He was just delaying the attack in the hope that help would arrive. Two more ladders clanged against opposite sides of the platform; other men were climbing up Gandhi's trunk, using her generous boughs as stepping stones. Simon didn't have time to think, there was no time to fear. He rushed back and forth, dislodging as many ladders as he could reach. Two men slithered from the trunk onto the platform at the same time. One grabbed Simon's arms and he braced himself for the punch. *The greater good*, he thought, as several more men joined the first two captors.

"Where's his fucking phone?" he heard one of them yell. His head exploded in a burst of pain as a fist connected with the side of his face.

Simon offered no resistance, letting himself go loose like a rag doll. And it really was only a few minutes.

∞ When Simon woke up, he was in hospital and his mother was by his side.

"How are you feeling?" she asked.

Simon touched his body gingerly. There was a bandage encircling his head, and his arm was in a cast, but he couldn't feel any pain at all. "I'm sorry to cause you all this worry, Mum."

She smiled through her tears. "My darling boy, don't worry about that. You are so brave."

Simon closed his eyes again. "Is my phone still in Gandhi's trunk? It was in a hole about six feet up from the platform, under some leaves," he whispered before he fell asleep.

The next time he woke up, Rakita asked how he had done it.

"What happens to me is irrelevant, in the face of human extinction."

Rakita placed his phone on his chest. "I hope you don't mind that I took the liberty of posting the video you took on your website. It's gone viral."

∞ When Simon was released from hospital, a barrage of media attention awaited him. He was inclined to ignore it, but both Sandra and Rakita urged him to capitalize on the media interest to spread his message nationally. When they found out that he called the tree Gandhi, he was dubbed "Gandhi" in the press. Sandra thought that was hysterical.

Simon didn't have to appear in court, as technically he hadn't had to be removed by police, but one of the protesters phoned to inform him that the court had ruled in their favour. The judge had taken the long view instead of the short-sighted argument for profit, and the old growth trees were saved. Rakita made her special pizza and Sandra joined them to celebrate.

Simon's days became a whirlwind of interviews and canvassing. Several days after he had arrived at home, Simon was catching buses to far-flung corners of the province again, usually with Sandra, going door to door and asking for three minutes of their time. More people knew of him, and TV crews followed him on several occasions, including some national ones.

He came back exhausted every day after dusk and ate a hasty meal with his father before falling into bed. Rakita saw him much less and worried he was over-doing it. She would waylay him when he returned from school and urge him to take it easy. If Sandra was there, she'd appeal to her. Wasn't Simon tired at school?

"I'm the one who's tired," Sandra answered, as they ate bread and jam in the kitchen prior to going out.

"Half the people end up promising to make changes in their life, Mum. This is the way to sway the tide of change. Person by person. My talisman showed me what to do."

"More than half," Sandra said through a mouthful of bread.

Rakita put her head in her hands. "I worry about you. You've been hurt so much. I don't want to come back and find you hurt, ever again."

"I haven't had a single bad experience, Mum. Knocking on doors, I mean."

"Not counting doors slammed in your face," Sandra said.

"After I've knocked on every door in my own province, I'll go right across the country, and then into the States," Simon said enthusiastically. "I'll have to stop going to school. This is more important." Day by day. Door by door.

"No way," Rakita said into her hands.

Sandra's jammy hand patted her shoulder awkwardly. "He really is making a difference. He's so good at it—he even manages to cry!"

Simon flushed slightly. The tears were real. Realizing that he was fighting for such basic rights as clean air and water did that to him.

Sandra was still talking. "And he talks so passionate and stuff, it makes people believe him."

Rakita lifted her head and smiled at them. "Politicians should learn from you."

"We ain't politicians," Sandra said. "We're like Terry Fox, going across the country on a journey."

"Yes," Simon said, smiling back at his mother. "Except I have to stop and talk at every door."

"So it's going to take us a lot friggin' longer than Terry Fox," Sandra muttered.

When Simon gestured that it was time to leave, Rakita didn't protest. Simon knew that she was proud of him.

CHAPTER NINETEEN

SIMON WAS LOOKING forward to his second summer with a great deal of anticipation. He couldn't wait to see his grandparents again, or the goats, or Sam and the swimming hole. Here, it felt like he was always on tenterhooks; he couldn't seem to relax. He was often tired, although he went to bed earlier and earlier. The constant canvassing was exhausting. On bad days, when people's doors remained shut or someone was so angry they shouted at the quiet boy looking at them compassionately from their doorstep, he wondered how long he could keep going. Would his whole life be like this?

He just needed a break. He just needed a quiet summer on the island.

It was a Tuesday night in June when Simon was wakened by shouting in the middle of the night. He peered at his watch; it was one in the morning. He felt groggy, and thought for a moment that he had imagined the noise, but then it came again, an enraged bellow from outside his window. And then what sounded like a multitude of voices began to chant:

Take our Jobs—No Way!
This pipeline is Here to Stay!

His body underwent a quantum leap from sleepy ease to rigid dread; he rolled off the bed onto his knees on the floor, and began to crawl towards the window. His room was dark, so he hoped that nobody would see his eye emerging from the corner of the window. There were people spread over the lawn, their angry faces raised towards the house. He searched the faces for Ratface and Hairy Nostrils, sure they were behind this new outrage, but he couldn't see them. Then someone shouted and pointed at his window, and he dropped to his knees and began to crawl towards the corridor. Toby, who had been sprawled on his back in an attitude of indifference, thought this was a fine game. He mimicked Simon, flattening his body to the ground and mincing along inch by inch. In this manner they reached John's room. Simon paused at the door, listening. The shouting seemed to be further away here, which probably meant they were mostly on the front lawn. He stood up and catapulted across the floor onto his father's bed. In the middle of the night, he was a kid again. Gone was the courage derived from the knowledge that his own body was irrelevant, except insofar as it could help him achieve his goals. He was simply frightened.

John woke up with a start to find his son cowering under the covers, straddled by Toby, who was grinning delightedly at this unexpected nocturnal drama. "Simon? What's the matter?"

"There are people shouting outside, Dad. They sound angry."

John listened for a moment. There did indeed seem to be muffled shouts coming from somewhere, although he couldn't hear what they were saying. "Stay here and don't move. I'm going to find out what's going on."

Simon didn't need to be told twice. He lay as still as a stone, pinned under Toby's comforting weight. After a few minutes John returned, and he looked grim. "Looks like some BigOilGramby employees, all worked up about the pipeline. Are they stupid? Don't they know whose house this is?"

Oh yeah, thought Simon. *They know whose house this is.*

"I'm going to go out there and get names and tell them if they don't go home this minute they'll be fired tomorrow." John snatched his iPhone from the bedside table and dialled the police. Simon could hear the impatience leaking from his voice as he gave his address, and then he was marching out the door with the phone still glued to his ear. Toby slithered to the side of the bed and looked back at Simon, as if to say, let's join the fun! His expression reminded Simon of Sandra. For a second he contemplated sneaking out of bed and downstairs to hear what his father was saying and whether anyone was listening or not, but then he worried that this idea had sprouted from a desire to meet Sandra's demands for juicy details. He stayed under the covers; juicy details were precisely what terrified him.

A crash reverberated up the staircase and Simon sat up in bed, his ears straining. A moment later, John burst through the door. His iPhone was still glued to his ear. "When are you getting here? They're trying to smash their way into the house. What the hell is taking you so long—we need you now!"

John's hand fell to his side and he looked at his son. "The crowd is too angry to listen to me, Simon. The police will be here very soon. Let me think."

The shouting amplified, and Simon jumped off the bed and dragged at the heavy, oaken door of the antique wardrobe. "Let's hide in here, Dad."

"Don't be silly. Just be quiet and let me think."

Simon felt his own voice amplifying. "There's no time to think. They'll kill us!"

Uncharacteristically, John shouted back. "Calm down and shut up for a minute!"

And then, suddenly, Rakita was between them, grabbing Simon by the shoulders and pulling him against her chest for a moment before thrusting something into his hand. "Let's go Simon. We haven't got much time."

Simon opened his hand. It was a talisman. He grinned at his mother, relief surging through his body. "They gave me my own talisman?"

"It's your Grandma's. Come on, Simon. Visit any year you want, but go."

John laid a heavy hand on Rakita's shoulder. "What about me?" he asked quietly.

Rakita looked at him with a distracted air. "Talismans won't work for you. They are going to throw a Molotov cocktail through the sitting room window downstairs, so the wardrobe would probably provide the most protection."

"How do you know?" Simon asked.

There was another crash from downstairs; either another window had smashed or they were in the house, breaking furniture. A smell of smoke wafted up the stairs.

"Go! Go!"

"Will I be with you in the future, if we choose the same year?"

"Probably not. Please go! I'm going."

Simon watched his father turn toward the wardrobe, his face closed. Then he clasped his hand over the talisman and said the first number that came into his head: "2037."

He vaguely heard his mother shout the same year before the strange whistling invaded his ears and the remembered blindfold slipped over his eyes. He relaxed as the wind took over his body, manipulating it like a rag doll before setting him gently onto grass. He opened his eyes and blinked; then he grinned. He knew this property! This long stretch of grass that blossomed into fruit trees encircled by the rows of bee hives. This was his grandparents' house. Still grinning, he looked toward the great oak where he knew the table to be; and there it was, sitting on grass that was much longer than it had been last year during his summer visit. He strained his eyes to see his grandparents, and saw instead an older version of himself, reclining comfortably and reading something from an iPad. What a contrast to his last visit to 2037! Then, he had been speaking to a crowd of millions. Now, he was relaxing in the sun. Simon looked around again for his grandparents, calculating what their age would have been in 2037. With a stab of pain, he realised that his grandparents must be dead. The realization made him think of his mother, and he looked around carefully to see if she had landed at the same moment in 2037. There was no sign of her. Remembering the rule about not interacting with one's other self, Simon approached cautiously, keeping the oak tree between him and the table. He got close enough to peer over his future shoulder, and saw he was reading the news. 'Earthquake Kills 100s,' ran the caption. Was he allowed to read about the future if he didn't influence it in any way? But couldn't learning about the future impact the present, in just the same dangerous way that meddling with the present could impact the future? What if the article showed that the world was in a dreadful state, with environmental calamities happening on a daily basis? Would that impact Simon's drive to change things now? If only his mother were here!

"Simon!" a musical voice called from the house. Simon turned his head to see a dark woman striding across the lawn, a pot of tea and two mugs clutched in her hands. A wail went up somewhere near the ground. Simon stood on tip toe so he could see. A tiny child was waddling determinedly through the long grass, crying as its mother receded. The woman reached the table and set the teapot and mugs down, then returned to scoop up the toddler. With a practiced hand she deposited the child on Future-Simon's knee; he merely raised his iPad so he could continue reading above the child's head. Simon watched in fascination as the woman turned and plunged into the grass again, only to bend down and grasp an inert bundle, which had been completely hidden in the long grass. She hugged this bundle to her chest and returned to the table. Simon saw with amazement that this was another child. Was this a family scene? Was this *his* family?

"Pour me some tea, Simon," the woman said. Her voice was soft and lilting. Future-him put his iPad on the table and leaned over the head of the toddler to pour the tea. "Me tea, Daddy?" lisped a childish voice.

"Too hot for Daniel. Would you like some water?"

Simon watched the toddler's face with amusement, wondering if it would suddenly break into howls at this obstacle to his desire, as he'd seen other toddlers do in public places at home. But Daniel seemed to accept the 'no' verdict peaceably, and gazed up at his father's Adam's apple as he swallowed his tea.

"Are you planning to fix the wobbly fence post today?" the woman asked. "Nanny keeps getting out. She's attracted to that wobbly post like a bee to nectar, even when I'm watching her and she knows perfectly well I'll lock her in the barn if she escapes. I've watched her saunter over to the post, eyeballing me the whole time, and lean on it with all her weight. The post starts to gracefully bend under her 120 pounds until it lies supine on the ground, pliable as a mistress. Then over she hops and away she goes."

Future-him laughed, and plopped little Daniel on the floor. He picked the bundle out of the woman's arms and laid it on the floor as well. Then he picked up his iPad again.

"I hope you're not doing any work," the woman said. "This is our day off."

When Future-him didn't respond immediately, the woman nudged his knee with her foot. "It's our first day off in two weeks. We're fighting for change every day and I am exhausted. I don't want to hear a single thing about that earthquake."

Future-him smiled and got to his feet. Bending over the woman, whom Simon assumed to be his wife, he put his arms around her, and kissed her. From the way he kissed her, Simon knew without a shadow of a doubt that this was his future family. When Future-him straightened up, Simon looked with interest at the woman's face. Her skin was the colour of milk chocolate. Her head was wrapped in a brightly-coloured scarf, kinky tendrils escaping to frame her face, which was a perfect oval. Her eyes were large and her lips were full, currently stretched into a grin. She was slim and muscular. She was beautiful, but she wasn't Sandra. What had happened to Sandra? Obviously this meant he wasn't going to marry her, but why not? What would happen to them? The thought that Sandra might not be in his life in the future drove through his innards like a shaft of anguish. What was good about seeing the future? It was crap. Simon looked over at the couple again. The woman had her head thrown back, the long, smooth column of her throat raised towards the sun, and Future-him was kneading her neck, massaging it slowly like he enjoyed the feel of it. It didn't look like the future was so very crap.

But Sandra, Sandra!

Simon followed Future-him as he retrieved his tools from the shed and began to mend the wobbly post. He had to stifle his giggles as Future-Nanny repeatedly attempted to bypass his bulk to get at her favourite post. Future-him huddled ever closer to the post, until his back curved over it like a protective horseshoe. Nanny tried to shove her head underneath his arm, and was repulsed. Then she went down on her knees to see if she could wiggle through his legs. Finally, in a burst of frustration, she rammed her head into his back. He jumped to his feet and yelled so loudly she galloped back towards the barn. But two minutes later she was slinking over again, pretending to eat grass on the way, her eyes fixed on her goal. She approached with more caution, leaning over his shoulder, but unfortunately getting side-tracked by his ear, which looked exceptionally nibble-able. Another bellow had her scurrying again towards the barn, but this time Future-him raced after her and slammed the door of the barn shut. Simon was quite impressed with his future ability to swear.

Watching became dull without Nanny, so he clasped his talisman: "2022."

Simon's eyes snapped open as soon as he felt something solid beneath him. He was sitting on his own bed, and Toby was regarding him with such a droll expression that he had to laugh. Then Toby flung himself on his chest, baptizing him with a hundred kisses.

Once Simon managed to extricate himself, the remembrance of the awful evening preceding his time travel rushed back to him. He went to the window and looked outside. A policeman stood near their front door, evidently guarding the house. Quelling the anxiety in his heart, Simon crept out the door towards his father's room. It was still pitch black and quiet, but Simon didn't turn on any lights. John lay on his back, stretched across the bed, snoring. Along with the relief came the realization of his own exhaustion—he hadn't slept most of the night. He tiptoed back to his room, pausing at the head of the stairs to peer down. An acrid smoke smell lingered in the air, but it was too dark to see anything.

When Simon woke up the next morning Toby had abandoned him, which meant his father was up. He glanced at the bedside clock and was surprised to see that it was almost midday. He'd missed school, and apparently his father was missing work. He took the stairs two at a time, skidding to a sudden stop half way down. The living room was a wreck. Wood, glass, and debris littered the room; chunks of plaster and wall paper drooped from the walls and ceiling. The sofa set was unrecognizable, and an unpleasant smell of smoke still loitered. He could hear his father in the kitchen, and tip-toed in that direction, anxious about what other discoveries awaited him. Toby ran towards him as he looked cautiously around. The blackened walls drooled dollops of plaster, but the table and chairs were intact. John had obviously been cleaning, because the floor was sparkly clean.

"Breakfast?"

Simon realised he was starving, and tucked into the pile of pancakes his father placed before him with gusto. He was half-way through before he realised his father wasn't eating, though he fiddled with his coffee mug. His face looked weary, pale, and closed.

"Are you all right, Dad?"

"Yes."

"You don't look all right. What happened last night?"

"Weren't you there?"

Simon stared at his father. After a minute John scraped his hands through his hair. "Sorry. It's just, I can't believe that my own workers would attack my house this way. Have they gone crazy? What if Alley hadn't come at that exact moment? What would have happened to us?"

Simon hoped his father had forgotten the uncomfortable memory of his mother saving only him. "What did happen, after we left?"

"I got into the wardrobe. There was the most godawful splintering and crashing noise from downstairs. The whole wardrobe shook." John closed his eyes briefly, as though the memory pained him.

After a moment of silence Simon asked, "Were you scared they'd find you?"

John sighed. "I think I prayed for the first time in my life, hypocritical though it felt. And that same moment I heard the whine of the police sirens."

Silence fell again. Simon wanted to know what the policemen had done; if they'd managed to catch the leaders, if they knew who it was. But something in his father's face stopped him from prodding him with questions.

"Today I've got to arrange for all the damage to be fixed and buy a new sofa set. At least we can be thankful that we didn't have a million possessions."

John stood up from the table, downing the rest of his coffee. "Are you going to school today?"

"Nah. I'm too tired to learn."

John moved towards the door. "By the way, did I mention this friend that I have, or rather, a friend of a friend, who has the ear of the PM?"

Simon sat up straighter in his seat. "Yes?"

"That's another thing on my to-do list today. I've asked that friend to ask his friend to talk to the Prime Minister about the pipeline. Inform him about all the nasty stuff going on, and how it would look, if the PM came out on the side of the nasty ones. Premier Smith has also scheduled a meeting with the PM in a couple of weeks, so he might get an earful from two quarters."

Simon jumped to his feet, wanting to throw his arms around his father and kiss him, but John had already melted out the door.

Simon went outdoors with Toby and smiled at the policeman guarding the house. His presence made him self-conscious about throwing Toby's ball, so he spent most of the afternoon inside, trying to restore the sitting room to a reasonable state. He gathered up bits of plaster and other debris into large garbage bags and swept the floor. He worked and worked, trying not to hear the insistent beep of his iPhone upstairs. No doubt it was Sandra, demanding to know the reason for his absence. Simon stopped his labours for a second. That was an uncharitable way of thinking about it. She wasn't 'demanding' anything. She just wanted to know. Naturally. Or perhaps she'd heard about the events of last night and was really worried. He should text her. But he continued to work steadily, until he heard a step behind him, and turned to hug his mother.

"You OK?" she asked.

"Yup. You?"

"Yes. Where did you end up last night?"

"I wanted to talk to you about that. Tea?"

"I'll make it. You finish cleaning the floor. You're a good boy, helping with this mess. Your father all right?"

Simon made a mental note to tell his father that Rakita had asked after him, first thing.

Ten minutes later, they were sitting in their favourite place overlooking the garden, Toby planted between their feet, salivating around the ball lodged in his mouth. The policeman had poked his head around the side of the house when he'd heard their voices, and given Rakita a very strange look. He'd made as if to approach, but she'd held up her hand. "We need to have a little chat here, is there anything you need?" With obvious reluctance, he had shaken his head and retreated.

"Was that rude?" Simon asked.

"No. He's probably just bored stiff; we don't want to talk to him, do we?"

Simon had to admit they didn't. On the other hand, he didn't quite know how to broach the subject he did want to talk about. Finally, he told her candidly what had happened during his time travel, in chronological order. When he had finished, a huge smile was plastered over her face. "I have to admit that I've met Marietta as well."

"Who?"

"Your wife. I've met your whole family several times during time travel. From what I've overheard, I think you're going to be blessed with a very happy union. That isn't easy these days, Simon. You are lucky."

It felt like something was lodged in his throat. He took him a few minutes to speak around the obstruction. "What ... what about Sandra?"

Rakita reached across the wide arms of her wooden chair to touch his hand. "Oh, that's what you're thinking of. I had completely forgotten Sandra."

The obstruction pricked his gullet. "You've never liked her!"

"Oh Simon, I like her just fine. You've discovered one of the serious downsides of time travel."

His mother was looking at him too intently; Simon got up and tugged Toby's ball from his resisting teeth, throwing it as far as he could across the garden. Toby pounded after it in delight, but Simon didn't return to his seat. He remained standing, half-turned away from his mother. "They have so many rules to prevent anyone impacting the future, but there aren't any rules to prevent the future from impacting the present."

"That's a great point," Rakita said. "I realised that when I was a bit older than you, and as a result, I more or less cut out my future time travelling. I still loved to travel to the past, but I wanted my future to be revealed to me like the surprises behind each door in an advent calendar."

"How's that supposed to help?" Simon muttered.

"I'm just telling you, in case you want to think more deeply about future time travel as well. As for Sandra, who knows what role she'll play in your life? How do you feel about her?"

Simon shrugged in an agony of irritation.

"Just go with the flow," Rakita said. "Life is long, you're going to love many people, in many different ways. Maybe Sandra is a vital link in your eventual successful connection with Marietta. Maybe you will have a wonderful few years with her, and remain best friends for the rest of your lives. Every single teen-in-love imagines that their relationships are going to last forever, but if they could think sensibly, they'd realise that the vast majority of people have more than one relationship."

"All right," Simon said, almost sullenly. "I get what you're saying."

Rakita stood up and gathered the mugs in one hand. "Go with the flow, Simon. If you are meant to love Sandra, love her."

She linked her arm through his as they walked back to the house together.

CHAPTER TWENTY

THE SCHOOL BAG dragged at his shoulders as Simon walked home, lugging a whole year's worth of school materials. Sandra tottered beside him, carting a similar load. It was the last day of school before the summer break, as well as the last day attending this school. Next year they were all going to the high school in the next town, where they would be amalgamated with several other schools.

"There will be so many kids, we might never see each other," Sandra had said during math class, plonking herself in the seat next to his. The teacher had told them to sit where they liked, as a last-day treat.

"We'll meet every lunch, silly. Just like now."

"Some people we'll be glad not to see," Sandra had muttered darkly.

Simon had looked over at Jake, Shawn and Tyler. How different this last day was, from his first day! He had been so miserable and scared, and now even the teachers treated him with respect. His former tormenters didn't treat him any way at all. Mostly they ignored him, but if they came face to face suddenly in the hallway or something, a look akin to fear seemed to cross their faces. Simon wasn't happy about that. Fear often generated resentment, and he would have preferred to end on a peaceful note. So on this last day he had brought a little packet of homemade cookies for each of them. When lunchtime rolled around, he suddenly felt nerdy, and stalked over brusquely, tossing the little packets onto the desk in front of them. "Peace offering," he said.

"Are you kidding me?" Sandra said, who had followed him. "If I punch you up a bit will I get cookies too?"

Simon gestured crossly for her to go away, but she stuck to him like a burr, determined not to miss anything.

The bullies looked at him warily, and then glanced at each other.

"Bystander effect," Sandra said.

"Shut up and go away," Simon said. He wondered if they were going to say anything, because it was pretty bloody awkward just standing there.

"Thanks?" Jake finally said.

Tyler opened his packet and shoved a whole cookie into his mouth and chewed. The others watched him.

"Waiting to see if he'll fall down dead?" Sandra said.

Simon elbowed her and she squawked theatrically. He stood for a moment more, but no further thanks were forthcoming, so he raised his hand in farewell and turned around to go.

"What the hell was that about?" Sandra asked loudly as they left the room.

"You're so bloody annoying. Why couldn't you just shut up for once?"

"With friends like you, who needs enemies?"

"Actually, I have a packet of cookies for you too."

Sandra brightened up immediately and slipped her hand into his.

A feeling of nostalgia assailed him during the afternoon. He kept thinking—this is the last time I'll see this room/talk to this teacher/ use my favourite toilet—even though he knew the minute he stepped through the doors for the last time, he'd probably never think of the place again.

Sandra had insisted on accompanying him home, despite him explaining that he had to pack for his trip to the island. He'd asked his mother whether he could travel there in a second with his grandmother's talisman, rather than trekking for days over the entire world.

"Sure," Rakita had replied. "I'm sure you'll land in the summer holidays some time."

"What, if it took me to the wrong place, who cares? I'd just try again."

"You can only try once, maybe twice a day. And there are 365 days in the year the talisman could take you to. The plane would be quicker."

Simon had to admit she had a point.

"I can't believe you're leaving me again," Sandra said, grumbling.

"And you're going to feel a lot better after you've watched me packing all afternoon, because that's what you'll be doing." Simon saw her scowl. "You wanted to come!"

In the end Sandra was quite helpful. She had a knack for folding clothes and storing them effectively in his backpack, or keeping Toby occupied while Simon searched for the items he wanted to take. This was particularly helpful, because Toby stuck his nose into everything, and seemed obsessed with the desire to climb right into the backpack.

"He knows you're going. He's sad," Sandra said.

"Projection."

He had to duck quickly to avoid the book she threw at him.

Soon after Simon had finished packing, they heard the roar of his father's car. Rakita hadn't visited that day, claiming that she wanted to give John a last day alone with his son before losing him for the summer. "But you're still sleeping here, right? So, you can be with me during the trip in real time?"

"Yes, of course."

"Still ... in the basement?" Simon had asked with curiosity. "Do you have to climb into that horrible dumbwaiter?"

She'd only laughed.

John entered the room and greeted them, while Toby did pirouettes of welcome that seemed calculated to trip him up. "I have some good news."

Instantly, both kids were standing in front of him, scrutinizing his face. "So my friend met with the Prime Minister today ..."

"Your friend of a friend?" Sandra said.

"Shut up," Simon said.

"Yes. Coincidentally, Premier Smith's meeting was scheduled for today too. Apparently, this friend of a friend told the Prime Minister that it was best to let this one go. He said there were important people trying to stop the pipeline, while the people supporting it were behaving so badly that it wouldn't be politically wise to back them."

John paused for impact and Sandra leapt into the silence. "Don't you guys talk about this serious stuff over tea in the back garden?"

"No, that's Mum," Simon said. "Would you *please* shut up? Dad?"

"Our PM is a malleable fellow, wisely relying on the information he's given to make his decisions. After two meetings on the same day from completely different quarters—a politician and an oilman—he has dropped support for the pipeline."

Simon launched himself into his father's arms, while Sandra danced around the room with a jubilant Toby.

"That's so brilliant, Dad. I thought I was going to hate the very word 'pipeline' for the rest of my life, but I'm so happy it ended like this!"

Sandra joined them for a three-way hug. "We did it!" she shouted, loud enough to trigger a ringing in Simon's left ear.

"And he got to this decision in the best way," Sandra said, pulling back from the hug.

Simon didn't understand her and, sure that it was just something stupid, felt annoyed. "What do you mean?"

"You said that it's good to gather information from different perspectives before making hard decisions. You said that was what the Leaders did."

Simon was surprised. She'd made a good point. Why had he been so *down* on her all day? He raised his head to his father. "It's true, Dad; that is the way to make a wise decision … or maybe we just got lucky. Damn, if we caught him on a good day, we should have asked him to fine companies producing one-use products."

John chuckled. It was the first time Simon had seen him laugh since Rakita had left him. He looked at his father. "What about your workers, Dad?"

John ruffled his son's hair. "You are right, Simon. This is more important."

∞ Sandra stayed for dinner, and then asked if she could accompany Simon on his nightly walk with Toby before John took her home. Already engrossed in the evening news, John agreed readily.

For the second time, Simon remembered that he'd been pretty bad-tempered with Sandra all day (though she'd been pretty annoying, too) so he resolved to be as pleasant as he could. It wasn't as if the only reason their friendship existed was so they could get married. She was his friend, and her friendship had made the hours and hours at school bearable. It was ridiculous to let his knowledge of the future undermine their current, precious friendship. He looked down at her cropped, orange hair. "I'll miss you."

"Liar."

"I will. I couldn't have survived this past year without you. Every time I'd had enough, your energy propelled me onward. Plus, you are my only friend at school."

She stopped and looked up at him. "Only a friend?"

And there was that mischievous glint in her eye, and then she was in his arms and her soft lips were touching his and he put his arms around her and strained her against him, oblivious as to what the neighbours might think or what the future might hold.

And Sandra responded, exploring his mouth with her own, her hands pulling him even closer. He shuddered, wondering if she could feel how much he wanted her. But he didn't feel self-conscious and he didn't pull away. He wanted her to know. And then she moved her head back to catch her breath, and he saw her pupils dilated with desire.

She knew.

"I like your way of saying good-bye," she said.

"It's so you don't forget me."

And they held hands all the way home, to Toby's disbelief, as it prevented them from throwing his ball.

∞ A few days later, Simon was sitting in his grandparents' garden, enjoying barbecued chicken and a variety of salads, and regaling his family with his adventures over the year. Ronny, who had recognized him instantly and greeted him with boundless love, sat between his knees, his eyes gazing at Simon's chewing jaw with a fascination that rivalled Toby's. It made Simon feel right at home.

He had had plenty of opportunity to talk about things with his mother during the trip, in between the barrage of texts and telephone calls flowing to his phone. After his father had taken Sandra home, Simon had used his last few hours in Canada to post the great news about the pipeline on his website. He'd also called some of the people who had been working diligently for the same cause, a couple of the First Nation Leaders and other devoted environmentalists. He'd thought he'd have the pleasure of surprising them, but the big news had already hit the media channels, so instead the conversations became mutual back-patting sessions and congratulations. It felt good. Surreal. He bombarded everyone, especially his mother, with questions like, what did we do that enabled us to win? No matter how many times he asked, the answers weren't satisfactory. It was luck, timing, the political climate at that particular instant. At first, Simon was sceptical about the role luck had played, sure that he'd contributed more than random luck to this huge achievement—the stopping of the pipeline. But as similar answers continued to trickle in from different sources, he was forced to admit that luck had played a big part. Luck that he had a father with high connections. Luck that Premier Smith was a reasonable man. Luck that the pro-pipeliners got so aggressive, so quickly. Luck that his own side didn't. Worse, there was the feeling that the decision could be reversed, as easily as it had been made. It wasn't the result of Simon helping to change the minds of enough people to constitute a critical mass. He'd won the battle, but he hadn't won the war—yet. Why, he'd barely traversed his own province—he had a whole country of doors to get to!

Simon checked his website frequently after posting, and was surprised and relieved to see that the expected hate mail wasn't materializing. Perhaps hate abated once issues were resolved, or at least was kept under wraps. Thank goodness for that. But Simon's iPhone beeped constantly throughout the first days of his trip: well-wishers, people he'd worked with, even media. Finally, Rakita had suggested he simply turn the thing off. Simon was surprised at the sense of relief he felt, as soon as he'd done so.

And now he was telling his grandparents the whole story, from his first post to the final congratulations. They were shocked at his account of the days of violence.

"I don't think a child that age should be placed in such danger," his grandmother muttered.

"It's a case of the end justifying the means," Harry boomed. The more his hearing deteriorated, the louder he talked.

Simon, his story finished, stuffed his face with salad. It was like eating a taste of spring. The difference in taste between these salads and the veggies in the store at home!

"They're just guessing as to the end, I always thought it was preposterous, the idea that Simon had to shoulder this heavy burden just because … umm …"

"… he wasn't supposed to exist?" Rakita finished her mother's sentence. "I think the real question is, how much are we willing to sacrifice for the sake of the world? The ultimate sacrifice? Our children?"

Simon was surprised at how easily they discussed whether he should be flung to the wolves or not. Then the question triggered a philosophical debate which didn't seem to have much to do with him, so he pushed his chair back to leave the table.

"Just wait Simon," Harry said. "We have something for you." He moved his plate to one side and Simon saw a white envelope hidden beneath it, addressed to him. He was surprised; who wrote letters these days? And who would write to him here? Everyone was looking at him with expectant pleasure, so he tore it open and saw it was an invitation to meet the Leaders of the island the following week.

"What do they want to see me for?"

"Maybe to thank you, for all your good work?" Rakita suggested.

"Who cares? They didn't seem to appreciate it when I was doing stuff that terrified me."

"Of course they did," his grandmother said in her shaky voice. "What do you mean, Simon?"

"They never helped me, even when my mother begged. If you hadn't lent me your talisman, I'd probably have died, Grandma."

"Oh rubbish," Rakita said. "Did your father die? Anyway, you can tell them these thoughts next week when we go to the meeting. I'm sure they'll have a reasonable explanation, as always. Now let's clear up here and get home to Nanny and the Henny Pennies."

Simon agreed cheerfully, and soon found himself on a little stool, pressing his forehead against Nanny's warm flank as he milked. Nanny stood very patiently (so long as there was food in her bucket), even though it took him twice as long to milk as it used to. His hands kept getting tired, but he knew that by the end of the summer his milking would be up to speed again. Every time Nanny finished her food, she'd crane her head around the post it was secured to and eyeball him steadfastly until he gave her more.

"I think she likes me, Mum."

"She knows she gets twice as much food when you're at the helm, so to speak. Come on, develop a steady rhythm; one hand, then the other, without a break. Don't you remember from last year?"

His mother had made a delicious stew on their second evening. Simon had asked for seconds, and then thirds. "What's in this, Mum? It's the best stew I've ever tasted."

"Do you remember there were two little black and white kids last year? That's the male."

Simon spat out his mouthful. "What? Churro? I loved him!"

"Rubbish. You held him a few times, that's all. He had a wonderful life, and when I took him to the butcher, I called him and he trotted right up, happy as anything. The butcher stunned him in one second; he didn't even know what was happening. I wish I could go like that."

"Mum! Don't talk like that!"

"Quick, easy, painless, without even knowing."

"I'm not eating any more of this."

"Suit yourself. Continue to buy meat at Sobeys without knowing or caring about the horrific lives those animals probably led, instead of eating a happy animal that lived well and died painlessly. Makes sense. Love your rationale."

Simon snatched up his spoon and finished his stew.

Nanny boasted two new twins this year, and Churro's sister was also pregnant. Both Nanny's kids were does, which pleased Rakita, who had to supply four does to the neighbour who had given her the pregnant Nanny when she'd returned to the island. Simon wasn't sure he'd ever get used to the killing part, especially if you knew and loved the animals, but he realised that this was a life he'd like to explore when it came time to settle down and raise his children. *With Marietta.*

"What about travelling and study?" Rakita asked.

"I'll do all of that first, but when I settle down, I'm going to have goats and chickens just like you. And a pig. And maybe a horse or two."

Rakita laughed.

Apart from new and missing goats, nothing seemed to have changed on the island. Sam came around with two fishing rods on his third day, and Simon happily plunged back into his swimming/hiking schedule. He kept his phone turned off, except on Saturdays, when he lay on his bed and texted for hours to Sandra.

Why can't U talk more?

Can't. Need to be quiet. Was anxious & scared all the time, for months. Need relax and clear head, walk swim milk animals, read. My days full.

U can't text me one thing during fucking reading time?

It's never one thing Sandra. I'm giving U my full attention now. My whole mind is devoted to U. Tell me what Yr doing. And I'll tell U.

Yeah, U already have.

Not about the nights. Do U know U are with me every night? I take U to bed with me. Simon couldn't believe he was writing this. But he wanted her to know that he thought of her always, and if he didn't want to text her all the time, that didn't matter.

We lie down side by side & we are kissing & I can feel your body against mine.

Simon, don't; I'm babysitting my brothers & sister and I can't keep my phone in my hand all the time.

OK. Did I tell you I have a meeting with the Leaders next week?

∞ On the day of the meeting, Simon couldn't eat—he had become accustomed to such scenarios.

The room with the comfortable sofas was now familiar to him, but instead of remaining sprawled in their seats, the same three Leaders he'd met last year sprang to their feet as he entered, coming towards him with arms outstretched to shake his hand. "You've launched a brilliant beginning, Simon."

"We are so proud of you."

The older woman and the two young men shook his hand, beaming into his face. Simon felt quite overwhelmed and shy. He smiled back as one led him to the sofa and the other placed a cup of tea in his hand. Rakita sat down too, watching Simon with a half-grin.

"We'd like to give you something, in return for all the excellent work you did on the pipeline," Mohammed said, picking up a rectangular-shaped box from the table.

"Wait Mohammed," Ji Su said. "You are always rushing. We have a few things to say first, no?"

"Second," Mohammed said, bounding forward and pushing the box into Simon's hands. Simon looked inquiringly into his face; he was nodding and grinning madly. His mother and Ji Su stepped forward also, and even Pierre, so that a little circle was formed. Simon blushed and opened the box. A talisman lay inside. He picked it up and held it close to his eyes, searching for the mother bird, carrying dinner home to the wide-open beak poking above the nest, striving upwards in expectation of food. Tears came to his eyes. "Thank you."

"We don't want you to waste all your bloody time playing with that," Ji Su said abruptly. "The world has not been saved. Even stopping the pipeline itself isn't guaranteed. You haven't really achieved anything yet."

"Both the Canadian and US governments were supporting the pipeline," Mohammed said, throwing his arm around Simon. "To stop it was a huge achievement."

Simon wanted to say that the old growth trees he'd chained himself to weren't going to be cut down either, but Ji Su intimidated him too much.

"But he's not finished, is my point. Every country must abide by the Global Climate Agreement if there's any hope of keeping the world's temperature below the disaster point. There's a lot of work to do. He must continue to live in Canada with his father, so it will be his permanent home."

"Obviously he's not finished. He's just starting. But he's achieved more in one year than we ever imagined he would. And this summer, he should relax and enjoy his talisman."

Simon put the chain around his neck. He liked the feel of the talisman nestling against his chest.

"Thank you for giving me one. I've wanted a talisman for so long."

"We held it back on purpose," Ji Su said.

"We were worried that you weren't ready," Mohammed said.

"For the talisman?" Simon asked.

"And for the role we thought you were destined to play."

"You know I am ready now?"

Mohammed smiled at him. "We know that you have gained the courage to do it on your own, without the aid of the talisman."

Simon opened his mouth to disagree. The talisman had helped him every step of the way! But what if his mother wasn't supposed to give him the talisman? After a minute, he was glad that he had remained silent, because he suddenly remembered the time the kids had beaten him outside the restaurant.

He didn't feel as fearful as the first time. It was almost as if he'd been terrified by the idea of being beaten up, but now he'd experienced the reality it wasn't so frightening.

Mohammed was still speaking. "You were a frightened kid when we first met you, and you had to find the necessary courage on your own, without attributing it to the talisman. The talisman can't give anyone courage—it has to come from inside."

Simon nodded. He understood, finally, why he'd been denied a talisman. He hadn't felt fear when the kids had attacked him. He remembered the baby bird. How he had felt differently. That was before the talisman took him to the rally in 2037 and he'd witnessed the triumph of humans against oligarchs and placatory governments. He had conquered his fear all by himself.

Simon heard Pierre's voice for the first time, a soft voice with a hint of a French accent in the vowels. "We also hoped that you would influence other kids, so your activism needed to be the kind they could imitate. In other words, not magic."

How he'd raged against being forced to take mini-steps, doing stuff that anyone else could do just as well, probably better. That had been the whole point!

"And you did a great job influencing other kids. Look how many joined you in the tree-saving campaign," Mohammed said warmly.

Suddenly, all the adults were on their feet. They raised their mugs of tea into the air and congratulated him, while Simon blushed and grinned.

He was going to time travel this summer. Every day. More if he could. Oh, how he was going to time travel!

CHAPTER TWENTY-ONE

SIMON WAS BEHIND a tree in a forest. He was relieved to be there. He kissed the trunk of the tree he was leaning against.

Throughout the summer, he had time travelled cautiously, edging forward in time in tiny increments, thinking carefully about each visit.

"Remember Marietta," his mother had warned. "Remember how that visit impacted your feelings for Sandra, for a time. You know the future can impact the present. Do you really want to know everything that happens to you?"

So Simon had intended to explore the future with tiny steps, but had gotten somewhat stuck in his 18th year, by which time he had become an environmental activist of international renown, while continuing to be a stellar student at school. Best of all, he was still loving Sandra, still together, and after one tantalising glimpse of his face buried in the most beautiful breasts, his visits to that time started to snowball. If she was letting him do stuff like that then surely he would be doing it a lot, so if he kept going back to that same time, it seemed logical that he'd glimpse them together again. Perhaps he'd catch Future-him and Sandra doing something really raunchy! But the wretched talisman refused to grant him another such vision, so he was reduced to tossing and turning in bed, fantasizing about pink cupids brushing his lips.

The end of summer loomed before his mother suggested that he was avoiding one future visit which, perhaps, should be made.

"Do I want to know whether my life's work actually does any good?" he asked his mother. "Do I want to know if I ultimately succeed or fail? How would that help me fight better?"

"It's just in case, you know."

"In case what?"

"OK. It's for me. I want you to do it for me. I need to know what the world is going to be like when you're at the end of your life. After I'm dead. Yes. I want to know if we survive. I have to know it."

"Mum ..."

"Don't if you don't want to. I'll understand. You're right really. What's the point of knowing? But I can't help it. I have a desperate desire to know."

And so Simon had grasped his talisman and asked to go to age 90. Nothing happened. He looked at his mother with a shocked expression. He would be dead at 90.

"Try 80," she said.

That was why Simon was relieved to be behind a tree in a forest, and kissed the trunk. He was relieved that he was alive at 80. He peeked around the tree. There he was, half-lying in the grass with a magnifying glass, inspecting some insect or other. Future-him still loved nature with the same passion. Warblings and cacklings drifted down from the tree canopy; buzzings and hummings wafted on the breeze. A fierce joy gripped Simon's heart. This must mean that they had won the war. This beautiful, deep-woods retreat, teeming with life, surely meant nature had been preserved in all its glory.

A red squirrel darted up the tree trunk nearest to the old man and balanced on the lowest branch, chittering furiously at Future-him's bent head. The old man manoeuvred himself slowly onto his knees and then pushed himself to his feet with the aid of a walking stick. He moved directly underneath the branch and looked up. The outraged squirrel tripled its vocalizations, flicking its tail and pummelling its back feet to emphasize its fury. Simon had to clap his hand over his mouth to stop himself from giggling, as Future-him grinned upwards in delight.

A boy suddenly came pounding over the forest floor, skidding to a stop beside the old man. "Grandfather, what are you doing?"

Simon craned his head to see his grandchild better. About 12 years of age—perhaps 14 if he was small like Simon had been—he sported the arresting combination of his grandmother's dark skin and his grandfather's blue eyes.

"There is an entire world on this forest floor, John, if you look closely enough."

"Grandpa, you know it's not safe to walk around like this."

"Why, what's happening? Who is the enemy?" the old man said expansively, looking around the quiet green space. "Nature? Is a nasty wolf going to come and eat me up?"

"No Grandpa, but Canada is at war. Remember?"

The old man sank to the ground, looking puzzled. "But Canada is such a peaceful country."

The boy crouched beside him. "Yes, but rising waters and shrinking agricultural land created a lot of hungry, desperate people. Remember I told you about the climate refugees at breakfast? They've invaded us because they're starving and desperate for our resources. I wish you wouldn't keep forgetting the refugees! There's a huge note pinned on both the back door and the front, commanding you to stay inside. You must have seen it when you left the house. And you have a note in your pocket, don't you, Grandpa?"

The old man fished around inside his pocket, his fingers closing over a piece of paper. He drew it slowly out of his pocket and unfolded it, eyeing the boy in surprise. Simon slipped from tree to tree quietly, until he was directly behind the couple on the ground. Luckily, the writing on the note was very large.

The world is at war.
I MUST NOT WANDER AROUND OUTSIDE BY MYSELF.

"Oh yes, I remember now," the old man said. "I know my memory is terrible. One of the gifts of old age, I'm afraid. I get immersed in what I'm doing—like studying insects—and I forget. I'm sorry."

The boy helped the old man get to his feet, and they began to shuffle away together. Simon didn't follow them immediately. He was trying to breathe. He was so flabbergasted, he could barely make sense of what he'd seen. The world at war? How could this be?

He needed to think. Think. Think. Had they got everything wrong? And hadn't he—without wanting to, without looking for it—stumbled on the truth about his own death?

He didn't want to know about his own death, even though he'd wondered about it, like every other human being. He had always been too afraid that the end might be nasty; perhaps some revengeful oil baron, who'd lost everything through the new government policies restricting fossil fuel use, would gun him down in his prime. Who'd want to know that?

Now he knew that he would live to 80 at least, a good, full life. And perhaps by that time he wouldn't mind so much about dying. Old people seemed to have really bad memories. He'd probably forget he was dying. As long as it wasn't a violent death, while he was still compos mentis.

But if the world was a dangerous place, even in the woods, had they got everything wrong?

Simon felt ill with all the thoughts ricocheting around his brain. The old man and the boy were talking, but he was too far away to hear. He slipped between tree trunks and came almost abreast of them.

"Do you see the chickadee?" his grandfather was saying. He pulled his grandson to a stop and shuffled forward one step at a time until he pointed at the branch just above their heads. "Look how close we can get; they're such friendly little birds." Simon squinted. The chickadee was barely a foot above their faces, tilting one bright eye towards them.

The boy, John, looked and smiled, but within a minute he was pulling at his grandfather's sleeve. "Come on, Granddad! Marauders were spotted in these woods yesterday."

"Marauders is a good word." The grandfather looked into the boy's eyes. "I am happy in the woods."

"I know Granddad, but it's not safe." The couple hobbled on.

The Grandfather kept pointing out birds and squirrels, once he blew gently at a spider's web. Once he stopped to encircle a blossom in his hand. He bent painfully to touch mushrooms. The boy looked at everything, then urged his grandfather on.

"Are biodiversity and nature thriving?" the old man asked.

"Yes, in many places."

"So we stopped emitting green house gas emissions in time?"

"In many places, yes," John repeated. He tugged on his grandfather's hand again to get him moving. Why did he have to stop walking every time he spoke! John saw savage, desperate men behind every tree trunk. He wanted to get home.

"Did I help that to happen? Was it my actions that changed the future? Did I reverse time?"

"Yes, Granddad," John said, pulling his grandfather steadily forward. "You led the way for humans to survive, and be civil about it. You started a massive movement getting people to simplify their lifestyles at a personal level." John realized that if he kept talking, his grandfather kept moving. "And you lobbied the government constantly, organizing political rallies to demand the government speed up its transition to renewable energy. The rally you organized in 2037 was the biggest human gathering in the history of humankind—including the wars. The government implemented the demands of its people and the changes happened faster. By 2040 emissions had been cut drastically. We did it. You can see the result around you—nature is thriving."

"But we're at war," the old man said sadly.

The boy pulled him forward. They were approaching a little house, hidden among the trees. "A lot of carbon was released from melting permafrost and stuff. Waters rose and food got scarce and people got desperate. But the human race is surviving, Granddad. Sure, we're doing what we've always done—fight—but we're here. And so are a lot of other species."

The old man beamed at the boy as they entered the house. Simon suddenly realised that the boy said these things to his granddad all the time. His ageing granddad, with his failing memory. He was soothing him. Driving away the sadness because his granddad couldn't roam in the woods he had helped to preserve.

∞ Simon asked his talisman to take him home. Rakita was in the garden, weeding the vegetables. He stumbled over to her and laid his head in her lap, like he used to do when he was a little boy. He told her every detail of what he'd seen, his eyes closed, his head reeling.

After he had finished, there was a short silence. Then Rakita began to laugh.

"The fact that my life ends in awful wars and senility is funny to you?"

Rakita stroked his head. "You changed the future, darling. It's just … that's great. We knew that the human race was in for a hard time whatever we did. But we also knew that great and rapid change was the only option that ensured our survival. That was our goal, darling, the survival of the human race. Not to have a perfect world where racism and inequality was extinguished. We aren't God!" And Rakita fell back on her chair laughing, because she didn't believe in God. She didn't believe that the moment in time the talismans landed you had meaning, either. But Simon remembered how the talisman had taken him to that massive rally in 2037 that changed the course of the government. He remembered how it had given him the strength to continue, even after his violent experiences. His mother lacked faith, and faith was a good thing, so long as you listened to science at the same time.

But it was hard to have faith in what he was doing if he ended up hiding in a rabbit hole slowly going senile. "I can't share your joy," he said to his mother. "The scene I just experienced didn't feel like a victory. It felt like evil humans had won."

His mother stopped laughing and sat up straight. "There are different levels of evil. The greatest evil is if our greed prevents us from changing our behaviour fast enough, and the world becomes uninhabitable and millions die. That's the worst. And it didn't happen, right? But we're hurtling towards that fate, right now, in 2022. So we have to keep doing what we're doing. Because that *is* what we're doing. That's the fate we're trying to avoid—and you have given me a glimpse that we might succeed. Thank you and bless you."

Simon blinked at his mother. "Canada will be invaded by starving hordes while the population hides in the woods and we're happy with that? I'd rather have any disease than senility! Take my legs, take my eyes, but leave me my mind!"

Rakita pulled his head towards her, so he was looking directly into her eyes. "We know that you are destined to make change; you've already changed history with the pipeline and you're just getting started." She gave his head a little shake. "You changed the future. What was going to happen, is no longer going to happen. You reversed history." A giggle burbled from her lips.

Simon began to smile. "I reversed time."

"Yes. We've reversed time once. Let's try to change history again. Let's impact this other, lesser evil!"

"So ... can we fight this?"

"Yes. In the exact same way; through education. Our message must change: instead of 'Transition Now,' it could be, 'Transition Now with Equity'.

"To draw attention to vulnerable populations?"

"Yes. To prevent their situation from getting so desperate that they are forced to attack us." Rakita burst into giggles again. Her whole belly jiggled against his head, and Simon stood up in irritation. Ronny came to lean heavily against his legs. "How is this funny?"

"I'm just ... happy. We can totally do this, too. We can prioritize aid to suffering countries to prevent desperation. Maybe those wars won't happen. We can do anything!"

Rakita stood up and did a little dance.

Simon thought she was completely mad.

Then he thought, perhaps they both were.

Then he jumped forward and began to boogie with his mother.

Acknowledgements

I would like to thank first and foremost my dear sisters Tessa, Anna, and Susie for their feedback and help as I wracked their brains for ideas and direction. Thank you Cam Farnell, for your valuable input about energy. Thanks to Michael Mirolla, Publisher at Guernica, for his brilliant editing—you transformed this book. I also appreciate the work that has gone into promoting *Reversing Time*, and thank Margo LaPierre, Anna Van Valkenburg and Dylan Curran for their excellent work. Thank you to David Moratto for his creative and eye-catching cover. I would like to thank my writing group for their thorough reading and patient advice as we leap from book to book without ever finishing one—Gwen Davies, Joseph Szostak and Nick Sumner! Special thanks to the kids who gave me feedback on my first YA novel: my kids Eytan and Abigail, various nieces and nephews, and Joseph Szostak's grandchildren. A genuine thanks to my husband Eli Elias (as opposed to the sarcastic thanks for being my anti-muse that I usually give him). This time, his knowledge of science fiction time travel books was deeply helpful. I am often amazed by the support of my readers—especially my family, friends, neighbours, teachers at my kids' schools—many of whom have gone out of their way to promote my book through word of mouth. Thank you for enjoying my writing.

About the Author

Charlotte R. Mendel was born in Canada, but has lived in many different countries. Her first novel, *Turn Us Again*, won the HR. Percy Novel Prize, the Beacon Award for Social Justice, and the Atlantic Book Award for First Novel. Her second novel, *A Hero*, was shortlisted for the 2016 William Saroyan International Prize for Writing, and was a Finalist in the 2016 International Book Awards in the General Fiction category. She currently lives in Nova Scotia with one husband, two children, two cats, three goats, four sheep, eleven chickens, and thousands of bees.

Printed in September 2021
by Gauvin Press,
Gatineau, Québec